ACCORDING TO
THEIR DEEDS

Books by
Paul Robertson

The Heir

Road to Nowhere

According to Their Deeds

PAUL ROBERTSON

ACCLAIMED AUTHOR OF *THE HEIR*

ACCORDING TO THEIR DEEDS

A NOVEL

BETHANY HOUSE

MINNEAPOLIS, MINNESOTA

Published by Bethany House Publishers
11400 Hampshire Avenue South
Bloomington, Minnesota 55438

Bethany House Publishers is a division of
Baker Publishing Group, Grand Rapids, Michigan.

Printed in the United States of America

Library of Congress Cataloging-in-Publication Data

Robertson, Paul, 1957–
    According to their deeds / Paul Robertson.
       p.   cm.
    ISBN 978-0-7642-0568-2 (pbk.)
    1. Antiquarian booksellers—Fiction. 2. Extortion—Fiction. 3. Murder—Investigation—Fiction. 4. Washington (D.C.)—Fiction. I. Title.

    PS3618.O3173A63   2009
    813'.6—dc22
                                                                2008051060

I am dedicating this book to my father,

Kenneth Robertson.

Let me tell you about him.

My earliest memory is of him reading. Even now, these many years later, it's not hard to find a present for him. I get him books.

His life is a demonstration of his values: God and family, education and responsibility, serving and living peacefully. My three brothers, my sister, and I can all tell you how wise, generous and accepting he is. He has been married fifty-three years (so far), has nineteen grandchildren (so far), and the tale of his great-grandchildren has only begun. He is a scientist and a teacher, he is respected by everyone who knows him, and he still reads more than I do.

I know that God my Father is loving, dependable, and a strong foundation for my life. I know because my own father has been all those things for me. My father is dedicated to his Savior, and I learned that from him, too.

So happy eightieth birthday, Dad.
Here's a book.

Lisa, we made it through another one together.
Thank you, love.

. . . and books were opened . . . and the dead were judged
from the things which were written in the books,
according to their deeds . . .

MONDAY

MORNING

Only one chair was empty.

"Sixteen thousand. Do I see seventeen?"

Charles slipped into the open seat. He paged through the catalog.

"The bid is seventeen. Do I see eighteen? Thank you, eighteen thousand dollars. Nineteen?"

A man beside him, in thick black-rimmed glasses, leaned over.

"I figured you'd show up."

"Which lot are we on?" Charles asked.

"Number sixty. The desk."

"Derek's desk."

"Nineteen, thank you. Twenty?"

"You knew him, right?" the man said.

"Yes."

"Twenty. The bid is twenty thousand dollars. Do I see twenty-one?"

Gold sconces on the pale blue walls pooled light on the white ceiling, and gold and crystal chandeliers showered light down on the fifty dark blue upholstered chairs. The carpet was even darker blue and very thick, a deep river, soaking up every sound but the auctioneer's voice.

The crowd was darkly upholstered as well.

"Do I see twenty-two?"

A wide young man in the front row lifted a wood paddle.

"Twenty-two, thank you. Do I see twenty-three?"

He did, somewhere else in the room.

"Everything's going high," the man in the glasses said. "Too many out-of-towners. I just wanted to buy back what I sold the guy, but I haven't won a bid yet."

"Who's bidding right now, Norman?" Charles asked.

"That guy with the frizzy hair, he looks like Einstein? He's from a big New York showroom. And up front, in the brown suit, he's from Houston. And that guy's from L.A. Everybody else has dropped out."

"The bid is twenty-eight thousand. Do I see twenty-nine?"

"Like I said, it's all going high," Norman said.

"It's a nice desk."

"Oh, yeah. Everything's real nice, all of it. The guy had great taste. Too bad he's gone, he was a great customer. But that desk, I'd have said twenty-six, twenty-eight for it, and we're blowing through thirty without a hiccup. But I don't do furniture, so what do I know."

Every sound of conversation sank into the carpet's downward pull. Wooden paddles rose and fell, or waved like water lilies on bottomless currents.

"I'm glad there was an empty seat," Charles said. A dozen people were standing at the back wall.

"A guy I knew was sitting there a minute ago."

"Oh—is it his chair?"

"No, I think he left."

"Thirty-four. Do I see thirty-five? The bid is now thirty-four thousand. Any bid?"

There seemed not to be. Mr. Einstein from New York, with his wild white hair and black mustache, had bid last and now stared straight and smugly forward.

"Thirty-four thousand. Going once, twice—" The auctioneer's eyes

darted, reacting to some new movement deep in the room. *"Thirty-five, thank you. The bid is now thirty-five thousand. Do I see thirty-six?"*

Heads turned and searched, but Mr. Einstein himself hardly reacted to this new unknown. He only raised his own paddle.

"Thirty-six. Do I see thirty-seven?"

He did, and everyone else did as well. A woman in a light gray suit and very improbable blond hair, standing against the back wall. She held her paddle out like a sword.

"Thirty-eight?"

Charles paged through his catalog. *Lot Sixty, Cherry Pedestal Desk, Philadelphia, 1876.* Other people were flipping pages as well.

"Not much of a description," Norman said. "Is there something special?"

"It's historic. Derek was proud of it."

"Oh, wait, that's where they found him, right? On top of it?"

Charles didn't answer. The bidding advanced, a conflict of deliberate and formal violence.

"Because that could be worth a premium," Norman said. "They'd clean it up, right? They wouldn't sell it with blood all over it. But you've got to be careful cleaning those old finishes. You can take them right off. I think it was a lot of blood, too."

"Do I see fifty? Fifty, thank you. Fifty-two?"

The formal quiet and the auctioneer's drone stretched a placid surface across the room. All that could be seen was slow and purposeful, apparently calm. But a tension was growing between the two bidders, like monsters beneath the surface sensing each other and edging into battle.

"Fifty-two. Do I see fifty-four?"

He did immediately.

"Fifty-four. The bid is fifty-four thousand dollars. Do I see fifty-six?"

"Fifty-six. Do I see fifty-eight?"

"Somebody's going to hit their limit," Norman said. "Fifty-eight grand! That's twice what it's worth."

"Do I see sixty?"

The blond woman's impudence was finally getting to the man from New York. He waved his paddle defiantly. It was, in the depths, a first ripping by sharp teeth; anger had been provoked.

"Thank you. The bid is sixty thousand. Do I see sixty-five? Sixty-five, thank you."

"Do you know who she is?" Charles said.

"I've never seen her."

"Sev-en-ty-five." Mr. Einstein had spoken it aloud, each syllable a separate word.

"Seventy-five. Do I see eighty?"

The woman's paddle jerked.

"Eighty. The bid is eighty thousand. Do I see eighty-five?"

"One hun-dred," Einstein said. The room gasped, every person, at the three distinct syllables.

"One hundred thousand dollars. Do I see one hundred five?"

Without hesitation, the woman thrust her paddle straight up, and through.

The man set his paddle under his chair.

It was over, suddenly. A leviathan had been vanquished and now sank away into ultimate deeps.

"One hundred five thousand. Do I see one hundred ten?"

"Not likely," Norman said. He would have been too loud, but the carpet sucked his voice right out of the air. "A hundred five, that had to hurt."

The victor had wounds to nurse, but the battle was past.

"One hundred five. Any other bid? Going once, twice." A pause. *"Sold. Lot sixty sold for one hundred five thousand dollars. Next will be lot sixty-one, a Tiffany lamp. Bidding will open at fifteen hundred. Do I see fifteen hundred?"*

"What was that?" Norman said. "Fifty was way over the line! A hundred grand? Now that was crazy!"

Ripples of conversation troubled the surface but that was all; the deeps were now still.

"There must be a reason," Charles murmured. The room was filled with murmuring.

"I'd like to know what reason. Twenty-five thousand for the desk and eighty thousand for the reason."

"*Thirty-two hundred. Any other bid? Going once, twice, sold. Lot sixty-one for three thousand two hundred dollars. Next will be lot sixty-two, a marble table. Bidding will open at three thousand. Do I see three thousand?*"

"So we're back to normal," Norman said. "Thirty-two hundred's high, but just a little. I guess when people fly in from up northeast and from the coast, they don't want to go home empty-handed."

"It's a large collection," Charles said. "It would pull people in from all over."

"I wish they'd stayed back where they came from. But if it's even just the dealers he bought stuff from, it could be this many people. The guy bought all over the place. All I wanted to do was buy back the stuff I sold him."

"Yes. I think you mentioned that."

"But it's all going too high. I'm not going to spend more on a lamp than I can sell it for. At least that blond lady is gone."

She was.

"I do wonder who she was," Charles said.

"Just as long as she's not here to bid on anything I want. Not that I'm getting anything anyway. A hundred grand for a desk! It's crazy."

"I wonder what Derek would have thought," Charles said.

Norman pointed at the next catalog page. "I bet that's the lot you're after."

"Yes."

"Number sixty-four. You got here just in time."

"*Going once, twice, sold. Lot sixty-two for five thousand six hundred dollars. Next will be lot sixty-three, two Windsor chairs. Bidding will open at five thousand. Do I see five thousand?*"

"Those are nice," Norman said. "I don't do furniture, but those are nice. From Vermont, 1920, all handmade. The real things. It must have taken a long time to pull all this stuff together."

"A lifetime."

"And poof, here it's all gone in three hours. Kind of funny, you know?"

The auctioneer's voice stabbed the air, slicing and cutting, on and on, relentlessly.

"And his wife doesn't want it." Norman said. "It's her selling it off, right?"

"I believe so."

"She's making a bundle. Especially after that desk! I wonder if she knew he was worth so much? His stuff, anyway. Did you get the list?"

"The catalog?" Charles asked, with it in his hand. "This?"

"No, the list from the police."

"I don't know of any list from the police."

"It's the stuff that got stolen, you know, that night he got killed."

"Any other bid? Going once, twice, sold. Lot sixty-three for thirteen thousand dollars."

"They want dealers to be looking for it," Norman said.

"No, I didn't get that list."

"Next will be lot sixty-four, a set of thirteen antique books. Bidding will open at ten thousand. Do I see ten thousand?"

"This is you, right?"

Charles nodded.

"Good luck," Norman said.

"Thanks."

"I guess no books got stolen."

"Ten thousand, thank you. Do I see eleven?"

Norman kept talking. "So that's why they didn't give you the list. Police and FBI, too. They're all looking."

Charles had his own paddle in his lap. He watched the bids increase.

"How much will it go for?" Norman said.

"Twenty-three, twenty-four for the set, maybe twenty-five."

"Remember, it's all going high. You sold them all to him in the first place?"

"Fifteen thousand. Do I see sixteen? Thank you, sixteen thousand."

"Yes. A book at a time, over the last six years."

Charles leaned forward, watching the different bidders.

"Do you know everyone bidding?" Norman said.

"So far."

"From around here?"

"No. Briary Roberts in New York. Jacob Leatherman himself from San Francisco."

"The old guy?"

"Yes."

"Did you know he was coming?"

"We had dinner last night."

His eyes were on the contest. The other bidders took turns, pushing the price up.

"Twenty thousand. Do I see twenty-one?"

Charles lifted his paddle. Now he was joined in the battle himself.

"Twenty-one thousand." For a moment, he owned the bid. *"Do I see twenty-two?"* And then he did not. *"Twenty-two, thank you. Do I see twenty-three?"*

Suddenly the bidding intensified with quick jabs from Jacob Leatherman, and then New York again.

"Twenty-five? Thank you. Do I see twenty-six?"

Jacob Leatherman's paddle quivered in the air.

"Twenty-six. Do I see twenty-seven?"

Charles signaled, quickly.

"Twenty-seven thousand. Do I see twenty-eight?"

Jacob was frowning from across the room, but his paddle was on the floor.

"Any other bid? The bid is twenty-seven thousand. Going once, twice, sold. Lot sixty-four sold for twenty-seven thousand dollars."

"But I thought you said it was only worth twenty-four," Norman said.

"Sentiment."

"Next will be lot sixty-five, a wood inlay chess set. Bidding will open at two thousand dollars."

15

"I don't do books," Norman said, "so what do I know. Oh, I sold this chess set. I'm just trying to get back what I sold him."

Charles stood and took a deep breath and moved toward the door.

Charles stepped out from the building into very bright sunlight.

It took a moment to adjust.

Traffic was heavy. On the sidewalk, a dozen people were scattered over the length of the block. The gray stone and mirrored windows of the office building across the street were very bright.

A cardboard box was in front of him, tight in both hands.

He turned south toward Pennsylvania Avenue, three blocks away. The faces he passed were stern and silent against the world, or talking on cell phones, alive, animated, in other worlds. Charles stopped at the first corner.

He was being followed.

Across the street a young man had stayed even with him. He was in torn jeans and a hooded sweatshirt, and he had stopped on his opposite corner. A well-dressed woman, passing him, instinctively drew back, and hurried past.

Charles waited.

Abruptly the man sprang from the curb and sprinted, dodging cars. His eyes were on the box in Charles's hands. A car squealed but the young man, lithe and quick, was already across.

Charles waited. The predator came to a halt, inches away.

"Hey, boss," he said, in a low voice.

"Don't cause a wreck, Angelo."

He shrugged. "You got that?"

"Twenty-seven thousand."

"For a little box." His accent was urban Hispanic and so were his black hair and shadowy face.

"You take it," Charles said.

"Back to the shop?"

Charles handed him the box.

"Take it to the shop. I'll be right there."

"Okay, boss, I'll take it, it's not any problem."

"Be careful."

"You are worrying for me, boss, or you are worrying for that box?"

"The box isn't going to do anything foolish."

Angelo smiled, a tiger showing its teeth. "I am smarter than that little box."

"Try to be."

With no other words he turned away, only walking but very quickly. Charles continued on his own way to a Metro station, and descended into the ground.

"King Street. Next stop Eisenhower Avenue." The doors whirred and Charles was on the platform, looking out at the streets of Alexandria. The escalator took him down to them.

The pocket around the station was in giant twelve-story scale, of offices and plazas, tied to the rest of the city only by it being brick. Beyond, though, a few blocks of King Street brought Charles to the three-story scale of real west Alexandria, authentic and shabby from a century of pawn and secondhand existence, now getting better but still not good.

Then another five blocks east and the buildings were solid and many were very good, and rents were high and the shop windows cleaner and the doors were appealing instead of simply peeling.

Charles crossed noisy Washington Street and into the heart of crowds and crowds. At Market Square he turned right into quiet streets, then one more block, and finally up two steps, and into a place that was very, very quiet.

The first impression was always the quiet. It was the special calm silence of books aging, books that were very practiced at aging.

"Hello, Alice."

"Good afternoon, Mr. Beale." Alice had a way of speaking that did not disturb the silence. "Mrs. Beale was just asking if I'd seen you."

The second impression was the quiet of color. Only the part of any color that could last decades was left in the room. Even loud colors were quiet.

"Is she upstairs?" he asked.

"Yes, sir."

Then the smell, which was faintest, half like a forest and half like old linen, but sharp.

"And have you seen Angelo?" he asked.

"No, sir." Her dress was the russet of a bright red cover faded over forty years.

"I didn't think he'd be back yet." The counter stretched across the right side of the room and stairs went up the left side, and a rail ran across the back.

"And have we sold anything?"

"A 1940 *Gone With the Wind.*"

"I can empathize with Scarlet," he said. "I feel like I've just come from the burning of Atlanta."

He opened the gate in the middle of the rail and climbed the steps.

"There you are."

Her voice was quicksilver and light and everything peaceful.

"Here I am," Charles said. "Dorothy, it was worse than I'd expected."

"I'm sorry." Her hair was slow silver, short and easy, and lovely. "Were you there long?"

"Twenty minutes. But I sat beside Norman Highberg."

"Oh, dear." She smiled, which was the moon at its brightest. "Did you get the books?"

"Yes, for twenty-seven. I had to outbid Jacob Leatherman just at the end. Oh, he scowled!"

"He'll get over it, and you will, too. I'm glad you got them. It helps to close the circle with Derek."

"It does help. And I have to tell you about Derek's desk." His own desk was at the front window, and he sat and pushed aside newspapers and magazines and catalogs to make space for an elbow.

"I suppose there was something special about it?" Anything would be special if she only spoke its name.

"Everything he had was special. But this was more than just ordinary special."

"It was auctioned today?"

"Yes, and sensationally." Now that he was sitting, he stretched his back, and put his hands behind his head. "I came in right in the middle of it. It should have gone twenty-five thousand, and it was about to go for thirty-four, and whoosh, two people bid it right up to a hundred and five thousand. There was a riot."

"A very calm one, I'm sure."

"People actually turned in their chairs and looked around. It was that drastic."

Her blue eyes widened in her own calm amazement. "Why would it sell for so much?"

"It's a complete mystery." He stared out the window at the street. "Poof."

"What?"

"A lifetime. Three hours and it's gone."

"Selling off all his things?"

"His world. Everything he was, all scattered." With his hands behind his head, the space on his desk he'd cleared for his elbow was empty now, abandoned.

"Life is more than what you own," Dorothy said. Her own desk was perfectly ordered, with a computer screen, a neat pile of papers, and two photographs. She put her elbows on the empty middle and looked at him.

"Oh, I know," Charles said. "But that's what's left at the end."

"He was an important person, wasn't he?"

"He was a bureaucrat in the Justice Department. Yes, he was important." He glanced at the newspaper. The first page was rancor in Congress, and the president refusing to cooperate, and officials denying any wrongdoing. "What would the *Post* print if there were no scandals?"

"Hollywood divorces, like everyone else."

"I guess that would be worse. Every story on the front page is about someone's failing."

The sun was overhead, in the west, full on the townhouses across the street. The shadow of his own building was creeping toward them.

He read a paragraph. "This poor man," he said. "A highly respected federal judge. Ten years on the bench. Then it comes out that he cheated on his exams back in law school. Over thirty years ago! First he was forced to resign, and now he's being disbarred."

"It does seem severe."

"There is more to life than what you own. There's also what you've done wrong."

"And what you've done right. Charles, you're getting moody. Did you bring the books home?"

"Angelo has them, speaking of lives lived questionably."

"I didn't know you took him." The two pictures on her desk were of Charles and of a teenage boy.

"I just decided at the last minute."

"Was he dressed all right?"

"No, he was not. There wasn't time. He wouldn't have come inside anyway."

"We have a delivery for him to make this afternoon in Arlington. And I was thinking we should get him a suit for his next probation review."

"His regular business clothes are fine." He dropped the newspaper into the wastebasket. "Felons in suits annoy me."

"Besides Angelo, how many felons do you know?"

"Aren't we all?"

"Mr. Beale?" Alice had come up the steps. "Mr. Leatherman is here to see you."

"Take a deep breath," Dorothy said.

Charles did.

"Jacob!" Charles said from the stairs. "Welcome!"

"What did you do that for?" It would have been a growl, but from such a small and fragile man it was a yip.

Charles reached the floor, smiling all the way. "Let me get you a chair." He swept through the gate and came to rest at his guest. "I'd invite you to the office but it's up all those stairs."

"I don't need a chair."

"I'm glad you could stop in. I was sorry you couldn't after dinner last night."

"I have time before my flight and I don't like sitting in airports. I told the taxi to bring me here."

"I'm so glad," Charles said.

Jacob smacked the floor with his walking stick. "You're glad? You're gloating, that's what it is, for outbidding me. What did you do that for?"

"You could have bid higher if you wanted them, Jacob."

"That's all they're worth. Now I'm going back without anything."

"I'm sorry your trip was a waste. I'll sell them to you, if you want."

"How much?"

"Thirty."

"Thirty?" He smacked the floor again. "They're not worth that. I'd have bid thirty if they were."

"Then I guess I'll keep them."

"I didn't come to have you gloat. I'll give you twenty-three." *Smack.*

"Thirty-five. And you're perfectly Dickensian when you do that."

"Bah, humbug then. Dickensian?" He rubbed his nose. "I like that. And you said thirty."

"You should have taken it while you could."

"Whippersnapper! Mocking an old man! You'll give me apoplexy, and I have all those airport lines to go through yet. You'll send me to an early grave."

"That's no longer possible, Jacob."

"I know when I'm not wanted. I'll leave if that's how it is." He narrowed his eyes. "The Locke, I'd have liked to look at that one. Is it as nice as you said it is?"

"It is, Jacob. Nothing special—I know you've seen better ones. But it's nice."

Jacob's scowl lightened a little. "I like looking at them. Do you have the books here?"

"No. I had a courier bring them."

"A courier? Why would you do that for?"

"Just common caution. Shall I call you a taxi?"

"I have one waiting outside. Did you say twenty-five?"

"Thirty-five."

"Thirty-five!" Whack. "Mocking an old man. I'll leave. I have to go."

Charles held open the door. "Then have a nice flight."

"No such thing." He started slowly and painfully down the first step, and then froze. "What's that?! Don't touch me!" He lifted his cane.

Angelo was four feet from him, also stopped, his eyes slits and his white teeth showing.

"Jacob—" Charles started.

"Street gangs!" Jacob yelped. "Here at your door! That's why you use a courier!"

"Jacob," Charles said. "This is Angelo Acevedo. He is my courier."

Angelo was silent.

"Just take the box in," Charles said.

Jacob shrank back as Angelo passed. "You let him touch your books?"

"I do," Charles said. "And it's fine. Let me help you to your taxi."

"Bah! I'll make it myself."

"Take care, Jacob."

"You too, Charles." Once Jacob was launched he moved quickly. The cab door was opened for him, the cab driver was scolded, and the cab drove away.

Charles closed the door and took a deep breath. "Angelo. Everything went okay?"

"Except that old crazy man."

"That's Mr. Leatherman, and he's actually very nice, just prickly."

Angelo frowned. "What is prickly?"

"Like a cactus."

"Like a little dog to bite at you."

"He doesn't bite, he just barks. But never mind. You took a long time."

"I came a different way from you, or why should I even carry the box instead of you?"

"You're right."

Angelo held out his hands. "So, boss, here is your box."

"Thank you." He took it, respectfully. "Go check with Mrs. Beale. I think she has a delivery for you to do this afternoon."

"Okay."

"And Angelo . . ."

He turned back from the steps and waited.

"Do you remember the delivery we made together, last November, and the man had the chess set on his desk, and he talked to you in Spanish?"

"I remember that house and that man."

"That is the man who died. These are his books that I bought back today."

"Oh, that man?" He shrugged. "That's too bad."

"It is too bad. That book we took him, it's here in this box."

Angelo glanced at the box with no greater interest than before, and then turned to his next task.

"I'll be in the basement," Charles said to Alice.

But he was interrupted. "Mr. Beale?"

Charles had just started for the basement.

"Yes, Morgan?"

As Angelo had ascended, Morgan had descended. He sat on a step halfway down. "There's a first edition *Odyssey* that just came up on eBay."

"Which translation?"

Morgan had stopped too high and he had to lean forward to see into the showroom. He bumped down one step, and all his pale face and red hair floated into view. "Alexander Pope."

"A 1725 Pope first edition?" Charles snorted. "I doubt it!"

"The listing says first edition. And it says it's signed by the author."

"The translator, you mean."

"It says the author."

Charles paused. "The *Odyssey*, signed by the author. That would certainly answer the question of whether it was written or oral. I suppose I should come and see."

"Do you think it could be anything you'd want?"

Charles squinted at the picture on Morgan's computer. "Not much of a picture."

"It's not a dealer," Morgan said. "Just an individual."

"Send an email. I want to know the usual—the publisher and city, number of pages, and the date. And I want a picture of the title page, and see if he'll tell us where he got it."

"How much would it be worth?"

"A 1725 Pope first edition? Even in poor condition, at least thirty thousand. But that's nothing like a first edition. I'd say it was nineteenth century. How long is the auction?"

"One week. It just started this afternoon."

"Keep an eye on it. We'll see how high it goes. I might decide to bid once we hear back from the seller."

"Yes, sir."

"Thank you, Morgan."

Charles stopped at the door to his office.

"Was Jacob all right?" Dorothy asked.

"Yes. Just being sociable. Have you ever read Homer's *Odyssey*?"

"Yes."

"Do you remember which translation?"

"No. It was in college." She noticed the box in his hands. "And that is the books?"

"This is Derek's books," he said. "Yes. I'm taking them to the basement right now to work on them." He looked at the box in his hand. "Or maybe I shouldn't."

"Why?"

"There might be Greeks hidden inside."

"That was the *Aeneid*, and that box is not a horse, and they would have to be very small Greeks."

"The Trojans didn't think they were in any danger either."

AFTERNOON

Down, down, down. He unlocked the door at the bottom and turned on the light.

The building was as old as most of the books, which was fitting. The basement had served many purposes; framed photographs in a corner showed what the renovation had uncovered. The floor had been bare earth for the first half century or so, and then quarters for two slaves, and then for two servants after the Civil War. Then it had been storage and children's rooms and disuse alternating over more years until it had finally become what it now was.

Now the walls were filled with shelves, and the shelves were filled with volumes, and the volumes were filled with . . . everything. They rested in their ordered ranks, contemplating the deepest and widest thoughts man had accumulated since contemplation had begun.

The floor, walls, and ceiling were thick and fireproof. The dry, cool air was thick with their philosophies, histories and literatures. It was a very safe place for books.

A few very valuable volumes were in the bank safe deposit, and the lesser items were in the display room upstairs, but this was always the foundation and the heart.

Charles set the box on the desk and turned on the computer.

Then he opened the cardboard box and lifted out the first package, wrapped in crisp brown paper. The paper fell open as he cut the tape.

He opened a drawer and took white gloves, thin clean cotton, to put on, and then he touched the book.

The boards and spine were the brown of soil walked on and worn hard and flat. The lettering was faint.

He lifted the volume and studied it. The spine was sturdy and the page edges were aligned, with none loose. He cradled it in one hand and opened the front board.

The Wealth of Nations by Adam Smith.

A two-inch square of light green paper slid off the first page. *Alexandria Rare Books* was printed on it, with the numbers 7273 2002 handwritten below.

He closed the book, turned it over, and opened the back board. Then he closed it again, turned it vertical, and opened to the center and then to a few other pages, efficiently and carefully, inspecting it at every angle.

Finally he set it back on its wrapping paper and turned to the computer. He typed 7273, read through the book's history on the screen, and then started typing: Purchased at auction 4/21/08, Derek Bastien Estate. Condition unchanged, very good. Price—

He paused and wrote the name of the book on a scrap of the brown paper. He wrote $3,100 beside it, and then typed that number onto the screen. He carried the book to a shelf and moved a ceramic block to make a space.

He typed 235 into the Location field on-screen.

Then he stared again at the brown paper, and paused.

". . . eleven . . . twelve . . . thirteen . . ." And he frowned.

But then he shrugged and started on the next package.

"Mr. Beale?"

"Yes?" He had four books and four prices listed on the brown paper. Two glass jars and a few small brushes were beside the book he was just closing.

Morgan had marched down the steps. "I'm getting the Anthony Trollope for Angelo to deliver."

"Do you need the computer?"

"For just a minute. And I think Alice was just answering a phone call for you."

"Mr. Beale?" Alice's voice marched down the steps. "There's a call for you, Mr. Edmund Cane."

Charles slid his book into its new space and picked up the phone. "Charles Beale."

"Good afternoon." A slow, deliberate voice. "My name is Edmund Cane."

"Yes, Mr. Cane? What can I do for you?"

"I understand you were at the Bastien auction this morning?" Every syllable was a distinct word.

"Yes, I was."

"You were present during the sale of the Honaker pedestal desk?"

"Derek Bastien's desk? I was."

"Perhaps you saw the young woman who purchased the desk?"

"Mr. Cane," Charles said. "I hope I'm not being impertinent. By any chance, do you happen to have white hair and a dark gray mustache?"

The phone was silent as Einstein contemplated an equation or two. "Yes, I do. I see you remember me."

"I certainly do, Mr. Cane. It was very dramatic."

"Do you have any idea who might have wanted the desk?"

"Well, you did," Charles said.

Time passed slowly, at least at Charles's end of the phone. Morgan slipped the green label in the front of the Trollope and started wrapping it in brown paper. "Anyone else?" Mr. Cane finally said.

"I am sorry. You might try Norman Highberg. He has a showroom in Georgetown, and he knows the general antiques market much better than I. I only do books."

"Actually, your name was among those given me by Mr. Highberg."

"Hey boss, do you have the box for me?"

They both turned toward the door. In dark pants, dark shirt and dark tie, Angelo was transformed.

"Yes," Charles said. "You're always quiet coming into a room."

"Everything is so always quiet here." There was no transformation of his voice, or his eyes.

"Mr. Cane?" Charles said into the telephone. "I'm sorry, I'll be just a moment."

Morgan sealed the cardboard package. "I'm done." He handed it to Angelo.

"Be very nice to the customer when you see him," Charles said.

"Oh, I am always nice."

"Do they think that you're being nice?"

"I don't know what they think."

"I should ask them. You have the receipt for them to sign?"

"I have that."

"Then we'll see you when you get back. Thank you, Angelo."

"Yes, boss." And then he was gone.

"I'm sorry," Charles said again to the telephone. "Is there anything else I can do to help you?"

"I would like to identify the young woman who bid against me. Do you know anything about her?"

"No, I don't. I'm sorry."

"You have never seen her before?"

"Not that I remember."

"How unfortunate."

"Actually, Mr. Cane, I did just think of something. I don't think it would be much use. But an employee of mine was waiting outside the building. He might have seen her leave."

"Could you ask him?"

"He just left for the afternoon. I'll ask him this evening. But I doubt it would be much help."

"That could be a great help."

"I guess it's all relative," Charles said.

"Good day, Mr. Beale."

"Good day, Mr. Cane."

Morgan was looking at the books on the desk. "Those are the Derek Bastien books?"

"Yes. It doesn't look like they've been touched since we sold them. They all still have their green labels in them."

Morgan picked up one of the glass jars. "Was something loose?"

"Not particularly. The Gibbon had a little spot on the spine. I remember gluing it back when Derek first bought it, but it must not have dried all the way."

"There are fourteen of them?"

"No, thirteen."

"Maybe the computer's wrong. Should I put them on the website?"

"Not yet. I'll tell you when. I think they need a little rest first."

The room was silent again. The invaders had all been repulsed.

Charles took the next book, the fifth, out of the box.

They were all books of law, government and human rights, by John Locke, Edmund Burke, Adam Smith, John Adams, David Hume; Rousseau, Voltaire, Montesquieu, de Tocqueville and more; man's nature and man's hopes of overcoming it, or at least containing it.

He held the wrapped book, staring at it. He slowly raised and lowered it, feeling its weight.

His eyes darkened and his brow lowered in anger.

He removed the paper, very slowly.

It was John Locke, *An Essay Concerning Human Understanding*. The first page was as it should have been, but there was no green paper square. The back cover was normal.

Even as he held it, though, his fingers tensed. He stopped until they had relaxed and he was ready.

Reluctantly, he put his finger against the pages. He took a deep breath and steeled himself. He opened the volume near the middle.

"No!"

He closed his eyes. When he opened them, it was still the same.

"Alice?" he called up the stairs, when he could, trying to sound normal. "Could you ask Mrs. Beale to come down here, please?"

"Look," he demanded, even as she was still in the doorway.

It was still on the desk where he'd set it. Defiled.

"What is it, Charles?" Her voice was the stillness that smoothed the waves, and her presence was the water's depths untouched by the storms above.

He touched it. "The pages are cut."

She came close, and she saw it, and his shock and grief was mirrored in her eyes. He waited for her to pass through the sorrow, as he had.

"What is that?"

He touched it, nestled in the hollow space, just a plain box of playing cards. The book had been hollowed for it.

"A card box."

"Which book is it?"

He sighed. "John Locke."

"Why?"

He could only stare. "I don't know."

Together, they could only stare. Then Dorothy asked the first practical question.

"Would Derek have done it?"

"Who else?" He shuddered. "It must have been." The book lay open, embarrassed, on its spine. The cut was exactly sized to fit the box; only a very sharp knife could have cut so cleanly. Charles shivered. "But I can't believe he would have."

"How are the other books?"

"I haven't finished them."

"You should." Encouraging, empathic, and a little stern, all together.

"I'll dread opening each one."

"I know. That's why you need to get through them."

"Just stay down here a little while, won't you?"

"I will," Dorothy said. The book was lying on its brown paper, and she closed it and pulled the whole thing to the side of the desk.

Charles lifted the next package from the cardboard box, took a breath, and opened it.

"That was the only one," Charles said, with the last of the other twelve books safely on their shelves.

"We'll have to do something with it," Dorothy said.

"We can't leave it here." He pulled the paper back to the center of the desk. "I don't know what to do. Just throw it away? I couldn't bear to."

"It's completely ruined."

"Thoroughly, through and through. I've never had to deal with such a thing. I can salvage the boards, and maybe we'd use them."

"I suppose we could just put it on the shelf."

"That would be as bad as throwing it away," Charles said, "and I'd see it every time I came down here."

"Then throw it away. I'll do it for you."

"Let's wait."

Dorothy had finished with sentiment. "The longer you wait, the harder it will be."

"But not today." Charles put his hand on the closed book. "I suppose we should see if anything is in the little box." He opened the book. The box of cards hadn't moved.

"What if there is?"

He looked at it bitterly. "Then I'll propose a couple rounds of poker." He put his fingers on the edges of the box. "It isn't even period." He worked it free and weighed it in his hand. "Not cards, anyway."

"I hope it wouldn't be." Her voice was always musical; now it had a note of curiosity.

"It's too light," he said, and opened the top flap. "No jewels, no money, no ancient treasures. Just some papers."

Dorothy moved closer to see. "They must be important."

"They'd better be." Several white sheets were folded together, and he opened the first. "I don't even know what this is. A list." Fifty or more handwritten lines, each two letters, a date, and a number. He showed it to Dorothy.

She read one from the middle of the page. "GJ, nine-twelve-oh-five, twenty-two fifty."

"His computer passwords," Charles said. "Or his automobile mileage."

"Why would he keep his mileage inside John Locke?"

"Why would he keep anything inside John Locke? I don't know." He opened another page. "A copy of four checks." He looked at them closely. "Cashier's checks. They are made out to . . . Karen Liu."

"That's a lot of money," Dorothy said.

"Five hundred thousand in all."

"I wonder who Karen Liu is."

"I remember Derek mentioning her name." He frowned. "She is a congressman. Congresswoman. Congressperson."

Then they both were silent. It was a silence of confusion, where thoughts were almost audible.

"Why—?" they both said. Dorothy finished the question.

"Why would Derek have that paper?"

Charles answered, staring, but not at anything. "I don't know."

"And what would the checks be for?"

"I don't know."

Dorothy took the paper. "They're dated eight years ago. When did you sell him that book?"

"Five years ago."

"I wonder where he kept the papers before that."

Charles broke from his reverie. "Oh, he must have had some other hiding place. Maybe he had a hole chiseled out of a Renaissance statue? Or a Ming vase? Or maybe thumbtacked to the back of a Van Gogh."

"Did he have a Van Gogh?"

"I don't think so. But I wonder why he had them hidden at all." Then slowly, he opened a third paper. It was a newspaper article. Charles and Dorothy both read the headline.

Man Killed, Police Search County for Wife.

"We shouldn't look at these," Charles said.

"Maybe we should return them."

"Yes," Charles said. "That's what we should do." But he sounded doubtful.

"Will you call his wife?"

"I don't know. I don't know whose they should be. Legally, they're mine."

"I don't think they were meant to be sold," Dorothy said.

"I'm sure they weren't. But sale at auction is absolute."

"You don't want to keep them, do you?"

"No. It just means that they are mine to figure out what to do with."

Now Dorothy was doubtful. "What did he do at the Justice Department?"

Charles folded the papers and put them back in the box. Distastefully, he pushed the box back into its lair. "Derek was Chief of Staff to the Deputy Assistant Attorney General for Legislative Affairs."

Dorothy frowned, and the solemnity that had watched over the room shifted its gaze elsewhere. "I had no idea such a position existed," she said. Her tone was plain that she saw no need that it should.

"It did. It does still, I suppose."

"Then those papers must have something to do with it. They don't have anything to do with us."

"It's still a poor place to keep them," Charles said.

Dorothy's attention was pulled back to the object on the desk. "What will you do with the book?"

He stared at the ruin of it. "That is the real difficulty. Oh my," he sighed. "I'm so disappointed."

"How much is it worth?"

"I was going to say four thousand," Charles said. "It was the most valuable book he had."

"How much did you sell it to him for?"

"Twenty-six hundred, five years ago. But it's not the money anyway."

"It's what it says about Derek."

Now they were back to the beginning. "Yes," Charles said. "Exactly. If he needed to hide something, there must have been a hundred other places that didn't require destroying something. I remember delivering that book myself, and we talked for an hour about just it. I even remember the chess game we had while we talked."

"He must have had a reason for doing what he did."

"I'd like to know the reason," Charles said.

EVENING

The clock's seven slow chimes sounded. Charles sat at the counter. "Good night, Alice," he said.

"Good night, Mr. Beale. Should I lock the door?"

"Yes, please. Alice?"

"Yes, sir?"

"What was the last thing we sold today?"

"A *Don Quixote.*"

Then she was gone and he was alone. He breathed in the calm. "Another day older and wiser," he said to the books. "Each of us."

Feet appeared from above, and Morgan followed them on the stairs. Charles moved aside from the computer.

"I already closed out from upstairs," Morgan said. "I just need to put together the deposit and balance the drawer."

"Go ahead," Charles said. "I'm just sitting."

Morgan counted checks and cash and anything else there was and finally let himself out, taking the blue deposit bag with him, secure beneath his coat, and leaving the quiet behind. Charles watched over it protectively.

A gentler tread descended, music in his ears.

"Are you ready, dear Dulcinea?" Charles said.

Dorothy had on her jacket and gloves against the April evening.

"Yes, señor."

As he stood, and as Dorothy came to the last step, the lock rattled in the front door, and the door opened.

"Hey, boss."

"Sancho Panza," Charles said.

"What do you say?" Angelo asked.

"Nothing. We're just leaving. Everything went okay?"

"Everything is always okay."

"Very good. We'll see you tomorrow."

He was across the room and on the stairs, mounting them in panther silence.

Charles set the alarm for the night. "And shall we go, Mrs. Beale?" he asked.

"Please, Mr. Beale," she answered, and they stepped out to the twilit street. The sharp lights and sounds replaced the quiet of the books, but nothing dislodged the linen and forest smell; it was irreplaceable.

"Do you have anything in mind?" Charles asked as they dawdled along.

"No. I'm sure I could find something in the freezer."

"You don't sound very convincing."

"I'm not trying to."

"Hah!" They'd reached Prince Street. "Then the world is our oyster. Let's find a pearl."

"Wherever you lead, Charles, I will follow."

He led from beside her, a knight errant with his fair maiden, zigzagging through busy lamp-lit sidewalks, beneath a salmon sky and still air the temperature of vichyssoise. At the door of a miniature black villa fit between townhouses, a large-nosed man bowed his jet-black hair to them.

"Madame Beale! Monsieur. So welcome!"

"Good evening, Henri," Charles said.

"The chef has *La croustade de veau braisé au Madère* tonight, very special."

They were whisked to a corner table framed by vines decanted from a ceramic row of cabbages, beets and onions above them. The table was polished ebony, and the chairs were plush and pink. They sat in them side by side, and their candle was lit.

"Ah, Dorothy!" A woman in a black evening dress and henna red curls flew across the room. "What a night! Did Henri tell you? The *veau braisé au Madère* is magnificent! I cried over it. It was so delicious."

"Of course he told us, Antoinette."

"Philippe! Come! Have a wonderful meal," Antoinette said, already racing toward another table.

"The veal pastry, of course," Charles told the waiter. And then they were alone.

"Oh! I was going to ask Angelo about something from the auction."

"You said he didn't go in."

"Something outside. I'll ask tomorrow."

"Do you like *La croustade de veau braisé*?"

"We'll soon find out."

In their corner, they were outside the mumble and buzz of the other diners and gymnastics of the waiters. Dorothy laid her hand on the table, free for the taking; and Charles took it, and held it. The candle flame danced.

"I want to meet Karen Liu," Charles said.

"What?" Dorothy straightened, and looked at him. "The congress-woman? Why?"

"I want to see what kind of person she is."

Dorothy adjusted to the subject, smiling and frowning, both. "You're worried about the checks."

"In many ways."

"Madame." The veal had arrived. They ate.

"Well, it is the best *La croustade de veau braisé au Madère* I've ever had," Charles said.

"The only one you've ever had?"

"If there had been another, I would have remembered."

"I'd have to say the same," she said. And then, "Tell me more about Derek Bastien."

"Yes. Let me see. Derek was a collector."

"There must be more to him than what he owned."

"I don't mean just that. But he certainly owned a lot. He lived in a grand house and everything in it was special."

"It was in Northwest, wasn't it?"

"Yes, in Foxhall. The floor was Italian marble. The wallpaper was a replica of Thomas Jefferson's. Everything was like that. His desk was originally Alphonso Taft's."

"Taft?" Dorothy smiled. "Is that a relation of President Taft?"

"His father. Alphonso was Attorney General in the 1870s. Derek didn't buy things; he acquired them."

"That's the desk you were talking about."

"Yes. It was typical. If he bought a toothbrush, it would probably have been ivory and once belonged to a Duke—or to the man who invented toothpaste."

Dorothy poked her veal pastry. "He must have been independently wealthy."

"He was, actually," Charles said.

"How nice for him," she said. "Did he have to work, then?"

"No. It was more of a hobby."

"Did you say something about the Attorney General?"

"Deputy Assistant Attorney General, and Derek was not that person. That person is named John Borchard, and Derek was that person's chief of staff."

"So this Mr. Borchard person must work for the Assistant Attorney General."

Charles shook his head. "No. The Deputy Assistant Attorney General reports to the Principal Deputy Assistant Attorney General, who reports to the Assistant Attorney General, who reports to the Attorney General."

"Charles, that's ridiculous."

"They have that whole big building to fill. This particular nest of Deputies was in charge of pushing Congress on laws the Justice Department was interested in."

"It sounds very bureaucratic."

"That would be an understatement. He only did it as a game. He liked to play games."

"You played chess with him?" Dorothy said.

"Yes. We would talk and play chess. Move and countermove and strategy."

"That job isn't my idea of a game."

"Not exactly mine either. But Derek thrived on it."

"How was he connected with Karen Liu?"

"I had Morgan look her up. She is on the House Judiciary Committee. She must have worked with Derek fairly often."

And after fending off dessert, they were again on the street and the sky was polished ebony, reflecting the lights of the town in its stars.

"Home?" Charles said.

"Please," Dorothy said, and they passed the incandescent shop windows and the curtained sitting-room windows; and where old trees reached over an even older street, and old brick sidewalks led past even older brick townhouses, they came to their own steps and front door.

"Were you serious?" Dorothy asked when they were inside, turning on their own sitting-room lights. "How do you meet a congresswoman?"

"I'll call and ask."

"They won't let you in."

"Then I won't go. And if she does let me in, I will go."

"But after that?"

"I will go on, wherever the wind blows."

Dorothy settled into a deeply plush wingback chair beside the fireplace and opened a book from the table beside it. Above the mantel was a framed photograph of a much younger two of them and a teenage boy, the same face on Dorothy's desk. "You will be tilting at windmills."

Charles took his own book from the table. "I've always wanted to do that."

"What do you think, Charles? Is Locke the greatest of the English enlightenment?"

"Now, come, Derek. You ask those questions just to be provocative. There's no answer to that."

"Who would rank with him, then? And don't say Hume, he's Scottish."

"Newton."

"Gravity is nice, but I'm speaking socially, politically."

"I'm speaking philosophically. There are laws that govern nature, and laws that govern man's nature. The Enlightenment isn't limited to politics."

"But, Charles! The end of philosophy is politics."

"Politics puts an end to philosophy, if that's what you mean. It's hardly the intellectual end."

"But politics is the practical end. And the practical purpose. What other use does philosophy have? Not personal, not for most people."

"It is personal for them, Derek. They don't call it philosophy. Most people call it values, or life purpose."

"And for most people it's a muddle. John Locke was concerned with the practical government of men, not some amorphous cloud of personal morals and beliefs."

"Morals were vital to him!"

"An Enlightenment philosopher, Charles? He was far past religion."

"Do you know his epitaph?"

"*I believe I do.*"

"*Let me try to remember. There's the part that says, 'Of good life, you have an example in the gospel, should you desire it; of vice, would there were none for you; of mortality, surely you have one here and everywhere, and may you learn from it.' That's the message of his Essay. His theories of government don't mean anything without his theory of human nature.*"

"*Yes, I know the epitaph. But he was a dying man when he wrote it. He'd lost his objectivity. What would you put on your tombstone, Charles?*"

"*Maybe the same as Locke. I hadn't thought about it. What about you, Derek?*"

"*Do you mean when I'm in my dotage and trying to curry favor in the next world?*"

"*Oh, let's say what you'd write now, still at the brazen height of your intellectual powers. If you were to die unexpectedly tonight, what would you want written as your memorial?*"

"*I would take the first part of Locke's, that says that 'His virtues were too few to mention, and may his faults die with him,' and paraphrase it.*"

"*How?*"

"*Virtue and vice are too subjective. I would take modern properties that I value: 'His knowledge of his fellow man was too great to describe, and may it die with him.' *"

TUESDAY

MORNING

"Good morning, Alice."

She beamed at him like the morning sun. "Good morning, Mr. Beale. Good morning, Mrs. Beale."

Charles climbed the stairs to the office. Morgan was already in his nook.

"On the hunt?" Charles asked.

"Yes, sir. There's an auction in San Francisco next month."

"Let me see." Charles stood over Morgan's shoulder and looked at the list. "A few things. I might call Jacob and see if he's going. Do you see anything we need?"

"I'll check against inventory. This is what's up on eBay since yesterday. And Briary Roberts just put a bunch of new stuff on their website."

"Did we sell anything?"

"Three volumes. Nothing big. I'll mail them this afternoon."

"Carry on."

Dorothy was just sitting at her desk. Charles plopped down at his and opened the newspaper.

"Do you have plans for the day?" she asked.

It was in the morning that her voice was the most musical. "Tell me what you'll be doing," Charles said.

"I'll finish this set of invoices and then I'm going to call Wilhelmina Stratton about the banquet Saturday evening. We have to start on the fall catalog this week . . . Charles, are you listening?"

His eyes were closed. "Of course, dear."

"Then what did I say?"

"Oh, I don't know. I just like to hear you talk. Your voice is a symphony to me, your words are pure notes—"

"Would you empty the trash, please?" Dorothy said.

He sat up. "First I need to read it." He opened the newspaper and scanned the front page.

"Anything?" Dorothy said.

"What a sordid world." He folded the paper and dropped it in the wastebasket. "What a human world. It's all scandals and failings."

"There's more to it than the front page of the *Washington Post*."

"Yes, there are other sections, but they are all still human."

"What in the world else would there be? Don't you have enough to do, Charles?"

"I have plenty to do."

"Because if you don't, you could file these invoices."

"I would love to, but I really have quite a bit to do."

"I was just asking."

Charles found his telephone book and looked up a number.

"Thank you for calling the office of Congresswoman Karen Liu," the telephone said.

"You're welcome. My name is Charles Beale, and I would like to meet with the congresswoman."

"Mr. Beale, is there anything I can help you with?"

"No, I'm sorry. It would need to be with her."

"She's very busy, of course." The voice was very polite. "Are you from her district in California?"

"No," Charles said. "I'm not a constituent, and I'm not a lobbyist or reporter."

"What would you want to discuss with the congresswoman?"

"I was a friend of a man named Derek Bastien, who died several months ago. He worked in the Justice Department."

The voice did not realize for a moment that Charles had finished his turn.

"Are you with the Justice Department?" it finally asked.

"No. I'm not with the government. I'm a bookseller, actually."

That was enough for the voice to be finished with the conversation. "Mr. Beale, let me take your number and I'll pass it on to her chief of staff. She is very busy, though, and she is usually not available."

"I'm not sure if you're serious," Dorothy said after he'd hung up.

"I am."

"You didn't give any good reason she should take time to meet you."

"I hope I didn't. And now I am going to visit Norman Highberg."

"You're going to Georgetown?"

"I need the exercise."

"I thought you had too much to do."

"This is one of the things."

"Then have a nice morning. I know better than to ask you questions when you don't want to answer."

"I don't have any answers. And I think it's important to find some."

The well-worn walk to the Metro station past the urban townhouses of Prince Street, and the bland Metro ride under the Potomac, brought Charles finally to the even more urban townhouses of Georgetown. The streets weren't very different from Alexandria, just wider and with more cars and more city and more important-looking people. The Capitol and the White House weren't far away; Georgetown was a closer planet to the sun and less likely to have its own native life.

Charles chose a doorway.

"Good morning. Is Mr. Highberg in?"

The young thing behind the counter gaped. "I don't know."

"Go find out."

The young thing went and Charles was alone to stroll. Somehow, it was a very nice showroom. Every manner of upscale antique was there, except of course furniture and books. Crystal sparkled, silver shone, wood glowed, and not an item was less than two hundred dollars or more than three thousand.

"Charles! What are you doing here?"

"You need to work on your customer service, Norman," Charles said.

"You're not a customer. What do you want?"

"I'm quite well, thank you. How are you?"

"Great except for taxes." The frames of his bulky glasses were as shiny and black as his hair. The lenses were smudged with gray fingerprints, and the hair was smudged with just gray. "My accountant just sent me last month's report. Taxes are killing me. You need an accountant? This guy's my brother-in-law and he's looking for clients."

"I don't need anyone."

"What are taxes in Virginia? It must be better than here. This place, you walk around with the mayor's hand in your pocket. You put a dollar in and he takes it out. You aren't a customer, right? Or maybe you are. Are you looking for anything?"

"I don't need anything."

"Sure you don't, but that doesn't keep people from buying this stuff anyway. Who needs any of it?"

"I don't, I'm afraid. But it is all very nice."

"You bet." He paused to breathe and look around, and he smiled. "Real nice. Because it's real. Every piece."

"I'm sure it is."

"I don't mean it's not fake. I mean there's something about it. You have to have the eye." He put his finger beside his eye and tapped. "If you have the eye, you can look at anything and tell. I'll go places and walk through somebody's showroom and nothing's real. It's not fake, but it's not real. And I can see it. I can see it a mile away. You know what I mean."

"I do know, Norman. I know exactly what you mean."

"Sure you do. Why else be in the business? You've got the eye,

Charles. You can see what's real. I don't do books, but I can tell, even with them."

"Anyway," Charles said, "I have a question."

"Maybe I even have an answer! What do you want?"

"Yesterday that man called me, Edmund Cane."

"Yeah, right, he was asking who I knew at the auction and I told him all the names I knew. He was trying to find out who the blonde was."

"Do you know if he found out?"

"Nope. I sure didn't know who she was. He might have found out, but I don't know."

"Who was he?"

"Cane? Oh, just a guy from a place in New York. He looks just like Einstein. Did you want to talk to him again?"

"Maybe. I'd at least like to know how to."

"Sure, you could look him up. The place in New York, it's called Horton's on Fortieth."

"Horton's."

"On Fortieth, that's part of the name. Big place. Say, that was some auction yesterday. All I was trying to do was just buy back the stuff I sold the guy."

"That reminds me, Norman. I have another question."

"I think I can do two, but don't push your luck!"

"I won't. You said the police gave you a list."

"Right. Stuff that got stolen from the house the night the guy got whacked. They want me to be looking for it."

"Yes. Do you have a copy?"

"Yeah, sure, somewhere back here. Give me a minute and I'll find it. You think you've seen something?"

"Probably not. I was just curious."

"I'll find it. It'll just take a minute."

Charles browsed. They were real things. The shelves and floor and tables were blanketed by a dizzying variety of shapes and materials and uses, but they were all very real.

Charles could tell.

Then the real Norman was again with him. "I got it. It's the list of the stuff that got stolen. You're supposed to keep an eye out for them, and if you see anything, call that number at the top. It's the police, and that's the detective to ask for, his name is Watts. And there's an FBI guy on it, Frank Kelly, since it's antiquities, and you can call him, too."

"I see. There are over fifty things here!"

"Oh. It's from all the burglaries. I think Bastien was the fifth one. Some guy going through the neighborhood."

"Norman—does it mean anything to you?"

"What, the list? It's stuff that got stolen."

"Yes," Charles said. "But the things that were stolen—do they say anything about who would have stolen them?"

"Huh? It's all kinds of stuff. A little French statue, a mahogany letter file, an ivory dolphin—that was a nice one, I sold him that one."

"They're all antiques."

"So the burglar's got good taste. And they're all small and valuable. He breaks in, grabs stuff, and runs. That neighborhood up there in Foxhall, every house is piled high with stuff."

"I have several customers up there," Charles said.

"Great place for a burglar. Except when Derek Bastien walks in on him right in the middle of his haul. Too bad. Wrong place, wrong time, and the guy panics. Grabs a marble statue and wham, wham, wham! You read about it, right?"

"I didn't read the details."

"I sold him that statue. I bet it weighed thirty pounds, at least. One whack would have been plenty, but the guy's panicked I guess. Blood everywhere. You know, I wonder if that's why the desk sold so high. But they wouldn't sell it with all the blood, would they? They'd clean it off. But you have to be careful cleaning those old finishes—"

"Thank you, Norman. It's been so nice to see you."

AFTERNOON

The return from Georgetown had been about the same as the trip to it.

"Mr. Beale," Alice said as he paused in the showroom, "there was a telephone call for you. Mrs. Beale has the message."

"Thank you. Have we sold anything this morning?"

"A Dickens. *The Olde Curiosity Shoppe*."

"There are shops where curiosity is a dangerous thing," he said.

"Hello, dear."

"Well, well," she said, with a lemon meringue tartness.

"Well what?"

"Congresswoman Karen Liu's office called and she would be pleased to see you tomorrow, Wednesday, at 7:30 in the morning."

"Tomorrow morning?" he said.

"Yes, and please call back to confirm."

"I will. How unexpected."

"Charles." The lemon had some sour. "What are you going to say to her?"

"I have until tomorrow to think of something."

"I still don't know why you are even going."

"I am going to look at her and tell if she's the real thing."

"The real what?"

"The real thing."

"How will you tell?"

He tapped his finger beside his eye. "I can see it."

"And did Norman Highberg answer any of your questions?"

"Some of them more than I wanted. Dorothy, I have some odd things to think about."

"It is because you are looking in odd places."

"Yes. And now, I think, bookstores in California should be open."

"Mr. Leatherman, please. This is Charles Beale."

He waited.

"Charles? Is that you?"

"Yes, Jacob. It is."

"Have you come to your senses? I'll give you twenty-three, and not a penny more."

"Did you have a nice trip home?"

"Of course not. If you're not calling about those books, what are you calling about?"

"I saw there was an auction in San Francisco next month."

"What about it? You're not coming out here, are you?"

"No. But I might want a few things from it, and I wondered if you were going."

"I might be. I might not be. I haven't looked at the list yet, but I don't think I want anything from it."

"Then if there is anything I want, and if you do go or send someone, and if you aren't bidding on the same things that I want, would you bid on them for me?"

"If, and if, and if, then I might."

"Thank you. I'll look at the list again and decide."

"Or I might just decide that whatever you want, I want it, too."

"I would expect no less of you, Jacob."

"And don't tell me you weren't the one who had that Edmund Cane call me this morning."

"I wasn't, actually. He called me, too. It was Norman Highberg that gave him my name, and probably yours."

"Who's that?"

"Just an antiques dealer who was at the auction. You should meet him sometime, you'd get along famously. Mr. Cane was asking you about the woman and the desk?"

"How would I know who she was? Do you think I know everybody in the country? If she's fool enough to pay a hundred thousand for a desk, she shouldn't be hard to find."

"It was intriguing," Charles said.

"It was a commotion and I hate commotions."

"You, Jacob? I don't believe it."

48

"I don't mind causing one myself; I just hate anyone else making one."

"I don't believe that either. I bet you were as intrigued as I was."

"Then you might be even more if you saw what I did."

"What did you see?"

Jacob chuckled. "When you've been around as long as I have, you learn to keep your eyes open."

"Then I would have a long time to go," Charles said.

"And you probably won't make it anyway. So I'll tell you what I saw. That chair you sat in?"

"Yes. It was the only one open."

"It hadn't been for long. There was a man in it, with long hair tied up. I don't know why they let him in, the way he looked, except they let anyone in any more."

"What about him?"

"He was bidding on the desk, too."

"But he'd left when I came in."

"Oh, you think so? You think you know everything, don't you?"

"Well—the chair was empty."

"He was still there. I saw him. He slid over to the side of the room, where you couldn't see him, and he tried bidding a couple times. He gave up, though."

"I didn't notice. You're right, Jacob, there are still plenty of things I miss."

"At least you admit it. That means you might learn someday."

"And that's all very intriguing, Jacob. I do wonder what it means."

"You wonder because you're still young and foolish."

"Idealistic," Charles said.

"Same thing."

"And I'm fifty-five."

"That's all? You look older than that."

"I only feel older. And you wonder, too, what it means, and you're certainly not young or foolish. Did you tell Mr. Cane?"

"Of course not. He didn't ask, and I didn't feel like telling him."

"Well thank you for telling me."

"I don't know why I'd take the time."

"I won't take any more of your time."

"I don't have that much left."

"Then goodbye, Jacob. Talk to you later."

"If I live that long."

Charles set the phone down very gently. "It takes a special person."

"To be friends with Jacob Leatherman?" Dorothy asked.

"To be Jacob Leatherman. It must require a tremendous amount of effort."

"Are you getting everything done?"

"Getting what done?"

"All those things you had to do," Dorothy said.

"The list is getting longer, and going to strange and stranger places."

"Where does it go next?"

"Upstairs."

Up the steps from the office to the third floor, which was three doors facing a tiny landing. Charles knocked on the one that faced him.

"What?" The door opened and Angelo was framed in its opening. He was not in his nice clothes. "Hey, boss."

"I have a question for you."

"What question?"

But Charles had to stop and stare. "Why do I feel like I'm about to get knifed?"

Something flickered deep in Angelo's eyes—maybe humor, maybe not. "Hey, you know, boss, I don't know why you feel some way, maybe it was something you ate." His voice was sibilant and low, like a lullaby through his smiling white teeth that were not smiling.

"I just hope you don't scare my customers silly."

Two white wires attached his ears to his pocket. "Oh no, boss, I don't ever scare those customers." The smile stayed not smiling. "That wouldn't be nice."

"No, it would not be nice, and I would hear about it. What are you listening to?"

Even the tiny speakers made the air throb.

"It's just music."

"I hope you don't go deaf. Anyway. Yesterday when you were waiting outside at the auction. Were you watching the door I came out of?"

"I was watching for you."

"Did you see other people leaving?"

"I saw people go in and go out."

"Lots of people?"

Angelo shrugged. "Some people."

"Did you see a woman in a gray suit, with bright blond hair?"

"Maybe I saw somebody who was that, I don't know."

"What did she do?"

"She walked away."

"That's what I thought. There is someone looking for her."

Angelo leaned against the door frame and narrowed his eyes into even tighter slits.

"She do something somebody doesn't like?"

"No. Nothing like that."

"So why does someone look for her?"

"It's business. It isn't a street gang or a drug ring."

"That is business. Hey, boss, you be careful if you get into people looking for someone."

"I will be. But this is a different world than the street, Angelo."

He replied with two seconds of silence. "You want anything else?"

"No, that was all."

"Whoever said that it was the Chinese who were inscrutable? I think Angelo is made of concrete."

Dorothy smiled, quite scrutably. "Did you find what you were looking for?"

"Yes, which turned out to be nothing."

"And now what are you going to do?"

He selected a catalog from his desk and leaned back in his chair. "I'm going to run my bookstore."

"Oh, how nice that you can spare us the time."

EVENING

The sun traipsed across the sky; hours that had once been future became past. Charles rambled up from the basement to the office and looked in on his wife.

"Is it time, Mrs. Beale?"

"It is, Mr. Beale."

"I was hoping so. And I believe it has chanced to rain."

He held her jacket, standing close to her, and stayed close down the stairs.

"Have we sold anything, Alice?"

"A Madeleine L'Engle."

"Just now?"

"Earlier." Alice frowned. "I didn't realize it was so late."

"Perhaps time has wrinkled a little. Have a good evening."

"Yes, sir. Good night, Mr. Beale, Mrs. Beale."

"Good night, Alice," they both said, while Charles opened the door, and the umbrella, and they both walked out under it.

Only April could have such gentle rain. The colors of the watercolor streets ran together from the slate roofs, down the dun and brick buildings, picked up the bright daubs of flower boxes and dark brilliant doors in every joyful hue that was respectable, spread across the footways in their own hard solid wet colors, and pooled into shining reflections in the streets. These were the old buildings' hidden colors that only came out in the rain, the shades of their youth buried under the dulling of their years.

"Do you remember . . . ?"

They knew every square of the pavement, which ones held puddles, which ones had root-lifted corners.

"Remember what?" Dorothy's voice was as soft as the rain.

"The open window."

"Of course I do."

The rain whispered.

"The rain makes me think of it," Charles said. "I would take you back there."

"It wouldn't be the same."

"It probably wasn't even then." They waited at a corner. The strolling water didn't wait but passed on.

"Sometimes I wonder if it really was the way I remember," she said. "But I would rather have the memory whether or not it's true."

"It is true. It's not what actually happened, the memory we have of it is truer than that."

"It's an irony, isn't it, Charles? Edmund Burke and now Thomas Paine, together on the shelf."

"Perhaps you shouldn't put them too close, Derek."

"No, side by side. Two men, two revolutions, and what different and radical reactions they had."

" 'Radical reaction.' That's a clever turn of phrase. Paine would have liked it."

"He had no humor, Charles. Radicals don't. Burke did. One of many contrasts between them."

"They make a good contrast. Burke was such a strong voice in the British Parliament in favor of the American Revolution, but so strongly against the French."

"And Paine never saw a revolution he didn't like, even when it almost cost him his own head."

"And I doubt, Derek, that you ever saw a revolution you did like."

"Never, except that they make good literature. I was reading Pasternak the other night."

"I agree that stable times are much more comfortable. But revolutions created the modern world."

"You sound like Jefferson, Charles. A little blood, now and then, to keep liberty fresh?"

"Maybe just a bit of personal revolution, as a fresh start. Do you have anything in your life that you would want overthrown, Derek?"

"A personal revolution? No. Besides, it's not a revolution unless there's blood."

WEDNESDAY

MORNING

"Mr. Beale, Ms. Liu will see you now."

"Thank you." Just 7:48.

The congresswoman liked flowers. They filled the waiting room in paintings and fresh-cut arrangements and pastel furniture.

The outer office was filled with people, at least photographs of them. It was an impressive cult of personality. Hundreds covered the walls, most of them of her and star-struck constituents, and hundreds of thank-you cards.

For surely the minuscule woman in the pictures celebrating the success of representative government service was the force driving the office and everyone in its fifty-yard vicinity. The face was a striking mix of features, Asian and African, which did not peacefully coexist but were proudly distinct.

The pictures hardly captured the vibrant energy that met him full force as he entered the inner office. The room was a sherbet bowl of lime, raspberry, orange and lemon, but the real brightness glowed from the dazzling smile and glittering eyes fixed on him.

Charles blinked.

"Mr. Beale! I am so *glad* to meet you."

With both perfect dignity and thorough eagerness, Karen Liu strode forward from her desk toward him, her hand extended at about the level of his waist. He leaned a little down, bowing before the queen, to reach her.

"Ms. Liu. I'm honored."

At this lower altitude he was chin to indomitable chin with her, and eye to mesmerizing eye.

"I am, too," she said. "Sit down."

Disobedience was unthinkable. He sat.

She did also, and they reached a middle-ground compromise to their vertical differences. It was a sign of favor; she didn't seem likely to compromise often.

"You were a friend of Derek Bastien," she said. "And that means you must be intriguing."

Charles was momentarily stunned.

"Well, I'm not," he said. "Not very."

She didn't believe him. "You must be. How did you know Derek?"

"I sold him books." He was beginning to get his breath back.

"Books. He had a lot of them."

Her eyes were disconcerting. He tried to concert.

"Antique books." He managed to meet her stare. "I have a shop in Alexandria. Derek was a customer." He tried to be intriguing. "And a friend."

"He was my friend, too," Karen Liu said. "And I was *proud* to be his friend."

"You worked with him, didn't you?"

Her stare shifted to distant horizons. "We accomplished so much. I could always *count* on his support at the Justice Department. What makes a book antique?" She suddenly returned.

"A long time."

"How much do they cost?"

"A lot."

She nodded. "Old and expensive. Derek must have loved them. And what can I do for you this morning?"

He smiled, his watts to her megawatts. "I just decided that I'd like to meet some of Derek's other friends. I hope I'm not wasting your time."

"No, you are *not*. He was a wonderful man, and we are all diminished by his loss."

Judging by her stature, the congresswoman had had many such losses. "I only talked with him occasionally," Charles said. "A few times a year when he came to the shop, or I delivered a book to him."

"I talked with him every week. My staff *worked* with his staff every day."

"Is that unusual? That's not the picture one usually gets of cooperation between Congress and the executive departments."

"It was unusual because Derek was unusual, and it has been quite different without him."

"Who took his place?"

"I wouldn't know." A dark cloud suddenly obscured the sun. "We have been instructed that all communication will pass through the Deputy Assistant Attorney General personally from now on, and not his staff." And the cloud became a thunderhead.

"I'm so sorry." Saying the wrong thing could bring torrential downpours, and Charles didn't have an umbrella.

"It is sorry. It is a *disgrace* for Mr. Borchard, who is an appointed official, to act this way."

"But tell me about yourself," he said. "If you don't mind. Derek spoke of you often."

Her smile flashed out like a lighthouse through the gloom, and the gloom went running for its life.

"Mr. Beale, I am living the most *wonderful* life in the world."

Somehow, no less an answer would have been right. "Tell me how you got to Congress. It must not have been easy."

Every sentence brought out a different light source. Now it was a laser. "Nothing has ever been easy."

"But I think you don't let that stop you. You must be quite a fighter."

"I have always fought, Mr. Beale. I *fought* my way into college, and into law school, and into every place I've ever been."

Charles had settled back into his chair. The conversation had turned into a stump speech, one that Karen Liu had given many times. But the passion was fresh and pungent.

"I *fought* my way out of an alcoholic mother and a father who disappeared when I was two, and out of *poverty* and *racism* and *bigotry* and I will *keep* fighting for the *people* who are still in *chains* to poverty and racism and bigotry. That is what I *have* been doing, and that is what I will *continue* to do. You can read my biography, Mr. Beale, it's on my website."

"I preferred to meet you first."

"Read it. Because when I looked at the *world* I lived in, the *ghettos* where I grew up, I had to *do* something about it. And I decided that here"—she waved her hand across the room—"*here* was the place to do it. And the people who *were* here *weren't* doing anything. So I took them on, and *I won.*

"And it was not easy. I had to fight an entrenched political machine that had everything, and I didn't have anything, and they spent every dollar and played every dirty trick they could. But they couldn't fight the *people*, and the *people* knew who was on their side, and I won that primary by three thousand votes. And I have *repaid* the faith that those voters placed in me, and fought for *them*."

There was a short break for applause from the audience.

"Ms. Liu," Charles said, and it was far inferior to the wild cheers that should have filled the room. "I see why Derek thought so highly of you. I know how important money is in politics, and an entrenched machine will have a lot of it. Beating them by three thousand votes is amazing."

"Many people were amazed," she said, and she was no longer on a platform speaking to thousands, but eye to eye with a single person.

"And I am even more appreciative of your time when I realize what important work I'm keeping you from." He shifted in his chair to stand, but the eyes did not release him.

"I am never too busy for a friend." She seemed to be waiting for him to say something else.

"I'm honored to be considered one," Charles said.

"I would like to see your books. Did you say that Derek came to your store?" No smile, just intensity.

"Yes, he did."

"Then I will, too." She smiled and the conversation became friendly again. "I'm *sure* it's fascinating."

"It is," Charles said. "Yes, please come."

"And did you have any other business with Derek?" There was still an undercurrent of expectation and questioning.

"No. That was all."

"Did he ever discuss his work with you?"

"Not often. We usually discussed more philosophic subjects."

"Did that include John Borchard?" It was a very direct question.

"Derek's boss? No. I know just the little that Derek told me about him."

"I would be interested to know what Derek told you." She smiled, and again the gloom dispersed. "And Derek told you about me? I hope that was always positive."

"Always."

"Well! I hope so, and I hope he meant it. And now it is time for me to keep moving along."

"Then thank you, Congresswoman. And I hope to see you at the shop sometime soon."

"You will! Nothing could keep me away!"

"You really met with a congressperson?" Dorothy asked.

"I did," Charles said as he got himself into his chair. "Really."

"Is *Liu* oriental?"

"Yes. She is both black and Chinese, and barely tall enough to be just one, let alone two. But she is energetic enough for three or four. We had a very nice talk."

"She must have had better things to do with her time." She was skeptical, and disapproving, and amused. "What did you talk about?"

"About Derek, and about herself. She was very open."

"To a perfect stranger?"

"It is her job to talk about herself. And I am hardly perfect."

"Hardly. But even you should have known better than to bother her."

"She could have said no," Charles said. "And I was nearly as surprised as you that she didn't."

"Nearly?"

"You underestimate Derek Bastien. His name is a little key to certain doors."

"There are other things that open doors. Did you ask her about those checks?"

"I did not, of course. But I hinted. I asked how hard it was to get elected that first time." He gazed out toward the horizon, his jaw set. "It was very hard. Very hard! But she prevailed!"

"With five hundred thousand dollars' worth of help."

"Please, dear," Charles said. "I am speaking of the people triumphing, and justice and all that, and you bring up sordid money?"

"I apologize," she said, not. "I suppose she did not take your hint."

"Well, it got fuzzy there. Or maybe I should say, it got very sharp. I don't know. I'll have to think it through."

"And now that you've met her, would you say she is the 'real thing'?"

"You know, despite what John Locke says about her, I think she is. But I need to make a comparison to be sure. Dorothy, who would you say was higher ranking—a congresswoman, or a Deputy Assistant Attorney General?"

"The congresswoman."

"The Deputy has more syllables, even with her extra one for being a lady. I'm going to try my little key again."

"You're not going to call him, too!"

"I am."

"Why are you doing this, Charles?"

"I'm wandering."

"You'll get lost."

"But I haven't come to a stopping place, yet."

She sighed. "Then just tell me when I should tell you to give up."

"I will." He found the telephone book under the magazines on his desk. "Or else you won't need to. I'm sure I'll hit a dead end with this very high-ranking official. It would be foolishness for him to waste his time speaking to me."

"Then why are you calling?"

"Just in case it isn't."

Dorothy turned back to her own desk while Charles found *Justice Department* under the government listing, and flamboyantly ignored him.

"I would like to speak with John Borchard," he said to the voice that answered, and he waited through clicks and beeps until another voice said, "Office of Legislative Affairs."

"I would like to speak with John Borchard," he said again, and this time waited through beeps and clicks until another voice said, "Mr. Borchard's office."

"I would like to speak with John Borchard," he said.

"Who is calling?"

"My name is Charles Beale."

"Thank you. What is your position, Mr. Beale?"

"I'm a bookseller."

For the first time in the whole smooth process, the gears clanked.

"Excuse me?"

"I sell antique books."

"Do you have business with Mr. Borchard?"

"Not really. I only wanted to speak with him."

"What about, Mr. Beale?" The gears were preparing to spin in the opposite direction, hard. Dorothy smirked.

"I used to do business with Derek Bastien."

"Just a moment."

All motion was brought to a halt. Charles waited. Dorothy did also, watching him over the top of her glasses.

"I am anticipating your rejection," she said.

The telephone spoke. "Mr. Beale, could you come to Mr. Borchard's office this afternoon at two thirty?"

He raised his left eyebrow right at her. "Two thirty," he said. "I will be there."

In Dorothy's eyes, even indignation was beautiful.

"Charles. Why are you pestering these people, and why are they letting you?"

"I can't guess their motives."

"Or even your own."

"Or yours. Why are you affronted?"

"It is embarrassing."

"You feel embarrassed?"

"No! You should. And even worse, it is a waste of time."

"Ah." Charles smiled. "The ultimate crime."

"It is. Go ahead, have your fun, and don't come running to me when they throw you in prison."

"I wouldn't be able to." He was suddenly startled. "Angelo. I didn't see you."

From the doorway, Angelo frowned. "Hey, boss. What do you do, that you go in a prison?"

"Impersonating an adult," Dorothy said.

"Oh." Angelo shrugged. "I am going out."

"All right," Charles said. "Thank you."

"How do you do that?"

"What?"

"What she said. *Impersonating*."

"You do things she does not approve of," Charles said.

Angelo jerked his head in disbelief. "And you go to jail?"

"Yes. She is a woman not to be trifled with, Angelo, and I know it well."

AFTERNOON

"I'll be out for the afternoon," Charles said to Alice as he passed through the showroom. "Have we sold anything?"

"That big, illustrated 1940 *Wizard of Oz*."

"That's who I'm off to see."

Behind was the bright yellow-brick road, and ahead was the Emerald City with its imposing sign: Department of Justice.

Charles stepped through the portal. "My name is Charles Beale. I'm here to see John Borchard. I have an appointment."

The woman and the counter both were wooden and imposing. "Just a moment, Mr. Beale."

It was a long, slow, wooden moment. Official ladies and gentlemen with badges and serious faces passed by.

"Someone will be down in a moment, Mr. Beale."

"Thank you."

"Please sign in. This is your badge."

"Thank you."

Another moment. The moments were very long here in the shadows.

"Please follow me, Mr. Beale."

He followed through dim corridors. Justice was indeed blind; anyone in these dark halls would be.

Then a doorway—from gray farmhouse into bright-colored Munchkinland.

"Just a moment, Mr. Beale."

He was in another of the building's many places to wait; but this bright-lit moment was brief.

An enormous bald head appeared. "How do you do? I'm John Borchard."

"Charles Beale."

There was a normal body beneath John Borchard's large head, clothed in a dark, serious suit. The face spread across the front of the head was serious, too, but capable of many emotions in only a few seconds. Even as Charles lifted his hand, the seriousness shifted through interest and anticipation to pleasure.

"I am so glad you called," he said. "Please come into my office."

The office was larger than the head. Charles was set on a supple, wine-red leather couch, beneath historic American paintings that needed as large a room as this in which to be properly displayed. Yards away, it seemed, was an immense desk, capable of properly displaying a Deputy Assistant Attorney General.

John Borchard chose a matching chair closer to Charles.

"Thank you so much for seeing me," Charles said.

"It's a pleasure." The voice was of bassoons and cellos. "So you knew Derek?" The head tilted at that profound thought. "What a tragedy."

"Certainly," Charles said. His own voice was rather reedy and oboe-ish.

"And you are an antiquarian?"

"I deal in antique books. I met Derek through his collecting."

"Yes, his collecting." Each phrase was a plaque in sound, dark wood with the words engraved in brass. "He was quite a collector. In many ways. But what can I do for you today, Mr. Beale—Charles?"

"Well . . . not really anything. I only wanted to meet you. As someone who knew Derek."

Mr. Borchard—John?—nodded. "I understand. Absolutely. An odd thing, isn't it? Yet I think anyone who knew him would understand. It was the quality of the man."

"There was a quality."

"There was. I can't tell you how much he is missed here. He'd been with me for over ten years."

"I'd known him about six years."

"How well?" One eyebrow climbed high. "Had you been his guest, even?"

"I did get in the front door a few times," Charles said.

The other eyebrow rose up to its fellow. "Ah. A game or two of chess?"

"A game or two."

A grand smile stretched the lower part of the face while the eyebrows expanded the upper. "He was quite good, wasn't he?"

"He was very good."

"Yes, I learned my lesson early on, that some battles are hopeless." What a big smile he had. "And I declined further contests. So you were quite into the inner circle, then."

"It was a large circle."

"Very, but close in, nonetheless. And your entrée was books."

"He purchased a dozen or so through the years."

"Did you supply all his books?"

"Only the antique volumes."

"I remember them on his shelves. Did he buy from anyone else?" Charles smiled. "Not that he told me."

"Nor would he have! Would he? He wouldn't have told you. So we don't really know."

"I never saw any others."

"Then we'll say he didn't. He wasn't usually so loyal with his dealers."

"It would have been fine, of course," Charles said. "Most collectors cultivate a network of suppliers."

"And he certainly cultivated his suppliers. He was absolutely a collector."

"He had a diverse collection."

"More than diverse." John Borchard was studying him. "Oh, you must realize. It wasn't antiques he was collecting. He collected people! He always was looking. For an interesting vase, for an interesting person. Maybe we should form a society, The Collected Works of Derek Bastien."

"What an odd thought, Mr. Borchard."

"Call me, John! Please! Those of us in it, we'd be quite a crew. What do the books on your shelves think of each other?"

"I think they get along," Charles said. "They have a lot in common."

"I wonder what we have in common, those of us in Derek's collection. It would be interesting to know what caught his eye. I expect you're quite an expert on books."

"It is my work."

"You have an interesting profession. That would make you collectable yourself, don't you think? Do you understand my point?"

"I do. But of course, everyone chooses their own friends."

"They do. To some extent. And why did you request this visit, Charles? Was it only to reminisce about Derek Bastien?"

Charles braced against the sudden swerve in direction. He frowned a thoughtful frown. "A little more than just that. It was to meet you. I know you were Derek's boss, and his colleague. And I appreciate having had the opportunity. I know you must be very busy."

"I am busy." There was no urgency or busyness in his manner. He seemed very relaxed. "So why did I accept your request?"

"You've decided to start collecting antique books?" Charles asked lightly.

The effect was immediate. John's smile sank into his teeth, and his eyes were pushed out by it. "Might I? Do you think I should? What are you offering?"

The force of the questions was more than necessary, an abrupt acceleration of the conversation. Charles was nearly knocked off-balance.

"Well . . . I have quite a few," he said. "It would depend on your interests."

"My interests. I have quite a few." John was very intent. His smile had been momentarily forgotten.

"Then you might want to come in to visit."

"I might." Then John remembered to be jovial. "Now that's intriguing. Absolutely!" He folded his arms and sank back into the deep chair. "I might. But I'm not sure if you've answered my question of why I wanted to meet you. The truth of it is that I was intrigued. You were a friend of Derek, the same reason you wanted to meet me."

Charles adjusted to match John's happiness. "As one specimen to another?"

"Yes, yes! That's it. One specimen to another! It speaks volumes about his collection, doesn't it? Ha! I apologize, Charles. No pun intended! And tell me, have you found any other of his specimens?"

"I had a short meeting with Karen Liu this morning."

The eyebrows rocketed. "Well! Derek's name opens doors, doesn't it?"

"I've noticed that."

"She's an impressive person."

"I was impressed."

"With good reason. And she has been a great ally of the Department. I've greatly enjoyed working with her. She's a good start, Charles, and I wonder who else you'll encounter." The eyebrows came down. "Anyway! It has been very interesting talking, Charles, absolutely so, and I'm very pleased you took the opportunity to call."

"The pleasure has been all mine."

"And I've done all the talking! It's my habit to question people, I'm afraid. My old days as a prosecutor."

"A prosecutor?"

"A life I led long ago. Back in Kansas." Smile. "I will stop in at your business sometime."

"I'm in Alexandria. Downtown."

"Very nice. I haven't been there in ages." He was standing. "In the meantime, if there is anything I can do for you, please let my secretary know."

"I will," Charles said. "Although I don't know what it could be."

"We often don't. And I do wonder what you mean, that I might start collecting. A very curious thought. I will think about it carefully."

EVENING

Dorothy had steel in her soft blue stare. "What did Mr. Borchard think of you?"

"He thought well of me. I will tell you all about it."

"Mr. Beale?" Alice flittered into their presence. "You have a call."

"Who is it?"

"Mr. Edmund Cane."

"Oh." Charles looked to Dorothy.

"He's called twice this afternoon," Alice said.

"This will just take a moment."

"Go ahead," Dorothy said.

"Thank you, Alice." He picked up his telephone. "This is Charles Beale."

"Mr. Beale. This is Edmund Cane."

"Yes, how do you do, Mr. Cane?"

"I am quite well. I am calling to inquire if you spoke with your employee, as we discussed? You thought perhaps he might have been watching outside the auction house." At his slow, syllabic pace, the sentences took quite a while.

"Yes, I did speak with him," Charles said. "I'm sorry I hadn't called you back."

"That is quite understandable. Did your employee have any information about the young woman who bought the desk?"

"Not really, I'm afraid. He thinks he may have seen her leaving the building and walking away, but it may not have been that person at all."

"I see. Well, Mr. Beale, I am sorry to have disturbed you."

"Not at all. In fact, I would be interested myself to know who she was representing."

"I am sorry I do not know."

"I've become quite interested in that desk myself." Charles was still looking at Dorothy as he spoke to Edmund Cane. "Perhaps you could tell me who you were representing?"

A short pause. "I'm afraid I can't give you that information, Mr. Beale."

"Oh, too bad. Because I think I'm actually interested in knowing! Maybe if I can find any information about the blond woman, we could trade."

"I would . . . I don't . . ." Mr. Cane was having difficulty answering. "That would . . ."

"Then never mind," Charles said. "Just a thought. But if I do find anything, I will certainly call you."

"As you wish. Thank you for your time, Mr. Beale."

"Thank you for calling, Mr. Cane."

"Are you done with your calls?" Dorothy asked.

"I think so."

"Are you going out to see anyone else?"

"Not right now," he said.

"Then Charles, dear," Dorothy said. "What is going on?"

"To tell the truth . . . I have no idea."

"You have an idea."

"All right, then, yes. I have an idea. Well . . . no, I don't. I don't know whether I do or not." He paused. "There is an idea, I just don't know what it is." He paused again. "It's not that I have an idea, it's that an idea has me."

"Just say it, Charles."

"I think that you want a cup of coffee."

"I think that I do. Would I need my jacket?"

"It's quite pleasant out."

"Will it still be when we come back?"

"The weather should still be, at least."

She took her jacket, and he led her down the stairs.

"Have we sold anything?" he asked Alice.

"The whole set of Tom Swift books."

Two feet of shelf was empty. "What a large space," he said hollowly.

"It is," she said, broadly.

"Have Morgan order a new set," he said, commandingly.

"I did it right away," she said, quickly.

The evening air was warm and floral. Pots and window boxes were the obvious sources, but there must have been whole gardens hidden behind the houses. The air was patched with the first fragrances of spring.

It was a short walk to the corner and a completely different fragrance.

"I love this smell," Dorothy said at the open door.

"What would you like?" he asked.

"Something a little sweet."

She sat, and Charles soon joined her, and they inhaled the dense bouquet of coffee and its café fellow travelers.

"Are you peaceful?" Charles asked presently.

"I think I am."

"Good. That will help."

"And I'm ready for you to begin."

He took one more deep breath. "I am intrigued by the papers that Derek had hidden in the book."

"Well, of course. Just 'intrigued'?"

"Tottering on the edge of deeply disturbed."

"What do you think they mean?"

"That is the point. I've decided not to jump to conclusions. I am going to follow the wind."

"Then where has it led you?"

"Karen Liu and John Borchard are both important, busy people. Both of them dropped everything at Derek's name and immediately welcomed me into their castles. Does that seem reasonable?"

"I have made my opinions on that known," Dorothy said.

"Strongly. Why should they? Is it because I'm so interesting?"

"I don't think so."

"I'm not interesting?"

"You are very interesting, dear," Dorothy said, with deep interest in him, "but they wouldn't know it."

"What a nice answer. So it must be because of Derek."

"Derek couldn't have been that fascinating."

"I will tell you about the two meetings. My conversation with Ms. Liu was pleasant and energetic but didn't tell me much except that she is quite a politician. My conversation with Mr. Borchard was more centered on Derek, and had a few sharp points, but was also not very informative. But both of them were undeniably interested in me."

"Just because of Derek."

"Kind of somewhat. The congresswoman particularly asked what I knew about John Borchard and what Derek had told me about him. John Borchard very particularly asked about my selling books to Derek."

"Selling them?"

"And if I would recommend any to him. That was the part where Oz was the most great and terrible. Those points in both conversations were actually rather tense, and I felt like I was supposed to do or say something."

Dorothy stirred her coffee. "What would they want you to do?"

"Whatever I must have come for in the first place."

"But you didn't go for any particular reason."

"Not really. Just to meet them."

"Well," Dorothy said. "And because of those checks to Karen Liu."

"And this is where it starts getting repetitive, doesn't it? And by the way, between the two of them, Ms. Liu and Mr. Borchard, she doesn't like him, he says he likes her, and they both thought Derek was wonderful."

"They are politicians. Were they being political?"

"Surely they were. So, that's where the wind has blown so far, and those are the windmills I've tilted at. And, to further tilt the conversation, there is, of course, Mr. Cane and the desk."

With a sudden growl, a huge locomotive-shaped roaster in the front of the shop roared to life. A man dug a scoop into a burlap bag and began feeding the roaster coffee beans.

"Is Mr. Cane just following the wind, also?" Dorothy said, raising her voice to speak over the thunder.

"Perhaps he is marching to the breeze of a different summer. But I'm holding my finger to that wind, too. Why would two people want Derek's desk so much, enough that the loser is pursuing the winner?"

"Where is that wind blowing?"

"Back through Norman Highberg, I'm afraid," Charles said. "So I'll call him tomorrow."

Puffs of smoke escaping the roaster blew past them. "And any other winds?"

"There are four winds, aren't there? And that's just two. So the wind blows where it wants but we don't know where it comes from or where it goes."

"You're sounding biblical."

Absently, he sipped his drink and looked deep into its swirls. "There's a feel about this, Dorothy, and I don't know what. Something deep and far-reaching. I want to not do anything wrong."

"What could you do wrong?"

"I don't know." His eyes were on her now, looking deep. "But reading about that judge in the newspaper, I think about how easy it is to do something harmful."

"I don't see the connection."

He smiled. "Never mind. I will just follow the wind and keep my eyes very open."

"Don't follow it too far."

"It may lead to the Emerald City."

"That's the wrong metaphor, dear," Dorothy said. "We are talking about the wind."

"All right, then, it might lift your whole house up and carry it to another country."

"If it gets that serious, you should talk to the police."

"If you drop a farmhouse, you don't know who it might land on. And you"—he pointed right at her—"should know that better than anyone."

"Me?"

"Yes, you. And Toto, too." He looked at his watch. "I think if we linger a bit longer we can get back to the shop just in time to leave for the day."

"The Federalist Papers. *Charles, what was it about that generation? Every one of them could write.*"

"*They had something to write about, perhaps.*"

"*Revolution. I said it made for good literature.*"

"*You don't like revolutions, Derek.*"

"*All right. I admit they have their uses. But they're uncontrollable once they're started and they create terrible vacuums. It took Europe nearly twenty years to rid itself of Napoleon. It's all about power, Charles. However it starts—even whatever 'it' is—it always ends in the hands of the ruthless and powerful.*"

"*Not always.*"

"*You're referring to George Washington? He's underrated. He understood power, and it did end up in his hands.*"

"*For the good of the country.*"

"*Remarkably. But, Charles, he is an example. He had great power, founded on his prestige and success, and used it to good.*"

"*And then gave it up.*"

"*When he had accomplished his purpose. I appreciate his example. Rule by power is necessary and it could be used to good purpose even today.*"

"*Are you a monarchist, Derek?*"

"*I guess we can't go that far. But within my own small sphere, it is an example I find very useful.*"

THURSDAY

MORNING

"Mr. Beale?"

"Good morning, Morgan."

"Good morning, sir." His red hair was really too bright to be growing in a place so hidden from the sun. "I have an answer back from the person on eBay selling the *Odyssey*."

"Yes, the hypothetical autographed first edition. What does he say?"

"He is moving and getting rid of stuff, and it was in a box."

"So he found Attica in his attic. Does he know where the box came from?"

"It was his grandfather's, who got it from an aunt in England as a present in the nineteen twenties, and she bought it for him at a bookstore."

"That's more than we usually get."

"There's a handwritten inscription to his grandfather inside the cover."

"Oh. Oh, dear. That's too bad. What about the title page?"

"Here's a picture he took of it."

Charles put his nose right up to the screen. "Hmm."

"Does that tell you anything?"

"It's not a proper title page."

"What is it?" Morgan asked.

Charles shrugged. "Some kind of half title page. It does have the title: *Homer's Odyssey;* Translated by Alexander Pope. But there's no publisher or city or date. Why does he say it's a first edition?"

" 'I believe it is a first edition because it is so old, and because the author signed it.' End quote."

"Of course."

"This picture is the inside front cover, with the inscription to his grandfather and the author signature."

"That?" A very faded smudge crawled along the top of the paper.

"I can make out sort of an *A* and sort of a *P*," Morgan said.

"I'm sure the book is nineteenth century, so Pope would have been dead a hundred years or so."

"Maybe that's why his signature is so shaky."

"Mine would be, too. Well, obviously it's not a first edition of anything. It's some other printing. Get the picture of the cover again."

Morgan quickly did so.

"But it's still interesting," Charles said. "I haven't seen anything just like that. It looks like very nice leather. How much longer on the auction?"

"Four and a half days. Until Monday afternoon."

"And where is the bidding?"

"Four hundred."

"Yes. The dealers all know it's not specifically valuable, and they're waiting."

"What is it worth if it isn't specifically valuable?"

"Three or four hundred, up to maybe fifteen if it's sort of specific. But it all depends. I'd have to actually see the book."

"You could fly to Denver. He wouldn't mail it here while it's under auction."

Charles stared at the book on the screen. "Morgan, I'm on an odyssey of my own at the moment. So I think I'll take a chance."

"Yes, sir. How much of a chance?"

"Fifteen hundred. I'm young and idealistic. Or foolish, I don't remember which. Make it two thousand."

"Yes, sir."

Charles watched the fingers flit. "It all still amazes me."

"I could show you how to do this."

"I know my limitations, Morgan."

"It isn't hard, sir."

"I mean that I'm already not very disciplined. If I were to start poking around eBay and all those other places, I would never escape. I'll just use my computer for email and leave the rest to you."

He slid around the corner to the main office. "Is Angelo's next probation meeting this Monday or the next Monday?"

Dorothy looked at her calendar. "A week from this Monday."

"I would like for him to learn better manners in dealing with people."

"I don't think we could have him wait on customers."

"No. I'll have to think about it."

The morning had progressed. Charles strolled down the stairs and wandered over to the front window to inspect a newly empty space on the shelf beside it. Outside the window a man on the sidewalk was inspecting the front of the building.

A brown tweed jacket draped the man's broad shoulders, and a fedora shaded his strong jaw and heavy forehead. He straightened his tie and strode up the steps.

The door opened. Charles still had his eye on the vacancy.

"Good morning," the man said, coming to a stop at the counter.

"Good morning," Alice said, accommodating as a traffic light turning green.

The conversation slowly accelerated. "Nice place you got here."

"Thank you, sir. May I help you with anything?"

"I'm actually looking for the owner."

Charles turned and merged in. "That would be me."

Blue eyes beneath the hat brim smiled. "Then that would make you Charles Beale. I'm Frank Kelly. How do you do, Mr. Beale?"

"I'm quite well, thank you, Mr. Kelly."

"Glad to hear it. I'm . . . um . . ." The blue eyes had focused on the wall behind Charles. "Well look at that!" He leaned closer to the shelves, and Charles moved aside. "Do you mind?"

"Not at all. Go ahead."

"Thanks." Mr. Kelly stared at the books, his eyes darting side to side, up and down. Then he gingerly put his hand to one and slid it out.

Charles waited attentively. Mr. Kelly's square jaw slipped slowly ajar; his broad forehead wrinkled.

"This is real Raymond Chandler?" he asked.

"Of course."

"Golly. First edition?"

"That one is."

"Well, get a load of that." He turned his intense blue stare back to Charles, and then to the shelves. "Are all of these—?"

"Not all first editions."

"Okay." He replaced the Chandler and pulled out a Ross Mac-Donald. "You know, I've seen these on the Internet. But I never really looked at one."

"Are you familiar with antique books, Mr. Kelly?"

"Oh, sure. All kinds of antiques." He shook his head wistfully as he put the book back. "It's my job. Say, you got a place where we could talk?"

"What about?"

"Well . . ." Mr. Kelly glanced around the room. Only Alice was with them, crisply. "It's business."

"Please, come with me."

Charles led him upstairs to the office.

"Mr. Kelly, this is my wife. Dorothy, this is Mr. Frank Kelly."

Their guest doffed his hat and held out his hand. "Pleased to meet you."

"It's my pleasure," Dorothy said. Bravely, she put her graceful hand into his.

"Great." He held it for a minute, scrutinizing her, especially studying her face and hair. Then he released her hand without any damage. "I guess I can talk with you both?"

"You might as well," Charles said.

"Then here goes." Faster than sight, he had a thin leather case in his hand. "I'm from the FBI," he said, flicking the case open to show his badge.

"How interesting!" Charles said.

"Man, is it!" Mr. Kelly grinned. "You wouldn't believe what comes up in this job."

"I couldn't even guess."

"It gets pretty strange sometimes." He shook his head. "But this isn't. I've got you on a list of dealers that Derek Bastien bought from."

"I see. Yes, Derek bought a number of books from me."

"That's it. I'm with the Artifacts and Antiquities division and I'm checking up on the stuff that got stolen from Bastien's house."

Charles frowned. "The FBI?"

"You see, we've got likely interstate commerce in stolen goods, plus those being antique objects. D.C. police reported it to us so I've got to ask around and fill in a report." He shrugged. "It's just my job."

"I only deal in books, Mr. Kelly. I wouldn't know much about any of the items that were stolen."

"Sure. Can I ask you some questions anyway?"

"Of course."

"Were you ever in his house?"

"Yes. A number of times."

"Did you talk about the things he owned? His collection."

"Yes. Of course."

"That's what I want to know about." Suddenly, Mr. Kelly realized he still had his hat on. He snatched it off, and nodded to Dorothy. "Sorry about that."

She smiled.

"Did you ever get the feeling someone was after any of his stuff?"

"Well . . . no," Charles said. "Not at all."

"Because we got a break-in where the intruder snags a French baroque ivory dolphin, a colonial pewter candlestick and matching snuffer, an 1856 Italian mother-of-pearl dueling pistol, non-operational, et cetera, et cetera. It's stuff that's not easy to pawn, so the guy must either have a channel or a customer, see?"

"I don't quite. Do you, dear?"

She smiled. "I'm afraid not."

Frank Kelly provided light. "Either he has somebody he can fence that kind of stuff to, or he already has a customer who really wants a pewter candlestick. With a snuffer."

"He stole the porpoise on purpose, you mean," Charles said. "That sounds unlikely."

"Yeah. Except there's a difference between a dolphin and a porpoise. A porpoise in the French Baroque is for Greek myths, and a dolphin is a symbol for the French crown prince." Mr. Kelly sneezed. "Sorry. Dust. You'd figure, you spend all your time with antiques, you should be used to dust. Anyway, it's obvious the guy has a channel. There were four other break-ins in the neighborhood in three weeks. A rash. Most all antiques. So he has a channel. I mean, what do you do with a Limoges vase?" He had turned back to Dorothy.

"Put flowers in it," she said.

"You could," he said, nodding. "Or peppermints. But you don't sell it to Mario the Fence in the back of the Italian restaurant like you do if it was jewelry or an iPod."

"How do you sell it?" Charles asked.

"There's ways. Fifty-fifty chance something'll turn up on eBay in a month or two. I've put the list in the database, and if anything shows up, we'll know right away."

"Surely the burglar would be smarter than that?"

"You'd think, right? But no. You'd be surprised how stupid some of these guys are. We get the piece, we get some fingerprints or DNA off it, and then we get him."

"I suppose you'd know."

"Yeah, break-ins like this, they happen all the time. Except how it went wrong with Bastien."

"Very wrong." Charles looked away from Mr. Kelly, and the room. The street was bright with light and life. Green leaves, breezes, people. "What about Derek himself? Are you investigating his death?"

"No. That's D.C. police. But, sure, if we find the burglar, they want him, too."

"How can I help you?" Charles asked. "I don't see how I can."

"Two ways. You deal in antiques, even if it isn't the right kind, so if you hear anything, let me know. And you knew the victim, so if you think of anything from that angle, let me know. Anything. Then I just follow the leads, it's my job. Anything you can think of now? Anything strange?"

"What about the desk?"

Mr. Kelly frowned. "That hundred-grand bidding war? Yeah, I don't know what that was about."

"You know about the bidding?"

"Sure, I was at the auction. Just keeping my eyes open. But I don't think the desk has anything to do with the break-in. You know, how could it? Somebody knew something special about the desk. The burglaries were all just smash and grabs. What, you know something about the guy who bought it?"

"No. The man who lost the bidding called me to try to find who won."

"If it really is to do with the burglaries, I can find out who bought the desk," Mr. Kelly said. "Who called you?"

"Edmund Cane. He is with Horton's on Fortieth in New York."

"Why'd he call you?"

"Apparently, just because I was there."

"Yeah. He's just following leads. I know all about it, that's my life. But that desk." He nodded, thinking. "That's a good point. I really don't think it has anything to do with the break-in, but I suppose it is kind of interesting. I might follow that. So you don't know anything about it?"

"Not the buyer. I know about the desk."

"I guess it was antique, right?"

"The desk was 1875; it was owned by President Taft's father."

"Right . . . and probably hard for a burglar to throw into his bag and run off with. But somebody did want it." He shrugged. "But you don't know why."

"I don't."

"Okay. It's a lead."

"Who else have you talked to?" Charles asked. "Or may I ask?"

"Sure, I'll tell you. I talked to dealers I know, to tell them to be on the watch for the stuff. I talked to a couple lowlifes that let me know things sometimes. I talked to the neighbors who had break-ins so they'd feel like someone cared, and his wife, too, so she'd feel like someone cared. None of that means anything; it's just for their feelings. It'll all come up on the Internet if it comes up anywhere. That's what'll actually mean anything. Or maybe we find the stuff somewhere, or else maybe we'll never see any of it again."

"You spoke with Derek's wife?"

"Lucy Bastien. I figured she'd like to know that someone cares, but she doesn't care. She could care less."

"I never met her."

"She's there in the house. Anyway, here's my card. Call my cell phone if you do think of anything."

"I certainly will."

"Anyway—thank you. Ma'am." He lifted his hand to tip his hat and it wasn't there. He grabbed it off his lap where he'd set it. Then he stopped, and looked at her again. "Do you mind if I ask? That's a real nice silver in your hair. It's natural, isn't it?"

"I don't color it," Dorothy said, somewhere between indignant and flattered.

"You see, I have this theory," Mr. Kelly said. "About that shade of silver. Not just any gray, but that real bright silver, I've seen that passed down mother to daughter. It's like blue eyes. Did your mother have that same silver hair? If you don't mind my asking."

Charles coughed.

Dorothy smiled, thinly.

"I'm sorry," Mr. Kelly said. "You do mind. I shouldn't ask personal questions."

"I never met my mother," Dorothy said.

"Oh. Okay, I'm sorry. Never mind, shouldn't have asked. Anyway, I'll find my way out."

"I'm going down," Charles said. He held open the office door and followed the broad shoulders down the stairs, and he and Alice received one more tip of the hat as the front door closed.

"I couldn't help but notice," Dorothy said as Charles returned to his desk.

"Notice what?"

"You didn't tell him what you found in the John Locke."

"He didn't ask."

"Charles, that's ridiculous. All right, what if he had asked?"

"I don't answer rhetorical questions. And, I doubt the papers have anything to do with his burglaries."

"They have to do with something. I think you're making a mistake."

"I'm trying not to make a mistake. And I couldn't help but notice," Charles said.

"Notice what?"

"How he noticed you."

"Oh . . . well . . ." Dorothy's cheeks blushed a delicate pink.

"Anyone would, of course. It's quite understandable."

"Don't be silly, Charles."

"When I am with you, it is everything else that seems silly. But I will try to attend to prosaic life."

Dorothy already had. "And what will that be?"

"I think I know another doorknob to try my key in." He found his telephone book.

"Who are you pestering now?"

"The wind is blowing toward Lucy Bastien."

"You should *not* pester her, Charles."

"I don't believe I will be. Apparently, she could care less."

"You know I have never liked that expression," Dorothy said.

"You know that I haven't either. Why is it supposed to mean the exact opposite of what it means?" He pushed buttons.

"It is a symptom of the hopeless state of our nation."

"Exactly." He waited as the telephone rang.

"Lucy," a voice said.

"Charles," he said.

"Charles?" The voice sounded puzzled, but amused. "What do you want?"

"To come see you."

"You do? Why?"

"I thought it would be interesting."

That was enough. "It sounds like it might be. Who are you, anyway?"

"Charles Beale. I knew Derek Bastien."

"Then maybe I'm not interested. I'm not going to buy anything. What do you sell?"

"Books. Antique books."

"Right. I hate antiques, and I don't like books either."

"I paid you twenty-seven thousand dollars for thirteen antique books last Monday. Isn't that worth letting me in?"

"Maybe. Okay, come on, I don't care."

"Thank you. Would this morning be all right?"

"Anytime you want. If I'm here, I'll answer the door."

"Thank you. Very much."

Charles looked at Dorothy.

"Just go," she said. "I will not discuss it."

"Yes, dear."

"Except that I can't believe you would say such things on the telephone to someone you've never met. Angelo isn't the one who needs to learn manners."

"Yes, dear."

Charles stood for a moment at the weighty oak door. There would be no chess game this time.

He rang the bell. The door opened.

There was no granite foyer table. No oval mirror on the wall above it.

He smiled. "Hello. I'm Charles Beale."

"Come in. I'm Lucy."

The foyer walls weren't gray-green. They were light yellowish tan.

"Thank you."

The floor wasn't white and black marble. It was bleached pine. It was the only wood in sight. There was no mahogany, no cherry, maple or even oak; there was no Chippendale, no Hitchcock or Windsor; there was no inlay or carving; no pediments, corbels, medallions, ball and claw, egg and dart, or any molding; the rococo trace work was gone; there was no dark blue or burgundy or umber or ebony; no silk, velvet, leather, tapestry; no statuary, nothing framed, no crystal—the list of what there was not was too long.

"Make yourself at home," she said.

Rattan. Everything. Yellow and white. The House of Bastien had become a Florida beach rental.

A poster of a palm tree hung where the mirror had been.

"I will."

He followed her into the front room and sat with a scrunch on the yellow cushion of a whitewashed wicker chair.

"Lemonade?"

"No, thank you."

Lucy perched on her own chair. "It looks like you've been here before."

"Yes." He forced his eyes back toward her. "A few times. It's quite different."

"That's what I wanted." She was not tall or thin. She was wrapped in beige and her long, dark, rough, graying brown hair was tied with a yellow ribbon.

"It's very light," he said.

"Finally. I can finally breathe." She took a deep breath to prove it. "You sold him books?"

"Antique books."

"Everything was antique around here. Fourteen books for twenty-seven grand?"

"Thirteen."

"I looked at the list. It said fourteen."

"The list?"

"He kept a list of everything he owned. He kept lists on everything. It had fourteen old books on it."

"I only bought thirteen. I'll need to check my computer."

"Whatever. Did you come here often?"

"Ten or twelve times over the years. I'm surprised I've never met you."

"Nobody's met me. I saw precious little of Derek, let alone his precious friends."

"I'm sorry I never had the pleasure."

"Blame Derek. That's what I do."

Charles took in his own breath, and nodded, and made a show of looking again around the bright room. "Well, then, thank you for letting me meet you now. I really didn't have a specific reason to come, even. I think I just wanted to see what you were like."

"Just like this. This is what Derek's wife looks like in her natural state. Released from captivity and readjusting to the wild."

"I'm sure it must be an adjustment."

"I've done it before. It's not hard."

"Done it before?"

"Derek wasn't the first husband I've buried. He was number two, not that he tried any harder."

"I'm sorry, I didn't realize."

"It doesn't matter. I married for love the first time, and money the second. What's left?"

"I'm still on love," Charles said.

"Marrying for money gives you a lot more time to watch television. The shopping's better, too." There was a sigh in her cynicism that rang it hollow. "What's it like to sell old books?"

"It's wonderful."

"Do you have a store, or do you just call on rich widows?"

"I have a shop. I'd be honored to show it to you sometime."

"Not likely, Charles. I don't ever want to see another antique as long as I live. So are you getting what you want out of meeting me?"

"Oh, yes. I couldn't even imagine what Derek's wife would be like."

"I sure couldn't," Derek's wife said. "Or him either."

"Yes. Quite a failing on his part. Why was that, do you think?"

"Well, you know, I just don't collect dust very well, and that was sort of a requirement of anything he had."

"He had quite a few friends, and they weren't the dust-collecting types either."

"You're about the first one I've met."

"And the strange thing is," Charles said, "you seem like just the interesting type of person he would have collected. Did you ever talk with him?"

"Not in years. I'd just see him around the house once in a while, and he'd say hello. Maybe I should have introduced myself."

"I am just amazed," Charles said. "It seems so unlike the Derek I knew."

"Well, you'll have to tell me about him sometime."

"Really?"

"No. I don't really care. And I'm just starting to get tired of talking now, if you get my drift."

"Of course. I do appreciate your time. You're a very interesting person, Mrs. Bastien."

"Cloverdale."

"Cloverdale?"

"Forget the Bastien. I made a mistake, so why should I be stuck with it the rest of my life?"

"I agree," Charles said. "Why be stuck with an old mistake for a whole life? Mrs. . . . Cloverdale." Charles stood and Lucy didn't. "I hope we have another opportunity sometime."

"Why would you want that?" she said.

"Because I think I deserve a second chance."

She had still not thought of an answer as he left the yellow world for the multihued one outside.

AFTERNOON

Trees were green, streets were black, the sky blue, and tucked between, in signs and flower boxes and cars, were red and orange and purple and white. There was no need for more yellow.

He set off with a brisk pace, passing large houses, fenced yards, aged trees. As the distance between him and Lucy increased, the dignity of the neighborhood decreased. It was a very nice day for a walk.

Charles tacked across Reservoir Road to Wisconsin Avenue and let the wind take him to M Street. The yards narrowed, then disappeared, and took the trees and gardens with them. The townhouses of George-town started.

Thirty minutes from the ruins of Derek's world to the oddities of Norman Highberg's.

"Mr. Highberg, please." Charles waited, for not too long. An amethyst horse that had been in the front window Tuesday had galloped away to greener pastures. Now there was a stained-glass, framed mirror.

"Charles? What are you doing here?"

"I have every right to be," he answered.

"Not around here," Norman said. "Nobody's got any rights. You want to put up an awning? You don't have the right; you've got to get permission. You want to put up a bigger sign? You would *never* get permission."

"Do you want an awning?"

"I want an awning. Too much sun in the front window. So I've spent the whole morning on the phone with city hall. The sun's going to burn out before I can get enough permits to do anything. I should move to Montana or someplace."

"How long have you been here?"

"Fifteen years. I bet they don't have architectural review boards in Montana."

"You wouldn't have many customers either."

"I could sell antiques and cow food. What do they feed cows, anyway?"

"I think you should stay here," Charles said. "I was in the neighborhood and I thought of another question for you."

"Everybody's got questions. Cane's got questions, the FBI guy has questions, now you've got more questions. Why is everybody asking questions?"

"It sounds like you have questions, too."

"It must be contagious. So what's your question this time?"

"You said there was a man who had been sitting beside you at the auction Monday, and he left just before I arrived."

"It wasn't because of you. What, you know him?"

"I don't even know who it was," Charles said.

"Galen Jones. What about him? I don't think he left because you got there. I figured you might come, but I didn't tell him to leave."

"Who is he?"

"Galen Jones. I just said it."

"But, Norman, who is he? How do you know him?"

"He's a matchmaker. You've got to know them in this business."

"A matchmaker."

"Yeah, sure. You have three antique chairs and you need one more for your table? He makes you a match."

"Oh, of course. I know what you mean. He makes replicas."

"Replicas, replacements. Yeah, people ask me all the time. I've got to know a few in this business for people who ask. I don't do furniture, but he does other work, too. And"—he narrowed his eyes—"I've got to know them to keep an eye on them." He tapped his eye.

"And why is that?"

"You know, somebody like Jones, if I find out he's had anything to do with a piece, I look at it real close."

"I see—it might be a fake."

"But I can tell. I know the real stuff, I can see it."

"Was he there when you arrived?"

"Yeah, I sat next to him to be sociable. And Jones, I never heard specific, but if you ask around, there's something back there, if you know what I mean."

"Not really," Charles said.

"Somewhere he got in trouble. I never heard specific, but if you ask around—"

"He tried to pass something he'd made as an antique?"

"Well, I don't know, I never heard specific—"

"That's very interesting, Norman."

"Anyway, his work's good and you'd have to look close to tell."

"Why would he have been at Derek Bastien's auction?"

"Oh, he did some work for him once. At least once, I don't know how much. Bastien, he asked me once if I knew someone who was good and I told him to call Galen Jones."

"What did he do for Derek?"

"I don't know. Probably made him an extra chair. That's what he does, if you have three chairs and you—"

"That's very interesting, Norman."

"Now if he did, it better not have been at the auction, or at least it should have said it was replica. That was all supposed to be real stuff. But I don't do furniture, so what do I know."

"And did you say an FBI person was asking questions?"

"That guy, what's his name. The antiquities guy. Nice guy, whatever his name is. Yeah, he called me, back when there were all those burglaries up in Foxhall. I mean, just the usual stuff. He always calls me. I keep an eye out for stuff for him. Once in a while I see something he's looking for. If I see it, I remember it. I remember a lot."

"You certainly do, Norman."

"And he called me yesterday. Checking in. I guess he was at the auction." Norman took off his glasses to wipe the smudges more evenly over the lenses. "I told him he should find that blonde."

"Sensible. I wonder, how would you look for her, Norman?"

"Why do I want to look for her?"

"I think I do." Charles frowned, thinking. "Say you wanted to bid on the desk, but you didn't want anyone to know who you were."

"Why should I want that desk?" Norman was fuddled. "I don't do furniture."

"How would you find an agent to bid for you?"

"I don't need an agent. I'd do my own bidding."

"But if you did want to find an agent?"

"There are agents all over the place. I used to do that myself. I'm too busy now."

Charles was lost in thought. "Maybe you don't even know how auctions work . . ."

"I've been to a million auctions. Where do you think I get my stuff?"

"First," Charles said, "you'd call the auction house."

"You're losing your mind," Norman said. "What are you talking about?"

"I need to call the auction house."

"So call them." Norman had found his place in the conversation.

"What?"

"You want to call Capital Auction? Call them."

"I will when I get back to the shop," Charles said.

"Why wait? Here's a phone. You should get yourself one of these."

Charles found a little cell phone in his hand. "I don't know the number."

"Give me that." Norman took the phone back, pushed numbers, and returned it to Charles.

"You have the number memorized?"

"I remember a lot. Anyway, it's only been a couple months since I called it last time."

"Capital Auction?" the phone said.

"Oh—yes, hello. I have a question."

"Yes, sir?"

"I would like to participate in one of your auctions, but I won't be in town. Is it possible to bid by telephone?"

"I'm sorry, sir, but we require bidding in person."

"Oh. I see. What do people do if they can't be there in person?"

"It's common to use an agent."

"An agent? How does that work?"

"You would have to make your own arrangement."

"Can you recommend anyone?"

"We can't recommend agents, sir. We do have a list for agents who have registered with us, but we can't specifically recommend any of them. That would have to be between you and that agent."

"I would like to get that list. Can you send it to me? Or is it on your website?"

"You would have to come here for it."

"Very good. Thank you."

He handed the phone back to Norman.

"Thank you."

"What are you, losing your mind? You know all that. And where are you going out of town?"

"Nowhere, and I was just asking."

"I could have told you any of that, anyway."

"But you don't like me asking you questions," Charles said. "Perhaps, Norman, the woman is somewhere on that list. Oh, and I do have one more question for you. Did you end up getting anything back that you sold to Derek?"

"Yeah, a chess set. Wood inlay. Real nice. It's the real thing, you know? You can tell. Austrian, 1890s. It's out of my range here in the shop, but I got it anyway. Somebody'll buy it."

"How much is it?"

"Four thousand. I paid thirty-one. You want it? I'll sell it to you for thirty-four. That's a deal. You try to find something this good."

"I don't think so. But my fondest memory of Derek is playing chess on that board."

"Thirty-four. Okay, thirty-three. Thirty-two seventy-five, and that's between friends. You're not going to turn around and sell it again? Because it'll go for four, and I'll sell it for that if somebody does."

"No, I wouldn't sell it. But three thousand is a little rich for my blood. I'll pass."

"Okay, but it'll be here if you want it. Until somebody else grabs it."

"Thank you, Norman. Thanks for everything."

The walk to downtown would have been as long as the walk to Georgetown. Charles took the Metro. The first train coming in from Arlington was too crowded and he had to wait for the next. Presently, though, he was back on the pavement and then at the same building where he'd been Monday.

The lobby oozed discretion and prosperity; the thickest concentration had solidified into the receptionist. "Good afternoon," he said. "I called a little earlier. I understand that you have a list of agents available to represent buyers in your auctions?"

"Yes, sir. I remember your call. I have one here for you."

"Thank you so much." The dark doors to the blue auction room were open. The rows of chairs were empty. "I wonder . . ."

"Yes, sir?"

"A friend of mine was at an auction here Monday, and he noticed an agent—he assumed it was an agent, anyway, a young woman about your age."

The woman at the desk was not very young. Her smile tightened.

"Sir, I don't know who that woman was, and if I did, I still wouldn't be able to tell you. I also don't know who else is looking for her, or why. I also can't give you any information about what she bought or what she did with anything that she did buy."

"I'm sorry," Charles said, "I didn't mean . . ."

"Yes, sir. Is there anything else I can do for you?"

"No. You've been very helpful. Thank you."

He hurried from the room, and from the building. On the sidewalk he looked at the paper; it had dozens of listings. He folded it and slid it into his pocket.

"Have we sold anything, Alice?" he asked.

Alice's dresses were invariably smart and new; but they were always the color of old things. "A volume of Robert Browning," she said.

"Not my favorite poet. Sometimes he seems to me rather overdone."

"If he were overdone, Mr. Beale, he would be Robert Burns."

Charles stopped in his tracks. "That's a terrible pun, Alice."

"Yes, sir."

"He is not some frozen turkey to put in the oven."

"Certainly not, sir."

"Because that would be Robert Frost."

"Yes, sir."

"There you are," Dorothy said, gliding down the stairs. "That was a long visit."

"I made a few other stops, including Norman."

She had a stack of envelopes, which she set on the counter. "Has the mailman already come?"

"No, Mrs. Beale," Alice said.

"Give him these." Charles and Dorothy climbed back up the steps to the office. "And what was Lucy like?"

"She was in the sky with diamonds."

The office had once been the master bedroom, and the other second-floor bedroom was now storage. The two closets had been combined, and then given their own door to the hall, and then they had been given Morgan.

"I have a search for you," Charles said.

"Yes, sir?"

"See if you can find the telephone number of a Galen Jones, somewhere local."

"Yes, sir. Just a second. Uh . . . it doesn't come up right away. There's thousands of Joneses. Any other clues?"

"He makes furniture."

"Oh. Okay. Yeah, here. Maybe this is it."

Charles copied the number from the computer screen. "Thank you, Morgan. And can you tell me the secret of life?"

"I could query Google."

"Never mind."

"Hello?" A tired female voice.

Charles settled into his own chair. "Hello. I'm calling for Mr. Galen Jones?"

"He's not home."

"My name is Charles Beale, and I'm trying to get hold of him."

"Give me your phone number, and I'll let him know."

Dorothy was quite settled into her own chair. "And who is Galen Jones?" she asked.

"A matchmaker."

"A what?"

"I am trying to find a wife for Angelo," Charles said.

"Get one who doesn't need lots of communication."

"A good point, dear. A matchmaker is a maker of replica antique furniture. He was at the auction Monday."

"Is this another gust of wind?"

"It's the one that blew me past Norman. And there was another breeze, too, that I think I'll send Angelo after. But first, I have to check up on my judge scandal."

"The man in the newspaper? And why are you interested in that?"

"I'm not sure. There is just something about him. Ah, he's only page six now." He skimmed paragraphs.

"Anything?"

"No. The reporter just wants to keep the story alive. Maybe he gets paid by the sneer."

"There's obviously some audience."

"Who would read this?"

"You are."

"I mean, besides me."

"Which brings up my original question. Why are you reading it?"

"Because . . . because . . . because it is a man who has been ruined by a piece of paper."

"What piece of paper?"

"Someone told the *Washington Post* about this cheating back in law school. I don't know if it was really a piece of paper or what, but that one little piece of information has destroyed him."

"There wouldn't have been a piece of paper if he hadn't done anything."

"But who hasn't?" He smiled. "Besides you, I mean."

"I'm not perfect, Charles, but I don't think I have any scandals hidden away."

"Then you are the exception, and besides, I think you are perfect. But just think what would happen if that paper about Karen Liu were sent to the *Post*?"

"The same thing that happened to the judge."

"At least. That is why I am reading about what has happened to him. It seems important to know."

"I wouldn't have thought of that."

"Because *you* are perfect, dear, and I *would* think of it because *I* am not."

"I never know how to answer when you say things like that," Dorothy said.

"That's why I do it. When you recover, I want to tell you about Lucy."

"When I recover, I will need to go out for the rest of the afternoon. However, I will look forward to another cup of coffee sometime *very* soon."

Charles knocked. Voices muttered from within. There was a scream, and a crash, then gunshots. Then silence.

The door opened with a sinister creak.

"Hey, boss," Angelo said. "What do you want?"

"I have a job for you."

Angelo turned off the tiny television and sat on his bed. "Okay, what is it?"

"It is a little complicated. May I come in?"

"It's your house."

Angelo's room was perfectly neat, although it would have been difficult to make a mess with the few possessions he had.

"It's your room, though," Charles said. He sat on the one chair.

"What job do you have?"

"I would like to find that woman I've asked you about."

Angelo shook his head. "Hey, boss, you start looking for people, they hear about it and you get lots of trouble."

"I only want to know who she is."

"There is something she has that you want?"

"I just want to find her, that's all."

Angelo shrugged and offered no further advice. "Where's she hang out?"

"Take this list." Charles spoke slowly. "Somebody hired that woman to be at the auction on Monday."

"Okay."

"Maybe, they got her name from this list."

"This doesn't have any name of a lady."

"No. It is a list of agents. Some of them are just individuals. Some of them are partnerships. Some of them are dealers who have regular businesses."

"Dealers. You want to be looking for dealers? That's not good, boss."

"They aren't that kind of dealer. They're antiques dealers or jewelers or art dealers."

"They're dealers," Angelo said. "Dealers you should stay away."

"I'm a dealer, Angelo. I can handle them. Now this is what I want you to do. I want you to go to each of these businesses that you can and look for that woman."

"You want me looking? I told that judge I wouldn't do any of that."

"This is not criminal, Angelo. You're just looking for her."

"You tell me to, so it's okay?"

"It's okay."

"How do I look? Look in a window? Look how?"

"This is where you get to practice your manners. Mrs. Beale and I think you need to learn proper professional behavior. Go to each place and go inside. Talk to the people. Look around and ask questions. See if this woman works there."

Angelo was processing. "These people in buildings, they don't talk to me. You they talk to, they don't talk to me."

"I think you can do it. Wear your good clothes. Be polite."

Again he shrugged. "But you don't want her to know you're looking?"

"That's right. Good. You understand."

"So for why do I say I'm asking them?"

"We'll think of something. We'll try the first one together tomorrow."

"Mr. Beale?" Angelo's door had just closed. "You have a telephone call. A Mr. Galen Jones."

"Oh, good! Thank you, Alice. I'll be right there."

He hurried back down to the office. "Yes, hello, this is Charles Beale."

"Right." A deep voice, gravelly, but it didn't sound like a big person. "I got a message you called?"

"Yes, I did. Thank you for calling back. Mr. Jones, I was a friend of a man named Derek Bastien. I've heard you may have known him?"

Charles waited.

"What do you want?" the voice asked.

"Well, to talk. Either on the phone, or to meet with you."

"Right." Another wait. "Who are you?"

"I sell books. Antique books. I sold some to Derek. That's really all.

And I heard your name, and a little more than that about you, and I wanted to talk."

"Talk about what? Look, do you want some work done?"

"No. I just want to talk. About Derek Bastien."

A long wait. "Okay, I'll talk. I'll come see you. Where are you?"

"At my shop right now. In Alexandria. I'll give you the address."

"I'll be there this afternoon."

Charles had only set the telephone down when it rang again. By reflex, he picked it up again, without waiting for Alice to get it.

"Alexandria Rare Books, this is Charles Beale."

"Answering your own phone?"

"Oh, hello, Jacob. How are you?"

The rusted, squeaking hinge of a voice answered, "Better than you are if you've lost all your help there."

"I haven't. I just had a feeling who it was, and I didn't want to inflict them with you."

"Someday you'll learn respect for your elders."

"You're about the only one, Jacob. What can I do for you?"

"It's what I can't do for you. I'm not going to that auction here, so you'll have to do your own bidding if you want anything."

"Oh, that's fine," Charles said. "There wasn't anything I wanted."

"So you would have had me go for nothing?"

"You're not going."

"Then it's a good thing I'm not."

"I would have told you. But I do have another question."

"Go ahead," Jacob said. "Run up my telephone bill."

"Thank you, I will. It is about the man at the auction Monday, who you saw bidding on that desk."

"What about him? I don't know anything but what I saw."

"I've found out that man's name. It's Galen Jones."

"Never heard of him."

"I'm not surprised. Even you, Jacob, have not heard of every person."

"Just most."

"Just most. This man, Galen Jones, is a maker of replica antique furniture."

"Oh, is he?" A conspiratorial tone entered Jacob Leatherman's voice. "Matchmaker? Bidding on the desk?"

"Exactly. Now, this is what I've pieced together. He was sitting in the back row. Norman Highberg came in and sat next to him. Norman is an antiques dealer and knows Mr. Jones. Then, when the bidding on the desk began, Mr. Jones went to where Norman wouldn't see him bid. And then, when the bidding escalated, Mr. Jones gave up and left. Would you say that was accurate by what you saw?"

"That's just what I saw, Charles." Jacob chuckled. "Are you after something?"

"I am, a little bit. I'm not sure what, it's actually rather complicated. But I just wanted to compare my guesses with what you saw."

"Now you tell me the whole story when you know it."

"Are you intrigued?"

"I'm young and foolish," Jacob said.

"Young, anyway," Charles said. "And you like puzzles, and so do I. I'll let you know."

He glanced across the room to Dorothy's empty desk, and then he opened his newspaper.

The newspaper was wrinkled and in the wastebasket. Charles was in his chair, pensively watching the street below his window.

He stood for a better view and hurried down the stairs to the showroom.

The front door opened and a long, drooping, gray mustache looked in. A long gray ponytail followed, and long wiry arms with long hands, and long, worn blue jeans, and a loose gray flannel shirt. And very sharp eyes.

"Mr. Jones?" Charles said.

"You're Beale?"

"I am."

"Right." The eyes swept the room. "Where do you want to talk?"

"Down here. Just follow me."

Galen Jones showed no hesitation, but loped right on behind Charles. But Charles hesitated. "Alice? Could you have Angelo come down to the basement for a moment?"

"Yes, Mr. Beale."

Then they went down the stairs.

Mr. Jones dropped into a chair like a bag of coat hangers.

"So, what can I do for you, Mr. Beale?"

Charles sat across the desk from him. "I really just have some questions."

"Okay. Go ahead."

"Of course. I think you must have some interesting customers, Mr. Jones?"

The eyes were power drills. "Once in a while. Most of them are pretty normal."

Charles nodded. "And you must have some interesting requests."

"So, Beale, where are we going with this?"

"Nowhere, Mr. Jones." Charles smiled, very openly. "I'm not accusing you of anything. I think I know what you do—you're a very skilled craftsman and you've made some beautiful things."

"That's what I tell people. You have a job you want done? We could skip all the talking."

"No, just questions."

"Hey, boss?"

Jones didn't move, but no one could have heard Angelo on the stairs.

"Oh, yes, Angelo."

"You wanted me?"

"Actually, not. I changed my mind."

"So you don't want anything."

"No, I'm sorry. Never mind."

"Whatever you say."

"Get on with it," Mr. Jones said, when Angelo was gone. "I don't like lots of questions."

"I was wondering about Derek Bastien's desk."

No reaction. "What are you wondering about it?"

"I wonder . . . if maybe there was something questionable about it."

Galen Jones shifted his position in the chair; he seemed to have hinges rather than joints. "Now, you think I'd answer a question like that?"

"I have been thinking about how you would answer it, Mr. Jones. You might not. But Derek is dead, and whoever owns the desk now may not even know about you."

"It doesn't matter to me who knows what."

"Did you know Derek at all?"

For the first time, the sharp eyes dulled. "I got to, a little."

"I knew him, too."

"So what are you saying?"

Charles sighed. "You tried to buy the desk at the auction Monday."

"You know a lot."

"I was there."

"It was a nice desk," Galen Jones said. "I liked it."

"I'm sure. You even moved away from Norman Highberg so he wouldn't see you bid on it."

"He talks too much."

"He does, but he didn't see anything, and he didn't say anything to me."

"I didn't get it, anyway."

"It went for over a hundred thousand dollars," Charles said.

"A lot more than I could pay for it."

"I think it was quite a surprise. Do you have any idea, Mr. Jones, why anyone might have been bidding so much for that desk? Was it a real antique? Or was it a clever copy? And if it was, I'd wonder what happened to the real desk. I assume there was a real desk. Do you know?"

"Now you're trying to be tricky, Beale."

"I'm not trying to be. I'm sorry."

"Well, you're barking up the wrong tree, anyway. So forget about the desk. There's nothing I have to say to you about it."

"I see."

They were both quiet, but neither seemed ready to be finished.

"What did you think of him?" Jones said at last.

"He was an interesting friend," Charles said. "And I'm learning quite a bit about him that I hadn't known."

"He got me talking, a lot better than you are. Too bad he got himself killed."

"Got himself killed? It wasn't his fault. It was a burglar."

"Then he shouldn't have had so much in his house worth stealing."

"I'll remember that for myself," Charles said. "Well—thank you, Mr. Jones. It's been very interesting to meet you. I might find another tree to bark at."

"You've got my number, Beale."

"Hey, boss."

Charles turned from the just closing front door. "Yes, Angelo, let me guess. You saw that man at the auction."

"He went out before you went out."

"I just wanted to check."

EVENING

The sky was dim, the streetlights were on. Charles sauntered down to the showroom just as Dorothy came marching in.

"Just in time," he said. "I was wondering whether to wait for you here or at home."

"I've spent the entire afternoon with Elizabeth Roper and Wilhelmina Stratton," Dorothy said. "We have the banquet completely under control, and I am worn out. They are too much like me, Charles."

"I hope it has renewed your appreciation for lackadaisical people."

"It has indeed." She set an armload of notebooks on the counter. "Alice, just set those underneath. I don't want to see them again until Saturday morning."

"Yes, Mrs. Beale."

"Thank you. And have you had a useful afternoon?" she said to Charles.

"More or less, and I can't wait to tell you about it. Are you ready for a cup of something?"

"I think I am. I suppose I can put up with your breezes as long as they blow me a whiff of coffee once in a while."

"We may set a record for caffeine before this is over," Charles said. "I also met Mr. Galen Jones while you were gone."

"The matchmaker?"

"Yes. I think I could go to a lamppost and say that I was a friend of Derek Bastien, and first it would invite me to its own private corner, and then it would tell me something that confuses me even deeper. It might also tell me it is only doing that because I am so interesting. I believe we've discussed how interesting everyone thinks I am?"

"We've discussed it," Dorothy said. "Why would anyone find you the least bit interesting?"

"Because my wife is extraordinarily beautiful." And then, before she could answer, "She has such a high opinion of me, I *must* be special."

"Then someone is in error," Dorothy said. "It will take me a moment to work out whom."

"Perhaps we should leave before you do, and before anyone comes looking for me."

"No one is looking for you."

"So far, not. Have we sold anything this afternoon, Alice?"

"Dickens' *A Christmas Carol*."

"Ah, now there was a person plagued by visitors."

"They were ghosts," Dorothy said.

The front door opened. A draft of chill air twirled in.

"Are you Charles Beale?"

Charles, Dorothy and Alice all turned to the tall, white-haired man standing in the door. His face would once have been handsome, but now it was worn and hollow. A strange light burned in his eyes. There was something shabby about his dark suit.

"I am," Charles said.

"You knew Derek Bastien?"

"I did."

The man did not move, but was motionless, lit from inside but black-framed from beyond. Charles stepped forward. He held out his hand. "Please, come in," he said.

Two steps forward and the man stopped again. He didn't match Charles's outstretched arm; he didn't seem to have noticed it.

"That's what he told me."

"He told you that he knew me?"

"He sent me."

Charles lowered his hand. He frowned. "Recently?"

"He's dead."

Charles smiled and stepped around the man to close the door. "I know. What can I do for you, Mr. . . . . ?"

The voice was bass with a couple strings a little too tight. The eyes seemed to focus a little past what he was looking at; which at the moment was somewhere around Charles's shoulder.

"You sell books?"

Charles swept his hand, from left to right, to show the room. "Here they are."

The odd-focused eyes only followed the hand and never raised to see the shelves covering every wall. Then they came back to some point inside Charles's nose. Abruptly he took hold of the hand, jiggled it, and let go.

"I'm Pat White."

"How nice to meet you, Mr. White," Charles said.

"Derek had a lot of books."

"He did. It was just the antique ones that he'd bought from me."

The eyes focused sharply onto Charles's. "How well did you know him?"

"Fairly well. I take it you knew him also?"

"I knew him. I know who killed him."

Crash! Alice and Dorothy dropped to their knees to pick up Dorothy's notebooks that had toppled to the floor.

After a moment, Charles answered. "I understood that he was killed by a burglar."

"Sure." Mr. White looked around the room, finally noticing the books. The pitch of his voice loosened. "What did he buy from you?"

"About a dozen volumes, mostly in law and government."

"Locke? Burke? Rousseau? Like that?"

"Yes. Exactly."

"Sounds right." The glances were sharp, spearing one volume and then another. "I'd be interested in those authors myself. Or I would have been."

"What do you do, Mr. White?"

"I'm retired."

"I see."

"No. You don't see. But it doesn't matter." He had become just a regular, slightly bedraggled person. He shrugged and his gaze came back to meet Charles's. "I used to be a judge."

"Oh." Then, unavoidably, Charles's changed. "Now I do see."

"And so does everyone else who reads the *Post* or watches the news. Well, it's been a pleasure, Mr. Beale."

"It has been. I am glad to have met you, and I mean that."

"What do you mean?"

"I've followed your story in the paper."

"Thanks. One of my admirers."

"I am, actually. I really would like to talk, Mr. White."

"I'll remember that."

"Why did you come?"

"Karen Liu told me you were asking around. I wanted to see what you were like, and now I have."

"You make it sound like I've disappointed you."

"No. As I was saying, it's been a pleasure." This time he started for the door.

"Perhaps we could have lunch," Charles said.

"I'll think about that."

And then he was gone into the night.

Cautiously, Dorothy stepped up beside Charles.

"That was the man in the newspaper?"

"Pat White. The *Washington Post* always calls him Patrick Henry White. It took me a moment to realize it was him."

"The judge. He knew Derek?"

"Yes. Bar the door before anyone else shows up," Charles said.

They both looked at the door, innocently closed. Alice crossed the room, turned the lock.

"I was joking," Charles said.

"It's closing time," Alice said.

"Well. It is. That was an odd visit."

"We get all kinds, Mr. Beale."

"I guess we do."

Morgan came. Charles watched him for a moment counting money and closing the shop. Slowly the air cleared.

He took Dorothy's hand. "Now are we ready to go?"

"I think so."

"Has Odysseus reached Ithaca yet?" he asked Morgan.

"Halfway," Morgan said. "And the bid is up to seven hundred. Is two thousand still okay?"

"If I bid too low, I will not get him; if I bid too high, I will pay more than he is worth. So shall I steer towards Scylla or Charybdis? I will stay the course and hold at two thousand."

"Yes, sir."

"Good night, Alice."

"Good night, Mr. Beale. Mrs. Beale."

"Morgan, we should get a new *Christmas Carol* in here right away."

"Yes, sir. And may God bless us, every one."

"Indeed," Charles said. "I wonder if Marley had ever been a judge."

"Do you still want a coffee? Or is it late enough for dinner?"

"Just a salad, I think," Dorothy said.

"A salad." Charles set his face resolutely forward. "Fortunately, Alexandria is one of their prime natural habitats. We will hunt one down."

They hunted, hand in hand. The first two blocks proved barren, but when they reached King Street there were many brightly lit, fern-filled lairs. A single shot brought down a fine trophy pair: plump, spinachy specimens, with grape tomatoes and blue cheese and raspberry glaze, and crusty floury French bread.

"Are we calm?" Dorothy asked.

"Enough."

"What was all that with Mr. White?"

"I don't know where to begin. He is a haunt of my philosophic musings." Charles munched an olive. "I meditate on what it would be like to be brought down by your past misdeeds, and presto, my meditation becomes a reality and walks in the door." He sipped his water. "It's rare when any part of philosophy actually becomes real."

"I think it's quite a coincidence." She sounded doubtful.

"Philosophy doesn't allow for coincidence," Charles said.

"Then what does it allow for?"

"The evil in human nature. And it only allows for it; it doesn't explain it."

"I don't think that the evil in human nature is the reason Patrick White fell out of the newspaper and into our shop."

"Oh, it is. You could say it's the reason for most things. But it *would* be nice to have something a little more specific in this case."

"Philosophy or not," Dorothy said, "I really don't think it's a coincidence."

"You think it's quite a coincidence, and you don't think it's a coincidence at all. Those two statements do not coincide."

"The first one is made negative by the tone of voice."

"Then let's see what connections there could be," Charles said. "He is—was—a judge. He could know people in the Justice Department, and he could apparently know Karen Liu in Congress."

"Lots of people know each other, Charles, but not at the same time we're reading about them in the newspaper."

"And he is in the newspaper because . . ." Charles stopped, suddenly somber.

"What?"

"He knew Derek, and he is in the newspaper because someone told them something about him. I need to think about this." He thought. "Now, say you were reading a mystery novel, and something like that happened. Could it be a coincidence?"

"No," she said. "Not in a well-written mystery, anyway."

"In real life, I suppose it could be. It must depend on how well written your life is."

"I don't think it is."

Charles frowned. "My life isn't well written?"

"I don't think it is a coincidence, as I have now said several times. Did he say he knew who killed Derek?"

"He said that."

"Who does he mean?"

"We would have to ask him. Oh, what does it all mean? Checks to Karen Liu. That article about the wife killing her husband."

"What about the other papers?"

"I'll need to look at them. I hadn't wanted to."

"Charles, I think you should talk to the police. I really do. I don't like this talk about killing."

"But what will happen if I do? We'd have the front page of the *Washington Post* all to ourselves for a month."

"They wouldn't have to find out. And is it really your choice to make?"

"So far. Just think about Congresswoman Liu. I like her. She is a driven person, and she is driven by very good things. I might even be glad she got those checks at that critical time."

"That sounds rather shaky."

"This is not a firm and stable world we live in. Anyway, I will look at the other papers. Now that I've met Karen Liu, and John Borchard, and Patrick White, and Lucy Bastien, the papers might make more sense to me. Once I've looked at them, we can discuss what comes next."

"And I need to get home," Dorothy said. "There are still calls to make about Saturday evening. Two hundred people are coming to this banquet."

"A blue-blooded and blue-haired two hundred. Yes, make your calls. We want them all to feel very comfortable and happy."

"We will. We have a surprise for them, too."

"Good. Then let's get moving and shaking, dear. I will tell you about Lucy and Galen tomorrow."

"Galen?"

"Jones. The matchmaker."

"Oh, yes" Dorothy said. "Did you have him look at Angelo?"

"No, I had Angelo look at him."

"Charles, how much would you say that the Enlightenment was based on laws?"

"Laws written by governments?"

"No, I mean natural laws. You mentioned Isaac Newton once."

"I think natural laws were very important, Derek. Once the Renaissance and the Reformation had overturned so much that people had once accepted, they were looking for something new to base their understanding of the world on. Newton and Pascal and the rest were describing the physical world with mathematic laws, so why not describe mankind the same way? That's what the Enlightenment fundamentally was: rebuilding the world rationally."

"Then it was fundamentally flawed. Nothing is less described by rules than human nature."

"On that, Derek, we completely agree. But what they built is the modern world we live in. We seem to govern ourselves and keep a semblance of order."

"Barely. Just barely. It's touch and go, and we live an inch from catastrophe. Charles, the reason there are no laws that govern human nature is that it is ungovernable."

"Some people are less governable than others."

"You're speaking of your own experience?"

"Yes, my son, as you know."

"I do. I know it isn't an easy subject for you."

"No, Derek, but it's all right. He would be a good example for a discussion of the ungovernable human spirit, but I don't think I would be objective."

"How old was he?"

"Seventeen. That was fifteen years ago."

"Fifteen years might not heal much."

"Believe me, Derek. It doesn't."

FRIDAY

MORNING

"Let me describe what Derek Bastien looked like."

The night had passed, the morning had come, and Dorothy, at her desk, looked very nice herself.

"Yes?" she said, peering over her reading glasses.

"I hope you're not too busy," Charles said.

"Please, dear," she said, "tell me what he was like."

"I'd be glad to." Charles's gaze drifted. "Did you ever see him?"

"You introduced me once, but I don't remember now."

"Exactly. Oddly nondescript for such a personality. Or maybe chameleon-like. He could just disappear in a room of people if he wanted."

"There must have been something not ordinary."

"First was his eyes. They were always studying. When you finally noticed it, it was unsettling for a while. Then his voice. It was deeper than you would think. Rumbly."

"And what did you talk about on your visits?"

"We played chess and discussed human nature. He studied it like a geologist would study rocks. His job was his laboratory."

"He said that?"

"No. I was studying his nature a little myself."

"While he studied yours?"

Charles laughed. "Wheels within wheels. I think I agree with John Borchard. He just referred to all of us as Derek Bastien's collected works. Himself, me, Karen Liu. All of Derek's friends."

"Mr. Beale?" said Alice, abruptly appearing. "You have a phone call. Mr. John Borchard."

Charles looked at Dorothy. "Speak of the devil."

"John. This is Charles."

"Good morning, Charles!" None of his rich baritone was lost through the telephone connection. "I hope I'm not interrupting anything?"

"I'm at your service."

"Well! What an opportunity! I shouldn't waste it."

"Please don't," Charles said. "What can I do for you?"

"I said that I wanted to drop in to your shop, there, but I just haven't had time."

"It was only two days ago that you said that."

"I am still very interested. And I was wondering, also, who else of Derek's friends you'd met."

"I have met a few more. His wife, Lucy, for one. I realized how odd it was that I'd never met her."

"I have only briefly myself! What did you think of her?"

"I might sound judgmental if I said anything."

"And that says quite a bit itself! I understand. Not precisely the grieving widow, I expect."

"Not precisely."

"And, I wonder," Charles said, "if you've ever heard of Patrick White?"

"Patrick White . . ." There was a long pause. "I should have guessed. Of course!" John said, bouncing back to life. "Very sad!"

"So you know him?"

"Oh yes, we've met. In fact, it's a bit of a long story, even before his present troubles. Well, that's interesting. Quite a path you're following!"

"I just take one step and the next one presents itself."

"And all from selling a few books. I doubt you had any idea where it would lead when he first came through your door!"

"I certainly didn't."

"I wonder where those books are now."

"I don't wonder that at all," Charles said.

Another pause. "You aren't curious?"

"I know where they are. I bought them back at the auction."

"Of course!" Jubilation! "Of course you would! Absolutely! So you have them?"

"I certainly do."

"That's very interesting to know!" The celebration died down. "All of them?"

"The thirteen offered at the auction."

"There weren't any missing?"

"No, I believe that was all."

"Well, I should have guessed. Do you plan to sell them?"

"I expect so. I haven't listed them yet."

"You haven't listed them." There was a feel of gathering for a leap. "When you do, let me know. I might be interested myself."

"I'll let you know," Charles said.

"Then I won't bother you anymore for now." Back to happiness and friendship. "Keep in touch, Charles! And remember, if there is anything at all I can do for you, let me know."

Piercing blue eyes were upon him as he hung up.

"Yes?" he said.

"Yes?" Dorothy said in reply.

"I should really think of something he can do for me."

"You could ask him about the papers in the book."

"I don't think I will," Charles said. "But I will look at them now myself."

"Give me a brief description of yesterday," she said.

"Of course. It keeps getting put off, doesn't it? I visited Lucy." The last shreds of his own happiness withered. "Did I say the auction was bad? This was much worse."

"Seeing the house."

"Wiped clean. I will never go back. Everything of Derek was purged, burnt with fire, consumed. Except that instead of black, it's all yellow, the one color he didn't like."

"And her?"

"She gave every appearance of cynical enjoyment at her new freedom and money. I wasn't there long enough to dig very deeply, but I don't think I would have found different emotions below that surface. This is her second widowhood. She didn't say what happened to her first husband. Anyway, then I met Galen Jones."

"Where did you find him?"

"Between Norman Highberg and Jacob Leatherman, I have pieced together that he is a maker of replica antiques, that he did some work for Derek, and that he tried to buy Derek's desk at the auction. I asked him if Derek's desk was actually a fake, and he declined to answer."

Dorothy was confused. "Where did you get that idea?"

"It was just a guess, and I won't even begin to work out what it might imply."

"As I have said," Dorothy said, "I think the police should be involved. However, as you have declined, I will admit that I am curious what it all means."

"Then I will find out and tell you. And, I have a project for Angelo, which I also need to tell you about. Will you be busy again this afternoon with the banquet?"

"I am afraid so. I will be putting out centerpieces and dealing with a catering crisis."

"What crisis?"

"I don't know yet. I'm just assuming there will be one."

"Then, until we meet again," he said. "Will you be finished by this evening?"

"I should be."

"Good. Perhaps we could spend it together."

"Alice? Have we sold anything this morning?

"A Jules Verne. *Journey to the Center of the Earth*."

Charles paused at the basement steps. "It is," he said. And down he went.

He stopped at the basement door to adjust to a proper attitude.

He crossed the threshold and locked the door behind him.

Without hesitation he went to the specific shelf, the specific, worn, unremarkable spine.

He set it on the desk and pulled on the white gloves. They weren't necessary—but it wasn't the book's fault what had been done to it.

Then he did hesitate.

And finally, when he did open the book, the crimes had not been erased. The book was still murdered and the box was still thrust deep into its ribs.

He pulled the box out.

He opened it again for this the second time. The papers hadn't dissolved or escaped. They were still there, and he removed them, and smoothed them open on the desk.

Six pages.

The first. The list of codes and dates. *GJ, 9/12/05, 2250; EF, 2/5/2003 1800; RM, 4/11/06, 750.* There was no order. The page was full, and half the back, with more than fifty entries.

The second. The four checks payable to Karen Liu, dated to her first campaign for Congress. The total was five hundred thousand dollars. They were cashier's checks with no indication of where the money had come from.

The third. The newspaper article. **Man Killed, Police Search County for Wife**. It was terrible, but at least brief, written in a small-town style.

A grisly scene met police yesterday morning when they were

called to a house on Washington Street. A man had been stabbed repeatedly by a large kitchen knife. Police are not yet releasing the name of the victim, but neighbors say it was the owner of the house.

Neighbors described a history of arguments and violence at the house, and said there had been many visits from the police during the year and a half the couple had lived in the neighborhood.

A neighbor across the street from the house described the couple to this reporter: "They were so in love when they came," she said. "They were such nice newlyweds. Then over a few months it changed. There was screaming and fighting at all hours."

The wife has not been seen since last night. Police have said the investigation is only getting started. They said they will make a statement after they finish their search of the house.

The fourth paper. This was another article, very short. **Drug Bust in Fairfax**—*Fairfax County police arrested more than a dozen members of an alleged drug importing ring. The early morning raids on five residences were the result of a three-month investigation. Drug-sniffing dogs uncovered over seventy pounds of cocaine hidden in furniture in one apartment.*

The fifth. The page was titled at the top, *Court Order, Fifth Circuit Court of Kansas,* then a typewritten list of names and numbers, *Howard Elias Finney, 2445993,* plus seven others, and below them, *To be released immediately,* then signed by *Quentin Osley, Judge,* and dated. The date was nearly twenty years old. There were several other case numbers and designations on the page.

The sixth paper, and last. It was a cover page of a report. *University of Virginia Honor Court Proceedings, 1974.* Beneath was a handwritten *Page 65.*

This last page, the emptiest, he stared at the longest.

Then he wrote a few notes in a small notebook and replaced the papers in the box, and the box in the book, and the book on the shelf.

AFTERNOON

"Morgan."

"Yes, Mr. Beale?"

"I have a couple little jobs for you."

"Yes, sir."

The pale face beneath the sandy red hair looked up at him through dense glasses.

"Do you need more sunlight, Morgan?"

"I get sunburn."

"Do you even get enough air?"

"I'm still breathing, sir."

"I suppose you are. First, here is an article about some drug arrests. Can you find out when it's from?" He put the handwritten copy in Morgan's long, thin fingers.

"Let's see." He entered a sentence from the article. "Looks like the *Washington Post*, March 20th, 2002."

"Thank you! That was easy."

"That one was."

"Hey, boss."

Charles turned. Angelo stood in the door, ragged and menacing.

"Yes?"

"You want us to go out now?"

"Yes, I'll be a few minutes. You'll need to look nice."

"What is that for drugs and arrests you are doing?"

"It's not me," Charles said. "Don't worry. I'll be down soon."

"Okay, boss."

Charles looked back to Morgan. "Here is another article."

Morgan read the words. "I hope these aren't anyone you know," he said.

"No. It's complicated. I'm trying to find out about a book."

"Yes, sir. I know how that can go off in all different directions. Let's see." He typed, then typed again, then a few other times. "That one isn't coming up."

"It isn't there?" Charles asked.

"I can't find it. It might be too old, or from some newspaper that doesn't have their back issues online, or they're hidden."

"Never mind, then. Next—this is the number and date of a court order from the Fifth Circuit Court of Kansas. Can you find anything about it?"

"That's probably online. Let me see."

There was more typing and clicking and passing of minutes, but finally Morgan nodded. "Right. It's some grand jury thing about, um, prosecutorial misconduct. Eight prisoners were released. Their trials had been overturned because the prosecutor had, um, whatever . . . I think it means he'd suppressed evidence . . . overzealous . . . jury tampering . . . Wow." His nose got closer and closer to the screen. "Hardcore ruthless. This guy would prosecute his own mother." He looked up at Charles. "Sir."

"That's good enough," Charles said. "Does it say who the prosecutor was?"

"No. Not here. But it does say no charges would be brought against him, apparently because of some technicality."

"All right, then, one more. There is a man in the news recently, Patrick Henry White. He was a judge, but he had to resign when someone told the newspaper that he'd cheated on some tests back in law school. I wonder if you can tell me where and when he was in school."

"Let's see." Morgan's fingers spoke with the computer and soon it answered. "It was in a *Washington Post* article six months ago. University of Virginia, 1972 to 1976."

"Thank you." He sighed. "I think that's all." He took the papers back. "And where is Odysseus?"

"Still sailing."

"Very well."

Charles walked slowly back to his own office. He took a porcelain soap dish from the bathroom, set his handwritten notes on it, lit them with a match, and slid the ashes into the wastebasket.

"Alice?"

"Yes, Mr. Beale?"

"Here is a list of books I would like you to pull for me."

"Did someone order them?"

"No, I'm just borrowing them. I'll need them in a couple hours and I'll have them back tomorrow."

"Hey, boss."

Charles regained his composure. "You must learn to make some sound when you come into a room, Angelo."

"I said, 'Hey, boss.' Are you ready for us to go?"

"Yes you did, and yes I am, and you look quite presentable. And have we sold anything else, Alice?"

"A volume of George Bernard Shaw's plays."

"*Pygmalion*. Well, Professor Higgins is taking Miss Doolittle to the ball."

"This is a jeweler," Charles said. "Very fancy. I doubt we'll find our lady here, so it will just be practice."

"People here don't talk to me," Angelo said.

"You look completely respectable," Charles said. "Come on." He pushed open the door.

Angelo stopped on the threshold. Even he was overwhelmed, his eyes wide open until he regained his blank, narrow stare.

Four pedestals interrupted the expansive royal blueness of the carpet, magnificent dark wood stands smothered in glittering sparkling dazzling flashing spot-lit jewels. Around the three walls facing them ran a blinding necklace of other crystalline displays.

Charles gave him time.

A velvet voice floated toward them. "May I help you?" The source, a crystalline young woman, had come from a side office door.

"I hope so," Charles said. "My name is Charles Beale, and I'm here with Mr. Acevedo."

"Good afternoon, Mr. Beale and Mr. Acevedo."

"Hey," Angelo said, still slightly blinded.

"We were given your name by Capital Auction."

"Yes?" the woman said.

"Mr. Acevedo is interested in acquiring some pieces that will be up for auction, but he would prefer to have someone more familiar with jewelry, and with bidding at auction, to represent him."

Angelo stood with his hands in his pockets, his eyes shifting side to side.

"I see." The woman smiled. "You would want to speak with Mr. Needham."

"Does he usually attend the auction himself, or does someone else?"

"That depends on the type of pieces, but he would work with you personally to begin with."

"I see. Is he in?"

"I believe he is engaged at the moment."

Charles smiled. "Perhaps we'll stop in later."

"Yes, sir. It would be good to call ahead of time."

"We will. Thank you."

"What do you think?" Charles asked.

"Hey, boss, that is the way you do it."

"What would you do?"

"You got another place to try?"

"Let's see . . . there is an office on the list that's close." He looked at the paper. "About three blocks."

"I will do that one."

"All right. Let's try it."

Three blocks was not far at Angelo's pace. Charles was the one gasping as they reached the solid gray stone slab within sight of Union Station.

"This is an office, not a retail store," he said. "You don't just wander in."

They rode an elevator to the third floor. When he wasn't moving, Angelo was very still, but when the doors opened he was moving before Charles had a chance to speak.

The door said Gallwood Imports. "You stay here," Angelo said.

He opened the door without knocking. Charles watched from the hall.

It was a small, crowded, untidy room with one occupied desk and two unoccupied. The occupant was a very thin man with dark hair and a beaklike nose.

"Yes?" he said.

Angelo waited.

"Yes? What do you want?" the man said.

"I am here for that package," Angelo said.

"What package?"

"That lady, she said to come get that package."

"What package? What are you talking about?"

"That lady said." Angelo was bored and impatient.

"What lady?"

"That lady, she called and said come get that package."

"Who?" the man said, confused but not yet annoyed.

"You got a lady who works here?"

"Ayala! There's a guy out here to pick up a package."

A woman looked in from a doorway, from under a pile of jet-black hair. "What?"

"Do you have something for this guy to pick up?"

"I don't have anything," she said.

Angelo stepped back to look at the name on the main door. "This is Gallwood, right?"

"Who called you? Where did you come from?" the man said.

"You got a package or you don't?"

"We don't have any package."

Angelo shrugged and turned and left. He closed the door and started down the hall.

"Wait," Charles said, and he stopped. "That was very good, Angelo."

"Thanks, boss."

"Can you do the rest of the list?"

"I can do that list."

They started walking again. In the elevator, Charles said, "Remember a few things. If someone starts getting mad, don't get into a fight."

"I won't fight."

"And don't make anyone suspicious. In a store they might think you are trying to shoplift."

"I know all that, boss."

"I suppose you do." The elevator door opened. "Angelo, do you know that I trust you?"

He shrugged. "You want I should go to the next place now?"

"No. We'll go back to the shop. You should just do a couple a day. The important thing is for you to practice talking to people."

"But you want that lady?"

"Yes. I don't know if you will find her or not."

"Okay, boss. I will talk to the people and I will look for that lady. What do you want I should do if I find her?"

"Don't do anything. Just tell me."

EVENING

"I have the books you wanted me to pull, Mr. Beale," Alice said as he and Angelo walked into the shop.

"Very good. Thank you." He looked into the box she had on the counter. "Have we sold anything while I was gone?"

"Yes, sir. A Mary Shelley *Frankenstein*."

Angelo disappeared silently up the steps to his room.

"Not a good sign," Charles said.

"You're back!" Charles said.

"I am," Dorothy said. "Alice said you were out with Angelo?"

"I didn't have a chance to tell you. I went to the auction house and asked for the list of agents who've registered with them. I am going to have Angelo go to each address and look for the blond woman who bought Derek's desk."

"Do you really want to know who she is?"

"No, the main purpose is for Angelo to get experience with professional situations."

"Do you think he might find her?"

"Who knows what he is capable of. We did two today and he will strike out on his own next week."

"Will he get along all right by himself?"

"As long as he doesn't get himself arrested. It was interesting to watch him. How would we act if someone like him came into our shop?"

"We'd wonder why he was there," Dorothy said. "We'd worry that he was going to steal something."

"That's how everyone looks at him. I wonder what it's like to know that no one trusts you. Everyone he sees is hostile or afraid."

"He gives them reason to be."

"Are you ever afraid of him?"

"No, not anymore. You know how I was at the beginning. But I trust him now."

"Why?"

"I know him."

"I wonder if we do. But anyway—he'll be busy with his list for a while. And, dear, for us, I've decided on a little outing."

"A what?" Dorothy said, suspicious.

"I've been neglecting you, and you've been working so hard. We are going on an outing."

"Where?"

"Far, but not far." He smiled. "It is an outing of the imagination."

"My imagination is more of the stay-at-home type."

"I will lead," he said. "Even imaginations need fresh air. Put on your jacket, dear."

Dusk streets opened to them. They strolled slowly into swarms of shoppers and walkers, and bicycles whisked around them and cars crawled slower than they walked. Windows illuminated and lines squeezed into ice-cream shops and bakeries. Very plain people mingled with very odd ones, and street musicians played. Charles led downhill.

Soon the river stopped them. They stepped out onto the boardwalk plaza and found a well-lit bench with waves lapping beneath them and restaurant balconies above them.

"You're wondering what is in the box," Charles said. It was in his lap.

"I see that it's books."

"Yes. They are our outing." He handed her a book with a black and white dust cover.

"*The Boys on the Bus*. Is it something political?"

"No. Here's the next one. Steinbeck."

"*Travels with Charlie*? A dog?"

"No, no, no. You don't know anyone by that name?"

"Well, you of course. But I still don't understand."

"All right. The next book."

"*Rebecca of Sunnybrook Farm*." She stared at the three books. "I'm sorry, dear …"

"Look at those three."

"Boys, Bus, Travels, Charlie, Rebecca, Sunnybrook Farm—oh! Oh, Charles! It's the day we went to the farm."

"The most important day of my life," he said. "Here."

She took the next book. "*A Light in the Window*. But there wasn't a light."

"You were the light, dear."

She smiled and proved his words true. Then she looked into the box. "What's next?"

"Guizot."

"*The Long Reign of Louis the Fourteenth*. I don't remember anything French."

"Well, the weather."

"The rain? Oh, the rain."

"The long rain."

"All day."

"What would have happened without the rain?" Charles asked.

"It wouldn't have made a difference."

"I don't think you would have noticed the lonely, gangly bus driver. You would have been frolicking all over the farm and whatnot, feeding the cows whatever you feed them."

"Nonsense. I noticed you the minute I got onto the bus."

"You've said that before, but you didn't show it."

"Of course I wouldn't. I was only seventeen."

"Anyway, it did rain, and the whole crowd of you were stuck in the barn for four hours, and I was stuck in the bus waiting. It was so nice of you to sit in the window for me to look at."

"And it was so nice of you to look at me," she said. "It didn't seem a waste of time at all. Are there any other books in there?"

"A couple more."

"*History of the English Language.* That would be our two college majors?"

"History and English. Notice the author."

"George Townsend."

"Do you get it? It's where we went to college."

"Oh, Georgetown. That's very cute, Charles."

"Serendipitous, and so was all of life back then." He took the pile of books she already had and handed her a new one from the box.

"*Sense and Sensibility.* That is the two of us?"

"Yes, romance and marriage. You are sensible and I live by feel."

"We are so different," Dorothy said, "and so alike. But it's our strength, isn't it?"

"It is a great strength. Especially with this next book, from the Broadway script shelf."

"*How to Succeed in Business Without Really Trying.* How funny! We did try so hard, didn't we?"

"But we succeeded anyway."

"It was all you, Charles."

"I think not. I could never run a business, and you could in your sleep."

"But there wouldn't be a reason. It's my occupation, but it's your dream."

"That's what I do in my sleep. Well, two more books. This one is the hard one."

She took it anyway. "*A Separate Peace.* I wondered what you would have." She stared at the cover for a while. "I was thinking the other day whether I had regrets."

"Do you?"

"I would still do it all over again."

"I would, too," he said. "My current regret is that I didn't talk with him more. Have I forgotten? We must have talked over dinner, and about his schoolwork."

"I'm afraid I mostly remember the arguments," Dorothy said.

"And compare that to Angelo, who never says anything."

Dorothy handed the book back. "I am so glad that you brought Angelo into the shop."

"Does he still remind you of William?"

"Now that I know him, he's his own person."

"Do you like Angelo?" Charles asked.

"I do!" Dorothy laughed. "As little as he says, he does have a personality. I don't know what he would be like if he was more open. I think I'd like him even more."

"I hope we have a chance to, eventually. Here's the last book."

He handed her *From Here to Eternity*.

Then, for a while, they sat silently and watched the water, while the sun set behind them, firing the far shore orange and red and then leaving it a dark ashen black. The windows of the buildings along it were bright sparks left from the burning; and all around where they were sitting were the bright lanterns of the riverfront and restaurants and streets.

And finally they started for home.

"I looked at the papers this morning."

The last of a simple dinner was between them on the dining room table.

"Were they bad?" Dorothy asked.

"Yes. Very bad."

"What?"

"One of them is about Patrick White."

Charles waited while she worked out what it meant. "About what he did in school?"

"Yes. It isn't obvious. It's just a cover page from a University of Virginia honor court. It doesn't say anything about Mr. White, just a page number, but it's from a year when he was a student there."

"It doesn't have his name?"

"It's him. I'm sure it is. A person would have to know that the paper was important, and then dig in to find what it meant. But if I were to send that paper to the *Washington Post* and tell them they could find a scandal behind it, then the damage would be done."

"But who did send it?"

"Maybe Derek Bastien. Or maybe someone else, but Derek had it. Dorothy, it is obvious to me that Derek was collecting incriminating documents about people."

"What were the other papers?"

"The checks to Karen Liu; the woman who killed her husband; the page from the University of Virginia; then there's the list of letters and numbers and dates, and a short article about police in Fairfax breaking up a drug gang."

"But you don't know what those are about."

"No, I don't. And there's one more. A copy of a court order releasing eight men from a prison in Kansas, from twenty years ago." He sighed. "I had Morgan look it up, and the men were released because the prosecutor at their trials had done something wrong."

"By mistake?"

"Apparently not. And it doesn't say who the prosecutor was, but John Borchard mentioned to me that he had been a prosecutor in Kansas long ago."

"That seems obvious," Dorothy said.

"It seems."

"It's difficult, isn't it?"

"Very difficult," Charles said. "Who would want to have a list of other people's sins?"

"Do you mean that literally?"

"I meant it rhetorically. But there is a literal answer in this case, isn't there?"

"I wish you could give it all to someone else," Dorothy said. "But I understand why you don't want to."

"When I looked at those papers this morning," Charles said, "I felt like a burden was coming down on my shoulders."

He stood from the table and carried his plate to the kitchen. Dorothy followed.

"How can you decide what to do?"

"I want to find out about Derek and why he had the papers, but I'll still have to decide what to do with them. I want to know the people themselves."

"But even then, what would you do?"

"I wonder . . ."

"What?"

"If there will be anything I can do to help them."

"I've been reading a volume of Jeremy Bentham's correspondence."

"I haven't sold you one, Derek."

"Ha! No, Charles, this is a modern version. But he certainly believed that people are controllable by innate laws."

"And his prison reforms prove him wrong. He was also firmly against the idea of innate, inalienable human rights."

" 'Nonsense on stilts.' "

"Exactly. Locke would not have been proud of him as a disciple. I wonder that you're wasting your time, Derek."

"I like to be provoked, Charles. He was voted an honorary citizen of the French Revolution."

"Not the best character reference."

"I am interested in his ideas of punishment. If someone commits a crime, why do we punish him by taking months or years of his life? You've stolen a loaf of bread, we seize ten years. What does it accomplish?"

"It is a deterrent threat."

"But for the one who isn't deterred?"

"I suppose it prevents them from stealing another loaf, at least for the next ten years. And, Derek, time is one thing everyone has. They might not have money for you to take from them, but they do have time."

"Bentham said that prison should be for correcting the individual, not punishing them. The Enlightenment had found its way into prison."

"I don't think he knew how to correct a person."

"If you had to decide a person's punishment, Charles, how would you do it?"

"I don't think a person can be corrected, Derek. I think he can only be redeemed."

SATURDAY

MORNING

Charles wandered down the stairs to the showroom. Dorothy was behind the counter talking with a middle-aged, upper-class lady with a large middle and larger upper.

"Mrs. Stratton," he said. "Good morning."

"Good morning, Mr. Beale," the woman said in a properly fruity voice. "Dorothy and I are discussing the banquet this evening."

"We're looking forward to it."

The front door opened.

"Good morning," Dorothy said in a bright greet-the-customer voice, and Charles turned to look toward the door, and then down slightly.

"Congresswoman Liu! What an honor!"

"Good morning, Mr. Beale." She nodded toward the ladies at the counter. "Good morning!"

"Dorothy!" Charles said. "Roll out the red carpet. This is her! An honest-to-goodness congresswoman!"

"Oh, Mr. Beale. Please!" Karen Liu beamed her searchlight-strength smile and without any hint of embarrassment. "Thank you!"

"This is my wife, Dorothy."

"Good morning, Mrs. Beale!"

"And our dear friend, Mrs. Wilhelmina Stratton."

"A congresswoman?" Mrs. Stratton said. "How do you do!"

A few tangled moments passed, of ebullient greetings and fulsome praises and self-effacing protestations, and of Mrs. Stratton seizing opportunity with both hands. But finally the air cleared and extraneous personalities realized they were no longer needed. Only Charles, Dorothy and the fully introduced congresswoman were left.

"And what an interesting shop!" she said as she finally had a chance to see it.

"Oh, it is," Charles said, "and I'm so glad to have you here. Let me show you around."

"Let me just look at it all first." They stood for a moment in the room's center, Karen Liu completely inflated, her eyes sharp and darting; and Charles and Dorothy respectfully silent.

"Now show me something."

"Of course," he said. He led her to the shelves under the stairs. "Books," he said. Dorothy watched from the counter.

"May I look at one?" Karen Liu said.

"Please."

She touched a spine and then a few more, reading the titles. "I thought you sold old books."

"These are a little bit old," he said. "The very old ones are downstairs. But even middle-aged books can be very interesting and valuable."

She slid one volume out. "Fishing?"

"A popular section."

Then her eyes got very big. "Two hundred dollars?"

Charles nodded. "*Fishing Salmon and Trout*, 1889. It's a fifth edition and the leather is still in excellent condition. Cholmondeley-Pennell is a standard for people who collect in fishing."

"What makes it worth two hundred dollars?"

"That people are willing to pay two hundred."

"There are people that would." She handed it to him. "But I wouldn't."

"It depends on what a person values," he said. "But books can be valuable in so many ways."

"The only use I would have for a book is to read it."

"Some people use, and some collect." Charles opened the book in his hand and softly turned the pages. "It means something to own a book. If a person enjoys fishing, this book can re-create that enjoyment. And this book, with its own collectible value, adds to the enjoyment. Some people collect antiques as an investment, but most do it because it enriches them in deeper ways."

Suddenly the charm and smile turned off. The change was striking.

"Do you have any books that are valuable because of what they say about people?" She was looking at him, not the book in his hand.

"What kind of things would they say?" he asked.

"Things they wouldn't want said."

Dorothy busied herself at the counter, actively not participating in the conversation.

"I have books about human nature," Charles said. "Some of them come to very bleak conclusions, and many people would rather not hear what they have to say. Is that what you mean?"

"It might be. What books did you sell to Derek Bastien?"

"Classic authors of the Enlightenment, the seventeenth and eighteenth centuries. They were books about government and law and human thought."

"Were they the kind you just described?"

"Some of those authors had a bleak view of mankind, but mostly they were hopeful."

The congressional brows furrowed, but the hearing room atmosphere had eased. "What if I wanted to buy something? What would you recommend?"

"I'd have to know what you value, Ms. Liu." He smiled. "I have to know who you are."

"All right." She was back to smiling, but a superficial one. "Pretend I wanted to buy something. Find out who I am."

"Do you have any hobbies?"

"Hobbies! Me?" The indignity was genuine.

"That's where some people start. Fishing, camping. Sports. Baseball is popular."

"I don't have time for hobbies."

"Do you have favorite authors?"

"Mr. Beale, I don't even remember the last time I read a book just to read it. I only read reports."

"Let's step back from reading. What would you like to experience?"

"Experience?"

Charles's own smile had faded. "What drives you, Congresswoman?"

She answered as seriously. "Struggle, Mr. Beale."

"For what?"

"For justice."

"I prefer mercy," he said.

She folded her arms and leaned her head. "Mercy is a whim. It is doled out by the powerful when they choose for a moment to lighten their oppression of the weak. Justice is equal and blind."

"Justice means getting what you deserve," Charles said. "I hope I don't."

"Some people just wish they could."

"Well." He sighed, and took a book from a different shelf. "You might like Sinclair Lewis. Or William Faulkner."

"They're old. The dead past doesn't interest me. I live in the present."

"Faulkner said, 'The past isn't dead. It isn't even past.' I think you would be fascinated by these stories because you would recognize everything in them and you would see how these characters dealt with the same struggles you have. You must know, Congresswoman, how tied our present is to our past. We've each gotten to where we are now through our past."

"It's been a hard road," she said.

"Just think how decisions you've made in your past affect your present," Charles said.

"Mr. Beale." She had returned to her hardest expression. "I don't know what that statement means. What exactly does it mean?"

"It was a general statement about all of us. I'm sure we've all made mistakes."

"Are you trying to say something specific about me?" She wasn't showing any emotion, just extreme attention. There was a short pause of measuring each other.

"I didn't mean to be, and I didn't mean to give any offense."

"I'm not taking offense. I'm just trying to understand what you mean."

He answered carefully. "I mean that I prefer mercy over justice."

She thought carefully. "Then I do, too."

"And my point," he said, picking up the speed of the conversation, "is that authors like these have explored that conflict. As I said, you might be fascinated by the ways they resolve it."

She joined the quicker flow. "I might just have to wait for the movie to come out," she said with her standard smile. "Did you really just want to meet me because I was a friend of Derek's? Was that the only reason?"

"Was that the only reason you let me come?"

"Let's say yes, Mr. Beale, to both of those."

"Let's do." He placed the books back on the shelves. "I had an interesting visit the other night. Pat White. He mentioned your name."

She frowned, but only some. "We've been good friends for a long time. I feel very sorry for him."

"Now, is that a case of injustice, or mercy losing to justice?"

"That, Mr. Beale, would be a very long answer, and I think I must have taken up quite a bit of your morning already."

"I'm sure your time is much more valuable than mine," he said. "I also met John Borchard."

She crumpled the name into a wad and tossed it back to him. "That would be another long discussion."

"Then let's not have it," he said, smoothing stiff creases out of the air. "Instead, Congresswoman—I wonder if you might want to look at something that isn't a struggle. Something peaceful instead."

"What do you mean?"

"A book that's just for looking. A very special volume." He crossed the corner to a shelf that was built tall to hold many sizes of books and took a small volume from it. "This was printed in 1892 in England. It's called a Wisdom Garden. They were a popular type at the turn of the century."

She opened to the middle.

"Oh," she said, and in a moment everything had changed.

"I was just remembering your waiting room. All the flowers."

Her mouth was still on *oh*.

Charles smiled. "The plates are engravings of English gardens."

"They're beautiful."

"Now this is how the book was used. You set it open on your desk and simply notice it from time to time throughout the day. It's meant to be calming."

"That's why I love flowers."

"And the captions are from Proverbs. I'd like to loan it to you. Would you mind?"

"You'd just let me take it?"

"I'd be honored if you would. This is how cultured ladies of a former time dealt with their stress."

"I could use less stress and more culture." She lingered over the page for a moment. "I'll be very careful with it."

"That's fine. That's all it needs."

The telephone rang, and Dorothy picked it up. "Alexandria Rare Books." She listened. "No, we close at two on Saturday," she said. "But we're open until seven through the week."

"And it's noon now," the congresswoman said. "I am so glad I came. And I know I will enjoy this book. When should I get it back to you?"

"Just when you've had time to look through it."

"I'll keep it for a few days and send it back. Thank you for our talk." She opened the door. "We might want to talk again."

"Whenever you'd like," he said.

And finally, she was gone.

"What do you think?" Charles asked.

"I'm impressed. She's a very strong personality."

"Is she authentic? Sincere?"

"I think so. A force for good."

"Corrupt?"

"I don't think so."

"What would happen if that paper became public?"

"I hope it doesn't."

"Does she think I know about her past misdeeds?"

"I think she wonders, Charles. You led her right up to that conversation."

"She was there waiting for me."

"Do you think you'll see her again?"

"That's up to her. We'll see if she returns the book herself or just sends it back, like she said."

EVENING

Charles waited.

He was in the front room of his house, in his comfortable chair. The clock on the mantel chimed six times.

He was in a gray suit, with a flamboyant red tie. Just waiting.

Then a door closed above and there was a rustle on the stairs. He jumped to his feet to watch.

Down she came! All in pale blue, like a quiet sapphire. Closer—and he got very close—the dress was damask textured; elegant from a distance, but intimately intricate. Her face was an exquisite cameo in a silver setting.

"You look so wonderful," he said.

"And you are quite debonair."

"We are made for each other."

"I told Wilhelmina we'd be there in fifteen minutes."

"You gather the mice, and I'll bring the pumpkin around."

"And now, ladies and gentlemen." The voice flowed like quiet thunder across the ballroom. "It is my pleasure to present to you our director, Mrs. Elizabeth Roper." Applause echoed back from the forty banquet tables.

"Thank you." The woman was tall and thin, and her silver dress matched her silver hair. "Thank you." The applause waned politely. "Before I begin my remarks this evening, I would like to introduce the board of directors of the FitzRobert Foundation. Our chairman, Mr. Thomas Grenville, of McMurty, Grenville and Cole. Stand up, Tom."

More applause. "Mr. Hamilton Kite of Alexandria Federal Bank. The honorable Mrs. Wilhelmina Stratton. Mrs. Dorothy Beale."

Dorothy stood, as the others had, but far more splendidly.

"Our special thanks to Wilhelmina and Dorothy for all their work on our banquet this year. And Dorothy dear, just keep standing. This marks the twentieth year Dorothy has been on our board." Much more applause. "I can't even begin to tell how much she has done for the Foundation in all those years."

"And of course, she is herself a graduate of the FitzRobert Home."

She sat, and Charles found her hand and held it while the rest of the names were called, and while the remarks began and plodded their slow path.

"With our new wing, which has now been open for three years, we have one hundred and forty children in the Home. As you see in your annual reports, there are still many needs that have arisen from our expansion. We will be presenting plans this evening for our new dining commons and kitchen. We also have many successes to share with you. And a special surprise."

A treasurer's report followed, and then an architect's presentation, all of it just short of being overlong. The director reclaimed the podium.

"Next is our surprise! Usually at this point in the evening we have a video presentation and we invite several of our older students to tell you how much they appreciate the support we receive from our donors. Tonight we have something different.

"This past year we have increased the faculty of our school by several instructors, especially in our arts and music department. The results have been extraordinary! And now for you, our donors and supporters, we will unveil our most closely held secret. For their inaugural concert, please allow me to introduce the FitzRobert Singers."

A door opened in a far corner of the ballroom. A small head appeared. It was nearly hidden between the tables, but its progress toward the front was obvious from the audience craning to see. It was followed by more small heads, and then heads with shoulders, and then tall, straight young men and women; they were all in white and black, shirts and blouses, pants and skirts, and they came and came, a dozen and another dozen and another, and then another.

When the final teen had taken her place, the whole array of them was spread across the front stage, forty-eight strong, each as dignified as his or her stature allowed.

An austere young woman, not apparently much older than her oldest students, severely in black including her long, very straight hair, stepped to the podium and turned it to face the faces.

She quietly hummed a pitch, but the whole room heard it. The silence was absolute and fiercely expectant.

She raised her hand. She waved it in four slow beats, and then the downbeat.

"Amazing grace . . ."

A single child's voice split the stratosphere, as thin and wafting as air but as piercing as a sword.

"how sweet the sound . . ."

The others joined him in harmony from the octaves below, their voices clean-scrubbed and as pure delight to hear as they were to see. Verse after verse the music poured, flawless to the last and to the music director's obvious relief.

The applause was thunderous.

Mrs. Elizabeth Roper, Director of the FitzRobert Home and Foundation, wasted not a moment afterwards.

"As you all know," she said, "our Foundation relies entirely on our donors. It costs one thousand dollars per month for each child, to provide food, clothing, a bed, and a quality education. We have always provided our services at no cost to our children, who of course, as orphans, do not have families to provide for them. Inside your annual reports, in the back cover, you will find an envelope for your donation this evening. After you've put your donation in and filled out the information on the front, the children will be coming to your tables to collect them."

As the words went on, Charles took a check from his wallet, already made out, and put it in the envelope. On the front of the envelope he filled in his name and checked the box for ONE TIME GIFT and wrote in the amount of the check, $12,000. Then he added, *William Beale Memorial Annual Scholarship.*

"What are you thinking?" he asked as they drove the dark streets back home.

"I know how those children felt," she said. "I was one of them there tonight."

"Do you remember the banquets they had when you lived there?"

"I think they had just a few donors, and they were very rich. They gave them tours. We would be so dressed up! They'd come walking through and we had to be just perfect. I didn't understand what it meant, just that they were so important and we should be so very grateful. It was frightening. I was sure I would do something wrong and these people would have me thrown out, or the whole Home would be shut down and it would be my fault."

"That was when you were very little."

"It was not my most positive memory," Dorothy said. "I don't remember as much about the donors and the fundraising from the later years."

"The children looked very nice this evening. I expect they aren't always so well behaved."

"Not unless they are much better than children were in my day. You would know that just from driving the bus."

"There were some very challenging episodes," he chuckled. "But I was still very glad for the job. I don't think an eighteen-year-old today would be trusted with a busload of children."

"They have adult drivers and chaperones now."

"Do they wear uniforms?"

"Not anymore. You were so handsome in yours, dear. And of course, you still are."

"Why are some men so much less governable than others, Charles?"

"We all are, Derek, to some degree."

"The degree varies so widely. It seems to be a critical property of any individual. I've been reading that it might be due to structure of the brain."

"When in doubt, blame it on chemistry."

"But, Charles, if some part of the brain that controls judgment and empathy isn't developed, then wouldn't that person be more apt toward crime?"

"But then all behavior is only neurons and synapses. Personality becomes just an equation of brain cells. I don't want to believe that."

"It's a natural progression from Newton. The physical world is just an expression of mathematic laws, and we are complex biological objects."

"Now you're blaming heredity, Derek. I think we're more than objects."

"Show me anything else."

"I think I am, just by having this conversation."

"Touché, Charles! All right, I admit, it is a stretch to explain human reason by chemistry."

"Human reason might be more reasonable if it could be explained that way."

"But I don't think we should leave heredity off the hook completely. We've touched on this before."

"Yes, with William."

"I'd value your opinions, Charles. You've paid dearly for them."

"Yes, they're dearly bought, Derek. But I don't know if that makes them valuable to anyone else."

"You said he was seventeen?"

"He was always troubled. We thought we could bring him through it, but in his last two years it became so much worse."

"Did you have any real warning, though? At the end?"

"No. Looking back, there were probably things we should have seen. But there was no real warning."

"Where did it all come from, Charles?"

"I wish I knew. It would help us so much, even now, to know why. Was it his upbringing or was it something he inherited? There is so much family history we don't know. Obviously it tortures Dorothy, especially. But we just don't know."

SUNDAY

MORNING

The pillars were a century old, and the stone was ages old, and the light ageless, and what they all held was eternal. Dorothy took a place and Charles beside her, an hour before the service, in the quiet. It was a different silence than of books, the silence of light and stone; not the silence of words but of Word.

The hour and the silence passed. There was music; they sang; words were song. Words were spoken; Word was spoken, and they listened.

" '*I am the Light of the world.*' Why do we need light? To see, to '*not walk in darkness but have the Light.*' Not in the world's light, but in the '*Light of the world.*' "

They listened.

" '*You judge according to the flesh; I am not judging anyone. But if I do judge, My judgment is true.*' "

They listened.

" '*His disciples asked, Who sinned, this man or his parents, that he was born blind?*' His judgment was true. '*It was neither that this man sinned, nor his parents; but it was so that the works of God might be displayed in him.*' "

They walked home in the world's sunlight, outside, where it was everywhere. "How should I judge?" Charles said. "Was it Karen Liu who sinned, or her parents?"

"But she isn't blind."

"I'm the one who's blind."

"No you aren't," Dorothy said.

"I'm walking in darkness, not in light. I can't see."

"Maybe it was neither she that sinned, nor her parents."

Charles stopped. "What could that mean?"

AFTERNOON

They sat at their own dining room table, just the two of them. An elegant platter of roast, potatoes and carrots was before them. Their china and silver and crystal shone. Charles served them both, still in his suit. The sun through the lace curtained window was a pillar. It was true perpendicular and the world was slanted against it.

"How could a person blame their sin on their parents?" Dorothy said.

"People will blame anyone. Just not themselves."

"What if I never knew them?"

"Would that make it easier to blame them?" Charles said.

"It doesn't," Dorothy said. "Not for me."

"And what about being a parent? How much blame can we take on ourselves for our child?"

"I take it all, Charles."

"You can't."

"I do anyway."

"Some of it is mine."

"We share it, then," Dorothy said.

"Besides, I have enough faults of my own."

She matched his sigh. "You're all I have, Charles. With all your faults, I still love you."

Hs smiled. "What did I ever do to deserve you?" he said.

"Whatever you did, I must have done the same thing."

"You deserve me?" Charles laughed. "Then whatever you did, it must have been very bad. I wonder who we can blame."

They finished their meal mostly in silence. Charles cleared the table and Dorothy put an apron over her dress to clean the kitchen. Then still with no words she took off the apron and Charles held out the jacket she'd worn in the morning. He held open the car door for her and then drove a short way to an open, quiet place.

There was another quiet here; not books, not words at all; but here there was also stone.

A slight chill wind attended them. They walked a gravel path around the brow of a low hill and through the shadow of a single old tree, then a few steps over emerald grass bursting with spring life, and stopped at a headstone among others. It said *William Beale and Our Dearly Beloved Son.*

EVENING

"Of all the books, I wonder why that one?" Charles said. He had a fire put up in the fireplace for the last cool evening of spring.

"What, dear?"

"Derek. Of all the books, why he would . . ." Charles couldn't help but smile. "Why did he pick the Locke?"

Dorothy closed the book she was reading. "I know that you and the employees do that, but I do not allow puns in this house."

"It was unavoidable."

"I don't think so."

"Anyway." He cleared his throat. "Why did he select the John Locke? He had hundreds of books just in his office. He didn't have to mangle an antique."

"Which antique books did he own?"

"Well let me see. I could look at the computer at the store. But I think I can remember from opening them last Monday."

"There were thirteen?"

"Yes. Write them down to make sure I remember them all. The first one was Adam Smith, *Wealth of Nations*. Then Gibbon, *Decline and Fall of the Roman Empire*. Thomas Paine, *Common Sense*, the *Rights of Man* and *Age of Reason*."

"One volume?"

"Yes, all in one volume. John Adams, *A Defence of the Constitutions of Government of the United States*. And then there was John Locke, of course, *An Essay Concerning Human Understanding*. That was the fifth one I opened."

"Then I was with you after that."

"And I was paying even closer attention. The next one was Thomas Hobbes, *Leviathan*. Then Montesquieu, *The Spirit of Laws*. Edmund Burke, *Reflections on the Revolution in France*. Voltaire's *Philosophical Dictionary*. Hume's *A Treatise of Human Nature*. Rousseau's *The Social Contract*, and de Tocqueville's *Democracy in America*. And *The Federalist Papers*."

"That was the last one?"

"Yes. How many was that?"

"Thirteen."

"Wait. That can't be all. That was thirteen?"

"That was thirteen. Is something missing?"

"Yes! It's obvious."

"What?"

"Immanuel Kant, *Critique of Pure Reason*. The de Tocqueville is an extra—we were starting on the nineteenth century—but the rest are all the standards of the Enlightenment. It wouldn't be complete without the Kant. Morgan thought it was fourteen, and Lucy Bastien said fourteen, too, but I knew I'd only bought thirteen at the auction. I didn't think that one would have been missing."

"Did you sell him a Kant?" Dorothy asked.

"Oh yes, I remember it now, and even the conversation we had about it. I'm embarrassed that I didn't notice it wasn't with the others. I would have realized it right at the time as I was opening the books, but I wasn't thinking straight."

"Why wouldn't it have been with the others?"

"I don't know. It should have been. I wonder where it is."

"Just more questions."

"More questions," he said. "And I told Mr. Kelly that no books were stolen." He fished through his wallet and pulled out a business card. "I suppose I should call him."

"On Sunday?"

"Just to leave a message." He pushed the buttons on the telephone.

"Frank Kelly of the FBI. Please leave a message."

"Mr. Kelly, this is Charles Beale of Alexandria Rare Books. You came by my shop Thursday morning. I said at the time that I had all of Derek Bastien's antique books, but I've realized I don't, that one is missing. I don't know if that's important but I wanted to correct the statement I made to you."

"*Immanuel Kant's* Critique of Pure Reason. *One German. He seems rather alone among the French and British, Charles.*"

"*You could give him Goethe as company.*"

"*I don't like Faust. For a government employee, it cuts too close to home.*"

"*Have you been making any deals lately, then, Derek?*"

"*Always, but not for my soul. It's usually just removing paragraph C from section Two in return for three more votes in the committee.*"

"*I suppose it depends on what paragraph C says.*"

"*Nothing, Charles. It was only put there in the first place so we could make a deal later on.*"

"*That Reason doesn't seem very Pure, Derek.*"

"*Kant would not approve? Germans are too logical for such nonsense, or at least they think they are. They always take their philosophy one step too far.*"

"*The Germans dive deeper—and come up muddier. I believe it was Henry Steeds who said that.*"

"*Quite. I prefer the mud of practical deal-making to the mud of philosophy, Charles.*"

"*Is that what you do, mainly, Derek? Make deals?*"

"*Mainly. Twist arms, give a little and take a little.*"

"*Do you usually get what you want?*"

"*Most of the time, Charles, most of the time.*"

"*But what do they want in return?*"

"*They give me their souls, and I give them unending life.*"

"*You're joking, of course, Derek.*"

"*Yes, of course, Charles. I'm joking.*"

MONDAY

MORNING

"Mr. Kelly!"

He was standing on the sidewalk outside the shop.

"Oh, good morning," he said, and stepped out of the way as Charles put his key in the doorknob. "I wasn't sure when you'd open."

"Not for a little while," Charles said. "But please come in."

"Thanks. Hope you don't mind."

"Not at all."

Charles crossed the showroom to the counter, turned on the lights and turned off the alarm. "You must have gotten my message."

"Yeah, last night. I would have just called you back, but I decided to drop in." He gave the room a swinging stare. "I love this place."

"Of course. Drop in anytime."

"I might. So, you said one of your books was missing?"

"Not exactly. One of the books I sold Derek Bastien is missing."

"From here?"

"No. It wasn't in the set I bought at the auction."

"Oh. I get it." He slid his little notebook from its little pocket. "And it should have been?"

"Well, I suppose so. Unless Mrs. Bastien kept it. It wasn't auctioned."

"So . . ." Mr. Kelly gave due consideration. "So maybe it was stolen the night he was killed?"

"I wouldn't know that at all, of course, but it might have been," Charles said. "Or Derek might have sold it himself sometime earlier. But I doubt that."

"What book was it?"

"*Critique of Pure Reason* by Kant. An 1830 edition and in reasonable shape."

"What's the market value?"

"Nine hundred."

"Okay. Unaccounted for. I'll check the inventory and see if it should have been there."

"That is the inventory that Derek kept?"

"Right. Real useful. That's the only way we knew about any of the other stuff that was stolen. The police looked at what he had on his inventory list, and they looked at what was left in the house, and whatever was missing got put on the list of stolen goods."

Charles nodded. "Actually, Lucy Bastien said she thought there were fourteen books on that list, and I only bought thirteen at the auction."

"There was a lot of stuff on that list. So, is that all you have to tell me?"

"That's all."

"Okay. Yeah, could be it was taken. That's how it was—just stuff. Whatever fit in the bag, I guess."

The door opened and Alice was with them, sliding off her jacket and beaming sweetness. "Good morning, Mr. Beale!"

"Good Monday morning," he said. "This is Mr. Kelly."

"I remember from last week!"

For a few moments, Alice was busy with morning chores. Frank Kelly gravitated to the mystery shelf, and Charles watched.

"Mr. Kelly?"

"Yeah?"

Charles took a slow breath. "Could you come up to the office for just a moment?"

Mr. Kelly caught the tone in Charles's voice. "Yeah, sure."

They climbed the stairs and Charles settled Mr. Kelly into the chair he'd had before.

Then he sat at his own desk.

Then he chewed his lip and Mr. Kelly waited.

"What do you know about the night Derek was killed?"

"What do I know?" The broad shoulders shrugged and the heavy brow crinkled. "Just what's in D.C. Homicide's report."

"I wondered. The newspaper said he was hit on the head."

"I think so. Burglary gone bad." Mr. Kelly waited.

"It really was a burglary?" Charles said.

"What do you mean?"

"I just wondered. It seems so random."

Mr. Kelly's shoulders rose and dropped again, but his eyes didn't move. "Hey, it happens. You think it wasn't?"

"Oh, not specifically. I don't really know anything. It just doesn't seem appropriate for someone like Derek Bastien."

"Tell you what," Mr. Kelly said, his stare still unmoving on Charles. "You want to look at the report?"

"Look at it?"

"Sure. You can't officially. But I could get you a look, if you wanted."

"Well . . . I don't know . . ."

Mr. Kelly leaned back, suddenly more relaxed. "Let me take you. It's no problem."

"I'm sure you're too busy."

"It's part of my job. Look, you were in his house enough. You knew him. Maybe you might see something in the report. I'm not just doing it to be nice; I think it's worth an hour because you might help me out."

"Well. All right," Charles said. "I would appreciate it."

"I would, too. Uh . . ." he was looking through his notebook. "Tomorrow morning. That work for you?"

"I'm sure it would."

"Hey, boss."

Even Frank Kelly was startled by the silent appearance.

"Yes, Angelo?"

"You want me to go to somebody on your list this morning?"

"Yes. I'll talk to you just as soon as I'm finished here."

Angelo nodded and silently disappeared.

"He works for you?" Mr. Kelly asked.

"Yes. It's a long story. He's my courier and night watchman."

"Courier, huh?"

"It's not really a necessity. When someone local buys one of the rare books, I send Angelo out to deliver it."

"Really?" Mr. Kelly was still staring at the empty door. "He ever go to Bastien's house?"

"I did take him once. Back when I was first training him."

"So he was at the house?"

"Yes, he was."

"Actually inside?"

"Yes. I took him in for just a while. Does that mean anything?"

"Huh? Oh, no." Mr. Kelly seemed distracted, but then he shook it off. "Anyway. So, tomorrow, ten o'clock? D.C. Police headquarters, front lobby."

"Tomorrow morning."

Charles climbed to the third floor and knocked on the closed door. Angelo opened it. His expression was a closed door.

"Let's pick which agent you should visit this morning," Charles said. He held up the list. "These two are close together."

"You want me to go to those two?"

"Yes. Do those. You'll have to take the Metro all the way to Maryland. Can you get there?"

"I can get there. Hey, boss."

"Yes?"

"That man," Angelo said. "He came out the door."

"Mr. Kelly? Where?"

"The auction door. He saw me waiting."

"He was at the auction," Charles said. "He's trying to find who stole things from Derek Bastien's house."

"He's police?"

"FBI. It's like police."

"They are all the same," Angelo said. "What things were stolen?"

"Antiques. Little statues and things."

"Oh. I remember. I see little things like that in people's houses. Who wants those?"

"The people that have them."

Apparently Angelo was feeling talkative. "To sell a thing like that, that's not easy."

"Exactly. It is Mr. Kelly's special job to find them. Angelo, if you had stolen things like that, would you know how to sell them?"

"Who says I was stealing those things?"

"No one. I just wondered."

"I don't steal those things."

"I know. Would you know how to sell them if you did?"

"I don't know anything."

"All right. I'm sorry. Never mind. I'll be in the basement for the morning if you need me before you leave."

AFTERNOON

Only the desk lamp was on. The computer was off. As still as the books, Charles leaned over the desk and just his eyes moved, and every few minutes his gloved hand as it turned a page with a silver spatula.

"There you are," Dorothy said. "You've been down here for hours."

"Time is much slower down here," he said. "It's like a horse pulling a cart. The books are so heavy they hold it back."

"What are you reading?"

"Chekhov. And I think he must have been reading me."

"There is someone here to see you."

"Then the further study of human nature will have to wait."

"Not necessarily," Dorothy said. "It's Patrick White."

"Then let's go up to say hello."

"Mr. White."

"Hello."

There was nothing eerie about him in the noon sunlight. The fever brightness in the eyes was veiled and the voice calm.

"I'm so glad to see you again," Charles said.

"You suggested lunch," Mr. White said.

"Lunch? Oh, yes. Of course. I'd be glad to."

"Let's go."

"Well—of course—I'll be right with you. Just a moment." He turned to Dorothy. "I'll be out for lunch."

"And perhaps we would do coffee afterwards?"

"Surely," he said.

Charles moved to the door, but Mr. White was suddenly not in a hurry.

"Did you have any place in mind?" Charles asked. The man did not budge.

"No."

Charles waited. "Is there anything you'd like to look at first?"

"No." Whatever he was looking at, it was not in the room. But then he snapped into the moment. "You pick someplace."

"Just down the street," Charles said, and Patrick White passed through the door with him.

Ten minutes later Mr. White spoke again, his first words since they had left the bookshop.

"Ham sandwich and coffee."

"Yes, sir," the waitress answered, and departed.

"What did you really know about Derek Bastien?" Patrick White said to Charles, and the conversation lurched to life.

"Well," Charles said. "I knew what his job was and I knew what his home was like and I knew what he liked to talk about."

"What do you know about blackmail?"

"Blackmail? Not very much, Mr. White! And I don't want to know more."

"It doesn't matter what you want." The tone did not match the words. Mr. White was apparently talking to himself. "It happens whether you want it to or not."

"What does that have to do with Derek?" Charles asked.

"You met John Borchard?"

"Well, yes, I did," Charles said, re-orienting. "Mr. White, I feel like this conversation is rather one-sided."

"I want to know where you are in this."

"I don't know where I am, and I don't know what *this* is. Perhaps you could enlighten me?"

Mr. White was again not with him. Several minutes came and went; the food came and Charles's went. The ham sandwich was not touched. Charles waited patiently.

Several tables cleared as the lunch crowd thinned. Charles watched passersby through the window. He shook off the waitress when she offered dessert. A group of motorcycles roared by on the street.

"Borchard killed Derek Bastien," Patrick White said.

"John Borchard?" It was fortunate that Charles was finished eating.

"It was blackmail."

"I don't understand at all."

"Borchard killed Derek over his blackmail."

"Blackmailing whom?"

"Me. Why don't you understand? He threatened me. And when I didn't do what he wanted, he told the *Post*, just like he said he would."

"He told them about you—about the law school?"

"He told them where to find the transcript of the honor court that found me guilty."

Charles had to take a breath. "Were you guilty?"

"Does it matter?"

"Well, wouldn't it?"

"It didn't. Okay, yes, I cheated. So I failed the class and I was on probation and I started over. And it *was* over. But what does a newspaper care? They came after me like I was a war criminal. There was no way to fight back."

"I see."

"But I did fight back. Even if I was ruined, I could still get my revenge. But then John Borchard killed Derek."

"Because he was blackmailing you?" Charles said.

"So now you understand."

Charles nodded, relieved. "I think I do. But why would John Borchard kill Derek for blackmailing you?"

Patrick White had frozen again, but this time his focus was straight on Charles and the thaw was quick.

"What do you mean?"

Charles said it again. "If Derek was blackmailing you, why would John Borchard kill him?"

A fierce light flashed in Mr. White's eyes. They were deep-set and dark-rimmed in his haggard face.

"It was John Borchard who blackmailed me! John Borchard sent the papers to the *Washington Post*."

Now it was Charles who had frozen. "John Borchard was the blackmailer?"

"Yes. Yes! Why don't you understand?"

"I . . . I'm sorry . . . I just got mixed up who you were talking about."

"Why do you think Derek Bastien was a blackmailer?"

"No, that's not what I meant. I was just confused. Please. Keep going. John Borchard had papers about you from your law school, and he threatened that he would expose you. And then he did. How was Derek involved?"

"I went to Derek for help. First, I went to get his help to stop Borchard. Then after Borchard told the newspaper, I went to Derek for help to get revenge. But Borchard found out and he killed Derek for talking to me."

"Why was he blackmailing you?"

But Charles had to wait. Mr. White's mental trips away from the physical world were becoming more frequent.

"Do you believe me?" was the answer when it came.

"I don't know. How sure are you of all of this?"

"Oh, I'm sure. I'm absolutely sure."

"John Borchard told you himself that he had this information and that he was going to use it?"

"He didn't tell me himself. But he made it obvious it was him. We both knew."

"All right, then. Did Derek know anything about it?"

"Not until I told him."

"And how do you know John Borchard killed him?"

"Who else would have? That's obvious, too."

Charles tried another direction. "Have you told all this to the police?"

"Of course I have."

"And they haven't done anything about it?"

"No. Nothing! Borchard's got them in his pocket."

"I see. So why are you telling me?"

This required another short trip away.

"Karen Liu said you knew Derek, and you were talking to people he knew. I thought maybe you knew something."

"I didn't know any of this that you've told me."

"Watch out for Borchard. That's the first thing," Mr. White said, oblivious to Charles's answer. "He's dangerous. But he might trust you. So see what you can find out. Maybe he'll let something slip."

"Really, Mr. White. I don't—"

"Derek Bastien was murdered. Somebody has to do something." And then, suddenly the conversation ended. Patrick White stood and dropped two twenty-dollar bills on the table. "Be careful," he said.

He left. Charles was left behind.

"Mr. Beale," Alice said. "You'll never guess what we sold while you were gone."

Charles closed the front door behind him, a cloud of bewilderment still swirling around his head. "I'm afraid to ask."

"*Moby-Dick*."

He stopped in his tracks and the cloud vanished. "The first edition? From downstairs?"

"Yes, sir."

"Who bought it?"

"One of our regular customers. Morgan has the order upstairs."

Charles climbed up to the office. "Did Alice tell you?" Dorothy said.

"Yes! Who bought it?"

"The same man who bought *The Scarlet Letter* two years ago."

"Oh—Abercrombie. In Arlington."

"That's it."

"Does he want it delivered?"

"Yes. He paid by credit card."

"Did we give him the regular discount?"

"Ten percent off twenty-seven thousand."

"Moby-Dick." Charles sank into his chair. "Oh my. He's been here so long. Are you sure?"

"Yes, dear." Dorothy smiled. "You look thoroughly befuddled."

"I'll go down to the basement and say goodbye." The jubilant mood sank slowly beneath the waves. "Dorothy, I've just had lunch with Captain Ahab."

"Patrick White?"

"I think he must be unbalanced. I hope he is."

"You hope he is unbalanced?"

"Otherwise what he said would be true."

"What did he say?" Dorothy caught his mood and began sinking with him.

"John Borchard is Moby-Dick."

"John Borchard is what?"

"There is a superficial resemblance," Charles said. "Dorothy, Patrick White is on a quest for revenge and Mr. Borchard is his target."

"Revenge? For what?"

"In this case, Captain Ahab has lost his judicial career rather than his leg."

"But . . ." Dorothy frowned. "But didn't . . ." She frowned more. "Charles, you have to tell me what you're talking about."

"All right. I can do it. I'm just still regaining my own balance. Mr. White believes that it was John Borchard who exposed his law school scandal to the newspaper."

"Why would he do that?"

"Mr. White did not elaborate. But beyond that, he says he went to Derek Bastien for help against John Borchard."

"Did Derek ever tell you anything about him?"

"No. I'm sure he never mentioned Patrick Henry White to me. But, Dorothy, this is the culmination. Patrick White says that John Borchard killed Derek Bastien."

She was momentarily speechless. "He said that?"

"Word for word. You look just like I must have."

"Killed him!"

"Yes."

She got her mouth closed, then opened it again. "Did he?"

"At this point, dear, I'm inclined to doubt it."

"I should hope so!"

"I would desperately hope he did not."

She had recovered. "And who are you that Mr. White would tell you all of this?"

"Me? Call me Ishmael."

"Hey, boss."

Charles rubbed his forehead. "Someday, Angelo, I will have a heart attack."

"You not feeling good, boss?"

"I'm fine. How did it go?"

161

"It was okay, that lady I didn't see her in those places. You want I should look at the next place tomorrow?"

"You have a delivery in the morning," Charles said. "A very important one. I'd do it myself, but I have another appointment. We can see if any of the places on the list are in the same area as your delivery."

"Mr. Beale?" Alice's voice from the stairs was panicked.

"Yes? I'm coming," he said, and Angelo followed.

"There's a man down here."

"Now who?" Charles stood and moved quickly. He reached the showroom.

"Beale."

"Mr. Jones," he said, as that was who it was.

"Talk."

The look in Galen Jones's eye was of an altogether different ferocity than Patrick White's.

Charles slid past the tall and centrally located Mr. Jones, and opened the front door. "We could step outside."

He pushed through the door and stopped on the front sidewalk. "You said you talked to the FBI?"

"I've talked to Mr. Kelly," Charles said. "I think I told you."

"What did you tell them about me?"

"About you? Nothing. I hadn't even met you."

"Nothing?"

"I never said your name or anything about you."

Mr. Jones searched the sidewalk for listeners. "So have you talked to anybody about me?"

"No. Well—Norman Highberg, and that was also before I'd met you. And my wife. What's wrong?"

"Kelly, the FBI, he came by my house this morning. He asked me about the desk. Just like you. Except he also wanted to know if anyone else was asking."

"I didn't say anything."

"Then how—? Never mind." Galen Jones was very frustrated. "Look, don't ever say my name to anyone. Ever."

"That's a hard thing to promise. I will try not to say your name to anyone."

"Then if you do, tell me."

"I will. I think I can promise that. Did you tell Mr. Kelly I'd been asking about the desk?"

"No way. I don't answer questions like that."

"I think it would have been all right. He and I have discussed the desk."

"My name, and that desk, those don't go together for anybody, okay? And I want to know how he ever got them together."

"Maybe from Norman. Norman told me that he'd recommended you to Derek. That's how I found you."

Mr. Jones paused. "Maybe. Yeah, that's it. But you're up to something, Beale, and you better be real careful."

"I'm just trying to do the right thing."

"As if anyone ever knew what that was."

And that was all. Charles watched as Galen Jones's long legs carried him swiftly away.

"Who was that?" Dorothy asked.

"Galen Jones. The matchmaker. Don't tell anyone about him. I just promised we wouldn't." He dropped into his chair. "Mr. Kelly from the FBI was asking him about the desk."

"So he does have some connection with it?"

"He didn't say that. It's more a question of why Mr. Kelly thinks he does." He rubbed his eyes. "Dorothy, I am now officially very worried about what is going on."

"Only now?"

"Only now officially and very. Who wanted so much to buy it? Two people were willing to pay a hundred thousand dollars for it." And then he took a deep, slow breath. "And no one special tried to buy the books."

"Who else would want the books?"

"John Borchard and Karen Liu, if they'd known what was in them."

"Maybe someone thought the papers were in the desk," Dorothy said.

"Exactly, dear. Why didn't we think of that before? That would mean that two people knew about the papers, and thought they were in the desk. But why would anyone try to buy the desk at this point? The drawers would all have been emptied."

"What would have happened to everything in the desk?" Dorothy asked.

"I think I'll call Lucy Bastien. Cloverdale. Whatever her name is."

Dorothy watched. "What are you doing?"

"Breathing."

"Why?"

"You don't know?"

"Charles! I mean why are you just sitting there."

"I just want to be calm." He took one more breath. "All right. I'm calm." He picked up the telephone.

"Mrs. Bastien. This is Charles Beale."

"Mr. Beale. The used-book salesman."

"That's right."

"Is that like a used-car salesman?"

"Pretty much the same thing."

"It's Cloverdale."

"Of course, I'm terribly sorry. Mrs. Cloverdale."

"That's better. What can I do for you?"

"I just wanted to ask you about Derek's desk."

"His desk? His desk?! What is it about this desk?"

"Oh? Have other people been asking?"

"Too many."

"I just have a simple question."

"Sorry. I have exceeded the allotted number of answers on that subject. Try something else."

"All right—another subject—what about the papers that were in the desk? That's a different subject."

"Barely, Charles. Just barely."

"Where are those papers? I doubt they were still in the desk when it was sold."

"How should I know? I didn't check any drawers. I think the place called and asked if I wanted them and I said to send them to his boss at work."

"John Borchard?"

"That's the one. Since he wanted them, anyway."

"Oh—he had asked for them?"

"He asked. It got real annoying, sort of like you. So I finally just told them to send him everything they found. Papers, paper clips, paper plates. Just send it all."

"I suppose we should be careful what we ask for."

"I never heard from him again so I guess it worked."

"Thank you, Lucy."

"Glad to help, Charles. Charles?"

"Yes?"

"I like it when I never hear from people again."

"You do?"

"Don't call back."

"Mr. John Borchard called while you were on the phone," Alice said at the door. "He said to tell you he really is planning to come by some time."

"I like it when I hear from people again," Charles said.

EVENING

They chose an aloof table far from the windows and outside light.

The confusion of smells assailed them: sweet caramel, bitter coffee, lemon, chocolate, salty meats, vegetables, thick cheeses, wood, hot sun-heated air and cold shadow, and people.

"There's too much," Charles said. "I don't know how to sort it out."

"Should you do something?" Dorothy asked.

"Dorothy, I don't know what to do."

"You don't know of *any*thing to do, or you don't know *which* thing to do?"

"Which."

"That's what I thought."

"Or any." They were silent, and their thoughts twined with the smells and sounds.

"But you have to do something," Dorothy said.

"Yes. Now that I'm worried, officially. No more just following the wind, anyway. Tomorrow morning Frank Kelly will show me the report on Derek's death."

"We keep hearing that it was just a burglary."

"The fifth in a series. Five different houses. It has to have been just an accidental tragedy. But it just couldn't have been."

"Do you think you'll see something that everyone else has missed?"

"No. But it seemed like an opportunity not to miss."

"I know it's all confusing, Charles, but I think that in the end, you're just going to have to give the papers to the police. There really isn't any other way."

"I keep hoping there is some other way. That's what I'm looking for." His fingers were drumming on the table, and he stopped them. Then he counted them off. "Six people. Karen Liu, John Borchard, Patrick White, and three more we don't even know. I open the book, and there I have their terrible secrets. Their sins. Their sins that can pull them down and destroy them." He looked at his open hands. "Am I being overly dramatic?"

"Not by too much. You could take it all to the police."

"That is a decision itself."

"But otherwise it's your decision, Charles, and I don't think it should be. Patrick White's secret is already exposed. We don't really know what it would mean to Karen Liu and John Borchard. We don't know if the other three are even secrets, or what they are."

"I think we can guess by the company they were keeping."

"And don't we have a responsibility to tell the police? They might be real crimes."

"And people should get what they deserve," Charles said. "The wages of sin is death."

"But the gift of Charles Beale is everlasting life?"

"I don't enjoy being in this position."

"I know that. And I understand why you don't feel free to give it up, either."

"The problem, Dorothy, is that you're right. I feel like I have godlike responsibility here, to deliver judgment that is true. It's just that I don't have wisdom, authority, omniscience or anything else. I'm not God."

"What happens if you don't do anything?"

"There will be some point where a decision is unavoidable. I just hope I can be ready when that comes."

"Maybe God will have delivered his own judgment by then."

Again they were silent, letting the coffee shop distract them.

"Did you enjoy your conversations with Derek?" Dorothy asked.

"Yes. They weren't always comfortable. He liked to provoke me, and I would push back at him. But they were very thoughtful and stimulating."

"Would I have liked him?"

"Only if he'd wanted you to."

"Where does evil come from, Charles?"

"Derek! How in the world do you expect an answer to that?"

"What is evil, then?"

"Well, what is good?"

"What we accept it to be, Charles. And evil, also."

"It's all subjective, then?"

"More or less. We're selfish over our possessions, so we call stealing 'evil.' You said, 'How in the world?' That's all we have, just 'in the world.' What is there outside of ourselves that we can measure against?"

"No, Derek. I think there is an external standard."

"Created by whom?"

"Let's say, God."

"Then why isn't this standard universally accepted? We both know it isn't, and it certainly isn't well enforced."

"If it were, Derek, I suppose there wouldn't be room for evil."

"Are we being circular, Charles?"

"Let's say there is an objective moral standard, but that there is also free will to disregard it. Would that give us a definition of evil?"

"That sounds like evil is built in."

"Or, Derek, what if the point of evil was to be an alternative to good?"

"What in the world do you mean, Charles? Why should there be any alternative to good?"

"So there could be something to forgive."

TUESDAY

MORNING

In a turbulent river of air, Charles struggled upstream. Trees held sturdily to their soil and tightly to their leaves; but with so many leaves, the trees couldn't mind every one, and a few were overlooked and carried away.

He caught the knob and steadied himself and then pulled.

One step over the threshold and everything changed. This air couldn't be the same substance as the muscular atmosphere outside. One swirl had come in with him, but the still wrestled it to the ground and pinned it.

"Have we sold anything today, Alice?" Charles asked. Strange how the abundance of air outside had taken his breath away.

"A *Wind in the Willows*."

"I should have known." And up the stairs.

"Good morning, Mr. Beale," Morgan said as he blew into the office.

"Good morning. Contrary winds out there. It took me a while to get through them."

"Yes, sir. But less than ten years."

"Ten years to get through the winds? They weren't that strong."

"Did you meet any monsters on the way?"

"Not many," Charles said. "Give me another clue what we're talking about."

"Did you pass any police hurrying by?"

"Police hurrying. With their sirens, you mean?"

"Yes, sir."

"We got it? The *Odyssey*?"

"Yes, sir."

"Good! Good for you, Morgan. Very good! . . . Well, maybe. How much was it?"

"Seventeen hundred forty."

"So if I'd stayed at fifteen, we would have missed it. I can't wait to see it."

"Do you think it was really worth that much?"

"Maybe not. But I always hope! When will we get it?"

"I paid right away, and I asked the seller to send it overnight. We should have it tomorrow."

"Very good, Morgan! So that will take away a little of the sting of losing the Melville. I'll go down and pack up *Moby-Dick*."

"Use a big box," Morgan said.

"Hey, boss."

"Oh. Good morning, Angelo." Charles looked at his watch. "Are you ready to go?"

"I'm ready to take the book."

"I'm sorry, I lost track of time. Let me wrap it."

"What are you doing with that book, boss?"

"I was reading it."

"What do you read all these books for?"

"I like to, Angelo."

"For what in the dark?"

"Oh, I don't know. It is less distracting. Or maybe I should say that it makes the book the only thing there is."

"What do you read in these books?"

"Everything. Everything there is. And there is always something new."

"In these books that are old?"

"Yes, especially. It is like being hungry and these are food. I am hungry to read these. And it is also like they are friends and I want to be with them and talk to them."

"That is what the people say about the drugs."

"It is a little like that. But these aren't bad for you. And they're legal."

"I will read one sometime."

"Yes, Angelo, please do. All right, here it is, all wrapped up. Do you have the receipt for them to sign?"

"I have that."

"Angelo, be very nice to this man. This is a very special, very expensive book. I would go with you but I have another appointment. Try to make the man feel like it is a special book."

"How do I make a man feel a way?"

"Treat the book very carefully. Hand it to him like you are handing him diamonds from that jewelry store. Act very grateful that he is buying it and say thank-you like you mean it. Look him right in the eye, but not to make him afraid. Make him feel that you are proud of him. *Be* proud and grateful that he is buying it. Do you feel like this book is precious?"

"It is lots of money."

"Because it is worth it. It really is."

"Okay, boss, but the man will feel the way he wants."

"Do the best you can."

The wind was just as wild across the Potomac, and clouds had joined it. Charles paddled undaunted through the canyon streets and the white-water breezes.

He docked at the District of Columbia Police station's grim landing and came ashore into its joyless lobby. But one smile greeted him.

"Hi! Mr. Beale! Morning. How are you doing?"

"Very well. Thank you, Mr. Kelly."

"I already told them we were coming. I won't even have to sneak you in."

In plain sight, the two passed the gauntlet of desks and halls; Frank Kelly showed his FBI badge twice at strategic moments. It was a very busy building and there were many policepersons.

A criminal would not have felt welcome.

On the third floor they came finally to a large room of desks and file cabinets, and once more the magic badge was shown.

"Most of this stuff is online," Mr. Kelly said. "But I don't have a password. It's easier to just drop in."

A file folder was retrieved and they chose a desk to take it to. Frank Kelly opened it and flipped pages, selecting a few to pull out. Charles sat and waited.

"Okay. Here are the ones you want."

He pushed a dozen papers across the desk.

"I may read them?" Charles said.

"Go ahead. Those you're allowed to see. And I took out the gory stuff."

"Thank you."

He started. It was a mash; everything about a murder scene and the people involved, circling out layer by layer to the outer reaches of Derek's life. There were interviews, narratives, forms, lists and descriptions.

Charles read for twenty minutes. Then he pushed the papers back across the desk.

"That's enough," he said.

"Not real great reading," Mr. Kelly said. "That answer your questions?"

"I suppose. There were five burglaries in the neighborhood in three weeks and they were all the same. Someone broke a window and climbed in, moved through the house very quickly and took small, valuable objects, and was out in just a few minutes."

"Those houses, they had plenty of small valuable objects."

"And the power had been cut."

"Right," Mr. Kelly said. "Which was not easy. It had to be done at the electric meter because all the lines are either underground or inside."

"Do most burglars know how to do that?"

"I don't think so. So that sure sets it off from a regular break-in. It must have been someone good. But most burglars aren't after antiques anyway.

"So usually the security company gets an alarm when the power goes out, but nothing happens at the house." Frank was looking through the pages. "The company calls the owners, and the owner probably just tells them no problem, the power's out. But the guy was gone in five minutes anyway, and it's too late even if the police do get called.

"So. At 2:15 in the morning something cut off the power at the Bastien residence, which set off an alarm back at the surveillance desk. We have that from the alarm company. Derek Bastien had instructed them to not immediately notify the police, which is a normal instruction. They were supposed to call his cell phone for further instructions, and if he didn't answer, then they would call the police.

"According to the alarm company, they did call and he answered. There was some kind of password he gave them to verify who he was. He told them to wait five minutes for him to call back and if he didn't, to send the police. He didn't call back.

"Apparently, he started looking around. He went into the office. The burglar must have heard him coming. By the angles, it looks like he was hiding behind the door when Bastien came in. He hit Bastien on the head with the marble statue, and that killed him. He probably never knew what hit him."

"I hope not," Charles said.

"Yeah, that's the part I never liked." Frank Kelly looked appropriately sad. "There's the victim, knowing he was about to get hit or killed. That must be a rotten feeling."

"It must be."

"At least it wouldn't last very long. Lots of blood on the desk, and lab analysis said it was all his."

"Mr. Kelly, would they have taken the desk to a lab to do that analysis?"

"Taken the desk?" Kelly scratched his head. "I don't think so." He looked through the papers still in the folder. "No. It was a pretty big desk. They just wiped samples of the blood. Crime scene techs would have done it. They didn't take the whole desk."

"Whoever paid so much for it, I'd hate to think it had been banged around and damaged being moved."

"They didn't take it. They only took the statue. 'Early eighteenth century Florentine marble statuette of James the Second of England, fourteen inches, thirty-five pounds.' No fingerprints. He would have been dead already, after he'd been in exile."

"In exile?" Charles was confused. "The burglar or Derek?"

"James. The Second. After he got deposed."

"Oh. Of course."

"Louis the Fifteenth had dozens of those statues made and sent them everywhere. Little presents to all his friends, you know, to stick the needle in George the First whenever he could. Eight thousand dollars market value. Wasn't sold at the auction. I guess they still have it here in evidence storage."

"Anyway," Charles said, "I think it does answer my questions. It really was just a random burglary."

"Looks like it. Fifth house in three weeks. If he'd just stayed in bed, he'd still be alive. Yeah, with somebody like Bastien, I bet D.C. Homicide checked real close to see if there was any way it could have been a real murder, and they didn't find anything."

"Have any of the things that were stolen appeared yet?"

"No. Nothing from any of the five houses."

"You said it was fifty-fifty whether they would?"

"Yeah, that's what I'd say. That many pieces, you can't sell them all individually without someone catching on. 'Someone' being me. But they might put them in a basement for a few years. Being connected with a murder makes all that stuff real hot."

"Of course."

"But now, you tell me. Do you see anything in there that sticks out?"

"Well, of course, the Kant wasn't on the list of things stolen."

"Right. And I looked—it was on the main inventory, the one Bastien kept himself. So somehow it was missed when they were figuring out what was stolen. What else do you see?"

"Not really anything else."

"Do you recognize many of the things on the list of stuff that was stolen?"

"I think so. I think they were all from his office."

"Huh. All of them?"

"I think so."

"Okay, so the guy started in the office and never got anywhere else. Probably doesn't mean anything."

"And Derek was lying across the desk?"

"He must have fallen onto it. There is a picture in here, but you don't want to look at it."

"I don't. The desk was several steps from the door. He would have gone well into the room to reach it."

"Yeah. That's pretty obvious in the pictures. Does that mean anything?"

"Just that he went to it. Had he turned the light on?"

"The light was off. Remember, no power."

"Of course. Well, no, I can't think of anything."

"Right—oh, hey, that's Watts out there. He's the detective. Hey, Harry!"

A very plain black man came at the call. He was a little stout, and a little gray.

"Hi, Frank. This your guy?"

"Charles Beale," Charles said.

"Nice to meet you," Mr. Watts said.

"I showed him some pages," Mr. Kelly said. "Nothing jumped out."

"I appreciate being allowed," Charles said.

"It's okay." Mr. Watts seemed only politely interested. "Here's my card, if you do think of something."

"Antiques, me," Frank Kelly said, "murder, him. I'll walk you back down to the lobby."

"Oh, dear."

"After me, the deluge," Frank Kelly said, watching the torrents of rain from the front door of the police station. "Speaking of Louis the Fifteenth."

"I think I'll wait until it's over."

"I'll give you a ride. I'm in the garage."

"After you," Charles said.

"*Après moi.*"

Charles followed again through more passages but this time going down, and then Mr. Kelly's car had to circle back up through the maze of the garage.

"Do you know anything about antique desks?" Charles asked.

"Bastien's desk? I asked a few people about it. Honaker four-drawer pedestal, 1875."

"What is Honaker?"

"Manufacturer. Honaker and Sons, Philadelphia."

"Could you find out who bought it at the auction?"

"Oh, yeah, sure. They'd probably just tell me if I asked, or else I'd get a warrant. But I don't know if it's hooked up with the art thefts. You've got to be careful." The car came out into brilliant sunlight.

"And now the rain is over," Charles said. "You could just drop me off at a Metro station if you want. You don't have to take me to Alexandria."

"No problem. I got a call to make in Leesburg next. That'll take the rest of the day. Yeah, you've got to be careful asking some people questions. Somebody important might have bought that desk for some reason, and they find out I was asking about it with no good reason, that'll be a mess. I'll go anywhere I need to, but I watch the lines real careful."

"Do you think there is any chance it is connected with the burglaries?"

"I don't see it. How could it?"

"I don't know."

"But, sure, I've thought about it, and I've been poking around a little. But I don't see enough connection yet to do any real investigating."

"Poking around?"

"Right. I read up on it, called a few crooks who might know anything."

"Crooks?"

"Shots in the dark. With crooks, you don't have to worry as much about them blowing a whistle because you're going outside the line."

"I see. Do you know a lot of crooks, Mr. Kelly?"

"That's my job. At least my guys are usually a little higher up the scale than muggers. And that makes me wonder what you're doing with that friend of yours."

"Which friend?"

"Your night watchman."

"Oh. Angelo. That's a long story."

"I know the story. I looked it up."

"You look up a lot, Mr. Kelly. Why would you do that?"

He shrugged. "Just following leads. That's my job."

"What lead would that be?"

"Nothing." Frank Kelly pulled up in front of the bookstore. "Anyway, let me know if you think of anything else."

"I will."

"Thanks."

"And thank you for the ride."

AFTERNOON

"Have we sold anything?" Charles asked, walking through the door.

"A Dostoevsky."

"*Crime and Punishment*?"

"Yes, sir." Alice's smile was stretched at its ends. "And you had a call. Mr. Abercrombie."

"The man who bought *Moby-Dick*?"

"Yes, sir. I think he has a complaint about Angelo."

"Is Angelo here?"

"Up in his room."

"Thank you."

"Alice said Mr. Abercrombie called?"

"He did," Dorothy said. "I talked with him briefly, but he wanted you."

"Was there a problem?"

"He said Angelo was touching things in his house."

"I'll talk to Angelo."

"Angelo?"

"Hey, boss." He was already back in his un-business clothes.

"How did it go?"

"That delivery? It was okay."

"Any problems?"

"Does that man say there was problems?"

"I haven't talked with him," Charles said.

"There was no problems, boss."

Charles looked into Angelo's face for any reaction. There was none.

"Mrs. Beale talked to him—he called here. He told her you were touching things in his house."

Silence.

"What kind of things did he have?"

"I didn't touch anything, boss."

"Did he have things by the door? How far in did you go?"

"I went in the door two steps. I did what you said to be nice."

"Were there things close by?"

Angelo shrugged. "He had those little statue things and glass and metal."

"Antiques. Or we could call them Art Objects."

"Yeah, he had those."

"Did you touch them?"

"I don't touch nothing ever, boss."

"Did he think you touched them?" Charles asked.

"Hey, boss, I don't know what people think."

"You really do know, though, don't you? You could tell he was looking at you and you knew what was going through his mind, because you see it all the time. I'm sorry, Angelo, that Mr. Abercrombie was suspicious of you. If you say you didn't touch anything, then I believe you."

"You think what you want."

"Maybe we could teach you to smile."

Angelo scowled.

"What did he say?" Dorothy asked.

"He said he didn't, and I believe him."

"What about Mr. Abercrombie?"

"I suppose he saw what he thought he would see."

"I hope Angelo isn't scaring everyone."

"At least he didn't actually grab any of Mr. Abercrombie's *objets d'art* and run them down to Mario the Fence in the back of the Italian restaurant. Or he could have just taken *Moby-Dick* to Mario in the first place."

"He wouldn't have."

"No, he wouldn't, since Mario only does jewelry and iPods. He'd have to know someone like Norman Highberg instead. All right, let me find Mr. Abercrombie's telephone number."

"I have it," Dorothy said.

"I'll call him and smooth the ruffled feathers. Oh, Dorothy, I actually got an expression on Angelo's face."

"What?"

"I suggested he learn to smile."

Dorothy brightened. "And did he smile?"

"Not exactly."

And did you have an interesting morning with Mr. Kelly?"

"It might be worth another *croustade de veau braisé*."

EVENING

"Something simple this evening, Philippe," Charles said. "What would you suggest?"

The waiter looked carefully around. "A hamburger, monsieur."

Charles was shocked. "A what?"

"A hamburger," he said even quieter than before. "The chef tried today to make a new dish, um . . ." He struggled to find the word. "It is like meatloaf." He shook his head. "She—" he glanced across the room at the hostess—"she did not like it."

"It wasn't good?" Dorothy asked.

Philippe shrugged. "It was not so good. But the ground beef is very good. In it he has garlic and tomato and basil. I will tell him to make a hamburger for you."

"Well, if that's all right."

"Yes," Philippe said. "Just don't tell . . ." He nodded toward Antoinette.

"She might see it," Dorothy said.

"If madame does not mind." He blew out the candle on their table, leaving their corner even dimmer. "And for you?"

"I wonder if I should order french fries and a Coke."

Philippe considered. "A baked potato? Or . . ." He paused, thinking carefully. "From yesterday, the soup was potato and leek. With mushrooms and shallots, and a touch of sherry. There is a little in the kitchen still. It is not so fresh, but for potatoes? So what if a potato is not fresh?"

"That sounds lovely," Dorothy said.

Philippe withdrew on his dangerous mission into the Parisian dark.

"Here's looking at you, kid," Charles said.

As silverware clinked and some semblance of Edith Piaf played on speakers, he and Dorothy sipped their water and watched the room.

There were diners who were obvious tourists, and others who likely were locals, and some from the suburbs or across the Potomac who had come for the food and atmosphere.

"I'm so glad to live here," Dorothy said.

"It's just right, isn't it?"

"It is. It's fun but not too much."

"Alexandria is nicely American, and just a little French," Charles said.

The illicit hamburger was stealthily delivered. Charles ate it furtively.

"And is there anything to say about Mr. Kelly?" Dorothy asked.

"Not really. I looked through the report about Derek, but I don't want to describe it to you. I also asked about Derek's desk. I don't see yet how anyone could have done anything to it. And I don't know yet why Mr. Kelly thought to ask Mr. Jones about it. Mr. Kelly said he asked around in general, although it sounds like rather a coincidence that he would happen to pick Galen Jones to talk to, or that he would even know of Galen Jones."

"Another coincidence?"

"It makes me wonder if Mr. Kelly has some other source of information. If I could find out who he was talking to, it might answer some questions."

"Could you ask him?"

"I might, but he would want to know why I was asking. So I'll tread carefully for now."

"Quick," Dorothy said. "She's coming."

Antoinette approached like a cavalry charge, and Charles stuffed in the last bite of his hamburger.

"*That finishes the trio. Montesquieu and Voltaire, and now Rousseau. Charles, you can be pithy: How would you compare them?*"

"*Is this a test of my vocabulary, Derek, or are you admitting you haven't read them yourself?*"

"*I never admit anything.*"

"*Because you are like Voltaire. He was the* bon vivant, *the consummate Man of Letters, the biting wit. He admired enlightened monarchs and he despised religion, he hobnobbed with Frederick the Great and Catherine the Great and all the other Greats. He would have sat right here to play chess and discuss—well, himself.*"

"*How am I like Montesquieu?*"

"*Not temperamentally. He wasn't subtle. But I think you share his insight into human nature. The* Spirit of Laws *introduces separation of powers as a form of government, because he knew how too much power in too few hands would lead to tyranny.*"

"*Although he didn't think that was necessarily bad, Charles.*"

"*You admit that you've read him.*"

"*Some of it. The part where he said despotism was preferable in some circumstances.*"

"*More stable. I wouldn't say he thought it preferable.*"

"*All right. And Rousseau?*"

"*You have nothing in common with him, Derek. Nothing at all. He was mystic, tragic and poor.*"

"And I am practical, complacent and rich."

"Your words, Derek, not mine."

"Again, I admit nothing. And yet, Charles, I think Rousseau was the most influential of the three."

"He didn't care about government. He cared about the individual and how we build societies out of individuals. Always based on the individual. Now you have his Social Contract. *That is the one you should read, Derek."*

"It's the one I least want to."

"Because it will upset your own ideology?"

"No, Charles, I have no fear of that. When he first wrote it, it was fashionable in Paris to cry while reading it, and I don't want to stain my desk."

WEDNESDAY

MORNING

A few minutes past ten, and Charles stopped on the walk in front of the shop. A much nicer day than Tuesday with downy breezes and feathery clouds.

He opened the door and smiled at Alice behind the counter. Her return smile was not all it could have been and her eyes were a bit wider than even they usually were. They darted from Charles to another point in the room, and Charles's eyes followed.

They were met by another pair of eyes, slitted beneath a brooding brow; the storms were inside the building.

"Mr. White," Charles said. "It's so good to see you."

"I came to ask again. I want to know where you are in this."

"Let's go upstairs, why don't we?"

Charles had to hurry to stay in front. In the office, he put Patrick White in Dorothy's chair and himself in his own.

"Now," he said, "Mr. White, I'm still trying to understand exactly what *this* is."

"I told you Monday."

"Yes, I know what you said. You believe John Borchard was behind the scandal that cost you your position. Then you said that he killed Derek Bastien."

"That's what he did."

"But those are very serious accusations. I can't just take your word for them."

The reaction was calm enough, but still hostile. "It doesn't matter to me what you think."

"Surely, as a judge, you understand."

"Former judge. And it doesn't matter. I'm not here to find out what you think. I'm here to find out how you got yourself involved. And why."

"I'm not sure why I should tell you anything," Charles said. "I don't know what you might do. I'm not even saying there would be anything of interest to you."

With that, Mr. White left the room, though not physically. His face was blank, pointed generally in Charles's direction. Charles waited. It wasn't too long.

"So he's gotten to you, too."

"Mr. Borchard, you mean? I've only spoken with him a few times," Charles said. "I mentioned that I'd met you. We didn't discuss anything further."

"That was enough. Now he'll try."

"Try what?"

"He knows I'm after him. First he'll tell you not to talk to me. Then he'll ask you what I know. Don't tell him anything."

"But that's my point, Mr. White. What do you really know? Of the things you've said, what do you have real evidence of?"

"I have this."

He leaned forward to take his wallet from his back pocket. He extracted a sheet of paper, folded small.

Charles took the paper and unfolded it.

Mr. White. Stop your efforts concerning the Sentencing Reform Act. University of Virginia Honor Court 1974.

"That was the first note," Mr. White said.

"What is the Sentencing Reform Act?"

"That's the proof it was Borchard. That was his project to strip every heartbeat of mercy out of the courts and replace them with his own hammer of stone."

"But how do you know the note is from Mr. Borchard?"

"Who else would it be? It was his bill from the start. He lives to punish. He always has. His veins flow with vengeance."

"What were you doing that he didn't like?"

"I was going to stop it. Karen Liu knew it was wrong, but they made a deal. I showed her how terrible it was. She was changing her mind—she was so close—and then this came."

"What happened?"

"I was ruined. And Karen Liu gave up. Borchard got to her! He was too strong. She had no choice. She let it through her committee and it went on and on, and now it's law."

"But what does the law do?"

Patrick White only shook his head. "It's too late now. All I have left is bringing Borchard to justice."

Charles handed the paper back. "You're sure this was from John Borchard?"

"He was the one who forced it through Congress. He was like a fiend—pushing, threatening, bribing." Then suddenly, he froze, off again to his other world.

"Mr. White?"

"How did you get involved in this?" The question was a sudden spotlight out of the dark.

"I would really rather not be." The spotlight stayed directly on him. "Derek Bastien was a friend. That's where it started. I don't like where it's gone."

"Karen Liu told me you were asking about Derek Bastien. That's how I knew you were suspicious of his death." The ferocious intensity of his stare was nearly blinding.

"I wasn't."

"Then you can't see."

"What would I even be able to do, Mr. White? What do you want?"

"I want revenge on John Borchard."

"I will not help you with that. I cannot, and I would not."

"He's killed once. He could do it again."

"Who would he kill?"

"Anyone who knows too much."

"I passed Patrick White in the showroom," Dorothy said. Charles looked up from his reverie.

"A moment sooner and you would have found him in your chair."

"What did he say this time?"

"Mostly the same. He accused John Borchard of being vengeful—rather ironic. Although he had a certain florid articulacy."

"I hope he doesn't make a habit of coming here," Dorothy said.

"They aren't pleasant visits." He returned to his meditation. "But I have to understand him. And what happened to him. And how it happened."

Dorothy began opening mail.

"It had to be Derek," Charles said.

"Derek who told the *Washington Post* about Patrick White?"

"It had to be."

Dorothy opened another few envelopes.

"And Patrick White says he went to Derek and told him about it."

"But Derek would already have known?" she asked.

"What a game he was playing."

Dorothy waited.

"And rather ruthless concerning John Borchard," Charles said.

"How did that work?"

Charles returned his full attention. "I don't know what Derek expected at first, but somehow Mr. White got the idea that John Borchard was the blackmailer. From then on, Derek apparently encouraged him in that. I wonder what John even knew."

"That does sound rather ruthless."

"But no more than the original attack on Patrick White. And now I wonder about Karen Liu."

"Do you think she was part of it, too?"

"She seems likely to be an additional victim," Charles said. "And Mr. White finally described more of what his original conflict with John Borchard was. It was some bill he was pushing through Congress, and which Mr. White didn't like. It was called the Sentencing Reform Act."

"What was it reforming?" Dorothy asked.

"Sentences. Perhaps they were simplifying English grammar. I wouldn't mind legalizing run-ons and comma splices, they're quite useful sometimes."

"That would not be a reform. That would be a travesty."

"That's what Mr. White considered it to be. He said it would remove every drop of mercy from the heart of the courts. And in a similar vein, he said John Borchard's blood flowed with vengeance."

"Mr. Borchard seems to be rather ruthless himself," Dorothy said. "We know he had some kind of problem back in Kansas."

"He seems to have intimidated Karen Liu enough to get the bill through her committee," Charles said. "So I wonder what form that intimidation took."

"It must have been the copy of her checks."

"That does seem likely, doesn't it? And she has a very negative opinion of John Borchard. But it was Derek who had the paper, and we don't know if John Borchard even knew that he did." Charles glanced at his telephone. "I think I need to talk to her."

"She might be back sometime soon to return the book you loaned her."

"I don't think I'll wait. I'll just call her."

"What if she won't talk to you?"

"I'll leave a message. It will be a test to see how anxious she is to hear what I have to say."

"My name is Charles Beale. I'd like to get a message to Congresswoman Liu."

"I'll take a message, Mr. Beale."

"Thank you. Please tell her I asked if she was enjoying the Wisdom Garden I loaned her and I had a question about Derek Bastien and a man named Patrick White."

"Yes, Mr. Beale. I'll give this message to her chief of staff."

"Thank you."

Charles leaned back in his chair.

"And now, dear, if you aren't too busy," Dorothy said.

"I'm never too busy for you, dear."

"We really should spend a few minutes discussing business."

"Business. Business? Oh, of course. The bookshop! How is that doing these days, anyway?"

"It is feeling neglected. I would like to discuss the fall catalog with you."

"Fall catalog. What did we say? We're featuring European literature, and travel literature, plus the usual."

"Yes."

"So I need to pick some."

"We need the pictures and the text to the designer by Monday."

"Monday. All right. We have sixty pages?"

"Sixty."

"Mr. Beale?" Alice chirped. "You have a phone call. Congresswoman Karen Liu."

"That was fast," Dorothy said.

Charles shook his head.

"Too fast. She is too anxious, Dorothy."

"Go ahead, dear. That is probably more important than catalog text."

He picked up his telephone.

"Well, Mr. Beale."

"Ah, Congresswoman. Thank you so much for calling back—I hardly expected it."

"I had to," she bubbled. "I've been looking through this garden book and I had to tell you how much I've been enjoying it."

"I'm so glad to hear that."

"I think I might even buy it."

"Whatever you like! Please don't feel at all obliged."

Charles waited.

"And, Mr. Beale," she said finally, with many fewer bubbles, "did you have a question about Pat White?"

"Well, I did. The only reason I'm bothering you with it is that he's mentioned you now a couple times. I wanted to make sure that you knew he had been."

"And what has he been saying?" There was no expression. Her voice had gone completely flat.

"I suppose you know what he's been saying about John Borchard?" Charles asked.

"What has he said to you, Mr. Beale?" Still flat.

"Some very serious things. I don't want to repeat them unless you've already heard them from him yourself."

"I have." The voice tried to perk up. "Mr. White has been under a great deal of pressure."

"I know he has," Charles said. "And I suppose that, in your position, you often are, too."

"This book you've loaned me has been a nice help with that."

"I'm very glad to hear it. I wonder if I could ever be of more help?"

"With another book?" she asked.

"I don't know. But I hope you aren't under the same pressure that Patrick White was."

There was a pause of several seconds, then Karen Liu's bright, happy voice was back. "I do hope I have a chance to get back over there to look at your other books. Maybe again this Saturday?"

"I'll be here," Charles said.

"Good! I will look forward to it!"

"What did that mean?" Dorothy asked.

"I think it means she has been under the same threat as Patrick White, and they've discussed it together."

"But she isn't unbalanced, is she?"

"No," Charles said. "She is still holding up. She will come Saturday, and I have to figure out what I will say."

"Will you tell her about Derek's papers?"

"I'm not sure. I've only met her twice. I don't know her well enough to be able to tell."

"Tell what?"

He tapped his eye. "If she is the real thing."

"The real what?"

"I don't know if I trust her. Anyway." He smiled and used his own bright, happy voice. "The fall catalog!"

"Well . . . you should start thinking about European literature and travel books."

"European travel—oh my!"

"What?"

"The UPS man will be here in an hour."

AFTERNOON

"Mr. Beale?" Alice asked. "Are you expecting someone?"

"Is it obvious?" he said.

"You've been looking out that window for twenty minutes."

"And I couldn't even tell you what's out there. I think I've been somewhere else entirely."

"Anyplace nice?"

"I've been wandering the Mediterranean."

"That would be nice!"

"Well . . ." He looked wistfully out the window. "It's been twenty years of war and dangers, and I'd really rather be home. And I don't know what to expect when I get there."

"I see." Alice nodded, very sympathetically. "Twenty years is a long time. They might think you're never coming back."

"I know my beloved will always be true." Suddenly he was alert, focused on the window. "There! There it is!"

The delivery truck came to a stop and the quick young man bounded up the steps. Charles had the front door open.

"Afternoon, Mr. Beale! Sign here."

"Thank you, Roger. I've been waiting for this one. Alice, could you ask Morgan to come downstairs?"

"What do you think?" Morgan asked.

"I'm not sure. It's very nice," Charles said. Both of them were just inches above the front cover. "Very, very nice. We'll open it."

He put his gloved finger against the page edges and lifted, opening it in the middle. "The typeset is at least 1800s. And the . . . oh my!"

"What?"

"Look close. At the paper."

"Is it parchment?"

"Vellum, even. This was a very expensive book."

"What about now?"

"I don't know yet." He turned back to the beginning. "Not much of a title page, is it?"

"No date, no publisher, no city," Morgan said. "Just the title and author."

"It could maybe be a half title if there were a regular title page after it." He shook his head. "But the book is still very nice."

"But you don't recognize it all?"

"No. It's not any printing I know of. Get that Barlow, will you? Thank you."

Morgan laid a heavy, modern book on the desk, modern at least compared to the other books in the room. Charles opened it with as much respect.

"Alexander Pope." He found the page. "Two dozen editions before

1850." He turned the pages of the *Odyssey* back to the first printed page. "I'll say 1830s."

"What about the signature?"

"Right." He turned back another page to the inside of the front cover. "That is supposed to be an *A*?"

"And that's the *P*," Morgan said.

"It isn't even two words. It's just one word. Even dead, I think Pope would have signed more clearly than that." He turned back to the first printed page. "Look. At the very inside edge. See?"

"It looks like . . ."

"Yes." Charles closed the book and looked at it from the top. "Yes. You can see here. There was another page, and it's been removed. You can see just the sliver that was left."

"That would have been the real title page?"

Charles had the book open. "It's been cut out."

"So it was the half title."

Charles was staring very hard. "I'm not sure. There's something about it."

Morgan waited. Charles looked up at the shelves. All four walls of shelves looked back. The shades varied, but they were all brooding hues of brown. The shelves were divided every three feet by vertical braces, and every section was numbered. Some sections were filled; many had spaces. Ceramic blocks held the books upright where the shelf wasn't filled.

"Get . . . um . . . there, over there, those three. Above the Grotes. The red ones. All three."

Morgan carried them to the desk. Charles opened the first.

"A Jane Austen set from 1820-something, isn't it? Yes, 1828. Now, see, the set title page. It has all the standard title page information, but it's the same for each volume except for the one line of the volume title. Then, the next page is the volume title page. Just like in our *Odyssey*."

"So this *Odyssey* is part of a set," Morgan said. "Is that good?"

"Well . . . yes and no. If we knew anything about the set, and then if we could actually locate any other volumes, that would be very good.

But we don't, so we probably couldn't, so it wouldn't. And the missing main title page is very damaging."

"Was it broken out?"

"Yes, to be framed. I'm sure it was. It's probably on someone's wall right now, or more likely in a box in someone else's attic."

"What will we do with this?"

"We could put it in the catalog and on the website, but just as it is— it's probably not worth more than eight hundred, and that's just because of its age and the quality of its materials. I wonder who was bidding it up to seventeen hundred."

"It was another dealer."

"Just taking a chance, like I was. And maybe I was the loser. Well . . . let me look at it for a while before I decide what to do."

"Yes, sir."

"Maybe I'll read it. I don't know if the Pope translation is even in print anymore. And this is a very nice volume." He turned away from the book. "What are you up to these days, Morgan?"

"Actually, sir, I've been looking through the inventory. I have a list to order."

"Anything special?"

"It's mostly replacements. I'll find them wherever I can. Briary Roberts has a lot of them."

"Anything expensive? We won't replace the Melville, of course."

"There is a nice Dante I found for about twelve thousand. Longfellow, eighteen sixty-seven. It's on one of the private auction sites."

"Eighteen sixty-seven? A first-edition Longfellow? That would be nice. I'll look at it."

"Mr. Beale?" Alice called down from above. "You have a telephone call. Mr. John Borchard."

"Hello, John, this is Charles Beale."

"Charles! I'm starting to feel like an old friend, calling you so often."

"I'm feeling the same way."

"Good. I think I've worked out a space in my schedule for tomorrow morning. I want to stop in and see you."

"Tomorrow morning would be fine."

"Wonderful! I'll look forward to it. Tomorrow morning then?"

"Yes, John, tomorrow morning."

"What time do you open?"

"Ten o'clock. But I'll be here earlier."

"Oh, no, I'm sure you'd be busy. Would ten-thirty be convenient?"

"That would be fine."

"Then tomorrow morning, at ten-thirty."

"Tomorrow morning at ten-thirty."

"Is that a customer?" Morgan asked as Charles set the telephone down.

"No, an old friend."

"He's coming by the store?"

"Yes. I think he might come tomorrow morning. Maybe around ten-thirty."

EVENING

"Good evening, ladies," Charles said, coming up from the basement. Alice and Dorothy were together at the counter.

"Are you ready?" Dorothy asked.

"Yes. I could walk out the door this instant. Are we going home for dinner?"

"I was going to get some fish out of the freezer."

Charles considered. "I don't know. After reading *Moby-Dick* all morning yesterday, I don't know if I'm in the mood for fish."

"I'm open to suggestions," Dorothy said.

"Have we sold anything this afternoon?" Charles asked Alice.

"Quite a few books, Mr. Beale. There was a Kipling, *Captains Courageous*."

"No, no more fish."

"A *Carry On, Mr. Bowditch*?"

"No."

"Several Patrick O'Brians."

"No!"

"A Jules Verne, *Twenty Thousand*—"

"No, no, no! Anything else?"

Alice smiled so sweetly. "And a Hemingway."

"Don't tell me," Charles said.

"*Old Man and the Sea*."

"Is that all?"

"Well, there was an F. Scott Fitzgerald, *The Great Gatsby*."

"Ah," Charles sighed. "That sounds like something we can work with."

Between four wild lanes of mired Duke Street traffic and their table were a wide brick sidewalk, a wider plate glass window, and a mild jazz trio. Between the two of them were two knives, two forks, and one steak.

"John Borchard is coming to the store tomorrow morning," Charles said during a pause in the music.

"I've heard so much about him," Dorothy said.

"In quantity and quality. Besides that he was Derek's boss, you've heard that he is harsh and cruel, that he put innocent people in prison in Kansas, that he blackmailed and ultimately destroyed Patrick White, and that he killed Derek. That's quite a tale."

"It does predispose me against him."

"He is also charming, jolly, thoughtful and very important."

"I'll keep an open mind. What do you think about him?"

"I'm trying to stay open myself," Charles said. "He is something between Derek's victim and his co-conspirator."

"Why is he coming?"

"To find out what I know, if anything, about Derek, including why I've put myself in the middle of his tussle with Karen Liu and Patrick White."

"Would he know about Derek's papers?"

"At this point, I'd put it at seventy percent that he does."

"Does he know you have them?"

"I give it forty percent that he at least suspects."

"What will you tell him?" Dorothy asked.

The jazz group fired up.

"I will play that by ear."

Did any of our philosophers play chess, Charles?"

"Chess? Why, I have no idea, Derek. What an interesting question."

"What would you guess?"

"Voltaire, if any of them. Hamilton might have."

"I picture most of them hunched over their writing desks scrawling by candlelight. Not gregarious or social."

"Nor cunning, either, Derek."

"You aren't cunning, Charles, are you? And you play chess quite well."

"I'm gregarious."

"What about Burke? Would he have played?"

"He might have been cunning, Derek. For the power he wielded in Parliament, he must have been. It wasn't all fiery speeches."

"The deals were struck at the gaming tables."

"So he played cards, not chess."

"I think I agree, Charles. Chess is pure intellect. Politics is much closer to gambling. Do you play any card games?"

"They've never appealed to me."

"Perhaps we should try. I think you'd be good at it."

"I'd have to learn any you'd suggest, Derek."

"I think I'll get a deck of cards."

THURSDAY

MORNING

Charles looked out the window from his desk. On the sidewalk below, across the street, John Borchard stood waiting.

The clock said 10:25.

"Should I invite him in?"

"Of course," Dorothy said, coming to look. "We're open. Why is he waiting?"

"Because he said 10:30."

"But that's ridiculous."

"A Deputy Assistant Attorney General isn't ridiculous," Charles said. "Well, maybe he is. But he isn't supposed to be."

John Borchard pulled a pocket watch from his suit vest, frowned, and returned it to its pocket.

"Now that is impressive," Charles said. "Did you see how he did that? It takes practice to do it with just the right pomposity."

"But why is he waiting?" Dorothy asked again.

Charles shook his head. "Because he's nervous."

"About what?"

"That's the question. I'll go down to be there when he comes in."

"Should I come?"

"In a few minutes. When you're ready."

"Have we sold anything yet this morning?" Charles asked. He and Alice were still alone. The clock said 10:29.

"There was a lady in to buy a book for her grandson," Alice said.

Charles had his hand on the doorknob. The seconds ticked down. Ten thirty. He opened the front door.

Mr. Borchard was six inches from it, his face down, staring at his watch on its chain. He looked up and an immense grin spread across his large face.

"Charles!"

"John. Come in."

John Borchard stuffed the watch back into his vest, took a vast breath, and stepped over the threshold. The room was suddenly filled.

He moved to his proper place in its center.

"This is Alice," Charles said. "Mr. Borchard."

"Oh! So good to meet you!" He shook her hand with both of his in a full body greeting, and then he returned his stare to the room itself.

"Absolutely amazing!"

He seemed absolutely lost in his amazement. His grin had been replaced by the pure fascination of a child in a wonderland.

Charles stepped back to the counter to be out of his way.

"What did the lady buy this morning?" Charles asked Alice.

"A *Peter Pan*."

For a moment the only sound was the ticking of John's pocket watch. Then he regained his speech.

"It is amazing. Charles, it's everything I thought it would be."

"It is just my humble shop."

"Hardly humble! It's impressive, quite impressive! Please, show me around."

"This is the showroom. Children's books—sports and hobbies—mysteries—general fiction—general nonfiction—and so on."

"But . . ." John moved to a shelf, wrinkles of doubt rippling across his forehead. "But they're special, aren't they?" He looked closer.

"These are all first editions or rare editions or signed copies. Yes, they are special."

"I see." He removed a *The Cat in the Hat* and gravely inspected it. He handed the book to Charles and looked again at the shelves.

Charles waited as Neverland slowly lost its magic.

"But surely, there is more?" John said.

"The older books?" Charles ventured.

"Yes! Yes, that's it! Exactly! I'd imagined older books. The ones that Derek would have bought."

Charles nodded. "Those are downstairs."

"Downstairs." The eyebrows raised in complicit understanding. "Downstairs! Of course. Of course they would be." And then, hoping against hope, "I wonder if I could see them?"

"Of course, John."

The eyebrows collapsed in gratitude.

"Thank you!" He beamed like the sun.

But a new moon had risen from above, and the center of the solar system was put in its shadow.

"John, this is my wife, Dorothy."

"Dorothy." It was profoundly stated, as if it revealed all truth.

"Mr. Borchard," she said. And she smiled, more gracious than truth. "Charles has told me so much about you."

His return smile made up in quantity what it lacked in quality. "And he's mentioned you as well." He took her hand and almost seemed to kiss it, but in fact only very gently and momentarily held it, and then released. "What an honor."

"We were just going downstairs," Charles said.

"Go ahead," Dorothy said. "I just need to talk with Alice."

John tore his attention from Dorothy and turned to follow Charles.

"Here we are," Charles said, unlocking the basement door and turning on the light.

John Borchard stared and blinked and stared again. "Incredible!" For a moment he was truly amazed. He walked slowly along the wall, studying each shelf. "What treasures!"

"This is more what you imagined?"

"Yes, quite." John took a breath. He had still not recovered his bluster. "May I look at one?"

"Here." Charles gave him white gloves from the desk, and then a volume from the shelf.

John peered closely to make out the title. "*Gulliver's Travels*. It is incredible! Is this a first edition?"

"No. That is a 1780 printing. If I had a first edition, it would be in a bank vault."

"This is quite a vault itself. Who would think, just walking past this old house, what treasures it has hidden!"

"Well, perhaps anyone who looked at the sign that says *Rare Books*."

"Well, perhaps! Absolutely. May I look inside?"

Charles carefully opened the book. "Some dealers don't touch them, but I hate to think of a book never opened. If it's in good condition like this, it won't hurt it."

John moved his finger across the page. "Absolutely amazing! And how much would this book be worth?"

"For its age and condition and rarity, about six thousand dollars."

"Amazing." He handed it back to Charles. Then a new expression emerged on his Brobdingnagian face as the cheeks pushed against the eyes, and the chin pushed up and out, and other features drew together conspiratorially. "And you said that you had Derek's books?"

"Yes. I bought them at the auction last week."

Then a whisper, but with a doglike eagerness. "They would be down here?"

"Yes, they are."

"All of them?"

"Well, actually, I've determined that one isn't. I hadn't realized at first, but one book that I'd sold him was not part of the set I bought back."

Then another new expression appeared, less dog-eager and more cat-watchful.

"I wonder where it went."

"I don't know, of course," Charles said. "He might have sold it. Or it might have been stolen the night he was killed."

"The night he was killed." John nodded at a chair. "May I?"

"Of course. Sit down." Charles sat at the desk. "Not as nice as the chairs in your office."

"But quite functional. The night he was killed . . ." John sighed, very deeply, but the cat eyes didn't share the unhappiness. They were only alert. "I keep thinking about that night. Derek must have been very courageous to walk into that office. In the dark. By himself."

"He was usually willing to take risks."

"Yes, he was." John seemed very satisfied with Charles's answer. "I knew him to take a number of risks through the years."

"You must have been very shocked the next morning."

"I was shocked when I found out. It was actually two days later."

"Two days?"

Now the eyes were veiled as the whole broad face went blank. "I was at the bottom of the Grand Canyon. Not much cell phone coverage there."

"The bottom of the Grand Canyon!" Charles said.

"My wife and I take a trip each year for our anniversary. Five days of rafting and camping."

Charles allowed a smile, between friends. "I would never have guessed you did such things, John."

"It wasn't what you would call roughing it." He matched Charles's smile, and raised it by an eyebrow. "We had comfortable tents and beds, and excellent food. Just right for a sedentary bureaucrat to pretend he was having an adventure!"

"I'm sure it was an adventure. A real one. But I can see that you wouldn't be getting much news from the outside world."

"It was only as we came out that I received the messages from my staff. And then it absolutely was a shock." John's face metamorphosed into a thoughtful frown. "But coming back to Derek's books. You say they're here in this room?"

"They are."

"May I see one?"

Charles smiled. "Of course." He stood and turned to a shelf behind the desk. John Borchard's eyes followed him exactly. "John Adams, *A Defence of the Constitutions of Government of the United States.*" He set the volume in the waiting hand.

"Like the other book, it isn't a first edition, I assume."

"No. But it was printed during Adams's presidency."

"Remarkable," he remarked. "Absolutely remarkable." He opened the book and shifted pages. "And it seems to be in good condition."

"That one, yes," Charles said. "Very good."

John lingered over the yellowed pages. "Are there actual ratings?"

"There are generally accepted criteria. Poor, fair, good, very good, excellent. Most dealers would understand what each means."

"And you would inspect a book to decide what condition it's in?"

"Yes," Charles said. "That's fairly straightforward."

John's lips had become dry. He paused a moment to wet them.

"Did you inspect Derek's books?" he asked.

Charles shrugged. "Having sold Derek the books in the first place, I already knew their condition. And of course he'd taken very good care of them. I knew they wouldn't have deteriorated."

"I'm sure he did take very good care of them," John said. "Absolutely sure."

Then Charles waited. John's face had again rearranged, with the brow down and the eyes squinted and the lips jutting, all with words pent up behind them.

"Charles, was there anything unusual about Derek's antique books?"

"He collected the standards of Enlightenment philosophy."

"The books themselves. I mean their physical condition."

"What do you mean, exactly, John?" Charles said.

John ran his finger along the line of his chin. "You know, Charles,

I'm still not completely sure why you came last week to see me. Was it really just innocent curiosity?"

"I did want to meet you."

"All these months had passed after Derek's death, but it was only two days after the auction that you decided to call me. I think there is more to be said."

Charles nodded. "I called because Karen Liu told me about you."

John regrouped. "Oh, of course. You had just spoken with her."

"And then, the day after I met with you, Patrick White came to see me. He actually mentioned your name, as well."

"Yes. You mentioned that to me on the telephone."

"He's been back twice since."

"Had you met him some other time before?" John was falling back in confusion. "I don't understand how you would have known him."

"Karen Liu gave him my name, I believe."

For the first time, Charles saw the face demonstrate a shade of anger; in this case, annoyance. "The congresswoman is dropping quite a few names, isn't she?"

"Mr. White did as well," Charles said. "Or maybe I should say he flung them."

Then irritation. "I can imagine."

"I suppose you know what he is saying?"

Resentment. "I know quite well. I hope that you realize he is not in his right mind?"

"I believe I used the word *unbalanced* when I described him to my wife."

"Unbalanced. Yes, that would do." The anger had melted into long-suffering, but there was still a snap in the words. "I've been patient with Mr. White, overly so. He's given me more than sufficient grounds for a slander suit. I've spoken with the police and I've consulted my lawyer."

Charles held up his hand. "I understand completely. Of course, I haven't taken anything he said seriously."

"Please continue not to. I will even suggest you not listen to him at all."

It was more than a snap. It was a command.

Charles smiled, very calm, very soothing. "I'm sure it's been very difficult."

"Very." John paper-clipped his own calm back together. "It comes with the territory, I suppose. Washington is a bare knuckles town."

"I would like to ask about one thing he said. He mentioned a Sentencing Reform bill."

"Yes, that was the particular spark that inflamed the conflict. It was simple enough—just rationalizing the sentencing guidelines for Federal crimes. It was long overdue. Mr. White thought otherwise."

"Did he feel the new guidelines were too harsh?"

"Oh, I don't know what he felt!" The paper clips were falling out. "He had no business involving himself, anyway. He was a judge, and this was between the Justice Department and Congress."

"Apparently, Karen Liu valued his opinion as a judge?"

"Apparently." A full-face scowl was magnificent. "Karen may have not used the best judgment in listening to him. Her subcommittee was working with us with the usual high level of cooperation, until he barged in. I don't think anyone realized at the time that he was already, as you said, off-balance. And my superior, the Principal Deputy, had given me the task of shepherding the bill through Congress as a very high priority. You can see how Mr. White and I developed quite a conflict."

"From his comments," Charles said, "he seems to consider it a very personal conflict."

"And what exactly were his comments?" John asked. "I'm only guessing what he might have told you."

"That you had sent the incriminating documents to the *Washington Post*."

"Yes, that's it. With absolutely no basis."

"Absolutely," Charles said. "I wonder who did send them."

"I have no idea. I don't want to know either."

"But the bill was passed by Congress?"

"It is law, now," John said. "It was a relief to get it over with."

"I appreciate you telling me all of this."

The conversation had recovered its balance. John's face was merely placid, whatever was going on behind it. At least the thought of leaving was, because he put his hands down together on the desk and pushed himself up out of the chair.

"I don't mind at all, Charles. I think I've taken enough of your valuable time."

"I'm very honored that you came to visit."

Together they climbed the stairs to the showroom.

Dorothy and Alice were still behind the counter in earnest conversation. But before John could even stretch any pleased look further than the corners of his mouth, every feature on his face fled backward in alarm.

"John," Charles said quickly. "This is Angelo."

"Who?"

John Borchard's incoherence was understandable. Angelo was not at his best. But even with the immobility of his face, he matched John in silent, eloquent hostility.

"My employee," Charles added. "Angelo, this is Mr. Borchard."

"That pipe, it does not leak now," Angelo said, his eyes still on John.

"Which pipe?" Charles said.

"In the sink upstairs," Dorothy said. "I noticed it this morning and I asked Angelo to look at it."

"Then thank you, Angelo," Charles said. "And, John, thank you again for stopping in. It was very interesting."

"My pleasure," John said, but all his face was still broadcasting his opinion of Angelo.

"That man," Angelo said, staring now at the door.

"Yes?"

"He came out from the building."

"Oh—the auction last week? I suppose that makes sense."

Angelo shrugged. "Do you want that I should go to a place on the list?"

"Yes. I guess you should just start picking them yourself."

Angelo's exit was his answer.

Dorothy was behind Charles as he ascended to the office.

"And what did you talk about with Mr. Borchard?" she asked.

"Books." Charles dropped into his chair and turned to stare out the window. "How would you describe his demeanor when he first came in?"

"He would have failed my theater class in college."

"What a good way to put it!" Charles spun his chair back toward her and laughed. "I've seldom seen such bad acting. He gave up on it once we got downstairs. He was too preoccupied with Derek's books."

"Does he know about Derek's papers?"

"I would put it at one hundred percent. He tried to ask if I did without admitting that he did. It was awkward."

"Did you tell him that you did?"

"No. I decided not to. But besides the papers, he also knows something about Derek's books."

"The John Locke?"

"Something. That's why he was here."

"Then what are you going to do? You're going to have to do something if he knows you have those papers. He'll do something first."

"For the moment, I will escape," Charles said. "I will go to the basement and call Jacob."

AFTERNOON

The *Odyssey* was open on the basement desk. Charles drummed his fingers beside it. He picked up the telephone.

"Mr. Leatherman, please. This is Charles Beale."

"Yes, Mr. Beale. I believe he's right here."

Charles prepared himself.

"Charles? What do you want?"

"The benefit of your immense experience and wisdom, Jacob."

"That's what everybody wants. Everybody thinks they know everything. Then when they get stuck, they call me."

"I have a question, and I am stuck. And besides, I call mainly as a favor to your staff, to keep you busy so they can have a few minutes of peace to get anything done. Anyway, I have a book, and it's a little odd."

"Odd, you say?" His voice changed. "Those are the ones that are worth anything."

"This is an *Odyssey*, the Pope translation, and it looks like it's about 1830, nice leather—"

"Wait a minute, you." Jacob's volume went up a notch. "That was the one in Denver?"

"That's right."

"You got that? Whippersnapper! I put a bid on that."

"How much?"

"Eight hundred dollars."

"Then you were quite outclassed. I got it for almost eighteen. There were more than just you and I bidding."

"What's it like? The picture wasn't worth anything."

"The title page is cut out. There's a volume title page. No half title."

"You think it's a part of a set?"

"I wonder if it's a private printing."

"Then you wasted your money. It won't be worth a thing except for the leather and the age. Wait, you don't know who owned it, do you?"

"I don't know. I wonder if that was on the true title page."

"It's been cut out, you say? That might be, Charles. That might be. They were broken that way, back in the twenties and thirties."

"It's only one page."

"But that was the fashion, about 1920 to 1935. People wanted that title page, nothing else out of it. Happened to a lot of books, mainly in England. And especially if the title page had something special about it. Have you collated the whole book?"

"I've been through every page, but I don't have anything to compare it to. What do you know about early nineteenth century private collection printings?"

"There were the cheap ones then like they make now—all the popular classics in matching volumes by subscription."

"No, it's not one of those. The leather is very nice." He paused for effect. "And Jacob, it's vellum."

"Vellum?" The telephone shook in Charles's hand. "Vellum? Are you sure?"

"I think I can tell."

"I suppose even you could," Jacob said. "So, 1830s and vellum?"

"Have you ever seen anything like that?"

"Only once. Twenty years ago. It was an 1820 Gibbon, in four volumes, and it was printed for the Duke of Wellington."

"Do you remember the publisher?"

"Padding and Brewster."

"What about the title page?" Charles asked.

"Besides the city and date, there was the Duke's name, the name of the collection, then the name of the volume."

"So that's what's been cut out."

"It would make a nice picture on a wall," Jacob said, very sarcastically. "I hate book breaking."

"I know your opinions on the subject. What do you think of it being the Alexander Pope translation?"

"That's an odd one, too, isn't it, Charles? That's an odd one. Long out of fashion by that point. Mostly. But it had a small following. Tutors used it. Private tutors."

Charles's eyes had not left the volume on the desk in front of him. "A wealthy child around 1830, studying Homer with a private tutor. A name springs to mind . . ."

Jacob cackled. "Don't get your hopes up, Charles! But that would be a catch if it were."

"There is an unreadable signature. I'm going to compare it to a few specimens. And I might run it up to the Library of Congress, to see what they think. It will just be so disappointing when they tell me I'm wrong."

"Have them call me, and I'll tell you. I'd look forward to it."

"I'm always glad to give you something to live for. Except I'm going to run out sooner or later."

"It's touch and go, Charles, but this will keep me going for a week or so. And say, what happened to that matchmaker you were after?"

"I met him, Jacob. A very interesting person. The story isn't over yet, but if you can stay alive for a couple more weeks, I might be able to tell it to you."

"You've been down here a long time," Dorothy said.

"I'm on the hunt," Charles said.

She sat beside him, worried. "I hope you haven't found more secret papers."

"No!" He had to laugh. "No, dear, not that at all. This is far more interesting."

"That's your *Odyssey*?"

"Literally, and literally literally. And literately. This *Odyssey* is my odyssey. Come, look at this signature. The first letter. What is it?"

"My first thought was an *A*, but it isn't. Maybe a *V*."

"Yes! That's what I think. An expensive leather set, 1830s, that includes Homer in a classic translation that was already out of date. And the letter *V*. Any guess?"

"No . . ."

"Possibly a private printing for a child, a student, per Jacob Leatherman. On vellum. Now compare that signature to this." Regally, he set a paper on the table next to the book, a printed image of a signature. "Do they look the same?"

"I—Charles—it couldn't be."

"Do they look the same?" he said again.

"Yes."

"Exactly the same." He sighed deeply. "Victoria."

"I don't believe it!" Dorothy said. "What are you going to do?"

"Going to do?" Charles laughed. "Just enjoy it as much as I can before I find out I'm wrong."

"Will you try to get it authenticated?"

"I might. I can call the Library of Congress and ask if they would inspect it."

"Would the title page have had her name?"

"That would be worth breaking out, don't you think? Jacob says it would have been done in the 1920s, which would have been about when our seller's grandfather would have received this as a gift."

"Would he have done it?"

"I think not. I think it was sold after it was broken. At that point, it was just another book. Now—I wonder whatever became of Victoria's library?"

"It must still be in England. In a castle or palace."

"This sounds like a job for Morgan."

He was up and moving, two steps at a time, with Dorothy far behind.

"Morgan?"

"Yes, Mr. Beale?"

"I am sending you on an odyssey."

"Yes, sir!"

"Start with Queen Victoria."

"Not Troy?"

"Start with young Vicky in her schoolroom reading about Troy, her stern classics tutor lecturing her on Homer and the legends of the Greeks."

Morgan rubbed his hands and grinned. "Yes, sir."

"And on her desk, a schoolbook fit for a queen, a private printing in deluxe leather and vellum."

"I can see it," Morgan said.

"And right beside it are matching volumes."

"How many?"

Charles squinted. "It's hard to tell. At least an *Iliad*. Probably an *Aeneid*. Possibly others."

"Yes, sir."

"But the question is about the *Odyssey*. Where is that book today?"

"I'll find it. I'll start in that schoolroom, and I'll trace it as far as I can. I'll find it, sir."

"Good. I hope, Morgan, that you'll find it in our basement. And find the others, too, if you can. I think they all want to be back together."

EVENING

The evening was warm and the windows were open. The breeze, dark and handsome, waltzed with the curtain, showing off its white lace to the whole room. In their chairs, Charles and Dorothy read, the turning pages keeping slow time in a dance of their own.

Until, finally, Dorothy set her book on the table beside her.

"Why are you reading *A Separate Peace*?" Charles asked.

"I want to decide if Gene meant to do it."

"If he rocked the branch on purpose?"

"I don't think it's that simple," she said. "Why did you pick this book for our outing last Friday?"

"It's about a young man who dies."

"I don't think it's that simple," she said again. "Gene resents Finny because he's athletic and popular, but they're still friends. At that one moment, though, on the tree branch, somehow Finny falls and breaks his leg, and it isn't set right, and he doesn't recover. Then Gene is forced to admit that he might have made Finny fall on purpose. Finny is so upset he runs off and breaks his leg again falling down the staircase. Then he dies during the operation to set it again."

"Gene didn't mean for Finny to die. He didn't know that he would."

"But Gene never really knows whether he meant for Finny to fall. Charles . . . what did we mean with William?"

"We didn't mean for him to die."

"We resented him."

"How could we not have?" Charles said, wryly. "We did love him, Dorothy, but you know how difficult he became."

"Were we glad when he died?"

"You know we weren't. But where would we be if he hadn't? Would we be sitting here now? Would we have the shop? We might not. We might have used all our money on legal costs, or we might have had to move somewhere remote to get him away from the city. Of course, I don't mean that I wouldn't trade anything to have him back."

"I know what you mean."

"Well, then yes, I knew that if I picked that book, an English major would realize what I was saying. So let me know whether Gene did it on purpose or even what that means, and we'll understand ourselves better for it. That's what books are supposed to do."

"Sometimes they explain us too well," Dorothy said.

"Derek Bastien said once that it was all chemistry, that behavior is just from the way a person's brain is wired."

"So why was William's wired that way?"

"That's what we don't know."

"What did you say to Derek?"

"I told him chemistry couldn't explain anything as complex as a human soul. Or as sublime."

"Ah, de Tocqueville. Democracy in America. *Wonderful, Charles."*

"You are expanding your range, Derek."

"Quite. What the Enlightenment sowed, the nineteenth century will now reap."

"But they will still bake their own unique loaf from it."

"You don't let anyone off the hook, do you, Charles?"

"We're all responsible for our own actions, Derek. De Tocqueville had America and France to compare. They both grew out of the Enlightenment, but very differently."

"And he was hardly the first—or the last—to compare them. Here is a challenge, Charles. Think of an original comparison."

"Between France and America?"

"In this period, yes. One that will surprise me."

"You never let me off the hook, do you, Derek? All right, I believe one springs to mind. John Adams and Lamoignon-Malesherbes."

"Malesherbes—he defended Louis the Sixteenth at his trial in the National Assembly, didn't he?"

"To no avail, of course. Compare him to Adams, who defended the British soldiers at the Boston Massacre, and got them acquitted."

"A slim comparison, Charles."

"But what became of them? Adams was elected president, while Malesherbes was guillotined a year after Louis."

"*A bit more interesting. But I'm thinking more of the years after, when America stayed a democracy and France returned to monarchy.*"

"*That's where I'm going, Derek. Adams's son became president himself, of course.*"

"*And what about the family of Malesherbes?*"

"*His daughter and granddaughter were also executed with him, but his great-grandson, Alexis, grew up and went in search of a better democracy than France.*"

"*Charles—don't tell me.*"

"*That's his book in your hand, Derek. He compares France and the United States.*"

"*A clever comparison yourself, Charles. Congratulations. But of course, he predicts many of the problems that American democracy would face.*"

"*I admit it, Derek. We're responsible for our actions, but we're also still human.*"

"*And who is responsible for that?*"

FRIDAY

MORNING

Even before Charles had the lights on and the alarm off, Morgan was sprinting down the stairs.

"Mr. Beale? Could you look at this?" Morgan was excited. Very excited.

"Here I come."

"It wasn't hard," Morgan said. "This one letter is the key. It's from Victoria to her great-granddaughter, Alexandra, in 1895. Alexandra was seven years old."

"How did you find it?"

"The London Museum had an archive." Morgan smirked. "It cost you two hundred dollars to subscribe to it."

"Money well spent, Morgan. What does it say?"

"It's this one line: 'I am sending you some books and toys from my own childhood.' That's all. But after Victoria died, there were no schoolbooks in the inventory."

"So there is a chance those are the books."

"Yes, sir, a chance. In 1912, Alexandra married this guy, Lord Bostwick. Then she died thirteen years later, in 1925."

"She was thirty-seven," Charles said.

"Influenza. Her husband sold off all her belongings."

"How?"

Morgan's grin got even bigger. "Sotheby's."

Charles's grin matched Morgan's. "Oh, how wonderful. Perfect. I will call them immediately."

"Mr. Beale?" Alice had arrived. "You have a telephone call. Mr. John Borchard."

"Hello, this is Charles Beale."

"Charles, John Borchard here."

"Good morning, John."

"Good morning! I hope it is for you."

"It is so far," Charles said.

"Very good! Charles, I wanted to call to follow up on our discussion yesterday morning. A specific point."

"Go ahead, then."

"Good. Thank you. The point is in regard to Patrick White. You may have wondered why I haven't taken stronger action against him for the things he's been saying about me."

"I think you've been very gracious so far, John."

"I have tried. There is a limit, of course, and some people might say he has already exceeded it, but I'm still reluctant to press charges. Let me tell you a story, Charles."

Dorothy was just sitting at her desk. Charles looked at his watch. "Go ahead, John," he said.

"Thank you. I want to tell you about a man I knew, back in my early days in Kansas. He was a fellow prosecutor in a neighboring county."

"Oh, yes. I remember you mentioning Kansas."

"Quite. This friend was quite zealous. He was young, idealistic, wanted to make his mark. He was even overzealous."

"I see," Charles said. "That's a little dangerous in a prosecutor, isn't it?"

John's answer was a little slow in coming. "Perhaps. In this case, a few lines were crossed."

"In what way?"

"Maybe we don't need to go into details," John said. "In fact, as this all happened to an acquaintance, I don't think I really know the details. Suffice it to say, there were a number of cases he prosecuted successfully but that later were overturned because these lines had been crossed."

"Were the people actually guilty of the charges he prosecuted?"

"He felt quite sure that they were, which would be why he felt justified in overlooking the niceties. However, the law is the law. The convictions were thrown out."

"Where is he now?"

"I'm not really sure. I've lost touch. He had already left the county, and at this point there wouldn't be any need to stir up his past. It could even be detrimental to his career. Um, for all I know, at least. As I've said, I've lost touch."

"And what does this have to do with Patrick White?" Charles asked.

"My friend later told me something he'd learned from the incident. He said he'd resolved to be much more careful in bringing charges against other people."

"Just more careful?" Charles asked. "So that he'd have more complete cases against them?"

"No, not exactly. We'll say he learned to be less anxious to see others punished."

"Something like mercy, John?"

"Yes. Something like mercy, Charles."

"I see. Well, that is a very interesting story. It does explain your lenience toward Patrick White."

"Good. I hoped it would. And I won't take any more of your time."

"I'm always at your service, John. And I actually have a quick question for you."

"Of course! What can I do for you?"

"Yesterday, you mentioned having gone on a camping and rafting trip through the Grand Canyon. I was thinking it might be just the thing for Dorothy and me."

"Absolutely, Charles! I would recommend it to anyone."

"Did you do it through a travel agency?"

"I did. I'll have to have my secretary dig that up. I'll have her send that over to you right away!"

"Thank you very much. I'd appreciate it."

Dorothy's eyes were as wide as the Grand Canyon when he'd hung up. "Camping and rafting?"

"John Borchard told me he was on vacation in the Grand Canyon when Derek was killed, and I was just curious about it. But I would take you! Would you like to?"

"I think I'd rather just see it from the top."

"Then let's do. When would you be ready? I'll take you anywhere!"

"I think I'd prefer Paris. But what are you curious about?"

"Oh, nothing."

"And what were you talking about before that?"

"His old friend, who was a prosecutor in Kansas. Actually, it was the person in Derek's paper."

"It wasn't John, then?"

"Oh, yes, it is John Borchard. He said it was a friend, but he was really describing himself."

"That sounds very complicated."

"It is very complicated. It will take me a while to work it out, and I have to call London." He looked at the computer screen on his desk. "And, I see that John Borchard's secretary is very efficient." He copied a telephone number from the screen. "I will be in the basement."

"Sotheby's," the telephone said, and it sounded just like it.

"Good morning," Charles said. "Or, it would be afternoon there, wouldn't it?"

"Yes, sir. It's 4:15."

"Good afternoon, then. My name is Charles Beale and I'm doing some research on an item that was sold through your house in 1925."

"Just a moment, Mr. Beale. I'll put you through to our records department."

"Thank you."

He waited, for a very short time.

"Mr. Beale?"

"Yes, this is Charles Beale."

"Good afternoon. I am Anthony Prescott." He sounded just like it, too. "How may we help you, sir?"

"I'm calling from Virginia in the United States. I am a rare-books dealer and I have a book, which I've just bought through eBay, and I'm trying to get more information about it. I believe the book may have been sold at a Sotheby's auction in London in 1925. Is there any information you can give me that might verify that?"

"I can look, sir. Could you describe the book or the auction?"

"It would have been a Lord Bostwick, selling the possessions of his deceased wife. The book itself is an Alexander Pope translation of Homer's *Odyssey*. I'm estimating the publication date to be in the 1830s. I don't know how it would have been described in the auction catalog."

"Mr. Beale," Mr. Prescott said. "I do see that sale for 1925. I'll need to do more research to find anything about that book."

"The particular things I'm interested in," Charles said, "are first, if this book was indeed sold through that auction, and second, if any other books were bought at that auction, and even possibly by whom."

"I may be able to help you with your first points, Mr. Beale, but we never release information about our buyers without their permission."

"I'm quite familiar with your policies, Mr. Prescott. I've bought a few things at Sotheby's through the years, so I'm one of your buyers myself! But anything I can find out would be useful, especially if I can determine that this book was one of a set. Oh, and one other request, if you don't mind."

"Go ahead, Mr. Beale. I see your record here in the computer. We'll be pleased to assist you."

"Thank you. I also wonder if there might have been a framed single page sold in that same auction. It would have been the title page of this book, broken out separately."

"I can check that as well, sir."

"Thank you so much. I do appreciate it."

Charles referred to his note and dialed another number.

"DuPont Travel," said another voice, which also sounded just like it.

"Hello, my name is Charles Beale. I have a friend who recommended your Grand Canyon tours very highly."

Smiles poured out of the receiver. "I'm so glad! They're very nice. Are you interested in one in particular?"

"My friend spoke very highly of the guides on his trip. I'd like to make sure we have the same ones."

"I'll have to see who they were. When did your friend take his trip?"

"It was last fall, in the middle of November. My friend's name is John Borchard."

"Let me see what I can find."

There was a moment of silence.

"Computers are wonderful things," Charles said.

"We couldn't get by without them! Now let's see . . . he was on the November seventeenth five-day trip. I'll have to call the tour operators to see about the guides. But if they're still available, I'm sure we can work it out!"

"Thank you so much! That would be so nice."

"Sure, Mr. Beale! Now, let me get a phone number and I'll call back as soon as I have that information."

AFTERNOON

"Have you worked out John Borchard's story?" Dorothy asked. They had returned to the salad hunting grounds, with similar results.

"I have worked a dozen different scenarios and ranked them in order of probability."

"What is the most probable, then?"

"None of them."

"*Most* is ordinal," Dorothy said. "There has to be one."

"*Probable* is qualitative, though, and none of them are."

"Charles, I am armed with the English language, and I know how to use it."

"Then I surrender! I will describe the least improbable scenario." He bit, chewed, and swallowed. "John thinks I have Derek's papers, which are incriminating to certain individuals. He does not know whether any of these papers concerns himself. Therefore, he told the story as if it were about someone else, and as a reason why he hasn't sued Patrick White over his alleged slanders."

"But why did he tell the story at all?"

"If I do have a paper about it, he wants to justify his actions to me. He wants to give me his side of the story. On the other hand, if I don't have the paper, I won't know what he is talking about."

"That seems improbable," Dorothy said.

"You admit it. You threatened me with the English language. Well, live by the pen, die by the pen."

"It is still the most probable, even if it is improbable."

"Just the type of nicety John Borchard would have ignored, and now it is haunting him. In my scenario he had to guess what Derek might have had on him, and that was it."

"Then he guessed right."

"I'm guessing what he is guessing that I am guessing."

"I never liked those."

"No, but that's how the game is played."

"What game?"

"Whatever game we're in," Charles said. "Derek's game. The game he played all the time. We have three papers worked out, I think. Karen Liu's checks, John Borchard's prosecutions, and Patrick White's cheating. There are three to go: The drug arrests, the woman who killed her husband, and the list of numbers and dates."

No light but the desk lamp, and the computer off. No one else but three thousand books. No sound but the rustling of papers.

The maimed volume was open on the desk, its card box removed, and Charles bent over a single sheet of paper.

He read it again:

Drug Bust in Fairfax—*Fairfax County police arrested more than a dozen members of an alleged drug importing ring. The early morning raids on five residences were the result of a three-month investigation. Drug-sniffing dogs uncovered over seventy pounds of cocaine hidden in furniture in one apartment.*

He picked up the telephone.

"Hello?" It was the same woman's voice, worn and plaintive.

"I'd like to speak with Galen Jones, please. This is Charles Beale."

"Just a minute."

And then, only a few seconds later, "Beale. What do you want?"

"I think I've found a new tree to bark up. I have a question."

"I don't care if you ask."

"Did you build a secret drawer into Derek's desk?"

Much longer pause. "That's one of those questions that I don't answer."

"One more, then. Have you put secret places in other furniture?"

"I never did like telephones, Beale."

"Those are real questions, Mr. Jones. I'm not trying to trap you. I hope there's some way you could answer them—but I don't like telephones either, to tell the truth."

"I'm hanging this one up."

And he did.

"Will you be busy this afternoon?" Dorothy asked as Charles settled into his desk.

"I'm not sure. I may have made an appointment."

"Who would you be meeting with?"

"Our matchmaker. In the meantime, I would like to take a break from my detective work. Are we still doing a fall catalog, dear?"

"I'm still hoping to."

"Good! Let me at it!"

"Mr. Beale?"

"Yes, Alice?"

"You have a telephone call. Mr. Anthony Prescott from Sotheby's in London."

"Thank you for your half hour," Dorothy said. "Back to work?"

"Not quite. This is actually bookstore business, so it will still count as play." He lifted his telephone. "Hello, this is Charles Beale."

"Mr. Beale, this is Anthony Prescott from Sotheby's in London. We spoke earlier today?"

"Yes, of course. Thank you for calling back, Mr. Prescott. It must be rather late for you. I hope you have some news for me?"

"I'm sorry, Mr. Beale. I can't give you any information about your book."

"What—nothing?"

"My apologies, sir, that we can't help you."

"Do you mean that you don't have any information, or that you can't give it to me?"

"I'm very sorry, sir. That's all I can say."

"Oh. Well, thank you very much, Mr. Prescott."

"Yes, sir. Have a pleasant day."

Charles set the telephone down and stared across the room at Dorothy.

"You look like someone just ran over your dog," she said.

"Yes, poor Argos. I'd finally landed on Ithaca," he said. "And the car that squashed him was Penelope running off with the mailman."

"That's terrible."

"It is." He frowned. "Except that it's seven o'clock in London."

"He must have been working late."

"And on Friday. Odd. Oh, well—that's what I get for hoping."

"I'm sorry, dear," Dorothy said.

"Not at all. Something might turn up. And besides, if someone wanted to buy Odysseus, I would have to sell him."

"And if you did, I might have to spend the money paying these bills."

"Pesky bills! Very well. Speaking of selling books, I need to pick a few more for the catalog. I think I'll look at the shelves downstairs."

Alice's smile was a passable antidepressant and the rows of books even more. Charles browsed them for a while, slipping past literature and travel and into sports.

"Mr. Beale?"

"Yes, Morgan?"

He was sitting on the stairs in his usual pose. "Mrs. Beale said Sotheby's stiffed you?"

"Yes. They did. Very politely."

"Shall I keep looking?"

"You can. Jacob mentioned Padding and Brewster as possible publishers. I know they've been out of business for a century, but there might be some trace still."

"Yes, sir. Didn't Sotheby's have any records of the auction?"

"He wouldn't say. He wouldn't say anything. It must have been some kind of secret."

The front door opened. "Hey, boss."

"Hello, Angelo. How was today's expedition?"

Angelo crossed the room. "I did not see that lady."

"I didn't find what I was looking for today either. How many places have you visited so far?"

He was already two steps up, but he stopped to pay attention. "I have seen ten places."

"Good. Have you done the same thing in each one, where you ask about picking up a package?"

"Every one is the same."

"Have you had any trouble in any of them?"

"No trouble."

"Have any of them treated you nicely?"

Angelo shrugged. "I talk and they talk."

"Do you treat them nicely?"

"I am always nice."

"We need to be sure we have a good definition for that word," Charles said.

The front door opened again.

"Beale."

Charles answered. "Mr. Jones. Good afternoon."

Mr. Jones only said, "Downstairs."

"Of course. This way."

Charles led, barely keeping ahead of the long, fast legs. Alice watched with wide eyes, and Angelo with narrowed ones.

Whump, the bag of coat hangers landed in the chair. *Whupp*, the long legs shot out.

"Okay, Beale, talk."

"I really just have the questions I asked on the telephone."

The chair leaned backward as Mr. Jones became straight, heel to head, at a thirty-degree angle to the floor. His arms crossed behind his head.

"I don't feel like answering them. Think of something else."

"All right. Let's try the auction. You were there, you saw how at least two people desperately wanted Derek Bastien's desk. They bid it up to a hundred thousand dollars. You bid on it, too."

"It's a nice desk."

"It is. But it's worth twenty-five thousand dollars, not a hundred thousand. There's some other reason those two people wanted it so badly."

"I'll tell you this, Beale. I don't know anything about it that's worth that much money."

"But you do know something, and that brings me back to my first question about a secret drawer. Do you put hidden compartments in furniture? Have you ever?"

"Beale, you're walking on thin ice."

"That's almost an answer by itself."

Mr. Jones leaned farther back, and his stare was even more acute. "What's your angle in this, anyway, Beale?"

"I'm trying to do the right thing."

His answer was a bitter, "Yeah, what's that?"

"I think you're not obtuse, Mr. Jones," Charles said. "This is what I'm working with. I saw a copy of a newspaper article about police finding cocaine hidden somehow in a piece of furniture."

Galen Jones leaned forward, slowly, his gray bushy mustache traveling a very long distance to barely a foot from Charles's nose.

"Where did you see that?"

"If you were Derek and you had that paper, where would you keep it?"

Mr. Jones showed he was not obtuse. A fierce light broke in his eyes.

"That lying—" The jaw clamped shut. "I'll kill him."

"He's already dead, of course," Charles said.

"Then he deserved it."

"So you did do something to the desk?"

"Yeah, it's a drawer." He leaned back to a less hostile distance. "So wait a minute. Where did you see that about the cocaine? Do you have the desk?"

"I don't, and I don't know who does. I've already told you a lot. Why don't you tell me what you know?"

"Okay, I'll tell you." He bent forward again, but this time it was to confide. "I met him first three years ago to fix some chess pieces. Highberg set me up with him."

"What was wrong with the chess pieces?"

"His wife broke them."

Charles paused. "Badly?"

"With a hammer. Smashed. I just made him new ones. The two queens."

"This was the wood inlay set in his office?"

"That's where I saw it, on his desk," Mr. Jones said. "So, a couple months later he called back and asked me to build him a hidden drawer in the desk."

"But you hadn't said anything about ever doing that."

"That's the kind of thing I never say."

"It got you in trouble before."

"A friend of a friend. I did him a favor and put a little space under a bed."

"That isn't wrong, is it?" Charles said.

"He made a deal with the cops when he got busted. Every name he could come up with was worth points."

"What happened?"

"It was ugly, but I hadn't done anything. But it won't do me any good if that desk ever gets my name on it. I didn't work for a year after that with all the dealers yakking about me. Do you get that, Beale?"

"I get it, Jones. That's why you tried to buy the desk back?"

"I wanted to just get it out of circulation. But some people have way too much money. For a desk."

"I think they wanted what was in it. Can you tell me what this drawer was like?"

"Yeah. There's eight inches behind the regular drawers on either side. That's just how it was made originally. It's empty space between the drawers and the back of the desk. On the left, there was a small drawer and a larger file drawer. This is what I did. You push them both *into* the desk at the same time, about an inch. If you push either one by itself, it won't go. Push them both and then pull them back out, and when you pull the bottom file drawer all the way out, there's a six-inch box behind that comes out with it. It hangs on the far back. Push the drawer back in, and next time you pull it out, there's no box."

Charles nodded slowly. "It wouldn't be easy to find."

"Depends on how hard someone's looking."

"Would someone just stumble onto it? The movers? The appraiser from the auction house?"

"I don't know. Probably not, if they kept it level. A regular appraisal, you wouldn't find it. If you pull the bottom drawer all the way out by itself and look in where it was, the box just looks like the inside of the desk."

"Whatever was in the drawer when Derek was killed—could it have still been there when the buyer picked it up last week?"

"For all I know, it could be."

"And if that person knew there was a compartment," Charles said, "they would find it."

"Soon enough, they would. They could tear the desk apart and it would be right there."

"Then it's possible that person would have the original contents right now."

"It sounds like you know a lot about what that was," Galen Jones said.

"I've seen some of the papers that may have been in it. How much would this box have held?"

"Six inches. At least a few hundred sheets of paper, or whatever else he put in it. So look, Beale." He backed off entirely, to his full straight length. "I've told you everything I know. From what you say, I don't think I want to know anything else."

"I will be glad not to tell you anything."

"Yeah, let's do that. Like including whatever you think you're doing."

"As I said, just the right thing."

"Lots of times that doesn't work. You might want to be careful."

"I will take your advice, Mr. Jones."

Mr. Jones was finished. He stood, and Charles did also.

"So Bastien had that paper about the cocaine, like it would do him any good."

"I don't know why he had it."

"And he was keeping it in the drawer I made him."

"You weren't the only one."

Mr. Jones was not finished. "I don't get involved." He flexed his fingers. "I just do my job, and I don't ever get involved in anyone else's. Because people that get into each other's business get killed sometimes."

"Are you talking about me or Derek Bastien?"

"Both of you. You really think you're doing the right thing?"

"I have no choice. I'm trying to undo what he did."

"Bastien betrayed me. You can't undo that."

"I'm feeling rather betrayed myself, Mr. Jones. But I still think I can do something for some of the people involved."

Mr. Jones nodded. "Look, you ever need help, call me. Because if you try to do some right thing, you'll probably need any help you can get."

Charles watched as Galen Jones left the shop.

"And have we sold anything, Alice?" he asked.

"Yes, sir, from the games shelf. A book on chess."

"Did you pick the last books?" Dorothy asked.

In slow motion, Charles walked across the office and lowered himself into his chair. "What did you say?"

"Did you pick any books?"

"What books?"

Dorothy took a slow motion breath. "For the catalog, dear. Weren't you downstairs looking?"

"Oh. No, Galen Jones came and we talked."

"He did come? You said he might. What did he want?"

"It's a long story. I need to make a telephone call."

"I can finish the catalog. We only have four more catalog pages to fill."

"Maybe you should, dear." He shook his head to clear it, and gave Dorothy a wistful smile. "This won't be a long call, but I'll have an errand to run after it."

"Who are you calling?"

He was already pushing buttons. "Norman Highberg, please," he said.

And he waited.

"Hello?"

"Norman? This is Charles Beale."

"Charles? I thought you were a customer. Why didn't you tell her who you were?"

"I am a customer."

"You are?" Norman was confused. "What? You mean you want to buy something?"

"Do you still have that chess set?"

"The Austrian wood inlay? Sure. What, you decided you want it?"

"Will you still give me that deal?"

"Thirty-two seventy-five, between friends. Okay. You're keeping it, right? You're not selling it?"

"It's for me."

"Because if someone's going to sell it for five grand, I will. It'll go for five, sooner or later."

"I want to buy it now."

"Okay, sold. Do you want to come get it?"

"Do you deliver?" Charles asked.

"Who, me? Sometimes. My wife's nephew, I send him out sometimes, but he breaks things."

"I wouldn't want it broken. Why don't you bring it, Norman. I think it's your turn to visit my shop, anyway."

"Okay. I can bring it. How about tomorrow?"

"Saturday? That would be fine. We're just open until two, but Dorothy and I will be here most of the day."

"And now, dear," he said, "I am going out."

"This was the errand?"

"I'm going to visit Lucy Bastien Cloverdale."

"Can't you just call her?"

"She told me not to call back."

"Well, Charles, that might mean she doesn't want you to visit either."

"She didn't say that. I don't think she'll turn me away."

"And you said it was terrible seeing the house changed," Dorothy said.

"I've gotten over it. It couldn't be as big a shock or insult this time."

"Anybody ever call you Charlie?" Lucy Bastien said, leaning against the front door.

Charles blinked.

"I was wrong."

"What?"

"Something I had just said to my wife. Never mind."

A stale, sticky smell drifted by.

"May I come in? I just wanted to talk for a moment. I won't be long. I hope you won't mind?"

"I don't mind anything. Why should I mind?"

She moved aside and Charles led the way into the front room. There was a loud crunch of wicker as they sat.

"What can I do you for, Charlie?" She threw a sloppy smile across the yellowness.

"I just had a question or two. I was looking at the books I bought at the auction."

"Auction. Oh, the auction! What about them?"

"I was wondering . . . I wondered if anyone might have done anythi' to them. Before the auction."

"Before." She frowned and thought very hard. "Maybe, um, who he was. Maybe he did."

"Who?"

"You know, started with a *D*. Derek. Maybe he did."

"I mean after . . ."

"After he got walloped, you mean?"

"Right."

"Well, let's see. The police were here and they didn't le'

233

in the house for a couple days. I called the auction place and they said they'd come when the police went away."

"How long was everything here in the house?"

"I wanted it out of here as fast as it could go. Figured it was worth bundles so why not sell it? I told the auction man to come get it."

"So, just a few days?"

"I needed to get rid of it all so I could get the place painted."

"Of course. They took everything? Even the furniture?"

"Every historic five-hundred-year-old Louis the Fortieth splinter of it. I said if it was older than the milk in my refrigerator, I wanted it out. I drink a lot of milk. You want some milk?"

"No thank you. I wonder—do you think anyone could have touched anything in the house before the auction people came and took it?"

"Nobody came."

"Could someone have broken in?"

"They already did. Why do it again?"

"Why, indeed? I suppose once was enough. There were all those police around, too."

"Gobs."

"I wonder, Lucy. Why did you smash Derek's chess set?"

A huge grin appeared. "Did he tell you I did? Well, goody! Maybe he did care!"

"Of course he'd care."

"You think he did? Wrong-oh, buddy. I figured I could get his attention. You think I did? He never said a word, and next thing I see, the pieces are back." Her eyes got big, and she whispered, "Spooky."

"He got new ones."

"Oh. That's what it was. I hope they cost him a bundle."

"I think they did. Did you smash many of his things?"

"No, that was the only time. I would have done more if he'd shown some appreciation."

Charles nodded sympathetically. "Do you tend toward violence, Lucy?"

"Not so much anymore. I get tired too easy."

"What did you say happened to your first husband?"

"He died." And so had the conversation. "See you later, Charlie. Time for my nap. The door's that way."

"I am back," Charles said.

"Just in time to go home. Is fish still emotionally disturbing?"

"No, I've regained my sea legs. And maybe some rice?"

"Yes, there will be rice. Did I hear from your call to Norman High-berg that we are getting a chess set?"

"Yes. Derek's set."

"What will we do with it?"

"I don't know," Charles said. "It's very nice. We could just have it in the showroom. It would fit right in."

"And will you tell me about your other adventures this afternoon? Mr. Jones, and Lucy Bastien?"

"They were adventures. But first, dear, I want to figure out the answers to all the questions you would ask."

EVENING

Dinner was over. The kitchen window was open to the evening air.

"What did Odysseus do to deserve such a punishment?"

Dorothy handed him a plate.

"He made Poseidon angry."

Charles put the plate in the cabinet. "Was that wrong?"

"No, it was Greek." She turned the water on in the sink and set a pot in it to fill. "I should have soaked this. It's hard as a rock."

"What did you do to deserve that?"

"I burned the rice."

"Please. Allow me." He took the scouring pad from her.

"Gladly, dear."

"Can you think of any place in classical Greek literature," Charles said, "where someone suffers on behalf of someone else?"

"Like you're doing for me with the pot?"

"Oh, maybe on a more epic scale." He scrubbed, hard. "Although this does seem Herculean."

"Alcestis. Do you remember? King Admetus was about to die, but Apollo talks the Fates into giving him a reprieve as long as he can get someone else to die in his place. He thinks maybe one of his aged parents will, but they won't. Finally his wife, Alcestis, says she will."

"I don't think I remember this at all," Charles said.

"There is a play by Euripides. As she is being taken to the underworld, Admetus realizes that Alcestis is better off than he is. He has to mourn for her, and his life will always be filled with sorrow and strife. But she will never suffer again."

"So she doesn't suffer on his behalf."

"In Greek mythology," Dorothy said, "everyone suffers. Hercules happens by on the day of the funeral, tears open the tomb, wrestles Thanatos, the god of death, to the ground and makes him let Alcestis go."

"So they all get to suffer on through life together." He gave up on the pot and left it to soak. "If a person does something wrong, what can they do? Do they have the stain forever?"

"Well, of course not."

"Exactly. There are two options: punishment and redemption. In the case of someone like Karen Liu, I know what the punishment would be. She would probably lose her position in Congress, and possibly go to jail. It would be worse than what happened to Patrick White."

"If those checks really represent a crime."

"Which we don't know for sure," Charles said. "But assuming they do, what is the alternate to punishment? What would redemption look like for her?"

"Everything she's done in Congress," Dorothy said. "You think she's accomplished lots of good things."

"Legally, that doesn't matter. But should it morally?"

"What difference would that make?"

"It makes a difference to me. If I have to decide what to do with the papers, should I consider that her good works outweigh the bad?"

"That's not exactly what redemption is."

"No," Charles said. "And that was where my question came from, about one person suffering for another. That's what redemption really is."

"In the case with Karen Liu, who would suffer for whom? In real redemption, not just anyone's suffering would count."

"No. It would have to be someone who's earned the right."

"I think your queen is in trouble, Charles."

"She has been from the fifth move, Derek. That's the problem with bringing her out so soon."

"You're usually more conservative with her."

"I thought I would try to upset your expectations."

"In this case, Charles, perhaps you shouldn't have. There."

"Then . . . there."

"It doesn't help. The lowly pawn moves . . . and there, you can't save her now."

"Perhaps. I'll try this."

"Wait. Let me see what that does. Ha! Very clever. And that means . . . at least I take your knight. Poor fellow. Nothing of his own doing, was it, Charles? The queen makes a mistake, and the knight pays for it."

"They are all in it together, Derek. Don't ask for whom the bell tolls, it tolls for thee. And there. That'll make up for it anyway."

SATURDAY

MORNING

The sky was a maze of light-punctured clouds. A clever beam could break through the shifting layers, evade fast-moving curls and strands, and attain the streets of Alexandria. An especially bright ray landed on the bookshop's steps at the same time Charles did.

The brightest light was already inside.

"Hello, dear," he said to her.

Dorothy looked up from behind the counter. "Was everything all right?"

"Yes. Packages are mailed and staples are bought."

"Thank you. And do you have any plans for the rest of the morning?"

"If nothing else comes along," he said, "I have some work to do in the basement. It looks like some of Morgan's inventory orders from Briary Roberts came in yesterday afternoon. Do you have anything you'd like me to do?"

"I'm low on change in the cash register."

"I will go out and get you some. And have we sold anything yet this morning?"

"I hesitate to tell you, Charles."

"Oh, good! It must be something fun! What is it?"

"A *Complete Shakespeare*."

"What outrageous fortune!"

"Please keep its slings and stones to yourself. Alice is not in on Saturdays, and I refuse to play your games."

"But it is who I am, dear."

"Then try not to be."

"That is the answer?"

"Yes, and I would like you to leave now, at least until you get it out of your system. You could go get my change. I need ones and fives."

"I'll go." Charles smiled. "I know a bank, where the—"

"Stop. Do not say anything else."

"For you, my love, I will be silent. My kingdom to be hoarse!"

Dorothy giggled. "You are incorrigible."

The sun had seized more of the sky by the time he again approached the front steps. He opened the door and stepped over its bright threshold.

"Congresswoman!" he cried. "I'm so glad to see you!"

"Thank you!" She glowed in emerald and gold, as if a beam of light had even found its way to the middle of the room. "I loved this!" She held the Proverbs Garden like evidence at a trial. "I just loved it."

"I'm so glad," Charles said, just reaching the floor.

"And I want to buy it."

He finally reached her. "You can get less expensive copies."

"I want this one," she said. "A copy wouldn't be the same."

"Then I'm honored."

"And I just loved talking to your wife."

"I always do, too," Charles said.

"Now I want you to show me more of your store."

"Then I need to take you downstairs."

"These are the old books."

The whole political exterior slid away. Karen Liu was as purely amazed as John Borchard had been.

"There are so many . . ." she said.

"About three thousand."

And finally she said, "I don't know what to say."

"I don't really either," Charles said. "The books just speak for themselves."

"They do." She began to recover. "How long have you been doing this?"

"Thirty years."

"How did you start?"

"Dorothy and I were just out of college and just married. We decided to give it a go."

"Why books?"

"Well, let's see. I was in history and Dorothy majored in English. We wanted to stay in Alexandria. And we both liked books." He smiled. "And it worked, despite our youth and inexperience. We started out of our house, and it took about five years to build up to a storefront."

"Did you have anything to start with?"

"I had four books that my grandfather owned."

"And now you have all this."

"We made a few fortunate discoveries early on. Prices have risen over three decades, so we rode the ups and downs and put the inventory together. Now we have to compete against the Internet, but it makes it easier to find things ourselves."

"What is all of this worth?"

"We could say about ten million, but it's very soft. It could drop by half overnight if something changed the market."

"That is amazing. I have never had a head for business."

"You've had your own successes, of course," Charles said.

She was done being amazed. "Yes. I have. Mr. Beale, when you were starting out—what compromises did you have to make?"

"I had to settle for less than I wanted many times."

"What if there had been an offer for help, but it meant compromising?

What if the only other choice meant giving up on ever having a store?" She was the most intense, and tense, that he had seen her. "Do you understand what I'm talking about, Mr. Beale?"

"I'm glad I never had to make that choice. Besides, I'm a different person now than I was then. I think I can only answer for what I'd do now. What would you do?"

"What would I do now?"

"What would you do now," Charles asked, "if you had to make a choice like that?"

She said flatly and firmly, "I would turn it down."

"I hope I would, too." Then, just as firmly, he said, "Please tell me about Patrick White."

It was hard to tell what was going on inside her.

"We've been friends a long time," she said, not so firmly.

"A professional relationship?"

"We met at a Bar Association luncheon the first year I was in Congress. He became my unofficial advisor on judicial matters."

"And you were friends?"

"We were kindred spirits. For both of us, the Law, and the legal system, was our lives. And occasionally, Mr. Beale, for social gatherings, a lady may appreciate a gallant escort. Even me."

"Even you." Charles sighed. "Then I especially convey my regrets."

"It is very regrettable." She was especially grim.

"But I take it you still communicate?"

"We still have a few things in common, even now."

"You mentioned that on the telephone," Charles said. "I understood there was some connection between you and Mr. White, and I think also John Borchard and Derek. Mr. White described a bill that Mr. Borchard wanted to pass through Congress."

"The Sentencing Reform Act. Yes, that is part of the connection between us all."

"Mr. White was against it, but you allowed it through your committee."

"Another compromise, Mr. Beale. I'm not proud of it. Patrick White was very disappointed."

"But you had to make a difficult decision," Charles said.

"It went against my values and it still troubles me very much."

"What could you do about it now?"

Karen Liu took her time to answer. "That law makes it difficult for judges to use their own judgment. It's very hard on people convicted of crimes, and those are the people I want to help."

"Hey, boss."

Charles was startled, more than usual; but Karen Liu nearly hit the roof, far from her head though it was.

"Angelo," Charles said. "Good morning."

"Do you want for me to go to any of the places today?"

"You could call and see if any are open on Saturday. Congresswoman, this is Angelo, my employee. Angelo, this is Congresswoman Liu."

Angelo's eyes shifted slightly to notice her. Karen Liu's reaction was more substantial. She stepped across the room, her hand stretched forward, her eyes full on him. Angelo was not sure for a moment what to do.

He drew back first like a cornered animal. Then, perhaps not consciously, he bared his teeth and tightened his shoulders, ready to fight.

Karen Liu didn't flinch. "It's a pleasure to meet you," she said, "Mr. . . . ?"

"Acevedo," Charles said. "You can shake her hand, Angelo."

He surrendered, very stiffly, and Charles watched.

"I am very glad to meet you, Mr. Acevedo," she said. "What do you do here for Mr. Beale?"

"Whatever he says to do." The voice was as hard as the hand.

"Angelo," Charles said, "you could ask Mrs. Beale to call any places on the list if you want. If none of them are open, just wait until Monday morning."

"On Monday morning is my probation meeting," he said.

"Oh, yes, of course we'll do that first."

Angelo nodded, barely, and stepped back onto the bottom step.

Only several stairs up did he have a safe enough distance to turn his back on them.

"Probation?" she said. Her intense stare was now fully back on Charles.

"Just a formality," he said.

"You go with him? Is he under your supervision?"

"Well, yes. It's a long story."

She thought for a few seconds. "What do you think of having someone under your control?"

"He's not under my control."

"I understand probation. If you are his supervisor, you have a lot of control."

"I don't like having control over someone else. It goes against my nature."

"Not everyone is like that. Please tell me the long story."

"I'll make it short," Charles said. "Let's see, it was last summer. I was walking home from the Metro station one night, fairly late, and I was on a dark street, and I met Angelo."

The congresswoman frowned. "And he was Hispanic, and dressed roughly, and he seemed threatening to you."

"Well, actually, he was holding a knife and he told me to give him my wallet."

The frown softened. "All right. Go on."

"So I did give him my wallet, and when I got home, I called the police. That was more out of civic duty. I wasn't hurt and it wasn't much money, and it was a good reminder to be more careful."

"What did your wife say?"

"Oh, I didn't tell her."

"You didn't tell your wife that you'd been held up?"

"I just said I'd lost my wallet. But then the police called back the next morning and said they'd found him. Then I had to tell her. We went down to the police station, and there he was, under arrest."

"For armed robbery? Why isn't he in jail now?"

"Actually, I found out who was assigned as his lawyer, and I talked to that person, and we went to the Alexandria Probation Office and worked out a proposal for the judge. Dorothy and I offered for Angelo to stay here and work for us and we would supervise him for the term of his probation."

The frown had softened all the way to bewilderment. Karen Liu was as expressive as John Borchard, even with a much smaller area to work with.

"Why?"

"That might be harder to answer." Charles smiled. "It certainly wasn't to gain power over him."

"You said last week that you preferred mercy," she said. "Now I understand what you meant. Some people might say they prefer mercy, but not many would put their money where their mouth was." She shook her head. "And the judge let you do it. There was no gun involved? Just a knife?"

"It was a very big knife." Charles laughed. "I was scared silly."

"How has he been as an employee?"

"There were a few adjustments, of course. He'd never had a job. But he lives in the attic now, and he's figured out some basic handyman skills, and he's our night guard and maintenance man and courier."

"You're turning his life around, Mr. Beale."

"He's doing it himself."

"How long is his probation?"

"Three years. We've finished the first six months. He has to provide satisfaction as an employee, keep us informed of his location, stay away from former associates, not break any laws, of course, and report to his probation officer every month."

Karen Liu seemed satisfied. Charles was released from her gaze, and his eyes wandered.

"Hey, boss."

"Yes, Angelo."

He was still and silent as usual, framed once more in the stairway door. His rooted stance seemed to show he had been there for a while.

"Mrs. Boss, she says no place on that list is open now."

"All right. I don't have anything else for you to do."

Angelo's eyes were black reflections of the room. He stood a moment longer, then left before the congresswoman had recovered enough to greet him again.

"I don't know what goes on inside him," Charles said, watching the empty space. "Anyway. Is there anything else we need to discuss?"

"No, Mr. Beale. I think I understand why Derek found you so fascinating."

"I'm really not."

"I think you are. I like your preference for mercy. I came here this morning to ask you about your talks with John Borchard, and with Patrick White, and especially with Derek. I don't think you're going to tell me anything, but I think I am going to trust you. Does that make any sense to you?"

"I know there is something wrong, Congresswoman. I don't know very much. But if there is anything I can do to help, I will."

"Then let's leave it at that."

"What did you talk about?" Dorothy asked. They were alone in the showroom.

"Books."

"Any books in particular?"

"I think we both decided to just trust each other, and not ask more questions." Charles shook his head. "We talked about Angelo."

"I called some of the offices on his list."

"Yes, he told me."

Then Charles held up one finger, and Dorothy was quiet. At the absolute limits of human perception, there was a creak from the hall upstairs.

"He's coming," Charles whispered.

They saw his tennis shoes on the stairs, then his ragged jeans, then him. He saw them watching.

"Hey, Angelo," Charles said.

"I am going out on the street," he said.

"All right. I don't think we'll need you today. I'll be downstairs unpacking boxes."

He crossed the room, but as he passed by Charles, he stopped, very close.

"You were not scared," he said.

"What?" Charles said, unsure.

"You were not scared. I know how people are scared. With that knife, you were not scared." Then he left.

All the lights in the basement were on. On the desk was a stacked mosaic of books, some with faded dust jackets and some with just faded covers, mortared together with printouts and price lists and catalogs. Charles put a final price sticker on a once-bright *Good Night, Moon,* and gave his attention to one last unopened box.

It was well packed inside and took a few minutes to burrow down to the one book inside.

The front cover was the same dun brown as many of the books watching from the shelves, but two of the corners were mashed round and wrinkled. The back cover had a jagged scar, but only skin deep. The spine was also torn, with its top pulled loose and hanging. The book was very thick, at least two inches.

Charles opened the cover to the title inside.

The Divine Comedy
Dante Alighieri
Transl. by Henry Wadsworth Longfellow

And then to the next page.

The Inferno: Canto I

And then to the first lines.

Midway upon the journey of our life
I found myself within a forest dark,
For the straightforward pathway had been lost.
Ah me! how hard a thing it is to say
What was this forest savage, rough, and stern,
Which in the very thought renews the fear.

AFTERNOON

"It's two o'clock. Shall we close the door?" Dorothy asked from above.

"Go ahead," Charles said. "But keep an eye out for Norman."

"Will you be down there much longer?"

"A little while more. Morgan managed to get quite a few books."

"Anything special?"

"Mostly standards. The Dante is nice. It'll take some repair."

"I can come to—oh, Charles, Norman Highberg is here."

"Norman! How are you?"

"I'm okay." Norman peered at the showroom walls. A large cardboard box was nestled in his two hands. "You sure have a lot of books."

"I do. That's what I sell. Thank you so much for coming."

"Gasoline costs more than I'm making on this."

"It isn't that bad. Maybe I can sell you something at a discount."

"Like what?"

"A book?"

"I don't do books."

"I don't do chess sets either. I'm not buying it to sell it, just to use it. You could just have a book for yourself."

Norman was very perplexed. "I don't get it. How do you use a book?"

"You open it and look at the words."

"Oh, you mean read it."

"That's exactly it," Charles said. "Anyway. I suppose that's the set?" He looked down at the box. "This is it."

"Let's crack it open," Charles said. "Here, on the counter."

Norman set the box on the counter. He scrunched his glasses up his nose and pushed his hair out of his eyes.

"I need a haircut," he said. "You know a good place? The place I go, it's no good. I've been going for years."

"Why do you go there?" Dorothy asked.

"I need to get my hair cut."

Charles said, "Is it somebody you're related to?"

"Me?" Norman said. "No."

"I just wondered," Charles said.

"He's related to my wife. It's her cousin. He's no good." He had the flaps of the box open and he started taking out individual wrapped packets. "You've got to wrap each one."

"So, we'll unwrap each one." He handed two to Dorothy and peeled the paper off another.

It was a knight. Norman paused to peer over his glasses.

"Mahogany. See the grain? The base is teak. The white pieces are chestnut and cherry. You can't get chestnut anymore. Now look at this. How they're joined? Perfect, right? And see, it's not glued. The pin goes through the base." He held the base and pulled the figure. There was no movement between them.

"Why wouldn't it just be glued?" Charles asked.

"Because that's too easy. This is show-off work. And talk about showing off? Here's the board."

His motions were pure grace as he took the paper off, and the board deserved every flourish. Every square was framed by the four woods inlaid, one on each side, creating an illusion of three-dimensional bevels. The outer frame was both intricate and elegant, a dense cascade of overlapping, variably sized squares like the froth of a wave.

"It's dazzling," Dorothy said. "It looks like a Klimt."

"It *is* Austrian, 1890s," Charles said. "Or maybe it's Sigmund Freud's psyche."

"I don't know about that stuff," Norman said. "But you can tell it's the real thing."

"What will we do with it, Charles?" Dorothy said.

"I want to have it here in the showroom," he said. "You wouldn't have some kind of table, would you, Norman?"

"I don't do furniture. There's a zillion places to buy tables."

"Just in Alexandria alone. Would there have been a stand for it?"

"Sure," Norman said. "Who knows where it is now, in Tokyo or someplace if it didn't get blown up in some war."

"What would it have looked like?"

"It would have been a square top, about four inches on each side, bigger than the board with a recess to fit it in and a big heavy column leg with some kind of flared bottom."

"Derek just kept the board on his desk, to one side. He'd move it to the center to play."

Norman shook his head. "I never figured that game out. I mean, who came up with it? Checkers, that makes sense. Everything moves the same way."

"If you appreciate that people are different, Norman, you appreciate that chess pieces are different."

"If everyone were the same, it'd be a lot simpler."

"Yes, it would."

"You played that game with him," Norman asked.

"Yes," Charles said. "Eight or ten times over the years."

"So who won?"

"I did."

"How many times?"

"Every time."

"You never told me that!" Dorothy said.

"That's why he kept playing me," Charles said. "You sold the set to Derek originally, didn't you?" he asked Norman.

"Yeah. First thing I sold him. Ten years ago at least."

"Where did you get it?"

"Germany. It was part of a bunch of loot left over from the Nazis. They got everything they could back to whoever owned it before the war, and then they auctioned the rest for the Jewish Reparation Fund. Good cause."

"And it had all been stolen by the Nazis," Charles said. "There must have been quite a variety."

"Some of them had good taste. It was everything—art, furniture, jewelry—everything. And that was just the stuff the government recovered after the war. A lot of it went underground."

"What do you know about that underground market, Norman? The market for stolen art."

"A little. I've got to, you know? In my business you've got to."

Dorothy had unwrapped the white queen, and Charles took it from her. There was no play in the pin holding the chestnut figure to the cherry base. "Where do you think Derek's stolen pieces are now?"

"Three places," Norman said. "In a basement somewhere, you know, or buried or something. Or in some rich guy's parlor that bought the whole bag. Or else at the bottom of the Potomac. That's where they'd be if the guy that stole them was smart."

"How would the guy that stole them find the rich guy that wanted to buy them?" Charles said.

"How do any of those guys find each other?" Norman said. "But they do. They always do."

"Could you find one?"

"Why should I want to? Except I could use the money, and that would be no taxes on the sale. You know how much I pay in taxes? What's it like in Virginia? It must be lower than D.C."

"I suppose," Charles said. "Here, Norman, look at this queen. What do you think?"

Norman looked close, then very close. "Let me see the other queen."

They found it, and Norman looked close again. "It doesn't exactly match the other pieces. The carving, you know? But the queens match each other. And the colors don't match exact either. But it's chestnut, and who can get chestnut? It must be from the same workshop." He looked very, very close. "I don't know. Maybe it was a different carver?"

"I think Lucy Bastien, Derek's wife, mentioned something about the queens. I hadn't ever looked close."

"Then she's got a good eye. It's good stuff. So maybe they don't match exactly, but you've got to have an eye to see it, and they're maybe the best work of the whole set."

"Very good, then," Charles said. "Here is a check, and I'm very glad to have the whole set. We'll keep it in the basement for now. I just wish I had someone to play with."

"I'd like to speak to Mr. Galen Jones, please. This is Charles Beale." He waited.

"Beale. Now what do you want?"

"I want you to build a table for me."

"What table?" There was some suspicion and a little curiosity.

"Do you remember Derek Bastien's chess set, Mr. Jones?"

"Sure. I told you I replaced the queens."

"I have that set now. Norman Highberg says it would have had a matching table once. I'd like for you to make one for me."

"Okay . . ." For the first time, there was less suspicion in his voice than interest. "I'll come look at it."

"Please. At your convenience."

"My convenience is Thursday. Are you always there?"

"Usually," Charles said. "You could call. Or no, we should meet up at Norman Highberg's. He'll know just how the table should look."

"Okay, ten o'clock?"

"Good. I'll bring the board."

"The pieces, too. But just don't tell Highberg I ever touched them. So, Beale, anybody asking you about the desk lately?"

"It's come up, but I haven't said your name."

"Just keep doing the right thing, okay?"

EVENING

" 'To be, or not to be? That is the question.' "

"Are you still being Shakespearian, Charles?" Dorothy said. They were together in their parlor, but Charles had no book in his hand.

"No, it is a question. Wasn't Hamlet's great flaw that he couldn't make up his mind?"

"He did have that problem."

"I do, too."

"You've been hoping for better choices."

"None have presented themselves," Charles said.

"I think I've lost track of all your conversations with everyone."

"There is one point, dear, that is especially troubling me. It is from Galen Jones, on Friday. I have been trying to work out what it means."

A breeze troubled the curtains.

"What, dear?"

"There was a hidden drawer in Derek's desk. Mr. Jones put it there."

The hidden breeze stirred the air in the room. "But Derek's papers were in the book you bought."

"Some papers were."

Some of the breeze swirled about him; some twirled about her.

"You think there were more papers?"

"I know he had a drawer and a book, and I have what was in the book."

"Then what was in the drawer?"

"I do not know," Charles said. "But the point that is most troubling to me isn't what was in each place, but why."

"I don't understand."

"What is it about the papers in the book that he chose to keep them there, instead of in the drawer?" The breeze died in a maze of eddies. "Alas, poor Derek, I thought I knew him well."

"Again! Five games, Charles, and I have yet to capture your elusive king."

"They have all been very close, Derek."

"And I think I see your methods. You hold back your stronger pieces longer than most players."

"They're wasted on a crowded board. Pawns are the power in the beginning, when they hold territory. All the other pieces' tactics have to cooperate with them."

"I've seen that you don't like giving them up."

"Sentiment, Derek. I don't have the ruthless streak a real master would."

"And you need to use your knights better."

"That is my other weakness. They have the greatest strategic potential, but I can't see far enough ahead with them."

"You did quite well in taking my castle, Charles."

"Sometimes I notice an opportunity, Derek! On the crowded board, they're very strong, but they weaken compared to the other pieces as the board clears. I trade them too quickly, while they're still more useful than a bishop. The key is to know the right moment, when their capabilities are becoming less useful."

"And then sacrifice them."

"Trade them. I think it's a better word."

"You mean it's a less ruthless word."

"No. A trade is for mutual advantage, and even as opponents, we choose *trades that benefit us both. A sacrifice is giving something up for no return. It might have no place in chess, Derek, but it has in real life."*

"Which is why I like chess, Charles. It mirrors my life quite well."

"I would think that was a callous statement, Derek, if I didn't know that you say such things just to provoke me."

"All right then, Charles, consider this: If I am the callous one, and chess is a ruthless game, why do you always beat me?"

SUNDAY

MORNING

The stone held away a steady rain.

Charles and Dorothy sat in the still dimness for their quiet hour. The muted, silent roar of sky-sent water on hard earth-anchored roof was the only answer to every thought and question.

The service began and they sang as they did every week, and the heavens replied with their streams.

They listened.

"Look at the world we have to live in. Our purpose might be to live the best we can in this world of decisions and challenges and tragedy. We would serve God, and the best lived life wouldn't be the most successful or accomplished, but the life that served God most sincerely. What would God's role be in a world like that? Just to watch and keep score in a grand game?

"No. The vast difference between our lives and a game, the great single fact of our lives, is Christ's sacrifice. Our lives cost him dearly, and that alone makes them desperately valuable. We have great worth because a great price was paid for us."

AFTERNOON

"He cost us dearly," Charles said. His suit was gray, and Dorothy's coat was black. The umbrella was black and the rain was gray.

"He was very dear to us," Dorothy said. The upright stone was gray. All the stones were gray and upright in the emerald grass, and the rain darkened them to black.

"Desperately valuable," Charles said. "If only I could have given enough."

"Oh, Charles. If only I knew why."

"If only we knew why."

He held the umbrella over them as seas fell around them, and seas rose within them.

EVENING

The rain had fallen and was all on its way to the sea. Only chill, moist winds were left, and the smell of the rain in the open window.

"I think I'm ready to be finished," Charles said.

"Finished with what?"

"Secrets and sins and confusions."

"How will you finish with them, Charles?"

"When we were out there this afternoon with William, I thought I knew."

"What did you know?"

But he shook his head. "Don't ask me yet."

"*Of our philosophers, Charles, did any practice what they preached?*"

"*Do you mean, were any of them more than theorists?*"

"*Yes. They could scribble their reams, but did they live any of their principles? Adams risked his life to put his signature on the Declaration.*"

"*Madison would be the real example. He was the real brains behind the Constitution, and then he had to govern by it for eight years.*"

"*Hoisted on his own petard, wasn't he, Charles? He had his theories about divided government, and then he had to pay the price when he was president. He must have wished at times he'd written the Constitution differently.*"

"*But he knew what he was getting into. You know, Derek, I think his experience in real governance would have convinced him that his theory of governance was correct. He would have been willing to pay the price.*"

"*And Thomas Hobbes was exiled to Paris.*"

"*And Voltaire was exiled from Paris.*"

"*I would have preferred Hobbes's position, Charles. Yes, I suppose many of them did pay some price for their ideas.*"

"*Derek, do you have any theories or ideals for which you would risk your life?*"

"*Not at all. Power and control aren't theories. What about you, Charles?*"

"*I do, Derek. Though I rather hope it doesn't come to that.*"

MONDAY

MORNING

"Good morning, Alice. A new week."

"Yes, Mr. Beale! And a man called a few minutes ago for you. I told him you'd be in about now."

"Who was it?"

"He didn't say, but he was British."

The telephone on the counter rang.

"Alexandria Rare Books," Alice said, and then she nodded. "It's him," she said.

"I'll get it up in the office."

Dorothy was at her desk. Charles popped over to his own and blew her a kiss.

"This is Charles Beale."

"Mr. Beale." The voice was very British. "My name is Mr. Smith."

"Good morning, Mr. Smith. Or afternoon?"

"Morning, and a very good morning to you." It wasn't clipped, nasal, competent British; it was unhurried, assured, very competent British. It wasn't British at all; it was English. "Mr. Beale, I think you might have something of interest to me."

"I hope I do. What would that be?"

"An Alexander Pope Homer."

Charles waved to get Dorothy's attention.

"The *Odyssey*?"

"Yes, that's it."

He had her attention.

"I do have a Pope *Odyssey*. I hadn't listed it for sale yet."

"All the better, Mr. Beale. Please don't. I'd rather discuss a private purchase."

"Well, certainly, Mr. . . . Smith. We can discuss that. I expect you'd like to see it?"

"I would very much."

"Do you know where we are in Alexandria?" Charles asked.

"Please allow me to suggest a different location."

The grammar was of a very polite request, but the tone, while also very polite, was not a request.

"Of course," Charles said. "Where would you like to meet?"

"I will be at Rusterman's on Twenty-eighth Street in Manhattan on Wednesday evening at nine o'clock."

Charles wrote quickly on a notepad. "Nine o'clock. Rusterman's. Yes, I'll be there. Is there any way to reach you, Mr. Smith, if I need to?"

"I'm sure there will be no need, Mr. Beale. I'm also sure there will be no need to mention this to anyone else."

"Certainly."

"Very good. Then, until Wednesday."

"I look forward to meeting you," Charles said.

"What is Rusterman's?" Dorothy asked.

"Apparently, a restaurant in New York."

"You're going to New York?"

"Apparently. On Wednesday. How interesting!"

"Did he say how he heard we had the book?"

"No. He was English, and said his name was Smith. Although he didn't sound like a Smith."

"What did he sound like?"

"Oh, a Hampton-Smythe, or a Bolingbroke or something like that. Or . . ." Charles stared back toward the telephone. "Or maybe a Saxe-Coburg-Gotha."

"A *what*?"

"Just a thought. Never mind. Anyway, did we ever finish the fall catalog?"

"Yes, dear," Dorothy said. "It is at the printer."

"Thank you, dear."

"And Angelo's meeting starts in thirty minutes."

"Mr. Beale?" Alice was smiling in the doorway.

"Yes?"

"You have a telephone call. Mr. Edmund Cane."

"New York again!" Charles said. "I wonder if he's still looking for the woman who bought Derek's desk?"

"Mr. Cane! Good morning! This is Charles Beale."

"Good morning, Mr. Beale." The syllables were as distinct and unconnected as ever.

"What can I do for you? Are you still looking for your desk?"

"No, Mr. Beale. I am afraid the Honaker desk is rather a dead subject at this point."

"A dead subject—not literally, I hope?"

Pause. "No. I didn't mean that literally."

"Of course. Anyway, what *can* I do for you?"

"I believe you purchased some books at that auction?"

"Yes," Charles said. "I did."

"I would like to purchase those from you."

"All of them?"

"I believe it was thirteen volumes? Yes, I would want all of them."

"Mr. Cane—I'm sorry, but they aren't for sale."

"I see. I hope they haven't been purchased by someone else?"

"No. I have them."

"Are they committed to someone else?" Mr. Cane said, inexorably.

"No."

"I am prepared to offer above market price."

"You certainly did for the desk."

Another confused pause. "Is price important to you?"

"No. Price is not the issue."

"Then may I ask what is?"

"It is simply that they aren't currently for sale," Charles said.

"I see. In that case, I hope you will let me know when they are. The offer would stand."

"Thank you, Mr. Cane. May I ask what your interest in them is? I suppose you have a client?"

"I won't comment on that."

"Well, then, I think we've run out of things to say."

"I will try again later, Mr. Beale."

"Please do."

"What was that?" Dorothy asked.

"Mr. Cane wants Derek's books."

"Charles—what does that mean?"

"It means too much to think about. However, it's time for me to leave."

And on cue, Angelo was standing in the doorway.

Charles checked his watch. Angelo stood beside him, patiently silent.

"It's time," Charles said. He opened the heavy door, and they passed from the sunlight into the courthouse lobby. The guard eyed them.

"Your knife?" Charles asked.

"I do not have any knife here."

Charles emptied his pockets to go through the metal detector; keys, wallet, change, his magnifying glass. Angelo had nothing.

Then corridors, up and down, left and right, back and forth, to and through the door that said *Probation Services*, into its small lobby, and sitting to wait.

"Angelo Acevedo."

They stood and passed through the open door into the cheap, plain little office, and closed the door behind them.

"Good morning, Angelo."

"Good morning, Mr. Conway."

Mr. Conway wasn't old, but he was shiny bald with a fringe of black. "And, Mr. Beale."

"Yes, good morning," Charles said.

Mr. Conway had an open folder on his desk. He read with his finger, which moved across the paper in front of him, line by line, inching down to the bottom. "How is everything?"

"It is good," Angelo said.

"Good. Mr. Beale?"

"Everything is going quite well, Mr. Conway."

"Did anything happen this month?"

Charles answered. "Angelo has been conscientious at his job, as usual. This last week I've had him out on business calls by himself and I believe he's been doing very well at that."

"Have there been any problems? Contacts with previous associates?"

"I really don't think so," Charles said.

"Okay." Mr. Conway closed the folder; his finger got out just in time. He looked up at them with a bureaucratic smile. "Then I think—"

And the door opened.

Everything plain and routine about the meeting collapsed. Mr. Conway's mouth dropped open and Angelo hardened into pure rock.

Charles blinked, and partly smiled, and said, "Congresswoman Liu! What a surprise!"

Karen Liu took in the room in a deliberate glance and planted herself directly behind Angelo.

"Good morning, Mr. Beale," she said.

"Mr. Conway," Charles said, almost up to normal conversational speed. "Allow me to introduce Congresswoman Karen Liu. This is Mr. Conway, our probation officer."

"Congresswoman . . . ?" Mr. Conway said.

"Every bit," Charles said.

"Good morning," Karen Liu said. "I am very pleased to meet you, Mr. Conway, and please excuse my interruption. I am here on behalf of Mr. Acevedo."

"I'm honored, ma'am," Mr. Conway said, very calmly. "What can I do for you?"

"I have taken an interest in this case," she said. "Please let me make it perfectly clear that I am *not* using my position in the Congress of the United States, and as the Chairwoman of the Subcommittee on Judicial Policy, to influence the due procedures of your office. I am here *only* as an advocate for Mr. Acevedo, to be sure that he is being treated fairly and according to the law."

"I can assure you he is," Charles said. "Mr. Conway has been extremely helpful and supportive."

"Ms. Liu," Mr. Conway said, "are you here as a character witness for Angelo?"

"I am here as a witness for Mr. Acevedo." The intensity of her stare had reached searchlight proportions. "I am also here as witness of the system. I am here on behalf of every person in this country who is struggling with a judicial system and an economic system that is too often set against them. Mr. Conway, I had my office review the public records of this case. I have interviewed Mr. Beale."

The spotlight beam dimmed dramatically to a quiet glow.

"I believe," she said, passionately, pleadingly, patiently, "that the terms of this probation should be reviewed immediately. There has been no violation of any of his probationary conditions. Mr. Acevedo has been a model employee and citizen, and I believe that an additional two years of probation is unnecessary." With a hint more firmness she added, "And excessive."

"The judge set the terms," Mr. Conway said, still very calm. "He would have to make any decision to change them. I only administer the court's orders."

"I am quite familiar with judicial procedures," she said. "So I would like your office to request an immediate hearing to reconsider whether the original terms are still in the best interest of Mr. Acevedo and of this state."

"Actually, Virginia is a Commonwealth," Mr. Conway said.

She rewarded his comment with a tight smile. "And I will be taking a *personal interest* in this case."

"I'll have my secretary call the clerk of the court right away. Judge Woody usually has a few open spots in his schedule."

"Thank you, and please inform my office of the time. It has been a sincere pleasure meeting you, Mr. Conway."

The door closed and the room shrank back to its normal size.

Charles jumped to his feet. "Mr. Conway—I am so sorry—I had no idea she would do such a thing."

"It's fine." Mr. Conway shrugged, still staring thoughtfully at the door.

"I'll talk to her." He had the door open again.

"I'm just going to toss this whole thing to the judge. I'm not going to tangle with someone like that."

"I'll be right back, Angelo," Charles said, and hurried out after Karen Liu.

"Congresswoman!"

In the front lobby, he caught her.

"Mr. Beale? Yes?"

"Just a moment. I'm sorry," he said, "I have to catch my breath."

He caught it.

"I needed to say," he said with his breath, "we're doing fine with Angelo. You really don't need to trouble yourself."

"It isn't any trouble."

"Then I'll be a little more direct. I think it's best for him to keep things the way they are."

"I understand. I'll be very direct." Her eyes, as always, were. "It might be best, or it might not." Her tone was friendlier than her words, somewhat. "But I have reasons of my own to take the trouble."

"Could you tell me what they are?"

"Not at this time, Mr. Beale. I have an important meeting I'm already late for. I'll repeat, though, that I have a very good reason for doing this. Now, if you'll excuse me."

Charles watched her push through the door and jump into a waiting car.

"I'd like to know the reason," he said.

" 'I am not *using* my position in the *Congress* of the United States and as the *Chairwoman* of the Subcommittee on Judicial Policy to influence you.' " Charles shook his head wearily.

"Was she overbearing?" Dorothy asked.

"Only in the friendliest and most cooperative way."

"What will the judge do?"

"We will have our hearing Wednesday morning."

"So soon?"

"So soon. People don't like to keep a congressperson waiting. Eight o'clock sharp."

"Will Judge Woody be offended by Karen Liu trying to browbeat him?"

"I hope not. Or I hope he is, and tells her to mind her own business."

"I hope he doesn't throw Angelo into prison just to show that he's not intimidated," Dorothy said.

"I don't know what he'll do. He might just do what she wants and let Angelo off completely."

"Charles, he wouldn't! What would happen to Angelo?"

"He'd be free. We don't want him to be our prisoner forever, do we?"

"He's not our prisoner," Dorothy said.

"You should be thinking about what we do want. The judge would like a written statement from us by tomorrow morning."

"What are we supposed to say?"

"Whatever we want."

Dorothy sounded plenty weary herself. "Why did Karen Liu do this?"

"She has a reason. She didn't have time to discuss it with me."

"I thought I liked her!"

Charles was very weary. "Then let's pull that copy of her checks out of the basement and send them to the *Washington Post*. That will stop her."

"That's not very funny, dear."

"Today I'm doing irony."

"Did Angelo say anything?"

"No, he's doing granite. Why would Karen Liu take such an interest in Angelo?"

"Mr. Beale?" Alice was never weary. "There's someone downstairs to see you. Mr. Frank Kelly."

"Mr. Kelly. Good morning."

"And you, too. Just stopping in. I was down in Mount Vernon."

"You're welcome anytime."

"Thanks." He lowered his voice. "And I've got a question."

Charles edged closer. "Go ahead."

"Your man, Angelo Acevedo. You said he was in the Bastien house?"

"Once, last fall. It was the first delivery I took him on."

"Okay. Look, um . . ." Mr. Kelly paused. "We got a couple of the stolen pieces back."

"Oh my! You did? How?"

"I won't say, for now. But yeah, it was that ivory dolphin and a couple other things."

"That's excellent, Mr. Kelly. Can that lead you to the burglar?"

"Maybe. It wasn't on eBay, it was somewhere else. So anyway, I need to ask you something. Your man, Acevedo. You think maybe he touched anything when he was in the house?"

"Touched anything?"

Mr. Kelly was speaking very quietly. "We've got some DNA off the ivory and his name came up on the computer."

"Angelo!"

"Right. I was just looking through the list of all the matches. Most of them were no match, and there was a match with Highberg."

"Norman? Did he sell that to Derek?"

"He did. And then one good match of your night guard."

"That would have been six months ago!"

"Right, but Highberg's would be that far back, too. Usually that's way out of range, so either it got touched recently or somehow it lasted longer than usual."

"How does DNA work?" Charles asked.

"It's great. The new equipment we've got, all you have to do is touch something and you leave behind enough trace cells that we can match you. We did it with Acevedo."

"He must have picked it up when we were there," Charles said. "Do you want to talk to him?"

"Uh, no. I don't think I'll rock that boat. But you think he could have picked it up or something. Then let's just say that's what it is. That's what I'll put in my report. So," he said, suddenly louder, "what do you think? Raymond Chandler?" His eyes darted toward the stairs, then back. "Would that be a good place to start if I wanted to get a few of these?"

"Chandler?" Charles was distracted. "Oh, of course. Or anything on the shelf there. Some of them are less expensive."

"Right. I'll think about it. Maybe next time." Mr. Kelly tipped his hat to Alice and turned his broad shoulders toward the door.

"Hey, boss." The front door had just closed. Angelo was on the stairs.

"Oh! Yes, Angelo?"

"I am going out to a place."

"All right. Yes, go ahead. When you get back, we need to talk."

"What did Mr. Kelly want?" Dorothy asked.

"Oh, nothing. Just stopping in. He's still interested in mysteries."

"Did Angelo leave?"

"He left. I told him we'd talk when he got back," Charles said. "Did you see him? How long after I went down did he go by?"

"He was right behind you when you went downstairs. There was a message from Vivian at Dupont Travel. She said she had the names of the guides you were asking about."

"Oh. Of course. Was she sure they had John Borchard on their tour?"

"She had a long story about how they needed to get a special helmet for him. His head was too big."

"So he really was gone when Derek was killed. Well, I need to think things through. I think I'll go down to the basement for a little peace."

"Mr. Beale?" More of Alice was almost more than he could take. "You have a telephone call. It's Mr. Leatherman. From California."

Charles paused. "That might be just what I need. I'll take it in the basement."

"Good morning, Jacob," Charles said.

"Too early to tell."

"That's the advantage to time zones. Ours is almost over. To tell the truth, it hasn't been the best."

"The afternoon will probably be worse."

"By all indications, it will be. What can I do for you, Jacob? Are you wanting the benefit of my immense experience and wisdom?"

"If you ever get any, I might, except you'd be old as I am."

"And you'll be wiser by decades then, so I'll never catch up. I won't even try."

"You're thirty years behind, Charles."

"Thirty years doesn't seem that long any more. So what can I do for you, Jacob?"

"I want to know if you found out anything about your Homer."

"I did. Good, and bad, and then strange."

"Strange? Tell me, Charles."

"I had Morgan track Victoria's schoolbooks through to possibly a 1925 Sotheby's auction."

"That's the good."

"Yes. Then Sotheby's was a brick wall. They wouldn't say a thing?"

"Not anything?"

"Nothing. No confirmation, no information, nothing."

"They should at least have told you something," Jacob said. "Is that the strange part?"

"No, that's the bad, because the strange is much stranger. This morning I had a call from a Mr. Smith. He was English."

"English?" There was an odd cackling sound. "English? Smith? Sounds like you might have caught a big fish there, Charles."

"Well, I wonder. What do you think? It must have been Sotheby's that alerted him. No one else would know I had it, besides the seller in Denver."

"But somebody's big enough to hush Sotheby's, and we both know who that would be."

"Yes, someone who'd be very interested in a book of Queen Victoria's," Charles said.

"Then I think what you think. What did this Mr. Smith say, then?"

"He will meet me in New York on Wednesday."

"Wednesday? When will you leave?"

"That afternoon. The appointment is for nine in the evening."

"Then I'll come in the morning."

"You'll come, Jacob?! Here?"

"How else am I going to see it before it's gone?"

"But you were just here two weeks ago."

"Then I'll come again. I want to see a book that Victoria studied Homer from."

"You are always welcome. Will you need a place to stay? Do you know when you'd arrive?"

"I'll have my girl here do all that. Maybe I'll take that overnight airplane."

"The red-eye? It'll kill you, Jacob."

"Something has to. I'll be there Wednesday morning."

"Then I'll be here. I have a meeting early Wednesday, but after that I'll be very glad to see you. Have a good flight, Jacob."

"No such thing."

AFTERNOON

"Jacob Leatherman wants to see the *Odyssey*. He's flying out."

"Just to see the book?"

"Just to see it. He'll be here Wednesday morning. I suppose Angelo's hearing won't take long."

"Did you have any peace in the basement?"

"A little. I'm still not sure what to write for the judge."

"Hey, boss."

Charles and Dorothy turned in unison toward the door.

"You're back," Charles said. "How did it go?"

"Do you still want that lady?"

"From the auction? Yes, of course."

"She is at that place I went."

"You mean, you saw her? Today?"

"She is at that place."

"What place?"

"It is this one." He handed the list to Charles, and pointed.

"Tyson Estate Agents. Tell me about it."

"I went to that place and I went into it and I said I was there to pick up their package and I said a lady called. And that lady comes out and says she never called for a package, and so I left."

Angelo finished and waited.

"What is this place like? Is it in an office building?"

"No, it is just a building and it has the office rooms in front and a warehouse building."

"I see. That would be for storage?"

"That building is to store things in."

"Well. Good for you, Angelo. That's very good."

"Do you want me to go to any more places?"

"No. That's enough. Tell me, Angelo, did you understand everything at the meeting this morning?"

"That lady, she's a boss over everybody?"

"She is an important person, but Judge Woody is the most important person for you. We'll go see him Wednesday morning." Charles glanced at Dorothy. "Sit down, Angelo."

He sat, as wary and taut as he always stood.

"At this meeting on Wednesday, the judge will decide whether to keep you on probation or not."

"I will go to jail?"

"No," Dorothy said, quickly. "No. Nothing will make you go to jail. The judge will be deciding if he will end the probation completely."

"You would be free," Charles said. "No probation, no jail. It would all be over."

"The probation is three years," Angelo said. He was paying very close attention, his face suspicious but still impassive.

"Congresswoman Liu thinks it has been long enough. She has asked the judge to cancel the rest of it."

"Why does she do that?"

"I don't exactly know," Charles said.

"But Angelo," Dorothy said, "what do you think of being off probation?"

"There is no jail?"

"There is no jail," she said. "Either nothing will change or the judge will just end the probation."

"Will the judge do this?"

"We don't know," Charles said. "He'll decide Wednesday morning. We're asking what you think about it."

Angelo didn't think. "That judge, he will think and he will decide." He stood. "Do you want anything else?"

"No. That's all."

When he had silently disappeared, Dorothy said, "You didn't tell him that we would tell the judge our opinion."

"Maybe we shouldn't."

"We shouldn't write a statement? But we need to."

"No, we shouldn't tell our opinion. We should just be objective. That judge, he will think and he will decide."

"But he might let Angelo go completely."

"He is a judge. And I am afraid of my own judgment. We'll work on it tonight at home."

EVENING

"Have we sold anything this evening?" Charles asked. Alice and Morgan were closing the shop.

"A few things," she said.

"What was the last one?"

"A Dumas. *The Count of Monte Christo*."

"Of course," Charles said. "The man who finally escapes from prison and revenges himself on the person who put him there."

"And gets rich, too," Alice said.

"Very rich, yes. And here is Dorothy. Good night, everyone."

"What should we say?" Dorothy said. They were sitting at the dining room table, her pen poised above the paper.

"What should we say?" Charles answered. "Dear Judge."

After a few seconds, "Yes?"

"I started," Charles said. "You go next."

"Dear Judge," she said. "Comma."

"That doesn't count."

"What do we want to say?"

"Let's look at the options," Charles said. "Dear Judge, Angelo is a changed man and a model citizen. We feel that society will be completely safe with him at large. There is nothing more that we can do for him. Please let him go."

"Next option."

"Next option . . . Dear Judge, Angelo has been well behaved, but we don't know what's going on inside his head, and it's rather frightening. We think he should remain under probation."

"That's too far in the other direction," she sighed. "What do we think? What would be the best thing for Angelo?"

Charles stared out the window, through the lace curtains. The street was dark except for all the lights—streetlights, headlights, houselights. "The best thing. Why am I having to decide that for so many people?"

"We asked for this responsibility."

"We didn't ask to judge him, just to supervise him."

"It all goes together," Dorothy said. She sighed. "I think everything should just stay the same. He could have been in prison. How much mercy should he receive?"

"There is no end to mercy."

Above the roofs there was no end to the dark.

"What is the best for Angelo?" Dorothy said again.

"Dorothy," Charles said, slowly, his eyes still on the dark. "I am not God. I don't know. How can I know?"

"I didn't say you were God," she said. "Are you all right, dear?"

"I'm sorry. I was talking to myself." His eyes were on the black night. "Why did Karen Liu intervene? If we hadn't found Derek's papers, we would never have met her."

"It just happened, dear."

"What would we do if he were our son?"

"Charles?" She watched him closely, as he still watched out the window. "I can take care of this. I'll just say that everything has been fine so far, we hope it won't change, but we don't want to push one way or the other."

Charles wiped his forehead and his hand was covered with sweat from it. "That's fine. That's what's best."

"You seem distracted this afternoon, Derek."

"A situation at the office, Charles. Somewhat out of control."

"Is it serious?"

"More than it should have been. I might have overplayed my hand."

"You often use game metaphors when you talk about your work, Derek."

"Everything is a game. Everyone is an opponent."

"I hope I'm not."

"Only in chess, Charles."

"I wouldn't want to play against you in anything more important, Derek."

"You would be a worthy adversary. But I have more than enough to worry about as it is."

"You have a very different view of life than I do, Derek. I see human interactions as generally cooperative."

"Then here's a game, Charles. Your view of life, or mine? Which would win?"

"Mine doesn't find value in winning. We could say, Which accomplishes the greatest good, yours or mine?"

"Mine doesn't find value in the greater good. We need an intersection, Charles, where our views cross."

"Personal contentment?"

"Personal success."

"Perhaps, Derek, the winner will be whichever of us believes he is winning."

"And how do we play, Charles?"

"Just living our lives, Derek."

"More than that. Let me think, Charles. Perhaps I'll find the proper game board for our game of lives."

"And if I don't want to play?"

"That's part of my side of the game, to set you to."

TUESDAY

MORNING

Storms rode the fast wind and in the wind rode everything that wasn't held fast. Loose clothing whipped around solid limbs, including Charles's jacket and the sleeves and legs of Patrick White's dark suit, standing on the front steps of the shop.

"Mr. White!" Charles's voice was whipped by the wind, too. "What can I do for you?"

"We need to talk," Mr. White said. He had no smile.

"Just a moment, and I'll open the door."

He turned the key and stepped into the abrupt tranquility. He turned the lights on and the alarm off. Mr. White turned the tranquility off.

"I've come to warn you," he said. He was in the center of the room, an emotional whirlwind. Every volume on the shelves was watching him.

"About what?" Charles said, trying to get some of the attention for himself.

"Borchard. He's getting ready."

"Ready for what?"

"His next murder."

The doorknob rattled.

Patrick White spun to face it. His back was now toward the counter, but Charles could still tell what his expression was because it was mirrored in Alice's face as she opened the door. There was a brief motionless moment, and then the wind hurled Alice over the threshold and almost into Mr. White's arms.

"Good morning, Alice," Charles said at his calmest.

Her keel evened, and she managed to get around the visitor and to safety behind the counter. "Good morning, Mr. Beale."

Charles had stepped forward and faced the bloodshot eyes of the storm.

"Let's go downstairs," he said at his even calmer calmest.

The books in the basement noticed Patrick White, but they were less impressionable. They knew human nature; they took his measure and then returned to their own business.

"Mr. White. Please, sit down."

The judge took his seat at the bench, and Charles slid around to his own chair behind the dock.

"Now," Charles said. "I will be candid. You've come four times now to rail against John Borchard. I want you to understand that I don't know if anything you've said is true. These accusations are very serious and you could get in trouble for making them. I also don't know why you're making them to me."

But Mr. White was gone, his jaw slack, and his blank eyes staring far away. Charles turned toward where he was looking, but the view was hidden.

He chose not to wait for the return. "Mr. White?"

"It's you."

Charles lost focus himself for a moment. "What?"

"He's going to kill you." Then the stare was on him full and ferocious. Charles's was still foggy.

"I don't believe it."

"Believe it. Believe it or die. You'll die if you don't believe it."

"I still don't."

"Then it won't be my fault." He shuddered in frustration. "I've done everything I can. I'm trying to save your life."

Charles wavered. "Why would he want to kill anyone?"

"He's mad."

Charles tried wavering in a different direction. "What makes you think he would want to do anything to me?"

"He's building a bomb."

Even the books were now paying attention again.

"How do you know?" Charles asked.

"I've seen him."

"You've seen John Borchard build a bomb?"

"Yes. I've been watching him. Look at this."

He opened his suit jacket and withdrew two folded sheets of paper. All eyes were on them as he flattened them out on the desk.

Each was a photograph of a book, the same book on the same dark, heavily grained wood surface, with the corner of a brass penholder. The book was closed in one picture and open in the other. The closed book was a browned and aged antique, identical to many in the room watching them.

"The Kant," Charles said.

"He can!" Patrick White said. "He is! See?"

The open book showed the yellowed pages cut, not in a rectangle as the Locke had been, but in a rounded, irregular shape. Exactly fitted inside was a black device, with one red and one gray button. The pictures were enlarged and grainy but still clear enough.

"Where did you get these?"

"I took them," Mr. White said, smirking. "Now you believe me?"

"I don't understand what they mean."

"He's making a bomb. What else could it be?"

"It can't be." Charles was still reacting slowly.

"And who else would it be for? An antique book! It's for you!"

"Where did he get it?" Charles was speaking to himself. Patrick Henry White answered for him.

"It's what he's going to do with it that matters. But we can stop him. I couldn't stop him before. This time I will."

"Wait," Charles said. "Let me think."

For once Mr. White was the one left behind. Charles stared at the pictures.

"What are you going to do?" he asked finally.

"I'm going to stop him."

"How?"

Suddenly, Patrick White stood. He took the papers from the desk and stuffed them away.

"Where are you going?" Charles said.

"I see what you're doing," Mr. White said. "He's got you. Hasn't he? If I tell you anything, you'll go to him. He has you in his control."

"But . . ." Charles shook his head. "If I'm on his side, why would he want to kill me?"

But Mr. White was beyond answering. "It's all too late, anyway. He has everyone else on his side. Everyone else but one."

"Who? Karen Liu?"

"Borchard has her, too." Then he was on the stairs, and Charles hurried after him. He caught up halfway across the showroom. Alice shrank back into a corner behind the counter.

"Wait," Charles said.

Patrick White stopped. "What?"

"You have no right."

"No right? For what?"

"To do anything to John Borchard."

"After what he's done to me? Who else will?"

"You are destroying yourself, Mr. White."

"I'm already destroyed."

Before Charles could answer, he threw the door open and let himself out. But the door didn't slam shut behind him. A customer was coming in, an older woman, in high heels and cashmere sweater and blue jeans. She shut the door softly and smiled sweetly.

"Excuse me," she said, "but would you have any Greek tragedies?"

"Alice said you were in the basement with someone," Dorothy said. She looked at him more closely. "And you look rather white."

"It's a Patrick White-white."

"He was here again?"

"Very much. I'm worried, Dorothy. I think he's going to do something."

"What?"

"I don't know."

"Is it serious, Charles?"

"I hope not."

"What did he say?"

Charles took a slow and deep breath. For a moment he was seeing something far beyond the room, and then he was seeing only Dorothy.

"Nothing specific. Dear, I'll be out for the rest of the morning. I'm going to talk to John Borchard."

"Was Mr. White saying more wild things about him?"

"Yes. That's what it mainly was." He stood. The wind rattled the window. "I think I'll take Angelo with me."

"Sit up here," Charles said.

Angelo shrugged, and closed the back car door and opened the front. Even that door was quiet closing by his hand.

"How do you do that?" Charles asked.

"How to do what?"

"How are you always so quiet?"

"That's not a *how* you do."

"Everything you do is silent."

"You just don't be noisy."

For a while Charles was not noisy. Then he said, "I'm trying to decide if that's not an answer or if it is."

281

Angelo said nothing else, and in the car it was quiet.

"That building is it," Angelo said, pointing. Charles pushed through the other cars into the left lane and turned into the parking lot. He parked at the front door. The first floor was painted cinder block. Above and to the side was sheet metal. The sign said *Tyson Estate Agents*.

"Hello?" Charles looked through the front room of two metal desks and cabinets.

"Just a minute," a voice said from a hall. Charles waited. Angelo stood.

A man in canvas work pants and a flannel shirt sauntered in. He frowned thoughtfully at Angelo.

"There's no package. Really."

Charles frowned thoughtfully back. "There is," he said. "But actually a different package. I wonder if I could speak to the lady who works here?"

"Jane! The guy's back again for that package."

A moment later, she entered. She wasn't in a gray suit as he'd seen her before, but she was obviously in charge, and obviously very blond.

"Hi."

"Hello," Charles said. "You don't remember me, but I've seen you before."

"Oh? Where?" She sat at a desk.

"About two weeks ago. My name is Charles Beale, and I was at the auction of Derek Bastien's estate."

The woman's expression changed to annoyance. "Are you police?"

"No. I don't think you've done anything wrong."

"I know I haven't. What do you want?"

"I want to see the desk you bought."

"Do you have a key?"

"No."

"Sorry. I can't let you into someone else's room."

"That's fine. I just wanted to make sure first that it was here. We'll have a key here in a few minutes. May I use your telephone?"

"Go ahead."

He dialed. "John Borchard, please." Then after many waits, he said, "Would you please get a message to him? Tell him Charles Beale is calling from Tyson Estate Agents, and it is extremely important. I'll wait."

It wasn't a very long wait.

"Charles. This is John."

"I'm very sorry to interrupt you, but we need to talk, urgently. Could you come meet me here?"

There was a last wait, different from the ones before because of the heavy breathing at the other end.

"You are at the warehouse?" John said.

"Yes."

"I'll be there in thirty minutes."

The front door opened.

Charles was sitting, waiting, and Angelo was leaning against the wall beside him.

"Mr. Borchard. Thank you for coming."

John Borchard's face had room for many emotions. Anger was in his jaw, annoyance in the set of his mouth, and menace over the expanse of his forehead. Deep in his eyes there was worry.

"Charles," he said, and all the emotions were in his voice as well. "Well. Why did you come here? Why didn't you just call me? We could have talked without the dramatic effects."

"I thought it would help us both to be truthful."

"Perhaps. And why now?"

"Patrick White came to see me this morning. And I had another reason for coming here, John. I want to see the desk."

"That isn't necessary."

"I do want to."

At first, annoyance was winning. But not for long.

"All right."

Blond Jane had only watched so far, but now she stood to lead the way to the hall and back, past locked metal doors in whitewashed walls to a door like all the others.

John Borchard unlocked it.

"Go ahead."

Jane retreated. Charles entered with the quiet shadow of Angelo close. John came in last.

The room was large, cinder block, cement, gray and empty, almost. Only the desk was in it, in the center, its rich dark wood and ornament in blunt tension with its prison. Its back panels had been roughly removed and leaned against it.

An intricate mechanism enclosed the exposed back of the drawers on one side.

Charles moved to the front of the desk and respectfully pushed the two left drawers in an inch, then pulled the lower drawer out. John Borchard watched. The box, no longer hidden, obeyed and came out with the drawer.

"That would have been helpful to know," John Borchard said. Annoyance was back, with real anger just beside it. "I suppose Derek showed you how it worked?" And then threat, a new expression not yet seen, appeared. "There is a great deal you need to explain to me, Charles."

But Charles was looking at the wooden box. It matched the desk perfectly. The stain was the same, the wood was the same, and even the joints were the same grooves and slots as the antique drawer. The only difference was that it wasn't as worn as the antique.

"It's beautiful work," Charles said. The box was empty.

"Yes, it is all very unfortunate."

"Yes, very. Do you know who made it?"

"The drawer? No."

"The desk itself," Charles said.

"No."

Charles moved slowly around it, stooping and peering. "It doesn't say." He felt the smoothness of the wood and the tight joining of the panels. Then he stood. "Now I'd like to see the papers."

"I won't allow that, Charles. Absolutely not."

"You'll need to, John. We're going to talk through this, all of it. You have as much to explain as I do."

His lower lip was quivering, and whatever emotion he was trying to show was incomplete without that part under control.

"They're at my house."

"Then let's go."

John Borchard held the door for Charles, and then locked it. Angelo barely got out before it closed; John had ignored him completely.

Charles twisted through the tangles of suburban roads, John Borchard's heavy silver Cadillac guiding him.

"You are making that man mad," Angelo said.

"Yes. It's unavoidable."

"That man, you should be careful with him. Does he have friends?"

"You mean his gang? No, there won't be anyone at his house. I know you wouldn't follow someone into his base like this, but I think he is a man who works on his own."

Angelo nodded. "I think he is. You are going into his house?"

"I expect so."

"I will not go in."

"That's probably best. He'll be more willing to talk with just me alone. He's in a difficult position and he needs my help, Angelo. I want to get information from him, but even more, I want to help him."

Finally they came to a driveway on a very new street of very large houses. Where Derek's house had been a painting, these were billboards. The landscaping was machined and the architecture generated.

John Borchard stood waiting in the driveway.

"Here we are," he said as Charles stepped from his car. "My wife is away for the morning."

"It's a very nice neighborhood, John."

"Please come in."

Angelo stayed in the front seat. John led Charles through the garage, not the front door, into an extensive kitchen of hard, polished surfaces, and through a dining room of designed colors and shapes, and a hallway of nothing comfortable, and to an office of deep and rich pretense, with nothing anywhere softened or wizened by any age.

"Please sit down."

Charles sat in a chair as plush as those in the Justice Department office. A clock ticked. Charles folded his hands.

"I am very disturbed," John Borchard said from behind his desk. Whether he wasn't trying, or the novelty had worn off, his face seemed less expressive. It was merely stern. "Charles, I accepted you for who you said you were and what you said you were doing. You gave no indication that you were anything but a friend of Derek's, simply looking at his life. But now it is obvious that you were misleading me."

"I apologize," Charles said. "However. Caution has been necessary, and John, I don't believe you were simply accepting me as Derek's friend. You assumed much more than that."

"And so I was correct. Then let's start over." John forced a forced smile. "And let's start with Derek's desk. How did you know about it?"

"I really didn't know anything about it at the time of the auction two weeks ago. Of course, everyone saw the bidding. The desk was worth over a hundred thousand dollars to two different people."

"But Derek had showed you the drawer?"

"No."

"Then how did you know about it?"

"That came later, and I'm under an obligation to not discuss it. But I did find out about the drawer, and about what it might have contained."

"And what do you think it might have contained?" John asked.

"I think caution is still in order," Charles said. "Instead, I'll mention Patrick White."

"I've warned you already to not listen to him."

"I know that he is mistaken about you, John. But someone threatened him and then carried out their threat. Someone."

"Apparently," John said.

"I believe it was Derek Bastien."

"Why?"

"I'll just say I've gotten to know Derek very well since he died. But that is what I think Derek kept in his desk."

"Evidence against Patrick White?"

"More than just Mr. White. And, John, I think you must have known what he was doing."

"What makes you think that, Charles?"

"Because you paid a hundred and five thousand dollars to get his desk."

John Borchard's face was out of control for a moment with a bewildering array of worries, angers and even bewilderments.

"But how did you know that I did? You're talking in circles."

"I guessed. At least two people knew about the drawer, to bid so high for it. Who else would it have been? You, or Karen Liu, or Patrick White. Possibly others. Mr. White didn't suspect Derek at all, and I don't believe Karen Liu did either. But Derek worked for you, and his interests in blackmail coincided very closely with yours. It seemed reasonable that you would know what he was doing. And not many people would have been close enough to him to specifically know about the drawer."

"But you were still guessing."

"I was guessing. I guessed that someone would get a list of agents from the auction house, which turned out to be true. Was that how you found Jane?"

"That isn't important."

"It seemed in character, though. So when I found her, I had a chance to try out my guess. If you hadn't responded the way you did, I would have tried Karen Liu next. Besides that, your questions about Derek's books were rather transparent."

"Yes, his books." John was back on firmer ground. "My questions were transparent. You could have answered me plainly."

"Why were you interested in his books?" Charles said.

This time, the expressions progressed through concentration, indecision, calculation, and finally firm resolution. John settled deep into his chair's padding. The final display of eyebrows, chin and lips was camaraderie and confiding.

"All right, Charles. I see that we need to work cooperatively here. I think we're working toward the same goal, and we'll need each other's help to get there." He leaned forward for a more intimate discussion. "Yes, I was aware of Derek's activities, but only slightly. I did see his drawer once and I knew what he had in it. I didn't ask for specifics. I only knew that he had some leverage over Karen Liu."

"So, it was unexpected when Patrick White began accusing you of blackmail?"

"Absolutely. I hadn't known that Derek also had incriminating evidence about him. It didn't take me long to realize what had happened, though. Derek engineered his downfall and made him think it had been me who did it."

"And that made it imperative for you to get the rest of his papers," Charles said.

"Exactly. Absolutely. I had to know what other schemes he had going."

"Couldn't you have gone to the police?"

"No. Not until I knew myself what was in the papers."

"And what was?" Charles asked.

"Too much." John grimaced. "And not enough. There were files on more people than I would have imagined, but the specific ones I was looking for were missing. Charles, my guess is that you have the papers that I don't."

Charles nodded. "I do have some papers."

"They were in one of the books?"

"Yes."

"So I was right," John said. "And that's how you became involved. Well, Charles, I would like to see them."

"You should, John. And I'd like to see the papers you have."

Their solidarity was shaken. John frowned.

"That would worry me," he said. "The papers concern a number of people. I'm sure they wouldn't want you to see them."

"They will never know that I have."

"It makes me wonder how you will use the information in them."

"I won't."

"Then why even look, Charles? It would be better if you didn't. You don't know most of them. They are his colleagues at work and people he knew socially. I have compelling reason to know, because I need to understand what damage has been done, and how it can be repaired. That's my responsibility as Derek's superior in the Department. I don't understand why you need to see them."

"John, it isn't that I want to. I also have my own compelling reason, but I can't tell you what it is."

John was not pleased. "A compelling reason?"

"I can't cooperate further until I've seen them."

John Borchard would have been a poor poker player. It was obvious he was going to fold, even as he tried to bluff.

"Tell me what you're looking for. I can tell you if you'd find it."

"I don't know. I have to look for myself."

"Oh, very well!" For the moment, they were not friends. "I'll ask you to excuse me for a moment."

"Of course." Charles stood to leave. "I'm sorry, John. I really don't want to see them. But I have to." He stepped outside.

The brief passage of the hall earlier had been enough to appreciate it. Now he had a much longer opportunity as three minutes passed. It was surprising how poor the Borchards' taste was; everything was expensive, but nothing was valuable. There was no feel to any of the house. The only consistency to any of the furniture was how soft the seats were, and the severe hardness of everything else.

The door opened.

"Please, come in."

A stack of folders was on the desk, about two inches high.

"It isn't as many as it looks," John said. "Each one is in its own folder. But there are still forty-six in all."

The folders were unmarked. Charles took the first and set it down off the stack onto the desk's surface. The wood was dark and heavily grained. He pushed a brass penholder out of the way.

Then he glanced up at a curtained window behind the desk chair.

"Need more light?" John said. "I sometimes do." He opened the curtains.

Charles looked out into the backyard. The black windows of the house behind them looked directly down and in.

Charles turned back to the folder. It held only a single page: a hotel bill from a Las Vegas resort, with a name and date.

"Nothing illegal," John Borchard said. "That is my peer, the other Deputy Assistant A.G. for Legislative Affairs. But he wouldn't want it known that he frequents casinos. He's quite a straight arrow."

Charles opened the next folder.

"And that is illegal," John said.

"I don't know what it is. A prescription?"

"For a steroid. That is our secretary. Her son is a college football player."

He opened the third folder. It was a two-thousand-dollar car repair bill.

"That is our personnel manager's wife. I casually asked him if he'd had any automobile problems lately, and he hadn't."

"So she wrecked her car and hid it from her husband. That's hardly blackmail material."

"Most of them aren't. And there isn't much need to blackmail your own secretary."

Charles opened another folder.

"Oh, dear!" The page had a dozen credit card charges from a hamburger restaurant.

"I didn't know that name," John said. "So I looked it up. He is the owner of a vegetarian restaurant that Derek frequented."

"That's absurd," Charles said.

"That is probably the most so. It's quite a collection. Some are illegal, some immoral."

"And some merely fattening." Charles sighed. "What a strange collection."

"The papers?"

"The people. You were right, John. He did collect people. Is this all the folders?" Charles asked.

"That's all of them."

"I need to look at each one."

"Then go ahead."

One by one he looked at the single pages, some for only a few seconds, some longer. John was silent, and the clock ticked. Fifteen minutes later he closed the last folder.

"Well," he said.

"Not a pretty picture," John said.

"Not at all. Of course, I don't know what many of them mean."

"Many of them, I did know. Most of the others I've found out what they mean. There are five that are still unclear."

"John, are there any people in your office that you'll have to take action about?"

"There may be. That will take a great deal of judgment."

"Their careers are in your hands," Charles said, pushing the stack of folders back toward John.

"They've made their own decisions. My judgment will have to be what is best for the Department. And now, Charles, did you find what you were looking for?"

Charles considered. "I think I did."

"Then I would like to show you something else that was in the hidden drawer of the desk." He took a small wrapped package from a desk drawer. He undid the tape and brown paper and held out an antique book.

"It's a *Critique of Pure Reason* by Immanuel Kant," he said. "But I'm sure you knew that."

"Yes, I know the book." Charles held the book closed.

"Which brings us to the subject of books. At first, when you came to me, I thought you might have been supplying Derek with some of his information, and you were offering to do the same for me. Then I went through the papers and I realized there were some missing. You've obviously noticed there is no mention among these of Karen Liu or Patrick White."

"Or you."

"Yes. Or me," John said. "So I had to assume those papers were elsewhere. If you open that book, you'll understand why I finally guessed that you had them."

Charles kept the book closed. "I really had no inkling there was anything in the books when I bought them at the auction."

"If I had known," John said, "you can be sure that you would not have bought them. But please, open it."

"I assume it's hollow."

"Yes, it is. But I want you to see what is in it."

"It was a shock, John, seeing the first one. I'm perhaps sentimental, but I don't want to see another antique ruined."

John shrugged. "I guessed what a hollowed book might mean, and when Derek's bookseller came calling, I felt my guess was confirmed. I knew the papers had to be somewhere—especially Patrick White's. So, Charles, I would like to see the papers you have."

"I don't have them with me, of course. I can tell you that Patrick White's is just a title page copied from the University of Virginia Honor Court proceedings, with an interior page number written on it. A person would have to get those proceedings and look at that inside page to make any sense of it."

"Hardly incriminating at all if someone found it," John said. "But if a newspaper reporter received a copy and knew it was important, he would quickly get all the details."

"Which is what happened," Charles said.

"With the consequences that everyone in Washington knows."

"And that brings me to the other reason I wanted to talk to you. Patrick White came to me this morning."

"More of the same, I suppose?"

"More than the same. John, I need to warn you. I think he might try to take justice into his own hands."

An odd new look came into John's eyes. It was mostly anger tinged with fear.

"So it has gone too far," John said. "What did he say?"

"It was vague, but it was very threatening. Last week he told me that you killed Derek."

"Yes, I've heard that."

"Today he said you were planning to kill again. He said he would stop you. He also said he had someone who would help him."

"In that case," John said, "I insist that you look inside that book." He handed it to Charles.

Charles held it for a moment, feeling its weight and balance. The lettering on the spine was still legible: Immanuel Kant, *Critique of Pure Reason*.

Charles opened the book.

The hole cut was smaller than the John Locke, but deeper into the thick volume. Resting in it was the black plastic object, a rounded rectangle, with the two buttons. It also had a speaker grill.

"A recorder?" Charles said.

"A small Dictaphone. A fairly common thing for an administrator to keep in his pocket."

Charles lifted it out of the book and pushed the Play button.

"Tell me about him," it rumbled.

Charles jerked in surprise, dropping the device.

"It's Derek," he said.

"Yes," John said. "Derek recorded a conversation. Go ahead. Listen to it."

He pushed the button again.

"Tell me about him."

"He called me last week." It was Patrick White's voice. *"He read about me in the newspaper and he knew it had to be Borchard behind the scandal. He said Borchard's been after him for a couple months, too."*

"After him? For what?"

"Something in the Justice Department. They're rivals. It's the same game—he's gotten the letters, too."

"What is this man's name?"

"He won't tell me. Maybe you could guess. You know everyone that Borchard does."

"I don't know who it would be," Derek's voice said.

"He says if he and I work together, we can bring Borchard down."

"How?"

"That's all we've said. He'll help us, Derek."

"I have to know what he's going to do. I have to know who he is."

"I'll find out," Patrick White said. *"But he's scared. He doesn't want me to know who he is. But he wants to be part of anything we do."*

And then there was silence.

"That's all there is," John Borchard said.

"It must be the same person Patrick White has mentioned to me. Who could they be talking about?"

"That's what I have to find out!" John said, suddenly vehement. "I have to know who it is. It isn't just Patrick White. There's someone else as well. It must be someone else that Derek was blackmailing."

"Could it be any of these people?" Charles put his hand on the stack of folders.

"It isn't. I've been through all of them. It must be one of the papers you have. That is why I have to see them." He was standing, pacing in the narrow space of the office.

"Karen Liu?"

"It's a man. White said *he*. And this man, he must know more than Patrick White does. He knew that the papers were in Derek's desk. He's the person who was bidding against me."

"Maybe . . ." Charles said, "maybe I could get Mr. White to tell me."

"Even if he doesn't know, he might have some clue. Something that could help me guess. Maybe the man at the auction who did the bidding. He was from New York."

"Edmund Cane."

"He might know. But I need to see the papers you have. That might be enough."

"I'll show them to you," Charles said. "And I'll talk to Mr. White."

"Do you know where he is?" John asked. "I haven't been able to find where he's living."

"No, I don't know where he liv—"

First, shaking.

Just afterward sound. Then the sorting of sounds—glass shattering, heavier objects falling. A percussion of air and then heat.

"Get down," Charles said. John collapsed to the floor.

But there was no more of the sound or motion. Charles stood enough to see out the window. John didn't move.

The neighboring house was buried in smoke. Charles watched in shock as the gray cleared. An upstairs window was gone, and also most of the wall that had held it, and the hole was black edged and jagged. Flames wavered inside.

"Call the police," Charles said, but John was immobile. Charles grabbed the telephone and pushed three digits.

"There's been an explosion," he said. "The house behind us—what is the address here?"

John didn't answer.

"I don't know the address. Whatever this phone number is."

"Who is calling?" the voice said.

"Charles Beale. I'm at the home of John Borchard in McLean. I don't know the address."

"We have your address. What happened?"

"Behind us. The house exploded—something in it—there's fire and smoke. It was a big explosion."

"We have help on the way. Has anyone been injured?"

"I don't know. I think—" The window that had looked directly down on John Borchard's office was destroyed. "I think someone must have been."

"Do you see anyone injured?"

"No. I'm calling from the neighbor's house. No one here was hurt."

"Mr. Beale, we have help on the way. Stay clear of the fire. Don't try to go into the house."

"I won't. We won't."

"That's all we need now. You can hang up."

Charles set the telephone down. "John. Are you all right?"

John Borchard was still not moving or speaking. He was on his knees, his mouth was open, his face was paper white, shining with sweat, his breath jerking, his eyes wide.

"John!"

Charles took his shoulder and shook it. The blank eyes suddenly moved.

"It was meant for me," he said, finally speaking.

"Who lives in that house?"

"Where?"

"The house right behind you!"

"They're gone. They've been gone."

Charles bent down, face-to-face with John Borchard. "Are you all right?"

John's face was a sagging ruin. "It was for me! They want to kill me!"

"You're fine," Charles said. "Sit up here."

John heaved himself up into his chair. His face was regaining color and his breath was becoming normal.

"The police!" he said.

"I called them."

"They'll see the files." John staggered to his feet. He pushed aside a small table and groped at the wood paneling behind it. The panel clicked open, uncovering the gray front of a safe.

A bitter smell had infiltrated the room.

"Hey, boss." Angelo's voice startled Charles. "Come on, get out of here."

"No. We're all right," Charles said.

John was on his knees, fumbling with the safe door. Finally, sirens were sounding.

"Who did that might come here," Angelo said.

Charles untangled the words. "No, I don't think anyone did it. It went off from inside the house."

"Come on, go!" Angelo's hiss was urgent and angry. "Get away."

"We'll wait for the police, Angelo."

"Boss, no police!"

"No police," John Borchard said, suddenly aware of them. The safe was still not open. "Not until I put the files away."

"Boss," Angelo pleaded. "Come! The police can't find me here!" His eyes were wide and white.

"Why are you so afraid?" Charles shouted at him.

A shudder passed from head to feet, and a thin sigh escaped the clenched mouth.

"I am not afraid."

"Then sit down."

Slowly the tense body settled into a chair, not sitting but perched. John was back at the safe, trying to open it. The sirens were close and car doors were opening.

AFTERNOON

"Mr. Beale?"

"Yes, Officer?" Charles was in his car in John Borchard's driveway. Angelo was beside him. The dashboard clock said 1:30.

The policeman leaned into his open window. "You can go."

"But I haven't spoken with anyone yet!"

"Yes, sir. I'm sorry you've had to wait so long. Detective Paisley may call you later."

"I really need to discuss this with him."

"I'll make sure he calls."

"Was anyone hurt?"

"We're not giving any information yet."

"Then please have your detective call me as soon as possible." Charles started the car and pulled out onto the street. "There," he said, angry and frustrated, to Angelo. "There was no reason to get away before the police came. We couldn't even get them to notice us."

Angelo didn't answer. He seethed.

"And then we just watched," Charles said. Dorothy's chair was close to his, and the office door was closed. "Police cars, fire trucks, ambulances. Everything. The electric company, the gas company. We finally just waited in the car."

"Was anyone hurt?" she asked.

"They wouldn't say. They didn't bring anyone out of the house while we were there."

Dorothy waited. "Charles. It can't have just happened by chance."

"No, I'm sure it didn't."

"Then what was it?"

"It was Patrick White."

Dorothy was shocked. "How? What would he have been doing there?"

"When he was here this morning, he said wild things. I think he was making an explosive—and it exploded."

"I don't understand, Charles. Do you mean it was . . . that he—"

"I don't know. He might have been trying to kill John, or maybe himself. I don't know."

"But did he live that close to John Borchard?"

"At least for the last days or weeks. Maybe he was renting, I don't know!"

"What did John Borchard say about it?"

"We didn't talk. He was with the police detective the last I saw him. Maybe that was why they couldn't talk to me."

"And what about Angelo? What did he think?"

Charles buried his head in his hands. "I called him a coward."

"You what?"

"He wanted to go. He was out in the car when the explosion happened and he came in to get me. He wanted to leave."

"But why would he want to go? He wouldn't have had anything to worry about."

"I suppose his instinct was too strong, to get away from the police, or from anything like this. So I asked him why he was so afraid. I was too upset! John was panicking, and Angelo was panicking, and I guess I panicked, too. I need to go talk to him."

"Angelo?"

The door opened. Angelo faced him, closed.

"I'm sorry," Charles said. "I shouldn't have said that."

Angelo didn't answer.

"I know you weren't afraid," Charles said. "You were trying to get us both out of danger."

Angelo answered. "Do you want anything else?"

"No."

Angelo closed the door.

"Mr. Beale?" Morgan was waiting for him in the office. "The information you wanted just came up on the computer."

"I'll come," Charles said, and Dorothy followed. They looked at Morgan's screen.

Former Judge Killed in McLean House Explosion—*Patrick White, who resigned last year from the Federal bench over a law school cheating scandal, was killed this afternoon when an explosion occurred in his rented house in McLean. Police have not released any details about the cause of the explosion, except that it was in an upstairs bedroom and that Mr. White was in the room at the time. Washington Gas has confirmed that the explosion was not gas related.*

"That's enough," Charles said.

"Wait," Morgan said. "This is new. It says the police think he was building some kind of explosive and it went off."

EVENING

"Charles?" Dorothy opened the basement door.

"Yes, dear?"

"It's nine o'clock. Shall we go home? Everyone else is gone."

"Did the police detective ever call? His name was Paisley,"

"Not yet."

"Have you seen Angelo?"

"No, his door's been closed."

Charles looked back down at the book open before him. "In the middle of life I find myself within a forest dark, for the straightforward pathway had been lost."

"It isn't lost, dear," Dorothy said. "He found it again."

"The path he found only lead to the door.

> *Through me the way is to the city dolent;*
> *Through me the way is to eternal dole;*
> *Through me the way among the people lost."*

"Charles ..."

"All hope abandon, ye who enter in!" Charles said.

"No! Charles. If you must be reading Dante, read *Paradise* instead."

He tried to smile. "Then be Beatrice and lead me."

"I'll take you home at least."

He did smile. "Yes. Let's go home."

"I saw in the newspaper there had been some burglaries near here, Derek."

"Yes, the neighbors. They really should get better alarm systems. Apparently you have hired your own guard. Is that why you brought that young man?"

"Not exactly, although living in a city always has its worries. And working for the government, too. When I saw you back in April, you mentioned a situation in your office. I hope that's resolved?"

"Actually not, Charles. In fact, I'm afraid it's gotten quite a bit more difficult."

"I'm sorry."

"The stakes continue to rise. I threaten your pawn, you return with an attack on my bishop, and suddenly the queens are face-to-face, and the whole game hangs in the balance."

"But in real life, Derek, we have other choices than defeat or victory."

"That reminds me, Charles. Which of us is winning at the moment?"

"Winning? Oh, of course! You mean your challenge from last time."

"Our views of life."

"I'm quite content at the moment, Derek, so I must be winning."

"I'm in a fight that takes all my wits and cunning, so I must be winning."

"Then let's call it a draw."

"But, Charles, for me, a draw is a loss."

"For me, it's a win."

"Exquisite, Charles! I like this game better than any of the others."

"It seems easy enough. Even though I don't know what I'm playing. All I do is be who I am and— Is something wrong, Derek?"

"No. No. I just had a thought."

"What was it?"

"Nothing exact, Charles. Just that, if somehow I lose the game playing by my rules, you might win it playing by yours."

WEDNESDAY

MORNING

Charles knocked. He was in his Sunday suit and Dorothy beside him wore a dark, respectable dress.

The door opened. Angelo was dressed in his own best clothes: a buttoned shirt and dark pants, leather shoes and combed hair.

"Are you ready?" Charles asked. Angelo answered by stepping past them and walking down the stairs.

"All rise. This court is now in session, the Honorable Judge Glenn Woody presiding."

"Please sit down."

Five people sat. Charles and Dorothy were on either side of Angelo, and behind them were Mr. Conway and one other man with a briefcase.

"I will be very brief," the judge said.

The back door opened.

Karen Liu staggered in. Her pace was slow, her energy dissipated, and her face haggard. There was nothing domineering about her; she looked no larger than she actually was.

"Congresswoman Liu?" the judge said.

"I am very sorry to interrupt," she said, falling into a seat in the back. "Please go on."

He did.

"Based on the facts of the initial case against Mr. Acevedo, the original probation arrangement was the minimum sentence the defendant deserved. Without the extenuating circumstance of the offer made by the supervisors, Mr. and Mrs. Beale, Mr. Acevedo would be in prison.

"Because of the special request filed by the Office of Probation, I have ordered a full report by Mr. Conway and by the supervisors. The reports showed good progress in keeping with the expectations of the original probation order."

He paused and his brow darkened. "I have also reviewed the special brief filed by Congresswoman Karen Liu's office." For a few seconds he seemed resolute, but then he sank back in his chair as if he had given up a struggle. When he went on, he was uncomfortable and visibly angry, but defeated; and his eyes were on the congresswoman in the back row.

"Therefore, it is my judgment that Angelo Acevedo will be released from probation. Mr. Acevedo, you have used this rare opportunity that was offered, and you have demonstrated that you are able to act responsibly and participate in society. Congratulations. This hearing is now adjourned."

Angelo stared.

"He just gave in to her!" Dorothy said, making her own judgments. "We have to talk to him."

"No, he's made his decision." Charles turned to Angelo, and then to Karen Liu, just leaving the room. "Take Angelo home. I'll be there as quickly as I can to talk with him. But I have to see Karen Liu."

"Congresswoman." He caught up with her much easier than the last time, still in the maze of courthouse halls. "Excuse me. We need to talk."

"I don't think I can," she said, and sounded even worse than she looked.

"Then let's walk first. Do you have some time?"

"I told them I wouldn't be in today."

It was still early and they had most of the sunlight to themselves. Charles crossed King Street from the courthouse, and Karen Liu followed. They came to an empty Market Square, the fountains in the wide pool playing and ignored. Self-absorbed City Hall paid them no attention either, but just sat to be watched itself.

The air was still cool. "Let's sit," Charles said, and he chose a bench in the sun.

"It's been very hard on you," he said, "about Patrick White."

"Oh, Mr. Beale." She was close to tears. "It's not just yesterday. It's his whole death, all six long months of it."

"I saw him yesterday morning. He came to the shop."

"I saw him Sunday," she said. "He was angry and accusing me of being John Borchard's tool. He said that to me! He said I was as bad as the rest, as everyone. After all we've been through together, those were his last words to me."

"Is that why you came to Angelo's meeting Monday?" Charles asked.

"I wanted to prove I could still show compassion. Even if Patrick didn't think I could, I wanted to prove it to myself." The political rally cadence emerged, but hollowly. "I will fight for people who are persecuted, who have been imprisoned by their poverty and circumstances. That is *why* I am here." But then the platform collapsed and a much weaker voice drifted out of the ruins. "But I can't fight forever."

"You'll get past this."

"I don't think so. I want to give up."

"But you're a fighter." They had both been facing forward toward the fountain, but Charles turned to her, eye to eye. "Why would you give up now?"

"He's beaten me." She looked down, away from Charles. "Borchard."

"He is not the one you're fighting."

By force of will she regained herself. "You wouldn't know, Mr. Beale."

"I would know."

"What do you know?"

"I know that eight years ago in your first election, someone gave you five hundred thousand dollars. It was illegal."

"Yes."

"And I know you've been threatened, that if you didn't do what you were supposed to, you would be exposed. Just like Patrick White."

"It's been three years since the first letter. What do you think those three years have been like?"

"I know it's been very hard."

"Yes, they have been very hard." She wasn't showing weakness now. Her voice was vehement and her expression wild.

"You sound like Patrick White," Charles said.

"Not yet, Mr. Beale, but I'm getting there."

"Then I want to ask you some questions, and they're very important."

"All right." She took a deep breath and composed herself. "Go ahead."

"Mr. White said there was someone who would help him against John Borchard. Did he ever tell you that?"

"Yes, he said that to me."

"Do you know who it was? I even wondered if it was you."

"It wasn't me. No, I don't know who it was."

"My other question is, how do you know it was John Borchard who was sending you these letters?"

"He made it obvious. Three times when we had conflicts, Derek arranged meetings. Mr. Borchard would say what he wanted in the meeting, and then a few days later I would get a letter. It would threaten me, saying the *Washington Post* would get copies of my checks if I didn't cooperate, and it would say what I had to do in the exact words Borchard had used at the meeting."

"Patrick White went to Derek for help."

"Yes, and I did, too. He said he would help, but then . . ."

"Then he was killed."

"How do you know so much, Mr. Beale?"

"I learned it from Derek."

"He told you about John Borchard?"

"No."

A mournful note played. A dozen feet away, a young man had put his lips to an oboe. His eyes closed, he played a slow scale upwards. The oboe case was open on the pavement in front of him for coins.

"But he told you what I told him," Karen Liu said.

"No. He already knew before you told him."

The oboe player had finished his beginning and he started a melody, peaceful and minor.

"But how? How would he know?"

"He was the one sending you the letters. Karen, Derek was blackmailing and threatening you. It wasn't John Borchard."

The reedy music circled them as Karen Liu fought to understand. "That can't be."

"I'm sure of it. I'm completely sure."

"He told you?"

"No. I didn't know anything before he died. I've only learned it since. But I know it's true."

"Not Derek Bastien. I can't believe it, Mr. Beale." But then she said, "Did you tell any of this to Patrick?"

"No."

"He was sure it was John Borchard."

"I know," Charles said. "If only I had told him."

"I didn't know what he was planning. I knew he had made some decision. That must have been it. The police said he was making a bomb and it went off."

The oboe tune sped in faster circles.

"John Borchard is afraid," Charles said. "He thinks the other person may still try to kill him. That's why I need to find out who it is."

"Why you, Mr. Beale?"

"I think Derek has challenged me to."

Karen Liu didn't question his statement. She had a different question. "What have you done, Mr. Beale?"

"What do you mean?"

"What have you done wrong? Everyone else has done something."

"I've done lots of things wrong."

"What is the worst?"

The oboe dove deep and then flew. "I killed my son."

Finally, Karen Liu said, "How?"

"His name was William. There was something wrong with him. We never knew what."

"What happened?"

"As he grew, he became hostile. Then he became violent. And then . . . I'll be brief. He took his own life. He found a gun, somewhere, and held it to his head."

"Mr. Beale—I'm sorry, I didn't know."

"It was a long time ago, and it's not a secret. I find I can usually talk about it now."

"But how can you say that you killed him?"

"He was only seventeen. He was still under my care and my protection."

"That wasn't your fault."

"Whose fault was it?" The oboe was passionate, wailing jaggedly high and low. "We don't know if it was something hereditary. There are adoptions in our family, you see. Even though Dorothy is on the board of directors at the orphanage, she still can't get any information about her own family." He caught himself. "I'm sorry. I lost control for a moment. Maybe I still can't talk about it."

"Thank you for telling me. It isn't the same as what I've done."

"I feel the same way about it."

They sat for a while, listening, until the notes died.

"I have to go see Angelo," Charles said. "Maybe he is a redemption for both of us."

"I've never had a congresswoman cry on my shoulder before," Charles said. He didn't sit in his chair. "Is Angelo upstairs?"

"Yes," Dorothy said.

"Have you talked with him?"

"We were waiting for you."

"I'll get him."

"Sit down." Charles had sat and Dorothy was sitting. Angelo lowered himself to the chair, bending but not yielding. He was absolutely expressionless.

Charles faced the black hair and narrowed eyes and swarthy skin that were all anyone saw of him.

"Do you understand what happened?"

"That judge, he said no more probation." His voice was as blank as his face.

"Yes. He did."

"And you said no jail."

"No jail, no probation. It's all over. You're free."

Silence.

"What will you do, Angelo?" Dorothy said.

More silence.

"You can do whatever you want now," Charles said.

It was unnerving.

"All right," Charles said. "We can talk again after you've thought about it."

Angelo stood and left.

"What did that mean?" Dorothy said.

"I don't know. He's never been closed up that tight."

"I'm almost scared, Charles."

"Mr. Beale?"

"Yes, Alice?"

"Mr. Leatherman is here."

"Jacob."

Charles held out his hand. Jacob Leatherman took it, frail as an autumn leaf, his other hand propped on his walking stick.

"Do you have it?"

"I have it. I'll bring it up." Charles looked closer at Jacob. "Alice, bring a chair."

"Whippersnapper." But he didn't complain, and he sat, his face the color of yellowed pages and faded ink. Charles knelt down on one knee.

"How are you, Jacob?"

"Just give me a minute."

"Alice, get Dorothy."

Jacob's color was getting better.

"Jacob!" Dorothy flew down the stairs. "Why in the world did you fly overnight? Let me look at you."

"I'm fine." He glared at the three of them around him, Charles, Dorothy and Alice. "Just get short of breath once in a while."

"And do you think you're flying back tonight?" Dorothy asked.

"It's this afternoon."

"Alice. Call Mr. Leatherman's store and tell them to change his flight to tomorrow. Then get a hotel room. Try the Marriott on Duke Street. Jacob, you need to take better care of yourself." Dorothy looked him straight in the eye. "You are not as young as you used to be."

"He never was," Charles said.

"I'm not staying over the night," Jacob said, but not firmly. Nothing about him was very firm.

"You need to do what she says," Charles said. "There's no use fighting. Believe me."

"Well." Jacob took a deep breath. "Maybe I could use a rest."

"Of course," Charles said.

"Flight was the worst I've ever had."

"I know the best thing to revive you," Charles said. "Can you make it downstairs? Dorothy, I think we'll be all right. Thank you."

It was a slow process going down the steps. Jacob was recovering, though, and at the bottom he clattered across the floor with his stick as fast as Charles could keep up with him. He put Jacob in the desk chair.

Jacob Leatherman took a few minutes to look around the room, and to breathe it in.

"You have a few nice books down here."

"They're all nice," Charles said.

"Yes. They are. You treat them with respect, Charles, and it'll show."

"Let me get you the Homer." He took it from the shelf and laid it on the desk. "Here it is."

"Here it is," Jacob said. He pushed his wrinkled hand into his pocket and pulled out a magnifying lens set in an eyepiece. He took off his glasses and fit the magnifier to his eye and tightened his cheek to hold it in place. "Now I can see."

Charles was silent as Jacob hunched over the book, the glass only an inch from the gold letters on the cover.

"Hand-stamped, of course. Give me gloves."

Charles handed him the white cotton gloves and the thin silver page turner. Jacob opened the front board.

For three minutes he stared at the faded signature, first moving side to side, then without any motion.

"Her own hand, Charles. Rested right there. She put her pen to the page and wrote the name of a queen."

"I assume it was hers. It hasn't been authenticated."

"It has been now." There was no strength in his wavering words, only absolute authority. "It was hers or I don't know anything."

"Then it was," Charles said.

Jacob turned the page. For a while he didn't move.

"I'll let you be by yourself," Charles said.

"Thank you."

"I'll be back down in a while."

"Is he all right?" Dorothy asked.

"Yes, he's fine. I'm still planning to go to New York this afternoon."

"Charles! With everything else happening? Can't you reschedule?"

"I can't. I don't have any way to communicate with Mr. Smith."

"If you don't show up, he'll call you."

"I don't think this is a meeting that I can miss," Charles said.

"What about Angelo? I . . . I don't think you should leave. We don't know what he might do."

"I'm going to take him with me. If he'll come."

Two quick knocks. The dark head peered out.

"Angelo. I would like you to come with me on a delivery. Would you do that?"

"Now?" He was still in his nice clothes from the morning.

"In a while. We'll be taking a train to New York."

"New York City?"

"Yes."

Angelo didn't speak. He might have been deliberating or he might just have been waiting.

"You don't have to," Charles said.

"You do not want to go alone?"

"I'd rather you went with me."

"Why?"

Charles did deliberate. "It's a very valuable book and I don't know exactly what will happen. I might want help."

"I will come."

"We'll leave in a couple of hours and we'll be back tonight, late."

"Angelo will come with me."

"I know you can't answer this," Dorothy said, "but could you tell at all what he was thinking?"

"I had one clue. When I asked him to come, he asked me why. He's never questioned me before."

"What did you tell him?"

"I made it sound like it might be dangerous, and I might need help."

"Will it be dangerous?" Dorothy said.

"I really don't think so," Charles said. "And while I'm up there, I think I will make one other stop. I wonder where I put Edmund Cane's telephone number."

"He was the man who bid on Derek's desk?"

"Yes. I would really like to know who he was representing."

"May I speak with Mr. Edmund Cane, please?"

"Who is calling?"

"This is Charles Beale, from Virginia. He and I have spoken before."

"Just a moment, sir."

Several moments passed.

"Mr. Beale?"

"Yes."

"This is Edmund Cane. It is so nice to speak with you again. I hope you are calling to discuss the sale of Derek Bastien's books?"

"Not on the telephone. I'm coming to New York on business, and I'd like to stop in for a moment if it's convenient for you."

"When would that be?"

"I'm leaving here by train in a few hours. I would be at your showroom about six. Is that too late?"

"We are open until nine. Would you prefer to meet later?"

"No, I have an evening meeting afterwards."

"Very well, Mr. Beale. We are on Fortieth Street, near Seventh Avenue."

"Good. I look forward to it."

Charles set the telephone down. "I just thought of one other clue," he said to Dorothy.

"About Mr. Cane?"

"About Angelo. One other clue about what he might be thinking. He didn't call me boss."

"I'm done," Jacob said.

Charles stood beside the desk. "I'm glad you came."

"Just an old man's folly."

"Your folly, Jacob, is beyond most men's wisdom. If you hadn't come, I might have taken it out to you."

"Brought it to me?" An ember spurted a few sparks. "Brought it? Why didn't you tell me? Would have saved me a trip."

"You need the exercise. May I take you to your hotel?"

"I should get back home."

"I think you should take the rest of the day off. I'd take you out to dinner tonight, but I'll be in New York."

"With your Mr. Smith?" His eyes glowed. "I'd like to meet him. But I'm not up to it."

"You'd scare him off, anyway. But if you're still here tomorrow, I can tell you about it."

"That's worth staying, then." He closed the book but stayed in the chair. "And how's your matchmaker? How's that story coming?"

"That's a good question," Charles said. "May I ask your advice?"

"That's what everyone wants. They think they know everything and then finally they ask someone who does."

"I'm glad that you do. The main thing is that I'm stuck. I don't know what to do. I won't tell you the whole story because it's too long and there are things that I shouldn't say."

"It won't matter anyway," Jacob said. "It's the same advice I'll tell you regardless."

"And what is that, Jacob?"

"If you don't know what to do, it's because you do know what to do but you don't want to do it."

"There are other people involved."

"There always are. That's no excuse."

Charles shook his head. "You don't even know what this is about."

"And I still know what you should do."

"Exactly, Jacob. You really do know everything. Let me take you to your hotel while I think about what it means."

"Jacob is settled," Charles said, "cantankerous and fulminating as good as new."

"He looked dreadful there," Dorothy said.

"More than usual. But I think he's revived. He really should get a rest. I hope he does."

"Are you ready to leave, then?"

"Almost. I'm going to call John Borchard. Sometime we'll need to finish our conversation."

"There's no answer at his house," Charles said, "and his office says he's not in today."

"Did you think he would be?"

"Not really. I'll have to wait until he's ready. And I wish the police detective would call."

"You could call him," Dorothy said.

"I will tomorrow. They must think I was just a witness to the explosion. They wouldn't know about the whole Derek Bastien story."

"John Borchard would have told them."

"Probably not."

"Is there anything to do about Patrick White?" Dorothy asked. "It doesn't seem right to just go on like nothing happened."

"I don't know what to do. The only thing I can think of is to talk to the police. But it will have to wait."

"Are you taking anything to New York?"

"Just the book. I'm planning to travel very light."

"Mr. Beale?" Morgan was at the office door. "I heard you're going to New York? I'm swapping a dozen volumes with Briary Roberts. Would you like to take them with you?"

"I'm planning to travel very heavy," Charles said to Dorothy.

"I could drive you to the train station?" Dorothy said.

"We'll take the Metro. Angelo can carry the books."

AFTERNOON

Angelo sat outside on the front steps, waiting.

"Be careful." She kissed him on his cheek. "I'd miss you if you didn't come back." She tried to sound cheerful.

"In that case, I will come back," Charles answered, trying more successfully. "Good bye, dear."

"Good bye."

"And don't worry," he said.

"I will."

"We'll be back tonight," Charles said. Morgan handed him a heavy satchel. "Even if it looks like we're staying until tomorrow."

"I'll meet you at the train station," she said. "Two fifteen?"

"Two fifteen. I'm sorry it will be so late at night." He opened the door. Angelo pulled himself upright.

"We are going now?" He took the large satchel, and in it the dozen books.

"Yes, finally."

From the sidewalk, Charles blew the kiss back to Dorothy. He had just a small briefcase, and in it just the *Odyssey*.

Charles was in thought and not seeing the world, and Angelo was not seeming to see. They walked half the ten blocks to the Metro in silence.

"Who knows you are taking that?" Angelo said, suddenly.

"This?" Charles was startled. "The book?"

"That book."

"Not anyone here, besides Morgan and Mrs. Beale."

And then the silence resumed.

At the Metro station, Angelo paused at the bottom of the escalator. Charles waited for him at the top. A train had just arrived, its doors briefly open.

"We can catch this," Charles said as Angelo reached the top.

"Wait."

Charles stopped.

"What for?"

"The next train."

The train doors closed. Angelo leaned against a pillar. Charles stood next to him. Five minutes passed before a new train opened its doors for them.

"Is this one all right?"

"It is okay."

Charles took a seat and Angelo stood, one hand on a pole. An assorted dozen passengers were already sitting; no one else had come onto the car with them.

The doors closed and the train swayed. Angelo, erect, did not.

"What was wrong with the first train?" Charles asked.

"The train was not wrong."

"What was?"

"That man."

Charles looked through the car again. "You saw someone?"

"He is two cars back. He waited when we waited."

"He followed us from the shop?"

"I saw him the first time when I asked you."

"What does he look like?"

"He wears blue jeans and a sweatshirt that is dark green. He has a baseball cap and he has a beard."

"Why didn't you tell me when you saw him?"

"Then you would look around to see him." Angelo opened his eyes wide and jerked his head side to side, for just a moment animated. "Like that," he said, mocking. "And then he knows I have seen him."

"Well. I probably would have."

"Do not look when we get out. I will tell you when to look."

"All right. What if he doesn't get out when we do?"

"Then we do not see him."

"How old is he?"

"Not old like you."

The train slid into the next station. Charles tightened his grip on the briefcase.

Twenty minutes later, they approached the Gallery Place station.

"We'll switch to the Red Line to Union Station," Charles said.

The train had become crowded, and when they exited, the platform had at least a hundred people. Charles tried not to look around.

They switched to the other platform, even as a train was coming in.

"He is in the car behind us," Angelo said as that train left the station.

Union Station was the second stop. They left the train, and Charles set a leisurely pace up through the halls and escalators. They left the Metro platforms and followed the signs and crowds.

"Make a look back now," Angelo said, "and then look away."

Charles turned. There was a large clock on the wall and he stared at it for a few seconds. Then he turned forward again.

"I don't recognize him," he said. "I'd remember that beard."

They approached the Amtrak ticket booths, where Charles stopped to look at the schedule board.

"We can take the train that's in fifteen minutes. You stay here while I get the tickets."

He bought two tickets and ambled back.

"He is watching from there," Angelo said. "He did not buy any ticket."

They waited five minutes and then climbed onto the train. It was crowded and they went through two cars before they found two seats together.

And finally it started moving. "I did not see him come on," Angelo said. "That man, do you know why he followed us?"

"Not specifically," Charles said.

"He is watching that book?"

"This? No one knows I have it."

"The man you will see. He has friends watching you to see that you are coming for the deal."

"I don't think it's that kind of people."

"We'll have two other errands besides our meeting at nine o'clock," Charles said. They had ridden in silence for an hour. "The first is an antiques showroom where I just need to talk to a man for a few minutes.

Then we will go to a very large bookstore called Briary Roberts. I need to give them the books in your bag."

"You do lots of deals," Angelo said.

"I sell lots of books. I buy lots of books. Would you want to learn more about books, Angelo?"

"No."

"What do you want to do?"

Angelo's shoulders might have lifted a tenth of an inch and dropped, or he might not have moved at all.

"You can do whatever you want," Charles said.

Angelo didn't move at all.

EVENING

The train came to a final stop. Charles exited and wandered toward an exit with his briefcase, Angelo a few steps behind with the satchel of books.

"Penn Station," Charles said, and they walked up the stairs and to the central hall.

"It is big."

"Have you seen anyone?"

"I don't see anyone."

"It's probably hard to tell here. There are so many people."

"Too many," Angelo said.

"First we're going to Horton's on Fortieth."

Angelo's face lifted as they left the station.

"It is tall," he said. He was not impressed.

"Yes. Most people notice. We have about a half mile to walk."

"Do they have a Metro?"

"The Subway. But I'd rather walk, I think."

They crossed to Seventh Avenue and turned left. The sidewalks were crammed and people moved much faster than in Alexandria. No one's eyes met theirs.

"I cannot see if anyone is watching us," Angelo said after a while.

"I don't know what we'd do if someone was."

"This is Horton's." It was.

"I will stay here." Angelo stopped outside the door.

"No, come in."

Angelo obeyed. He stepped over the threshold, and then stopped.

Six of Norman Highberg's shop could have fit inside; and besides antiques, Horton's did furniture. The display tables and cases were works of art by themselves. Thousands of pieces were ranged around them: Byzantine, Baroque, Beaux Arts, Bauhaus; porcelain, pewter, paintings. Not much of human history or geography was *not* represented.

"Do you remember Derek Bastien's house? The man who was killed."

"I remember."

"He had lots of things like these."

"I never touched them."

Charles paused. "I know you didn't. Here," he picked up a candlestick from a display of silver in the front aisle, "hold it for a moment."

Angelo took it, turned it from one side to another, and handed it back.

Charles replaced it on the table. "Angelo, I don't believe you've ever touched a valuable antique before in your life."

"What do you mean?"

"Nothing. Just the way you held it."

"Mr. Beale. I am Edmund Cane."

Charles turned and extended his hand. "Mr. Cane. Thank you so much for seeing me."

"So good to see you again."

"Thank you. Although we've only barely seen each other before."

"I do remember," Mr. Cane said. "You were in the back row?"

"Yes, I was. I came in during the bidding for the desk."

"Of course. I believe I said that I'm no longer interested in the desk."

"Yes, you did say that."

"I am, however, interested in the books you purchased at the auction. The thirteen volumes mentioned in the catalog."

"As it turns out, there were actually fourteen," Charles said.

"The catalog was incorrect?" Mr. Cane's enunciation was as stiff as his white hair was riotous. "I believe it said thirteen volumes?"

"There were thirteen volumes at the auction. Derek Bastien had fourteen, but one had been separated from the others."

"I would want them all."

"Yes. I don't have that particular one in my possession."

"I would take the ones you do have."

Charles nodded. "I think I would like to know who is actually trying to buy them."

Edmund Cane's speech had been robotic. Now he seemed to have blown out his transistors. He froze, jerked slightly, and finally computed an answer.

"I'm very sorry, Mr. Beale, but of course I can't give you that information."

"That's too bad," Charles said. "It is quite a mystery, isn't it? First the desk, and now the books."

"I really can't comment."

"There's a lot of mystery surrounding the whole Bastien estate. I've been told that a few of the pieces stolen from the house have been recovered by the FBI."

"I am currently only interested in the books."

"Yes," Charles said. "I only deal in books, but the FBI actually questioned me concerning the other pieces."

"I suppose they would be interested in the stolen antiques."

"Yes, exactly. Did any of them come from here?"

"Here?"

"I wondered if Derek Bastien had bought anything from Horton's. Did the FBI ask you about them?"

Mr. Cane wasn't sure of any reason not to answer. "No one from

the FBI has been here about anything stolen from the Derek Bastien
estate. I don't believe he had purchased any of them or any pieces at
all from us." At about two syllables per second, the sentence took a
long time.

"No one at all? You're quite a large dealer in antiques."

"We do cooperate with the FBI. It is our normal procedure to compare our pieces with their lists. But no one has been here in specific
reference to the Bastien estate."

"I see. I suppose you deal with their New York office?"

"Of course."

"I wish you could tell me who you were representing," Charles said.

"I am sorry, Mr. Beale, that I can't help you. I would still want to
purchase the thirteen volumes you have."

"I am sorry, Mr. Cane, that I can't help you."

"I see." Mr. Cane dealt with the sorrow. "Then I hope your trip hasn't
been wasted. What else are you doing in the city, Mr. Beale?"

"As I said, I have a meeting at nine. Just book business. And no,
stopping in hasn't been a waste."

The next walk was twenty minutes.

"This is Briary Roberts," Charles said. "It's a very old antique bookstore. It's been here more than a hundred and fifty years."

"I will stay out."

"You could at least bring those books in."

So again Angelo followed Charles over a threshold. At the counter,
Charles said, "Is Mr. Peake in?"

The Alice-ish young woman said, "May I tell him who is asking?"

"Charles Beale. I have some books for him, and I also want to ask
him a question."

"I'll see if he can come down. Just a moment."

Charles used the moment to stroll. Angelo stood beside the counter,
the book satchel at his side.

"Come look at this," Charles said.

Angelo came.

"It's just a book of photographs," Charles said. "These are New York tenements a hundred years ago. They would have hundreds of people in a building like this. There would be six or eight people in a room the size of yours, but no window."

The page held Angelo's interest. "Where do they come from?"

"They're immigrants. They came from Italy and Poland and other countries in Europe."

"People still live in these buildings?"

"There are new immigrants there, but it isn't nearly this bad. These people"—he touched some of the faces on the pages—"their great-grandchildren live in houses out in the suburbs, all over the country. They have jobs and families. That was why these people came, so that their children could live better lives."

Angelo turned a page. "What are these people?"

"That's Ellis Island. They are just arriving in America, maybe that very day. They've left everything they know behind to come to a place they've never seen. They don't speak any English. They have hope, but here, I think they are mostly afraid. When you came to our shop the first day, it was something like that."

"I was not afraid."

"Oh no, I didn't mean it that way. I know you weren't."

"Charles!"

A teapot of a man, short and stout, came bubbling and whistling toward them.

"Ah, Mervyn, here you are. Here, I'd like you to take a quick look at something. Angelo, they have some books to trade for the ones in your bag. I'll be back in a few minutes."

"What do you think?" Charles said. Mervyn Peake was bent as much as he could be over the *Odyssey*.

"The quality's good. The title page, or whatever you call it, doesn't look good. Where'd you get it?"

"Off eBay. Just someone clearing out their attic."

He gave it one more critical look. "Seven hundred."

"I paid seventeen."

"You've been snookered, then." He gave Charles a critical look. "What do you think's so funny?"

"I'm not laughing!"

"You're rolling in the aisles. What's the hook?"

"Mervyn, have you ever heard of a man called Mr. Smith?"

"Are you kidding me? Half the people who want to sell me books are Mr. Smith."

"This Mr. Smith wants to buy a book. This book. He's British, and I'm meeting him this evening at a restaurant called Rusterman's."

"On Twenty-eighth? I've been there."

"Did you meet a Mr. Smith there?"

"No Smith. We had a dinner there once when the manager of our London branch came over."

"Any particular reason you had the dinner there?"

"The British Consul in New York came, too. He picked it. He had some connection with the owner. It didn't have anything to do with books."

"We're ready," Charles said to Angelo. "Did you get the books?"

"I have those books from the lady."

"Very good. It looks like we have plenty of time to get to Twenty-eighth Street."

The sky was finally black, what little could be seen beyond the high walls and lights. The windows of Rusterman's were bright but only looked into the lobby. The dining room was hidden.

"I will stay here," Angelo said for the third time that evening.

"You are completely respectable, Angelo," Charles said, "and it would be fine for you to come in. But Mr. Smith is expecting me alone."

"That man, he knows I am here, he is watching. He doesn't show up if I come in. I will wait outside and watch."

"That's fine. I don't think he's watching us, but maybe he is. I don't know how long I will be."

"Thirty minutes and I will look in there for you," Angelo said.

"Charles Beale."

"Yes, sir," the maitre d' said. "Please come this way."

Through the foyer, but they did not turn into the dining room. Farther back in the hall, the master opened a door and stood back. Charles entered.

The room was comfortably sized for the single table, and at the table, very comfortably, sat a middle-aged man. He was impeccably dressed in a dark suit and silk tie.

"Thank you," he said, and the maitre d' bowed and slid out. "Mr. Beale. Please sit down."

"Thank you. Mr. Smith?"

"Mr. Smith, yes." His tone left no doubt that he was not. "I trust you had a pleasant trip."

"Very pleasant."

"Good. We won't take extra time this evening. May I see the book?"

"Of course." There was no place setting or food on the table, just a large flat envelope and a brick-shaped wrapped bundle. Charles opened his briefcase and set the paper package in the center. The man waited and didn't move.

Charles took his white gloves from his pocket and pulled them on. He pulled the paper apart and lifted the book from its cushioning and held it forward.

Mr. Smith took a magnifying glass from his pocket and inspected the cover. "Please open it to the signature."

Gently, he did.

The signature was considered.

"Turn the page, please."

Charles turned to the half title. The imperturbable Mr. Smith tensed slightly.

"The full title page has been removed," Charles said. "Evidently long ago."

Mr. Smith took the large flat envelope from the table, and from it extracted a clear plastic sheaf enclosing a single, yellowed book page.

"Oh my," Charles said.

Her Royal Highness
Princess Victoria
History of the War of Troy and the Greeks
The Odyssey
Padding & Brewster, London, 1827

"There is a slight notch from the cutting," Mr. Smith said. "I'd like to see that it matches."

Charles held the book while the man compared his page to it.

Then the man leaned back. "I accept that it is authentic." A tiny charge of excitement made the convivial smile he'd had from the beginning tremble, just a little.

Then Mr. Smith returned to his perfect poise. Pleasantly, he said, "I propose one hundred thousand dollars for the book."

Charles paused. "It's a very rare book, of course, but I wouldn't have asked that much."

"I have made inquiries into your business, Mr. Beale, and I don't feel that negotiations are necessary."

"But—"

"And this is the only offer that I'm authorized to make."

Charles gestured with his empty hands. "Then by all means. I accept, very gratefully."

He re-wrapped the book and held it out.

Mr. Smith received it, and in return handed him the brick-shaped package. "I hope you find that in order."

Charles opened the end. "This is cash!" He recovered. "I'm sorry, I hadn't expected it."

"It is one hundred thousand dollars."

"Mr. Smith, I'm very sorry—a cash transaction of this size, I would need some idea of who you are—"

"I hope you can deal with the formalities. I would prefer that there is no idea of who I am."

"I see." Charles smiled. "Yes, I can deal with the formalities. And please tell me, do you have the other volumes in the set? I suppose there would be an *Iliad* and an *Aeneid*?"

"They will all be together. Thank you, Mr. Beale. It has been a pleasure."

"Thank you very much," Charles said. "And please give Her Majesty my regards."

Mr. Smith chortled as only an Englishman of his bearing could. "What a romantic thought. But if I ever were to see her, I will."

Charles stopped ten feet out from the front door. He still had the package in his hand.

"The deal is good?" Angelo appeared from the empty air.

"Um, yes, I think so."

"That is the cash?"

"Yes, it is. How did you know it would be cash?"

"A deal is always cash. Did you count it?"

"I didn't. It would have taken too long."

Angelo's eyes were on the package, but he managed a brief look of scorn at Charles.

"You don't even count it?"

"I'm sure it's fine."

"Don't carry it out in your hand."

Charles opened his empty briefcase and put the package inside. "All right. We'll just go back to the train station, then, and head home."

Angelo swept the street with a quick glance and then fixed again on the briefcase in Charles's hand.

Dorothy was parked in front of the deserted train station. The sky was moonless black.

"Hello, dear," Charles said. He took the driver's seat. "We did make it home." Angelo slid silently into the back.

"Thank you," she said. "Did you sell your book?"

"I did. It was all very interesting."

It was 2:30 a.m. as they crossed the Potomac and ten minutes later when they stopped in front of the bookstore.

"Here we are," Charles said to Dorothy. The street and the shop were as dark and empty as they could be. "I'll only be a minute."

"I'll come in."

Angelo followed with the book satchel. Charles turned on the light and put his code into the alarm.

"Thank you for coming, Angelo," he said. "I'll put those books down in the basement for Morgan."

"Good night," Dorothy said as Angelo disappeared.

The desk was empty except for its computer and one volume that hadn't been returned to its shelf. Charles set the book satchel next to them. Then he opened the briefcase and took the package out and unwrapped it. There were ten banded stacks. It took over a minute to count one stack of one hundred hundred-dollar bills.

He didn't count the others. He wrapped the stacks back together and set the package on a shelf behind a row of books.

He looked closer at the volume on the desk. It was the Dante; he opened it and read a few lines at random.

> *For all the gold that is beneath the moon,*
> *Or ever has been, of these weary souls*
> *Could never make a single one respose.*

Then he put it up on the same shelf as the package of money.

"Is everything all right?"

"Yes, it's fine." Charles turned the alarm on and the light off. He and Dorothy walked out into the night. The streetlamp sent their shadows flying.

Charles stretched his fingers as he opened Dorothy's car door. "I've been carrying that briefcase all day. It's nice to have my hands free."

On the third floor, Angelo's light turned off.

"One hundred thousand?" Dorothy was shocked.

"It was the only offer he was authorized to make."

"Who was he?"

"Just Mr. Smith."

"That's how he signed the check?"

"No check, dear. Just hundred-dollar bills. A thousand of them."

Dorothy was very shocked.

"Where is it?"

"In the basement at the store."

They reached their house. Charles parked on the street in front.

"Does Angelo know?"

"Know what?"

"That there is a hundred thousand dollars of cash just downstairs from him."

"Um, not necessarily."

"Why didn't you bring it home?"

"I thought it would be safer locked in the basement of the store."

"Is it just lying out?"

"It's not lying. It's telling the truth."

"Charles."

"It's on the shelf behind the Dante."

They were finally settling into bed at three o'clock in the morning.

"You could sleep late tomorrow," Dorothy said.

"Maybe I will. I'm not as young as I used to be."

"You always will be, dear."

"I'm too tired to think what that means. The only thing I have to do tomorrow is to call the police detective."

"Did you see Mr. Horton?"

"Cane. Edmund Cane. Of Horton's. Yes."

"Did he tell you anything about the desk?"

"No, except that he never told the FBI anything about it. But someone must have."

"Told them what?"

"I'm too tired to think what that means either. Oh, Dorothy, what was Derek doing? What was going on?"

"Someone must know."

"I keep thinking about the conversations I had with him. Especially the last one."

"What did you talk about?"

"Just a game we had started. It was about how we lived our lives, but it was mostly just an exercise in repartee. That's what I thought, but suddenly I wonder what he really meant." He turned off the light. "How I wish I could have one more talk with him."

"So, Charles, how do you like the game now?"

"I don't, Derek. It's quite unfair that you've put me up to it. I'd rather not be playing."

"I think you need to be. We'll see if the principles you've spouted all these years will stand up to a real test."

"Is that the point, Derek? Is that why you put the papers in the book? To embroil me in all of this?"

"It seems to have worked."

"But surely you didn't expect to be killed. Was it just a common burglary, or was it one of your victims?"

"You're only imagining me, Charles. You know I can't answer that."

"Were you really a blackmailer, Derek? Was that the game you were playing, and your 'situation' at the office?"

"You don't sound content, Charles. You must be losing our game."

"But you're dead, Derek, so I don't think you've won it."

"No. It isn't pleasant here. The circles go deeper and deeper and I still haven't found my depth."

"Who killed you, Derek?"

"Have I passed that circle yet? I believe I have. The murderers. Yes, that was one or two back. I hope I'm not headed to the ninth circle, to the circle of traitors."

"Who was the other person you were blackmailing? The person who tried to buy your desk? The person Patrick White had helping him. Who was it, Derek? Was that who killed you?"

"Patrick White? Yes, he's down here now, too. I don't know where they'll put him. There's a circle for everyone. I hope I'm not in for the traitors, the betrayers. That's the worst judgment of all, way down at the very bottom of the Inferno. Am I a traitor? Did I betray you, Charles? Is that why I'm still going down?"

"No, Derek. You're no traitor. I forgive you."

THURSDAY

MORNING

"Charles."

"The Inferno."

"Charles!"

"What?"

The room was dark. Dorothy was beside him. He sat up awake.

"You were dreaming. You were saying something."

The clock said 3:40.

"I know who it is," Charles said.

"What?"

"I know who killed Derek."

The telephone rang.

Or was it sirens? He was still disoriented. He found the screaming telephone.

"Hello?"

"Is this Charles Beale?" the voice said.

"Yes, it is."

"This is Alexandria Emergency Services. We have a call that your building on South Fairfax street has a fire."

"In the building?"

"Yes, sir. We've dispatched trucks."

"Fire?"

Dorothy gasped.

"Yes, sir."

"I'll be right there."

"Mr. Beale, the Fire Department trucks are just leaving now. They'll be there in two minutes. Stay away from the building."

"Yes, yes. But I have to go."

He put down the telephone. Dorothy was up from the bed getting dressed very quickly.

They did hear sirens.

He ran. The streets were empty and black. He didn't even think of driving until he was already on the sidewalk running, panting, then walking, then running and coughing and pushing.

The streets were black and red and blue and white. The colors flickered ahead. An infernal world was before him and he raced to it as fast as his slow, uncooperative legs could.

He turned the last corner and it was all before him, bright and screaming.

The grinding lights filled everything and they were still coming.

There was sound, sirens as demonic as the lights.

He was close and he didn't know how to stop running. But he was halted by a wall of smoke and everything else was unreal; the smoke was real. And the smoke was born of burning.

The smell told him what was burning, not just bitter and choking but horrible with the taste of forest and of old linen. He stumbled closer.

He was stopped by arms and voices, and then he couldn't move at all but was made stone by the smoke and red light that was inside.

Dorothy stood beside him.

The white spotlight glare made the beautiful old building grotesque and drowned the red light inside. There was only smoke. He choked on the smoke.

It was gray and poured out in an upended waterfall, gushing from windows and streaming from everywhere else. Terrible smoke, full of fragments of pages; they were tiny glittering sparks, scattering everywhere. Scattering everything. Everything that they were.

All of the books.

The men were breaking open the front door. The flames in the window flared and forced out huge planets of smoke. The whole street was smoke.

Water poured in, but the flames were unquenchable. All the windows were full of flames, every story of the building was in flame. Every story in every book was in flame.

The top floor was in flame. Angelo's window was filled with smoke. Men with hoses pushed through the smoke at the front door.

Something central inside surrendered and broke apart and fell, and waves of heat and smoke and fire crashed against everything. The men fell back from the door.

Now the whole building was a chimney, pulling in oxygen at the base and feeding itself to the inferno. The flames were insatiable.

Something central inside Charles surrendered and broke apart and fell.

Rivers of water rained in, and how could the fire still burn?

Despair crashed against everything and minutes or years passed.

The flames faltered under the onslaught, finally, or because everything was consumed. The men renewed their attack on the door. There were shouts above the siren howling. There was nothing but smoke; everything was only smoke now. Everything that had been was only smoke now.

More men were in the front door. Why would so many go in?

There was no end of the smoke. Charles could smell every book in it, and everything else that was in it. What else was in the smoke?

The men came back out. They were carrying something. It took three of them.

Charles could move again, but he was stopped, held back.

"Who is it?"

The men carrying didn't hurry once they were out from the smoke.

They carried to an ambulance. They laid on a stretcher, slowly, and covered with a sheet and set up into the open doors and the ambulance drove off.

All of the men had come out of the building. Water still rained down on it. There was no flame, only smoke.

"There's a basement," Charles said. "It's a fireproof room."

"It's too dangerous," they said. "We have to wait."

It was 4:30 in the morning.

Dorothy stayed with him. He stood and waited.

The hoses stopped. The smoke only oozed now, swamp-like. The street cleared. Only a few men stayed.

A police car arrived and a grim man from it came to him. The man wore a jacket, and Charles shivered. It had been so hot before.

"Mr. Beale?"

"I'm Charles Beale. I own the building."

"Yes, sir." The man spoke with the weight of death. "Detective Mondelli. We recovered a body from the fire." The man wasn't weighed down by it, though. He was doing his job.

"I saw them," Charles said.

"Can you help us identify it?"

Charles walked away. The man went to Dorothy, but she was crying. Charles took her away and the man waited.

Charles and Dorothy stood and looked at the smoke and black window holes and the black door hole. A fireman stepped up to it and looked in.

"I want to get to the basement," Charles said to a fireman.

"I don't think—"

"Now!" Charles pushed him away. "I'm going in. Are you coming with me?"

They did come. Three of the four firemen still there came. Charles crossed the threshold into the black gaping hole.

The fire still raged inside, but a fire of silence and blackness and an unbreathable sopping smoky stench. It was much worse than the fire of heat and light.

He didn't stop. He didn't stare at the charred walls and open ceiling or anything else the flashlights touched. It was too different from what it had been to possibly be the same room. The floor held.

He hurried to where the stairs had been. The upper stairs had fallen but the stairs down were still passable.

"Watch out!"

But he didn't care. He had to get to the bottom. The steps held.

The lights fell onto the door. The knob wouldn't turn. The walls and door weren't burned. He used his key and the knob was free, but the door still wouldn't open.

He pushed but it did not yield. The bottom landing was filled with water, over his shoes.

He was pulled back and stronger shoulders went against the door. It moved a little and then an axe came down on it and it cracked and fell inward.

Heavy, evil smoke roiled out. The lights could not penetrate. They fell back from Hadean gate coughing and daunted and the smoke came and came, darkness itself.

Charles abandoned hope. Without hope, he still went on.

He dropped to his knees and crawled under the smoke. He felt it running over his back like sand. His eyes were closed. His face was just over the face of the waters and sometimes dipped into them.

His head rammed into something hard as above him came a cracking and then a heavy, rigid weight came down on his back, forcing him down and submerging his face. He pushed up against it, choking and drowning.

The weight was pulled off. He sputtered, forcing water out of his lungs but filling them only with poison air, and he was still blind.

He found what he had run into. A chair, against the door. He pushed it aside and the broken door that had fallen on him, and crawled on, faster now.

The lights were behind him, just dim, dull spears into the Cerberus of smoke.

He reached the desk. A portion of the black air had drained out and clear air had begun to fill in, up to a foot now above the level of the water; but still no light could pierce the smoke.

He felt his way around the desk. He could sense the other men behind him.

Finally a shaft of white cut through the clear air between water and smoke and found the wall.

"Look at that," a voice said, a voice that sounded like sound through smoke.

Like light through smoke, only faintly more than shadows, a dim row of ghostly books stood silent above the ruin of the room.

"I don't believe it," said another voice.

But Charles didn't care. The chair was all important. It meant more than all the books.

His hand in the water touched something else solid, but not hard.

"Here!" Then he coughed again from breathing in enough air to speak. "Down here!"

The lights found him and what he was holding up out of the water, a hand.

Movement became urgent. He pulled the hand, and arm, and he saw black hair. Angelo's black hair.

Angelo's black hair. Angelo's black hair. Charles touched the hair.

Stronger arms and shoulders again took hold, and he slid through the water, getting out of the way. His back found the desk and he sat against it. There was only one more thing.

Pulling and lifting, the men drove, burdened, toward the door and stairs. For one moment a light passed over the black hair and closed eyes and white teeth, and the jaw convulsed and choked in the wicked air.

He was alive. That was the one thing.

The men staggered away up the stairs, and the room went black and still.

Then Charles rested. The water was cold and he was soaked. The air was foul but could be breathed. Slowly his eyes could see thin gray light from the doorway, from the street or the beginning of morning. Even here, the night was not absolute always.

The light touched the walls and the books, or Charles could see them without light. They had also survived for a while longer, even if nothing would last forever, and what a story they must have seen played out in the smoke.

"Hey! Buddy! You still down there?"

The lights came back and the air was clear.

"I'm here," Charles said.

"You all right?"

"I will be."

"Your wife's throwing a fit up there."

They helped him stand but he wouldn't leave yet. Through the weird girders of light, he grabbed a book and then the package he'd left last night. Only then they slogged through the debris and murk and up into the world of the living.

Charles walked slowly out into the open air and light, gray from ash and dawn. Dorothy ran to him.

"Charles." She buried her head in his soaked, sooted shoulder. "They have Angelo."

"He was in the basement."

He put his arms around her and they fell onto the front steps to sit and weep together. They sat alone together and ignored the ruins behind them.

But not for long. In the street, still blocked by barricades, two paramedics were kneeling and Charles stumbled over beside them. Angelo was propped between them, breathing at least, a living man.

"How is he?" Charles asked.

"Okay, maybe," one said. "Smoke, but that's probably all."

"Could we just take him to my house? It's very close."

"He should go to the hospital."

"I want to take him to my house," Charles said to the driver. "It's just three blocks."

"You what? Wait a minute."

Now there was a swarm around Angelo, and a stretcher, but Charles pushed in. "Does he need to go to a hospital?"

The paramedics were talking. "Are you related or anything?"

"I'm his probation supervisor. I can sign papers."

"Let me just check him out."

Charles stepped back. But then another voice interrupted.

"Mr. Beale?"

"Detective. Yes? I don't remember your name."

"Mondelli. That's somebody you know?"

"My employee. He lives in—lived in the top floor."

"Anybody else would have been in the house?"

"No one," Charles said. "No one should have been."

"So, you have any idea who it was? Um, we don't have a lot left of him to work with."

Charles breathed in the clear, cool air. "There is a man named John Borchard."

"Spell that?"

Charles did. "He works at the Justice Department downtown. He lives out in McLean. Or it might be someone else."

The detective was staring at the name. "So why would he be in your building?"

"I'm sorry, Mr. Mondelli. If it's him I'll tell the whole story. But I have to get my wife back home." He turned away to find a fireman. "Sir. The books in the basement. I have to get them out."

"We'll have an inspector look at it. He'll tell you if you can get anything out."

"They're rare books. It's ten million dollars."

"Uh, okay, we'll have the guy here in a couple hours. I'll get the water pumped out."

"Thank you."

Angelo had not been moved. A pillow was under his head and Dorothy was beside him.

A pillow was under Angelo's head, and Charles and Dorothy were still beside him. Daybreak pierced the lace curtains.

"Look at him," Dorothy said.

The suspicion and hardness had receded from him and uncovered a tranquility that was natural to his still features. "That's who I always thought he was."

A clock chimed six times.

The telephone rang.

"I'm so tired," Charles said. "And it's going to be such a long day." He picked up the telephone. "This is Charles Beale."

"Detective Mondelli. Okay, tell me your story."

"Mr. Mondelli. Yes. I don't remember what I said before."

"What would this Borchard be doing in your building at three in the morning lighting fires?"

Charles closed his eyes. He set the receiver on the side table for a moment, then picked it up.

"Was it John Borchard?"

"We can't find him and we've got some forensics that match and I have Detective Paisley from Fairfax on the other line who wants to talk to you."

"You've done quite a lot."

"So why was he in your place? And you were at his place Tuesday when the judge blew himself up."

Charles spoke slowly and wearily, keeping his words straight. "There are some papers. Important government papers. He didn't want anyone to see them and he thought I might have them."

"Okay, wait. Government papers. What kind of papers?"

"I don't really know."

"Why would you have them?"

"That's what we were talking about at his house. He thought a former employee gave them to me."

"Okay, we'll get to that. What about the fire? So what you're saying is, he would have broken in to your place to what, burn it down just to get rid of these papers?"

"I don't know," Charles said. "I don't know what he was doing."

"You have sprinklers?"

"We have fire sprinklers and an alarm."

"Did any of it go off?"

"I haven't heard that it did."

"Okay. So he went in to burn the place and he cut off the alarm and water somehow. We'll get a report from the fire chief, but he already says it was gasoline. Maybe he used too much and the fire was too fast and he got caught. Okay, Mr. Beale, I'm going to need to find out about these papers, but this is enough for now. I need to get a statement."

"I'll be glad to do that a little later, Mr. Mondelli."

"That's okay. I want to talk to your night guy, Acevedo, too."

"He's not awake yet."

"Okay. I'll call this afternoon. You going anywhere?"

"We're not going anywhere."

"Thanks."

The rising sun was inches lower on the wall, creeping toward the bed. It touched a shelf, and the John Locke and the wrapped package of money on the shelf. Dorothy lowered a blind.

An hour had passed and Charles woke, still sitting beside Angelo. Dorothy was gone.

He found her in the front room, in her chair.

"I'm sorry," he said. "I closed my eyes."

"You needed to."

She had been crying. He pulled his chair beside hers and held her hands.

"Here we are."

"What will we do now?" she asked.

"We're fine. We have insurance. We can salvage a lot from the basement. We're fine."

"It's all we had."

"We have each other."

"It's all you had," she said.

"I have you."

"Why can't we ever have anything, Charles? It's just like losing William. I feel like we can never have anything important."

"We can start back up."

"There's nothing I can ever hold on to. You're everything I have."

"Hold on to me."

She did, and he held on to her, until they looked toward the stairs and Angelo was watching them.

"Angelo. Come." Charles pulled a third chair from the dining room table. "Sit down."

He was wearing Charles's clothes that Dorothy had left for him, loose on his thin frame. His face was closed and shrouded in silence, but something inside was shaken. He sat by them quickly, and his eyes were further open than the narrow slits that usually were the windows between him and the world.

"How are you?" Dorothy asked.

"I am okay."

"You look all right. Are you hungry? What do you need?"

"I am okay."

"He is," Charles said. "He's fine. Angelo. I'm so glad you're all right." His hand, which had been holding Dorothy's before, clamped on to Angelo's. "I'm so glad."

Angelo didn't answer, but it wasn't a hard silence. The yearning in his eyes said more than he ever had in words.

"I don't know where we'll put you now," Dorothy said. "Your room is gone. You'll have to stay in the guest room."

"What room?" Angelo asked.

"Your room at the shop is gone. You'll have to stay here," Dorothy said.

"I will not leave?" He was frowning, trying to understand.

"Why would you leave?" Charles said.

"That judge said there is no more probation."

Charles's mouth dropped. "No! Angelo! That never meant you had to leave! Of course not." And then seeing the bewilderment in Angelo's face, he started to laugh. "Is that what you thought? Angelo, if you want to, you can stay forever."

"I will stay," Angelo said, and very firmly.

"Well good, then. That's taken care of." Charles let go of his hand. "But we don't have a shop anymore. It will be a while before you have anything to do."

"Your books?" Angelo asked. "There was fire."

"There was fire." The joy burned away. "Yes. We lost the whole building except the basement. Angelo, tell me what happened."

"I was in the basement."

"Why were you in the basement?"

"I went to watch that money."

"How did you know it was down there?"

"You did not take it away in your car."

"Why did you go to watch it?"

"That man following, that was bad. He wanted the money."

"What man?" Dorothy asked.

"We saw someone on the way to New York," Charles said. "So you were in the basement. Just waiting?"

"I was waiting. And then the door opened."

"The front door?"

"That door opened and I heard walking up there, then walking on the stairs down."

"What about the door?"

"He tried to open but I had it locked already. But he unlocked it."

"He had a key?" Charles asked.

"That lock, it is too easy," Angelo said.

"What happened when he opened the door?"

"That door didn't open."

"The chair," Charles said. "You had it against the door?"

"That man pushed, but I held it closed and the chair held it."

Charles stopped. Dorothy was hardly breathing and her face was white.

"It's all right," Charles said. "Angelo is sitting right here with us. Whatever he tells us, he made it through."

"It's terrible," she said.

"But it's over. Go ahead, Angelo. Did he ever get the door open?"

"No, it didn't open. Then he went back up the stairs. Then the light went off."

"He turned off the electricity."

"I locked the door again if he would come back. Then I waited and then I smelled fire."

"Did you go up to see?" Charles asked.

"I looked up the stairs, but it was all fire."

"Could you have gotten out?"

"That man, he might be waiting for me to come out."

"So you went back down."

"He would get that money if I went out."

"The money isn't as important to me as you are, Angelo!" Charles shook his head. "You could have died down there."

"I think it was a very big fire," Angelo said. "You say that room doesn't burn in fires. Then the smoke came."

"Maybe it was the better thing to do. You probably wouldn't have gotten through it. John Borchard didn't."

"That man did the fire?"

"That's what the police say. He didn't get out, Angelo. He died right above you."

"He was not a good man. I said be careful."

"Yes, you did. We both had to be careful."

Angelo's perils had taken Dorothy's thoughts from her own. "I think that's enough," she said. "Come into the kitchen, both of you. We need to eat. We'll have a long day. We need to get back over there to get the books out. I'll call Morgan and Alice."

"You get something for Angelo," Charles said. "Tell Morgan to meet me at the store in twenty minutes, and tell Alice to bring boxes. Have her buy a couple hundred somewhere. And lots of packing."

"Don't you want anything?" she said. "You must be starving."

"I need to think what it means. Angelo, are you sure you had the door locked in the basement?"

"It was locked."

"But he still got it open?"

"That man, he must be good on locks."

Charles stared out the window. The sun had gone. In just a few minutes, clouds had covered it.

In just a few minutes more a car had arrived, loudly. Its door slammed and the doorbell rang, while a voice called through the window.

"Mr. Beale? Are you in there?"

Charles jumped to the door. "Congresswoman. Come in. Dorothy, Karen Liu is here."

"I just heard," Karen Liu said. Charles had barely gotten her seated. "My staff got a call that John Borchard was killed in a fire. Then they said it was in a bookstore in Alexandria. Oh, Mr. Beale! I drove right over. The street was closed. I called and found out where you lived."

"You found us," Charles said.

"I have some coffee," Dorothy said.

"Yes, please. What happened? What was he doing?"

"I don't know for sure. The police think he was trying to burn down the building and he didn't get out in time."

"That's horrible! Mr. Beale, you know how I felt about him, but I never wanted anything like this! Did he . . . ?" Suddenly her momentum stalled. She started again, much slower. "What was he doing?"

"It had to do with Derek," Charles said. "He thought I had Derek's papers."

"And he burned down a whole building to get them? Oh, Mr. Beale! I can't believe it. He could have killed people." She stopped again. "He killed himself." She lurched forward. "Do you think he did it on purpose?"

"I don't know," Charles said. "No, he wouldn't. Not like that."

"What about your books?"

"The showroom was destroyed. The basement may be salvageable."

"Oh my. Oh, Mr. Beale. If there is anything I can do, anything, I will. Anything."

Dorothy handed her a coffee cup and she took it without noticing.

"We're only getting started," Charles said. "I need to go back and look. I need to get the books out as quickly as I can. Congresswoman—"

"Please call me Karen. You already have, once."

"Karen. Would you stay with Dorothy and Angelo?"

"I'll go with you," Dorothy said.

"No, you stay and get some rest. There won't be a lot to do yet. I'll take a flashlight." He went up the stairs to the bedroom and took a flashlight from the nightstand. Then he opened the John Locke and took one paper from the card box.

He looked into the kitchen. "Angelo, I'm leaving. Take care of Dorothy for me."

"Take care how?"

"If she needs anything." He turned back to Dorothy. "Goodbye, dear."

Charles stepped out onto the brick sidewalk that he walked so many times, and so many others had walked before him. He looked for a moment at the old townhouse and the lace curtains in the windows.

Then he chose a quick pace, down two blocks, over one block, past the firemen carrying away barricades and people clotting the way. He squeezed through.

In the full light, the ruin of the building was entire and terrible, but only pitiable, not profound as it had been in the night. Charles stood and pitied it. The face was intact but charred with great black stains leaking upward from the blank holes of the windows. Just from the way it stood, it was obvious that it was hollow and dead inside.

There was one sign of life, a man in a hard hat coming out of what had been the doorway, and Charles hurried toward him.

"Excuse me," he said. "I'm Charles Beale. I own the building. Are you inspecting it?"

"Yeah. Good morning. They said you want to get books out of the basement?"

"Yes, very quickly. May I get them?"

"Okay, look, Mr. Beale," the man said. "This place isn't safe. But how much did you say the books are worth?"

"About ten million dollars."

He nodded. "I'm going to let you in. It's not going to fall in today, I don't think, but you're doing this at your own risk. I'm giving you one day."

"Thank you. I'll go down now and look."

He walked in and stopped. There could never have been anything like books in such a place. There were no shelves, no counter, nothing to make it a room. There was only black, enough to suck the light out of air. There was no ceiling. He looked straight up to where the office had been and it was only more of the same black, lightless space.

He walked down the stairs. The splintered door was the first thing visible, and he pushed it aside with his foot. The water was mostly gone. He turned his light onto the walls.

The books stared back at him and their thoughts were unknowable, whether it was relief or reproach or resignation. He took a volume from a shelf and gently opened it. The cover was strong and straight and the pages were dry.

> Now, as they went on, Mr. Great-heart drew his sword, with intent to make a way for the pilgrims in spite of the lions. Then there appeared one that, it seems, had taken upon him to back the lions; and he said to the pilgrims' guide, What is the cause of your coming hither? Now the name of that man was Grim, or Bloody-man because of his slaying of pilgrims; and he was of the race of the giants.
>
> MR. GREAT-HEART: Then said the pilgrims' guide, These women and children are going on pilgrimage, and this is the way they must go; and go it they shall, in spite of thee and the lions.

GRIM: This is not their way, neither shall they go therein. I am come forth to withstand them, and to that end will back the lions.

"Yes, Pilgrim," Charles said. "Keep making your progress. I will fight for you all that I can."

He stood for a very long time looking, at shelves, at books, at the room, and at the precious value of everything, everything at all.

"I've so enjoyed knowing all of you," he said.

Slowly he climbed the stairs, back into the light.

Morgan was standing in the street, gape-mouthed, wide-eyed and blinking.

"Good morning," Charles said.

"Oh."

"Yes. It's all right, Morgan. There's a lot of work to do. The basement looks good. Everything's down there."

"What happened?"

"We'll talk about it later. For now, we need to get the books out. Do you have boxes?"

"Some. Alice is getting everything." Morgan blinked once more. "I should just start?"

"Yes, get started. Take them to my house, we'll find room. I need to go out for a while."

But he had only turned when a taxi blocked his way, and its door opened, and a walking stick jutted.

"Get me out," a voice said, and Charles reached down and gently lifted. It didn't take much force.

"Jacob," he said. "We've had a bad accident, I'm afraid."

"Bad accident? That's nothing. I've seen plenty worse."

"It's bad enough."

"You think you're trying to get free advertising? It's all over the television."

"Oh. I haven't been watching."

"Of course not, there's work to do. What's left, anything?"

"The basement came through, Jacob. Everything's still down there. Morgan has already started and Alice is coming."

"Then it's not bad at all. Just work, and I know you don't mind that. Buck up, Charles."

"Thank you. Thank you very much. I'm glad you're here, Jacob. Would you like to go over to the house for the morning? When is your flight?"

"I cancelled it. I'm here to take care of your books, and someday you'll learn how to yourself and keep your store from burning down. Stop there! Let me see!"

Morgan had just emerged with his first box and Jacob scuttled over to him.

"Leave the top off," he commanded. "Let them dry. Not too many to a box. Now you'll pack them special to let them dry. I'll tell you how."

"Oh, Mr. Beale!" Alice had arrived.

"Everything is fine," he said. "We won't sell much today, but everything's fine."

She burst into tears.

"Leave the boxes," Charles said, "and go over to the house to see Dorothy. Everything will be fine. Come back and help when you're ready."

"Yes, sir," she sniffed.

"And thank you so much," he said. "For everything." Her lip was too stiff to talk so she just nodded. "Morgan. Just keep working, slow and steady. Angelo could help, and Alice will too when she's calmed down."

"Will you be back soon?" Morgan asked.

"When I can. I need to take your little telephone."

"Yes, sir. Here."

"Thank you very much, Morgan. You've been such a help over the years."

Morgan set the first box next to his car and went in for the second.

"Jacob," Charles said. "I need to go out for a while. If you could just watch and help them pack."

"What are you doing, Charles?" Jacob looked at him suspiciously.

"Just some business."

"What business?"

"Doing what I know I have to do."

Jacob searched him with a single glance.

"Then I'll take care of this."

Charles returned to his quick pace. He took a smart left onto King Street and crossed to Market Square. The crowds were thicker than the day before, with brisk-moving suited office workers squeezing between slow tourists. Most of the benches were empty and Charles picked a solitary one. He took Morgan's telephone from his pocket, and a business card, and pushed the little buttons.

"Frank Kelly."

"Mr. Kelly. This is Charles Beale."

"Oh, hey. What can I do for you?"

"I need your help."

"Sure. What?"

"Mr. Kelly, this is about Derek Bastien, and it's a very long story. I just have one question, though. When we talked about Derek's desk, you called it a Honaker."

"Um, yeah. I think that's right."

"Who told you that it was?"

"Somebody. Let me think. Why do you want to know?"

"It's part of the long story."

"Go ahead," Frank Kelly said. "I like stories."

"Do you remember the auction where it was sold? Two people tried to buy it. One of them hired a man from New York as an agent. I've spoken to Edmund Cane, that agent, and he called the desk a Honaker, too." The little telephone was awkward to hold, and Charles switched it to his other ear. "No one else so far has known that detail about the desk. Whoever told you might be the person who also told Mr. Cane. I need to find that person."

"Okay, just a minute. I'm looking at my notes. So is it something to do with the burglary?"

"It might be."

"Should you be talking to Harry Watts over in D.C. Homicide?"

"I don't know yet. I'm not really sure."

"Okay, here it is. Right after the burglary in November. Interview with Norman Highberg."

"Norman," Charles said. "You're sure?"

"It's right here. Okay, Mr. Beale, I feel like I need to know more about this long story."

"Would you like to meet?" Charles said.

"I could come right over. Are you at your place?"

Charles sighed. "No. We had a fire last night."

"A fire!? Oh, man, I hope it wasn't bad. What happened?"

"It was very bad. The building was destroyed."

The telephone gasped. "All the way? What? Everything?"

"The basement survived, where the rare books were. That was very fortunate."

"So, wait. I mean . . ." Mr. Kelly struggled for words. "Was anybody hurt?"

"Yes. The man who set the fire was killed."

"Oh, man! Oh, man. Right in the store? I don't know what to say. Are you all right?"

"Yes, all of us are all right."

"That's such a great place! Oh, I'm really sorry." And then Mr. Kelly's investigative mind finally caught up. "Hey, what, is there something up? It doesn't have anything to do with Bastien, does it?" A longer pause and a grimmer voice. "Where was your night guy?"

"He's all right. He was there, but he's all right."

"Mr. Beale, we need to talk, and we need Watts in on this. Who's covering it in Alexandria?"

"It's a Detective Mondelli."

"Okay, never heard of him, but we need him, too. Look, I've been getting some stuff up on your Acevedo guy, and I think I need to start moving."

"Mr. Kelly," Charles said. "There's a lot more to say and many more questions. Could you meet me at Norman Highberg's shop in Georgetown? I think we can find our answers there."

"I'll be right there."

"Give me a little while to get there," Charles said.

Charles took his time. He walked the familiar length of King Street, looking in windows and watching people, but never stopping. He rode the escalator to the Metro platform with the usual dozens of other people and waited until the doors whooshed open. He chose a seat and watched Alexandria accelerate away.

The ride was uneventful. He took the Blue Line past the airport and under the Pentagon, through Arlington and finally under the river to Georgetown, a familiar and comfortable course, and very finally left the Metro behind beneath the Georgetown streets. And then he was on the streets, which were very busy and crowded. He walked the blocks he needed to, passing the storefronts and so many people. At one last door he paused, and walked in.

"Is Mr. Highberg here?"

"Charles." Norman had his finger on his nose, pushing up his glasses. "You want to just move in here? You've been up here all the time. Don't tell me you have more of your questions."

"No, I don't have questions."

The little telephone in his pocket made a funny sound. When he looked, it showed his home telephone number. He closed it and it stopped ringing.

"So you're just browsing?" Norman said. "Maybe now that you have that chess set, you might want to look at some other things." When Charles didn't answer, he said, "Are you waiting for something?"

"For someone." But then they weren't waiting, as Frank Kelly stood in the door. "Norman, you know Mr. Kelly, of the FBI?"

Norman squinted at the silhouette. "Yeah, sure. Hi. What do you want? Did something get stolen or did something get found? It's always one of those, right?"

"Mr. Highberg," Frank Kelly said. "Do you have a room we can talk in? Just us three."

"I got all kinds of rooms. Come on up."

He led them away from the light through the sparkling windows and all within that sparkled in the light, upstairs and through a dusty corridor and into a room. It was a stockroom with unpacked empty boxes and unopened full boxes and a bench and packing litter and chairs.

"So, what do you want?" Norman asked. "You don't look happy, Charles. Usually you look a lot better."

Charles looked at Mr. Kelly. "How shall we do this?"

"Okay, this isn't very good," Mr. Kelly said. "I'm not sure if I have jurisdiction or what, yet, or whether I need to get Harry Watts. Do this. I just won't be here officially. You say what you know, and I'll figure it out as we go along."

"Well." Charles rubbed his eyes; they were red and weary. "Mr. Kelly, I'll tell you my story now, and you'll see how the burglaries are part of it. I'm very tired and I'll try to make it short."

"What are you talking about?" Norman Highberg said.

"Just listen," Frank Kelly answered.

"Derek Bastien was a blackmailer," Charles said. "He kept papers on people he worked with. He manipulated these people with threats, and fooled them into thinking it was his boss, John Borchard, who was doing it."

"Borchard?" Frank had his notebook out. "He's the one—"

"Yes, he was the one this morning."

"I read the police report after you called."

Charles went on. "One of the people Derek was blackmailing was a judge, Patrick White."

"White?" Frank put his notebook down. "He's the one—"

"Yes, who died Tuesday. Do you know the rest of his story?"

"All the stuff in the newspaper. Yeah, I know."

"Derek Bastien was the one who told the newspaper about him," Charles said. "Mr. White was one of his victims."

"What are you talking about?" Norman was acting very confused. "What is all this?"

"But Patrick White thought John Borchard was his tormentor, and he planned revenge."

"Is that what the bomb thing was about?" Frank Kelly said.

"It was supposed to look that way," Charles said. "But there was another blackmail victim. Someone who went to Mr. White and offered to help. But I think he only helped Mr. White die."

"Keep going," Frank Kelly said. "I think I'm following it."

"I'm not!" Norman Highberg said. "What is this, anyway?"

Charles did keep going. "I think he also helped John Borchard die. John was desperate to get Derek's papers. He bought Derek's desk."

"Borchard bought it." Frank was writing furiously, but still intensely attentive. "The papers were in it?"

"In a hidden drawer, and they were still there. I saw them Tuesday. John showed them to me."

"I get it," Frank said. "Because someone else tried to buy the desk, too. That's this other victim, right?"

"Yes. It has to be."

"The one that you say, um, what? That he booby-trapped White's bomb?"

"I guess that would be it," Charles said.

"Okay, that would be tricky. And then Borchard?"

"They would have been there in the shop together. He made sure John Borchard didn't get out after the fire was started. Maybe he was already dead."

"What . . . what, what fire?" Norman was beside himself. "Somebody tell me what you're telling me? What fire? And who's dead? Where?"

Frank was shaking his head. "Do you have any clue that he wasn't there by himself? The police report says he was."

"I don't think he was. He picked locks and turned off my alarm system and sprinklers. I don't think John Borchard could have, but I think the man who broke into Derek's house, and the other houses, could have."

"Okay." Frank was very pleased. "I got you. That's real good." Then his smile deflated. "Except I've got bad news for you."

"What is that?"

"I've got about two-thirds of a case against your guy Acevedo on that."

"Angelo?" Charles was too tired to react.

"DNA for one thing, and that stuff we recovered, too. I've got a link between a guy he knew and the attic we found the stuff in."

"I was afraid you would say that."

Mr. Kelly was still figuring. "And he'd be in your shop, and he knows the alarm and everything else."

"Wait," Norman erupted again. "Where was the fire? Did you have a fire, Charles? What, at your place?"

"But Acevedo isn't anybody Bastien would be blackmailing," Mr. Kelly said. "So Acevedo's working with someone else? I'm getting mixed up."

"I'm getting mixed up," Norman said.

"It comes back to the desk," Charles said. "The man from New York, Edmund Cane. He was the agent for that other victim, the one I want to find. And Mr. Cane called the desk a Honaker."

"Honaker?" Norman said. "It was a Honaker?"

"Does that make a difference?"

"No. No way that desk was worth a hundred five grand, even if it was a Honaker. But I don't do furniture, so what do I know."

"What do you know, Norman?" Charles asked. "John Borchard didn't know. The only two people who knew that the desk was a Honaker were Edmund Cane and the FBI. I think Mr. Cane must have heard it from his client, and I think Mr. Kelly must have heard it from the same person as well. Norman, I think that was you."

Norman Highberg tried to make sounds but nothing came, and his face contorted in an indecipherable expression. But finally, he choked out words.

"Are you crazy?"

"I'm not," Charles said.

"You're crazy, you both are. What is this? What are you doing here?" Now that the words had broken loose, they came in a torrent. "You're both wacko! You think I even know what you're talking about?"

But Frank was already moving on. "Okay, I can handle this. I'll get Harry Watts in here. I should have called him before. I just figured Highberg's DNA on the stuff we recovered was old, but it must have been recent."

"I don't have DNA!" Norman said.

"But look," Frank Kelly said, "we need to get hold of Acevedo. Where is he?"

"Back in Alexandria," Charles said.

"Does he know what you're doing right now? I mean, does he know we'll be after him?" He took a slow breath. "Where's your wife?"

"I'm getting out of here," Norman said. "This is too crazy."

Charles rubbed his eyes again, and they were much redder and wearier. "Yes, Norman, go ahead. Leave."

"What?" Frank Kelly's head jerked up from his notebook.

"Leave, Norman," Charles said. "I'm sorry. Just go away."

"Now?"

"Yes."

Frank Kelly set his jaw. "Yeah. Get lost."

Norman didn't move, but then he did quickly, and left them.

"Okay," Frank said. "Start over."

Starting over took a great deal of energy. Charles had to wait to gather it.

"You killed Derek, and Patrick White, and John Borchard," he said.

"Just keep talking."

"I'm very tired," Charles said.

"I've got a gun right here, and you're only alive as long as you keep talking."

"Norman knows you're here and he heard everything I said."

"I'll deal with that when I have to. First, just talk. Start with the desk."

"All right." Charles kept his eyes on Mr. Kelly's face, and not on his hands. "I always knew there were two people who wanted the desk. As I worked out what Derek was doing, I knew who they must be. John Borchard was obvious after I talked with Patrick White. The other person was elusive. I knew who he was; I just didn't know his name.

"There was always the big question that I never saw an answer to. How did Derek get all these papers? When did he have time to find court records in Kansas and class records in Virginia, and how did he ever get bank records? And all those dozens of other papers? And then I knew who the other person must be. It was his spy, his agent, his burrower. There was one paper I had, a list of dates and amounts and people's initials. It was his list of his payments to you. A lot of money, but not enough to outbid John Borchard for the desk. When did you know there were papers in the book as well?"

"Just keep talking."

"It must have been when you talked with John Borchard, the evening that Patrick White was killed; or earlier, because you had Mr. Cane trying to buy the books on Monday.

"One thing I knew about the spy was that he was always showing up somewhere. Once Patrick White was exposed in the newspaper, a mysterious fellow victim approached him. Did you hear the recording that John Borchard had?"

"Just keep talking. Don't ask questions."

"I thought about it. If I had supplied Derek with that information about Patrick White, and then I saw the huge drama playing out in public, I would have been worried for myself. What would you do? I think you would have felt at risk. So you became Mr. White's confidante, so that you could know everything he knew. Probably that was when you knew that there was only one way out of your business with Derek. How did you get into it in the first place?"

"I said no questions."

"Well, it will come out. I can think of several ways you might cross paths. The Justice Department and the FBI, his collection of antiques and your job hunting them. It looks like he paid you a lot of money. And then, after the auction, you showed up at my shop. You were just following leads. One of them was that I asked Edmund Cane some pointed questions about who he was representing. It was just the next morning that you arrived. Just like with Patrick White, you wanted to be close to know what was happening. Looking back, I remember you following me in that one morning, and standing there as I turned off the alarm.

"I don't know what you said to John, to get him to come with you to my shop, to recover the papers. Maybe you even told him you were with the FBI and you needed his help? I know that you gained my confidence, Mr. Kelly. I'm sure you could gain everyone else's.

"I'm rambling, I'm sorry. As I said, I'm very tired. I guess that once you saw that the Patrick White scandal was getting out of hand, you saw the danger of Derek being exposed as the source. And, if Derek would do that to Mr. White, could you trust him yourself? So you ran a quick series of burglaries to camouflage your attack on Derek. Was it a rotten feeling for him, Mr. Kelly, when he saw you? Or did he not see you?"

"Just. Keep. Talking."

"I'm almost finished. You went through such efforts to hide yourself. All those burglaries, that was really lots of effort, and risky, although you must have a lot of useful skills and you surely know how burglaries are done. But also keeping Patrick White so close that you could kill him if you needed to, and getting John Borchard to the bookstore.

"I also suppose that was you following us to the train station, after Edmund Cane called to tell you we were coming to New York. We had that suitcase of books, so you would have assumed we were packed for the night, and there wouldn't be anyone in the building. You might really have been successful with making those all look like accidents.

"And now, I don't know what you were planning next. You claim that you recovered the things stolen from Derek's house and you've tried to involve Angelo, of all people. I think you were setting up the next death, where Angelo would kill me, but die himself somehow. And Norman?

That was ridiculous. You recovered those stolen items from your own attic, and there wasn't any DNA on them. Certainly not any that was months old. That was ridiculous, too.

"But at least it gave me a way to get you here for this conversation. So now I do have some questions, and you need to answer them."

"I don't need to do anything."

"But you've been exposed now, Mr. Kelly. It's over."

"I don't think so." Frank Kelly tapped his fingers on the packing bench beside him. "I don't think so, because it's just the two of us sitting here. You could have taken this whole thing to Watts and D.C. Homicide yourself. So why are we just sitting here together?"

"I wanted to be sure."

"It's more than that. What papers did you have in that book, anyway?"

"Karen Liu's checks, John Borchard's overturned convictions, Patrick White's law school paper, the list of payments to you, and Galen Jones's drug connection. And one other."

"Sounds like the top-sellers, there," Frank said. "Borchard knew about Bastien's secret drawer and so did I, so he couldn't keep those first four papers there. Jones knew about the drawer, too. I think I know what the last one was. You looked through the papers that Borchard got from the desk. What were you looking for?" He waited, but Charles didn't answer. "You wanted to know what he had on you."

"I didn't find anything."

"You already had it. That one other paper."

"I was afraid so," Charles said. "I'd hoped it wasn't."

"That's straight from the files at the orphanage, the FitzRobert place." Frank Kelly folded his arms. "Let's say I let you out of here alive. If this goes to trial, all that stuff will come out. Karen Liu is going to sink like a stone. But your main problem is that you've got homicidal maniacs in your family tree. Hey, sorry to be blunt, but that's the clinical name. How's your Dorothy going to feel when she finds out her mother was crazy, and that her son inherited it right down the line?"

Charles didn't answer.

"So here's a deal. We just walk away. You don't tell anyone about me, and I don't tell anyone everything I know. Just pretend we never had this conversation."

"I don't think I'd feel very safe about that."

"You can make some arrangements. Write the whole long story and put it in a safe place where it goes to the newspaper if anything ever happens to you. I admit it's messy but I don't see any alternative."

"You would have killed three people and nothing would happen to you?"

"They were not nice people. Right?"

"That doesn't matter."

"I think it does. You could almost say they got what they deserved."

"And would you get what you deserve? You've killed two people in the last two days. What kind of homicidal maniac have you become?"

"Hey, watch it," Frank said. "Did your man Angelo get what he deserved? Aren't you all about second chances, Beale? Why didn't you drop those papers in the police department's inbox the day you found them? Because you didn't want Borchard or Liu to get shoved out the same window that poor Patrick did. I've been reading you like a book."

"I think at this point, Karen Liu is ready to face her charges."

"You should worry more about yourself."

"It would be very hard on Dorothy to know the truth," Charles said. "But we'll get past it."

"Get past it? I think you're underestimating what this will do to her. She's going to realize that your William killed himself because he inherited a defective mind from his mother. Think about something like that long enough and you might go crazy."

"How did you get that paper?" Charles asked.

"I looked in her file at the orphanage."

"Then you've made a mistake," Charles said. "We've seen her file. Her mother never killed anyone. She and Dorothy's father were missionaries in China. They died there when she was an infant."

"This was a separate file. It was marked closed. You never saw it."

"I know what file you mean. We never did see what was in it. But it wasn't Dorothy's. It was William's. Didn't you know that we adopted him?"

The telephone in his pocket rang again. He reached for it, but even faster Mr. Kelly had his hand inside his jacket.

"Don't touch it."

Charles put his hand down. "My wife is getting very worried. She doesn't know where I am."

"Who does?"

"No one."

Mr. Kelly shook his head. "Then there's something else going on here. Why would you walk into this room if you knew you were never coming out? You should at least have kept Highberg in here."

"I wanted him away from danger."

"Where's the paper you talked about? The list of money Derek Bastien paid me?"

"I have it with me. I didn't want it found before I talked to you. You see, it's part of the reason I didn't give the papers to the police either. I can't save you from your punishment, Mr. Kelly, and I wouldn't. But I was hoping there was something I could do to rescue you. Something." He sighed. "You're right. I am all about second chances."

"Then you're all about being a complete idiot. You're going to save other people and you can't even save yourself?"

"For whatever you've done to me," Charles said, "I forgive you."

The door opened.

A long gray mustache looked into the room, and Galen Jones's bright eyes above it.

Frank Kelly suddenly smiled. "Jones? Right? Galen Jones. What do you want?" His eyes stayed on Charles. "We're just talking antiques."

Mr. Jones hesitated. "I was meeting Beale. I'm making a chess table for him. It's ten o'clock, right? Thursday? Highberg said you were up here." His eyes stayed on Frank Kelly. "Something wrong?"

"No, nothing's wrong," Mr. Kelly said. "He'll be done in a few minutes. You could wait downstairs."

"Okay." Mr. Jones stood for a moment more. Then he shook his head. "What's happening?"

"I said nothing." The smile was gone. "Get lost."

"Highberg said you were talking about Bastien's desk."

Charles nodded slowly, and his eyes stayed on Galen Jones. "I'm just trying to do the right thing."

Mr. Jones visibly tensed, and his eyes went to Frank Kelly's hand resting on his lap, but tense and not at rest. "What are you—"

"I said get lost!"

"Nobody talks to me that way!"

The hand twitched. "If you don't—"

Jones stepped forward. "I've had enough of you."

Mr. Kelly's hand moved, deliberate and threatening. His eyes were full on Galen Jones.

But another hand moved fast. With all his strength Charles pulled at a box on the bench beside him and hurled it as hard as he could. Its whole weight seemed to hang for an endless moment in the space between them. Then it half caught Frank Kelly's shoulder but didn't slow or veer, and an awful, heavy blow hit him full in the face, carrying him and his chair backward, still in the same shattering crash, all the way to the floor.

He only shuddered once, and then was still except for the rattle of his breathing.

"Thank you," Charles said, his own breath in gasps. "Thank you for coming."

Galen Jones pulled the box away. A cascade of what had once been a Chinese vase poured out of it. "What was . . . ?"

"No. Don't ask. Just call the police."

"You get his gun, I'm not touching it."

Frank Kelly didn't stir; a dark bruise was already covering half his face. Charles eased the gun from the holster and set it on the bench behind him.

"Mr. Jones, I had completely forgotten that you and I were meeting here today."

FRIDAY

EVENING

"What do you suggest tonight, Philippe?" Charles said.

"Monsieur." Philippe bowed low. "For you tonight we have a very special dinner," he said in his most deferential voice. "All day we have been preparing for you."

"Charles! Dorothy! Oh!" Henna red hair came flying across the room, with the hostess beneath it. "Oh, how terrible it has been!" She nearly fainted, or did for a moment and recovered, without interrupting the flowing words. "I was in the kitchen when Henri told me you had arrived. We have talked of nothing else since yesterday! Nothing! Such tragedy!"

"I think we've recovered, Antoinette," Dorothy said. "The police were over all day yesterday asking questions, but we've finally had some rest today."

"What will you do?" she asked. "Can you even dream of starting again?"

"I think we can dream," Charles said.

A thin, beautiful note strung itself from one corner of the room to the other. A wandering violinist planted himself beside them and began to play.

"But for tonight," the hostess continued, unabated, "you will have no cares. Tonight everything is for you. I will return to the kitchen, so that everything will be perfect for you!" And she left them, perfectly.

"I thought about not calling this morning," Charles said, "and just showing up like we usually do. Who knows what else they might have in store."

The violin's haunting melody wrapped about them like linguini.

"It is perfect," Dorothy said. "They're all enjoying themselves so much."

"Are we recovered?" Charles asked.

"We've started to be. I do want to start over."

"We'll build a new shop."

"But then it wouldn't be old!"

"No, it's a new start, Dorothy. The old is gone. The past is gone. What do you think of that?"

"Well . . . I liked our past. Most of it."

"We still have most of it," Charles said. "But it's more than just the building that will be new."

"What else has been changed? Charles, what would have happened if you'd just taken the papers to the police in the first place?"

"They might have figured out how Derek was killed, and prevented the other deaths. They might not have. I don't know how my decisions affected John Borchard and Patrick White."

"There hasn't been anything in the paper about Karen Liu," Dorothy said.

"I think she'll come forward herself. She wants the fight."

"It would have to be a relief for her."

"In the end, none of them escaped," Charles said. "I couldn't save anyone from their own pasts and their own decisions."

"Did you think you could?"

"I tried."

"Angelo escaped," Dorothy said.

"He's been through the fire, and I think it was a refiner's fire. I think we're going to see gold."

"And what about you, dear?"

"Me?"

Like the tide, the music and murmur slowly swept against them in waves, foam-crested with their own thoughts. Charles sat quietly staring away, and Dorothy at him. He sighed.

"Do you remember," he said, finally, "talking about coincidences? In a well written story there shouldn't be any. I went in to Frank Kelly and I closed every door out, because I wanted . . ." He had to pause to think. "I knew what he'd done. I knew what he would do. But I couldn't make myself be the one who brought about his destruction. I only could hope that there was some forgiveness, or something, that I could give him. And at the very moment I needed him, Galen Jones walked in. I hadn't even thought of him, and there he was."

"I don't even want to think about it."

"But it's over."

"It does sound like a coincidence," Dorothy said.

"No, I think the story is too well written for that."

"What story, Charles?"

"My story, and we know who it is who's writing that. And your story, and Angelo's story, and everyone's. What a book that must be."

ACKNOWLEDGMENTS

I would like to thank my friends the Honorable Judge Woody Lookabill; and Blacksburg, VA, Fire Chief Keith Bolte; and especially the very special Sharon Dilles for the help and information they provided.

ABOUT THE AUTHOR

Paul Robertson, author of the acclaimed novels *The Heir* and *Road to Nowhere,* is a computer programming consultant and a part-time high school math and science teacher. He is also a former independent bookstore owner. Paul lives with his family in Blacksburg, Virginia.